<u>**** DID I READ THIS ALREADY? ****</u>

Place your initials or unique symbol in a
square as a reminder to you that you have
read this title.

JH Mw				☆	
JM					

Heartbreak Creek

**Center Point
Large Print**

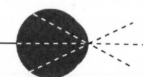

**This Large Print Book carries the
Seal of Approval of N.A.V.H.**

Heartbreak Creek

Kaki Warner

CENTER POINT LARGE PRINT
THORNDIKE, MAINE

This Center Point Large Print edition is published
in the year 2011 by arrangement with
The Berkley Publishing Group,
a member of Penguin Group (USA) Inc.

The text of this Large Print edition is unabridged.
In other aspects, this book may
vary from the original edition.
Printed in the United States of America.
Set in 16-point Times New Roman type.

ISBN: 978-1-61173-242-9

Library of Congress Cataloging-in-Publication Data

Warner, Kaki.
Heartbreak creek : a runaway brides novel / Kaki Warner.
    p. cm.
ISBN 978-1-61173-242-9 (library binding : alk. paper)
1. Mail order brides—Fiction. 2. Ranch life—Fiction.
   3. Colorado—Fiction. 4. Large type books. I. Title.
PS3623.A8633H43 2011b
813′.6—dc22
                                                    2011028102

If friends are more valuable than gold,
then I am rich indeed.
Thank you Cyndi and Janet
for being there when I need you.

Heartbreak Creek

PROLOGUE

Edwina Ladoux stood at the window in her late father's office and watched a small two-wheeled carriage swing through the front gate.

Or rather, what was left of the front gate. The filigreed ironwork had been torn off years ago —rumor was it now graced the back garden of a bordello up by Bossier City—and the lovely stone pillars had toppled soon after. Quarry stone was hard to come by in bayou country, so back when there had still been hope of rebuilding, she and Pru had laboriously carried the stones around to the orchard to fill in the gaps in the garden wall. But now that wall had fallen, too.

The carriage rolled briskly down the oyster shell drive beneath the long-armed oaks and their streamers of moss. Only three of the original trees remained. The fourth had burned the night the Yankees came but had stood until high winds toppled it two years later. Now it sprawled across the lawn like a blackened skeleton, slowly sinking into the overgrowth.

The carriage stopped and the driver stepped down, a tall, thin man Edwina knew well. Bernard

Alexander, and his father before him, and his grandfather before that, had been bankers for the Whitneys for almost seventy-five years. He probably dreaded this meeting as much as Edwina did. And he hadn't come alone, she noted, recognizing the other occupant as he came around the back of the carriage. He'd brought Reverend Morton.

Reinforcements? In case the distraught Widow Ladoux needed a tut-tut and a pat on the shoulder to help soften the loss of the home that had been in her family for three-quarters of a century? Bless his heart.

The front door opened and closed. Murmured greetings. Without furniture or carpets to muffle sound, voices carried through the empty house. A moment later, footfalls thudded in the hall. Clasping her hands at her waist to hide the shaking, Edwina turned as the door opened.

But only her sister, Prudence, stepped inside. "Mr. Alexander is here. Reverend Morton has come with him."

"I saw. Is he expecting a ruckus, do you think?"
"Oh, dear."

Edwina gave a brittle laugh to cover the fear gripping her throat. "Don't worry, I'll behave."

Pru hated scenes. Edwina—the impulsive, high-spirited sister—thrived on them. As with any well-bred, well-trained southern lady of quality, drama was her weapon, just as pride was her strength. Like the whalebone corsets and hoops under her dress, they shaped her and supported her, hiding beneath the bows and ruffles and hospitable smile the core of determination that gave her the strength to endure what she must.

Today would be a test of that. Today she had a task to perform—her last as the sole survivor of the Whitney family and inheritor of Rose Hill. With the flourish of a pen, her own personal drama would be over. She could finally drop the mask of brave but impoverished southern widow struggling to cling to her home while the last shreds of a way of life crumbled around her. She was so very weary of the pretense.

It was liberating, in a way. This final act had been so long in coming she was almost glad to have it done. She was ready for a new role.

More or less.

Pru walked toward her, her footfalls echoing hollowly off the stripped walls and empty shelves and bare wood floor. "Do you want me to stay?"

Edwina saw the worry in her sister's dark eyes and forced a smile. "What I want is for you to keep Reverend Morton occupied. If I have to suffer through one more pitying glance or murmured platitude, I declare I will throw myself out the window."

Pru arched a dark brow. "And fall the entire twelve inches onto the veranda? You brave thing." Reaching out, she gave Edwina's clasped hands a gentle squeeze. "He's only trying to help."

"Like he helps all the lonely widows?" Seeing Pru was about to scold, Edwina waved her away. "Fine. I'll be nice. But really. Doesn't the man realize we're Catholic?"

"He came to stand witness, not preach. And he brought the mail." Pru reached into her apron pocket and pulled out an envelope. She studied the address. "That's a dismal name. Heartbreak Creek."

Finally. Snatching the letter from her sister's grip, Edwina stuffed it into her skirt pocket. "I saw an advertisement for an employment opportunity and inquired about it, that's all."

"In Colorado Territory? Over a thousand miles away?"

To forestall further questions, Edwina nodded toward the door. "I think we've left the gentlemen waiting long enough. Show them in. I want this over with as soon as possible."

Pru hesitated. "You're sure you don't need me to stay?"

"I'll be fine. This is simply a formality." Edwina forced a smile. "We knew Rose Hill was lost months ago. I'm just glad it's going to our banker, rather than that Yankee scalawag tax man."

Pru nodded and turned away. She took a step, then paused to swing her gaze around the room that was empty of all but their father's desk and three mismatched chairs—one behind the desk, and two in front. "I shall miss the books."

Edwina heard the quaver in her sister's voice and strove for a lighter tone. "I don't know why. You read every one of them."

But Pru didn't seem to hear. "They were like friends. I felt safe among them."

Safe. Something twisted in Edwina's chest. Guilt, no doubt. She wanted to blurt out that those days of hiding—under beds, behind drapes, inside the pages of books—were over. She had a plan. A desperate, foolish, outrageous plan that was already in motion and, if successful, would allow them a new start far away from this place of destruction and despair.

It wasn't just the war-torn South Edwina hoped to escape but their own desperate childhoods. Years ago Pru had been Edwina's protector—and would bear the scars from that selfless act for the rest of her life. Now it was Edwina's turn to step out from behind her sister's skirts and do what she must to save them both.

Again, that feeling of liberation swept through her. She might be leaping from the fat into the fire, but at least for that brief moment she hung suspended between the two, she would be totally free. Clasping her hands once more at her waist, she stiffened her back and lifted her chin. "I'm ready, Pru. Send them in."

A scant fifteen minutes later, the papers were signed and witnessed. Rose Hill Plantation was now the property of Bayou Bank & Trust of

Sycamore Parish, to be auctioned off at a later date for back taxes.

Before the ink had dried, Edwina was slipping out the office door and down the veranda steps into the south lawn.

Hardly a lawn anymore. Mostly ragweed and dandelions. More weeds choked the azalea and camellia beds. The crepe myrtles had been left untended for so long they hardly bloomed anymore, and the arbor where she and Pru had hidden from Mother was now a tangled mass of ropey wisteria vines. With no one left to fight back the undergrowth, Rose Hill, like most of the grand houses throughout southern Louisiana, was slowly falling into neglect, disappearing beneath a mountain of untamed vegetation.

Blood was an excellent fertilizer, Edwina had heard.

Chased by so many memories and emotions she couldn't separate one from the other, she quickened her pace. By the time she reached the resting place on the rise above the bayou, she was almost running.

The gate creaked as she pushed it open. Slowing to catch her breath, she followed the weed-choked path past the raised vaults of all those who had lived and died at Rose Hill. Here, in this quiet place, nothing changed. The same birds nested among the wide, glossy leaves of the magnolias. The same squirrels scurried by with their acorns. The stately oak still stood guard over the dead, its outstretched arms trailing long streamers of moss like gray tattered scarves.

When she came to the newest graves, where the lime-washed concrete was still starkly white, unscarred by war and time, she sank down on a stone bench and dropped her head into her hands.

It was over. Gone. Her home, this resting place, an entire way of life . . . lost with the signing of her name.

"Daddy, I'm sorry. I'm so sorry."

After a while, disgusted with herself for giving way to useless tears, she blotted her cheeks and straightened. She had cried and wrung her hands for years, and it had gotten her nothing. Now she would do what she must to protect herself and Pru, even if that meant going all the way to Colorado Territory.

Gathering what courage she had left, she pulled the letter from her pocket and broke the seal.

A bank draft and several railroad vouchers slipped from a folded piece of paper and into her lap. Edwina carefully studied them. One voucher was for passage on the Texas and New Orleans Railroad dated five days hence. Another was for a later date on the Missouri Pacific, and the third was for the Colorado and Nevada.

It's happening, she thought, her heart starting to pound. *It's really happening.* With trembling fingers, she unfolded the sheet of paper.

I accept your terms. Enclosed find train vouchers and travel funds. I will meet you in Heartbreak Creek on the eleventh of April, 1870. Bring proxy papers. Brodie.

Edwina stifled a sudden urge to break into hysterical laughter. Or maybe wails of despair. It didn't matter which. It was done. Her fate was sealed. Within less than a month, she would serve herself up like a timorous virgin to a man she had never met, in a place she had never been, for a purpose that made her cringe.

Except, of course, she was neither timorous nor a virgin, and this time, she knew exactly what was in store for her.

A shadow passed overhead, and Edwina looked up to see a brown pelican wing by, the pouch beneath its beak full. She doubted they had pelicans in Colorado. Or magnolias, or shrimp gumbo, or long sultry days when even the alligators didn't venture far from the slow, murky waters.

But they had mountains. And snow. And since she had never seen either, she at least had that to look forward to.

"You're *what?*"

Pru's voice had risen to a near shriek. Her eyes were as round as a carp's, and her brows had moved halfway up to her tight dark curls as she'd stared at the papers in her hands.

16

It might have been comical had Edwina been in a laughing mood. Hoping to avoid arguments, she had planned to put off this confrontation until tomorrow, the day before their departure. But her sister had found the proxy papers, so Edwina was forced to tell her all.

"A mail-order bride." Edwina flopped down on the narrow bed in the room they shared in Mrs. Hebert's boardinghouse. "It's the perfect solution. And please don't try to talk me out of it, because as you can see by those papers, the deed is already done."

"You're married?"

"This morning. In Judge Aucoin's chambers. His assistant stood as witness. It was all rather humdrum." And somewhat sordid, but she didn't mention that. She'd been through one grand wedding. She certainly didn't need another.

"Married?"

"To Declan Brodie. He seems a nice enough man." Seeing that her sister was about to start yelling, Edwina dumped the contents of her reticule on the bed and riffled through the papers and vouchers until she found the tattered newspaper clipping. "Here," she said, handing it to Pru. "Read for yourself."

Edwina already knew the words by heart:

Honest, hard-working widower, age thirty-three, seeks sturdy English-speaking woman to help with mountain ranch and four children.

17

Drinkers, whores, and gamblers need not apply.

Such a romantic.

And one with rather low standards, she thought. Yet she qualified—except for the "sturdy" part. Since she had lost so much worry weight over the last months, her once "willowy" figure now had all the appeal of a flagpole.

"You actually responded to this?" Pru's voice was starting to rise again. "An advertisement in a common newspaper?"

"It's not common," Edwina defended. "It's the *Matrimonial News*. And it's famous. Everybody has heard of it."

"I haven't."

Edwina waved that aside. "And he wrote a very nice letter back." Digging again through the papers on the bed, she came up with a crumpled envelope, which she handed to her sister. "A rather nice assessment, I think."

"As well it should be," Pru snapped when she saw the signature. "Since the man wrote it himself."

"Not that one. The one from the traveling circuit judge."

Another terse appraisal that Edwina knew by heart:

Mr. Brodie is a man of strong determination who is well respected and tall.

Tall?

"And he also sent this." She held up a tiny

tintype of an unsmiling, clean-shaven, dark-haired man in a dark coat and banded collarless shirt.

Pru studied the tintype, then handed it back along with the letters of recommendation. "I just wish you'd talked to me first," she said, crossing her arms over her chest.

Edwina recognized the pose and braced for a scolding.

"Why would you do such a thing, Edwina? I know it was hard losing Rose Hill, but—"

"It isn't just Rose Hill, Pru. It's . . ." Edwina spread her hands in a helpless gesture. "It's everything. That man spitting on you, the vile things that Yankee upstart said to me, those horrid men in Crappo Town who are terrorizing everyone. This isn't home anymore. Everything has changed. And if there's nothing left for us here, why should we stay?"

"We? You're dragging me into this?"

"You're my sister. Did you think I would leave you behind?"

"Well . . . I . . ."

"They have mountains, Pru. Huge mountains! And all kinds of things we've never seen. And look!" Edwina bent to pull from beneath the bed the book that had arrived only yesterday. Beaming, she held it out. "Knowing what a glutton for information you are, and how curious you would be about our new home, I had this sent all the way from a New Orleans bookstore." And it had cost her dearly, but seeing the smile on her sister's face convinced Edwina it was worth every penny.

"*Our* new home?"

"Our new home. Mr. Brodie has a place for you in his household, too." Or he would, as soon as Edwina talked him into it.

Pru laughed and rolled her eyes. "He'd better. Since his new bride doesn't know a thing about cooking or tending children."

ONE

COLORADO, APRIL 1870

Twenty-seven days after signing over her childhood home to the Bayou Bank & Trust of Sycamore Parish, Edwina Ladoux stared bleakly out the soot-streaked window at her shoulder.

Just a few more miles. An hour, at most. And they would finally arrive in Heartbreak Creek and begin the exciting new life awaiting them.

The thought filled her with absolute terror.

Not that she wanted to put off this meeting forever. Or could. The signed proxy papers were in her carpetbag, all nice and tidy and legal. She had spent the man's money and had used the train tickets he had sent. She was obligated. Married. A wife again.

Thank heavens she had had the foresight to insist upon a two-month waiting period before actual consummation took place—God, how she dreaded going through that again—so for now, anyway, her husband couldn't force his attentions on her. *Her husband.*

It was madness. Ridiculous. The very idea that Edwina Whitney Ladoux, once the reigning belle of Sycamore Parish, should be reduced to marrying a complete stranger—a man who apparently was so hard-pressed he had to advertise for a wife in a newspaper—was ludicrous. Absurd.

Yet here she was, so terrified at the thought of having a husband again, her stomach felt like it was stuffed with hot nails.

Especially when the train began to slow. She clutched at Pru's arm. "Are we there? So soon?"

"Soon? It's been almost three weeks, Edwina. I, for one, am ready for this journey to end."

"Maybe something has happened." Edwina peered out the window toward the front of the slowing train, but saw nothing untoward. "We just stopped to put water in the tender, so it can't be that. Perhaps there's been a rockslide. Or a tree has fallen across the tracks."

She hoped so. She hoped it was something so catastrophic she could delay the meeting looming ahead of her for weeks. Months. Forever.

"Second thoughts, Edwina?"

Of course she had second thoughts. Hundreds

of them. Thousands. What had seemed like a viable solution back when penury was panting in her face now seemed like the most foolish thing she had ever done. Not that she would ever admit such a thing to her sister after tearing her from the only home she had ever known and dragging her halfway across the country. It was too late, anyway. Edwina had given her word and had signed her name. There was no stopping it now.

Unless she died. Or the train fell into the ravine. But that seemed a bit drastic. "Maybe it's another herd of buffalo."

"Oh, I doubt that." Beside her, Pru fussed with the front of her traveling cloak, then checked the tilt of her black horsehair bonnet. "They rarely range this high into the mountains."

Ever neat, Pru was. Sometimes such excessive attention to detail drove the imp in Edwina to do or say something to mess up that perfect order. But not today.

Today—assuming a host of guardian angels didn't swoop down to rescue them—they would arrive at the small depot five miles south of Heartbreak Creek, where her husband would be waiting. With his four children. Arms out-stretched to welcome his bride.

The thought almost made her vomit.

"I suppose it could be a herd of bighorn sheep," Pru mused. "Or elk. The book said both are common in mountainous terrain."

Oh, who cares? Biting back her mounting apprehension, Edwina stared stoically out the window. She wished she could be more like her sister, eagerly devouring each new tidbit of information, delighting in every long-winded description of the fauna and flora of the Rocky Mountains, as if this journey was some grand adventure rather than an act of pure desperation.

But then, Pru wasn't the one who would soon have a strange man coming at her with consummation in mind.

Edwina shuddered. In sudden panic, she reached over and gave her sister's hand a hard squeeze. "Thank you for coming with me, Pru. I couldn't have come without you."

"And I couldn't have stayed without you."

With a sigh, Edwina tipped her head against the cool glass and studied the small canyon below with its fast-moving stream and toppled boulders and deep, dark forests pushing right up to the edge of the churning water. Back home, the bayous and rivers were sluggish and warm and brown, shaded by sycamores, stately cypress, and moss-draped oaks. By now, the redbuds and dogwoods would be blooming and the magnolia buds would be fattening for their annual summer display of fragrant, showy blossoms.

A sudden, intense swell of homesickness almost choked her.

Gone. All of it. Forever.

The *clackety-clack* of the slowing train wheels gave way to the *screech* of brakes. Finally the train shuddered to a full stop. Passengers twisted in their seats, trying to see past the vapor from the smokestack that coiled around the windows like lost clouds.

The door at the front of the passenger coach swung open, and the conductor stepped inside. Stopping in the aisle between the two long rows of bench seats, he hooked his thumbs into his vest pockets and studied the expectant faces turned his way, his lips pursed beneath a bushy gray mustache that looped around his red-veined cheeks to join equally bushy muttonchop sideburns. He didn't look happy.

"There's a problem, folks," he announced. "Three miles up, a washout took out the Damnation Creek trestle."

The passengers moved restively. "What does that mean?" one asked.

"Means we'll be stuck for a while."

Edwina perked up. A while? How long was "a while"?

Raising his hands to quiet the angry muttering, the conductor explained. "They're sending wagons to carry you around the washout to Heartbreak Creek. The railroad will put you up there until the trestle is repaired."

"How long?" a man called out.

"A week. Maybe two."

Immediately, more voices rose. The conductor had to shout to continue, but Edwina scarcely heard a word. With something akin to giddiness, she turned to Pru. "We're saved, praise the Lord."

"A reprieve only." When Edwina started to say something more, Pru shushed her and leaned forward to attend the conductor's words.

But Edwina was feeling too euphoric to heed more than a word or phrase here and there—"hotel . . . meals . . . don't drink the water." To her, it all meant the same thing. A delay. A blessed reprieve. She wouldn't be meeting her new husband in Heartbreak Creek today as expected.

Thank you, Lord.

The conductor concluded his announcements and left, promising the wagons would arrive within an hour or so.

Pru fidgeted and sighed. "At least they'll be covering the cost of our accommodations in Heartbreak Creek until the tracks are repaired." She shot Edwina a look. "Stop grinning. And what makes you think your new husband won't travel the extra distance around the washout and be there waiting?"

"Oh, Sister, pray he doesn't."

Pru's elbow poked her ribs. "Hush," she warned in a low voice. "You must stop referring to me as your sister."

Edwina almost snorted. Prudence was more than her sister. She was her lifelong best friend, her confidant, the one who gave her courage when everything seemed so bleak. "You *are* my sister," she argued, rubbing her bruised side.

"Half sister. And to call attention to that fact is unseemly and casts your father in a poor light."

"*Our* father."

Pru pressed her full lips in a tight line, a clear indication she was losing patience. "Must you be so obstinate? If you're trying to make a new start, Edwina, why carry old baggage along?"

"Old baggage?" Edwina gave her a look of haughty disbelief. "Even though you're twenty-seven and an *entire* year older than me, *Sister,* I have never considered you *'baggage.'* "

Waving that aside, Pru went on in the same low voice. "There is no need to bandy it about that your father—"

"*Our* father. Who adored *your* mother. As well he should." Edwina was growing weary of this endless argument. Back home, Pru's parentage had been common knowledge. Everyone at Rose Hill had loved Ester, who had taken on the role of Edwina's mammy as soon as it had become apparent that Pricilla Whitney was incapable of caring for her own child. Had he been able, Charles Whitney would have gladly married Pru's mother; as it was, he had been utterly devoted to her until the night the Yankees had swept through Sycamore Parish, leaving death and destruction in their wake.

In truth, Edwina had loved Pru's mother more than her own.

Her gaze dropped to the fine, pale web of scars marring the brown skin that showed between the cuff and glove on Pru's right wrist. Other scars, hidden by the long sleeve of her gray bombazine, stretched up her right arm and halfway across her chest and back. Burn scars, given to her by Edwina's mother when Pru had tried to protect her little sister.

Edwina had scars, too, although other than a few pale stripes across her back, they were of a more subtle kind, the kind that festered in the soul and left behind invisible wounds of doubt and guilt and distrust.

She owed Pru her sanity, if not her life. And she loved her for it.

"Be that as it may," Pru went on, regaining Edwina's attention. "Races don't mix. It's against the laws of man and God, and you know it."

"Here we go again." Edwina faked a yawn behind her gloved hand. "If reason fails, bring out the Scriptures."

"Edwina!"

"Well, really, Pru. If it's true that white and black shouldn't mix, you would be a drooling, crossed-eyed hunchback with an extra ear. Instead you're beautiful."

Pru snorted. "Except for the hair and nose."

"Not as bad as the wart on my elbow," Edwina

chimed in. "And my less-than-ample bosom and—"

A soft, feminine chuckle interrupted Edwina's self-deprecation. Looking past Pru, she saw the blond lady across the aisle was smiling at them. Edwina had seen the smartly dressed young woman several times over the last days, nearly always seated with another young, attractive lady toward the rear of the coach. But today, after the train had stopped in Santa Lucia to fill the tender with water, both women had moved to the vacant bench across the aisle from Pru.

"Are you truly arguing about which of you is less attractive?" the woman asked, her green eyes dancing with amusement. Beautiful eyes, with a slight upward tilt at the outside corners that might have hinted at wide-eyed innocence if not for the hard knowledge behind the knowing smile. A Yankee, by her accent. Poor thing. No wonder she seemed jaded.

Before Edwina could respond to the comment, the other woman, seated next to the window, looked over with a wide smile. Where the blond had shown a worldly-wise weariness beneath her cool green eyes, this auburn-haired lady seemed without artifice. An ingenuous, dimpled smile complemented intense chocolate brown eyes that sparkled with such life and intelligence Edwina couldn't help but smile back. "You are both too beautiful by half," the woman said in a clipped

English accent. "Your bone structure is superb, both of you. And I assure you, I would know."

Edwina wasn't sure what to make of that. Usually, any compliments she received—mostly from men—involved her magnolia skin, which always sounded a bit sickly to her—or her glorious hair, which she thought was abysmally average, ranging from mouse brown to light brown, depending on how many lemons were available—and her soulful blue eyes, which were admittedly her best feature and the exact shade of the early spring forget-me-nots that had bloomed along the garden wall back home.

How sad that they, and the wall, and all the handsome young men with their pretty compliments were gone forever.

"Excuse me for intruding." The blond woman held out a hand encased in a finely sewn white kid glove. "I'm Lucinda Hathaway."

"Edwina Ladoux . . . Brodie." Leaning past Pru to take the proffered hand, she noted the gold ear bobs, the fine fabric of the blond's traveling cloak, the shiny button-top boots planted protectively against an expensive leather valise stowed under her seat. Even though Edwina had supported herself and Pru as a seamstress—barely— and was skilled at refitting made-over dresses to look stylish, she couldn't help but feel dowdy in comparison to this pretty woman. "And this is, Prudence, my—"

"Traveling companion," Pru cut in, ignoring Edwina's sharp look. "So pleased to meet you."

"Madeline Wallace, but I prefer Maddie," the auburn-haired woman chimed in with a wave in Edwina's and Pru's direction. She wore no gloves, and a thick signet ring was visible on her left hand.

"You're married?" Edwina was taken aback by the notion that a married woman would be traveling alone if she didn't have to. Then realizing how rude that sounded, she quickly added, "I saw your ring."

Maddie held up her hand, palm out. She studied the thick gold band for a moment, then shrugged. "I suppose I am married, although I haven't heard from Angus in over three years. Perhaps he's dead." A brief flash of distress at that startling announcement, then she let her hand fall back into her lap and smiled. "He's Scottish," she clarified, which clarified nothing. "A soldier. I couldn't bear to stay another day with his family —they have low regard for the English, you know, and little hesitation in showing it—so I left."

"Good girl," Lucinda murmured.

"Left?" Edwina parroted, shocked by the notion of a woman simply heading off on her own to a foreign country just because she didn't like living with her husband's family.

"I'm an expeditionary photographer. A tintypist, really, specializing in *cartes de visite*." Maddie

30

smiled as if that explained everything, which it didn't. "The *Illustrated London News* is paying me to capture the American West from a woman's perspective. Isn't that grand?"

It was unbelievable. A female photographer? Edwina couldn't imagine such a thing. It had taken all her courage to travel a thousand miles, yet this tiny woman had taken on a man's occupation and crossed an ocean to an unknown country. How daring. And terrifying. And admirable.

"And you?" Lucinda inquired, jarring Edwina back to the conversation. "Do you live in this area?"

Edwina blinked at her, wondering how to answer. "Yes. I mean, I plan to. That is to say, I will. Soon."

"She's traveling to meet her husband," Pru piped up in an attempt to translate Edwina's garbled response.

"How nice." Lucinda's voice carried a noticeable lack of enthusiasm.

"Not really."

"Oh, dear," Pru murmured.

The two women across the aisle stared at her with brows raised and expectant expressions, so Edwina felt compelled to explain. "I've never met him, you see. We married in a proxy ceremony."

A moment of awkward, if not stunned, silence. A pitying look came into Lucinda's eyes, but Maddie clapped her hands in delight. "A mail-order bride! How perfect! How utterly western! You shall be my first subject! Won't that be delightful?"

Delightful in a ghoulish, horrifying way, Edwina thought, not sure she wanted her misery captured on tintype for all time.

That afternoon, when the wagon transporting the passengers rolled to a muddy stop outside the hotel, Edwina decided that if Heartbreak Creek was an example of divine intervention on her behalf, then God was either extremely angry with her or had a macabre sense of humor.

But she still offered up a grateful prayer of thanks that no tall, dark-haired, unsmiling man rushed forward to greet her.

"Oh, my," Maddie breathed, eyes sparkling with enthusiasm as she peered over the side rails. "I could take photographs here for a month."

"If we live that long," Lucinda muttered. Clutching her leather valise in one hand and raising her skirts with the other—much to the glee of three reprobates grinning from the doorway of the Red Eye Saloon next door to the hotel—she gingerly stepped out of the wagon, onto the mounting block, then up onto the boardwalk. With a look of distaste, she dropped her skirts and looked around. "Two weeks. Here. Surely they're jesting."

Edwina climbed up onto the boardwalk beside

her, followed by Maddie, then Prudence. Moving aside to make room for the other passengers clambering out of the wagon, the four women studied the town.

It was a dismal place.

Situated at the bottom of a steep-sided canyon, the town was a rat's nest of unpainted plank-sided buildings, sagging tents, dilapidated sheds and lean-tos, all sandwiched between a flooded creek and a single muddy dunghill of a street. And the crowning glory, perched on the rocky hillside north of the wretched town, was a sprawling, many-scaffolded edifice that looked more like a monstrous spider poised to strike than a working mine. The entire town had a haphazard, unfinished feel to it, like a collection of random afterthoughts thrown together by a confused mind.

And yet, Edwina realized, looking around a second time, if one looked beyond the eyesore of the mine, and the squalor and taint of decay that seemed to hang in the air like stale wood smoke, there was astounding beauty to be seen. Tall conifers rising a hundred feet. Stark cliffs sheened by cascading waterfalls winding down the rock face like frothy ribbons. High, white-capped peaks cutting a jagged edge against a cloudless blue sky. It was savage and mysterious . . . but it was also blessedly free of the ravages of war, and for that reason more than any other, Edwina liked it.

"I wonder what they mine?" Maddie asked, squinting up at the sprawling hillside monstrosity.

"Nothing lucrative," Lucinda murmured, eyeing the ill-kempt, wide-eyed gawkers now spilling out of the saloon to get a better look at the ladies. "This place is one step from being a ghost town."

"A ghost town!" Maddie fairly glowed with excitement. "Two weeks won't be long enough to do justice to this marvelous place. And look at those faces! Each one tells a story. I can't wait to get to work."

"Then you'd best start unpacking," Lucinda advised, eyeing the boxes of photography equipment crowding the boardwalk.

Prudence nudged Edwina's arm and nodded to where the conductor was crossing names off a list as the other passengers filed into the hotel. "Let's get settled."

The Heartbreak Creek Hotel might have been—for a month or two, anyway—a thriving place. But years of neglect had reduced it to a bedraggled, rickety old dowager, barely clinging to the threadbare remnants of her brief glory. Sun-faded drapes, scuffed wainscoting against peeling wallpaper, once-lovely oil sconces now caked with soot and dust. Even the air that met them when they stepped through the open double doors smelled musty, laced with the lingering scents of stale cooking odors, tobacco smoke, and moldy carpets.

As they waited their turn before the conductor, Edwina scanned the lobby. Directly across from the entry doors was a high paneled counter that showed remarkable, if grimy, workmanship, manned by a harried elderly clerk passing out brass keys as the passengers signed in. Beside the counter rose a steep staircase that led to a banistered mezzanine off which doors into the upstairs rooms opened. To the right of the entry, an archway opened into a dining area, now deserted in the midafternoon lull, while to the left stood a closed door, which led, judging by the tinkling piano music and loud voices, directly into the reprobates' saloon.

"She with you?" a voice asked.

Turning, Edwina found the conductor frowning at her, his small, faded blue eyes flicking to Pru, who stood slightly behind her. Edwina read disapproval in his expression and felt her ire rise. "She is."

The conductor's lips thinned beneath his bushy gray mustache. "You'll have to share a room. That all right by you?"

"Of course it's all right." Edwina started to add, *and why wouldn't it be, you pinhead?* when a sharp tug on the back of her coat choked off the angry retort. Pru hated scenes.

The conductor licked the tip of his stubby pencil and squinted at his list. "Names?"

"Edwina Ladoux . . . Brodie. And this lovely

35

lady with me"—ignoring her sister's warning glare, Edwina swept a hand in her direction—"is my—" Another jerk almost pulled her backward. Before she could recover, Pru stepped forward to say, "Maid. Prudence Lincoln, sir."

While Edwina coughed, Pru accepted their room assignment, nodded her thanks, and shoved Edwina on into the lobby, where the front desk clerk was directing passengers to their rooms.

"You almost choked me," Edwina accused, rubbing her throat.

"Hush. People are looking."

"At my vicious *maid,* no doubt."

"Welcome, ladies. I'm Yancey." Showing stained teeth—what few were left, anyway—in a broad smile, the hotel clerk, a grizzled old man with eyebrows as fat as white caterpillars, beckoned them forward. "Room number?"

Before Pru could answer, Lucinda stepped past them and up to the counter. "Room twenty." Setting her valise on the floor, she gave Pru and Edwina an apologetic smile. "I told the conductor we would share. I hope you don't mind. It'll be safer," she added in a whisper. Then without waiting for a response, she turned back to the slack-faced clerk, plucked the pen from its holder, dipped it in the inkwell, and smiled sweetly. "Where shall I sign?"

"Twenty?" The old man was clearly aghast. "But that—that's the Presidential Suite!"

"So I've been told."

"But you're not the president."

"Alas, no." Turning the full force of those dazzling green eyes on the befuddled Yancey, Lucinda leaned closer to whisper, "But Uncle insisted I take it if I ever came to Heartbreak Creek. Will that be a problem?"

"Goddamn."

Apparently, that meant it wasn't. After ordering a freckled boy to take fresh linens and water to "the big suite," he reverently placed the key in Lucinda's gloved hand and bowed them toward the stairs. "Last room at the end of the hall, ladies. The boy is setting it up now."

As they headed toward the staircase, Edwina gave Lucinda a wondering look. "Are you really Grant's niece?"

"Grant? Who said I was Grant's niece?"

"But, I thought . . . you mean, you're not?"

Lucinda laughed. "That old drunk?"

Not much of an answer, but apparently all Lucinda was willing to give. As they trooped up the stairs, Edwina mused that there were a lot of unanswered questions about Lucinda, not the least of which was what was in that valise that she guarded so protectively. Edwina sensed that like her, Lucinda had been through hard times and devastating loss. But Lucinda had chosen to fight back, while Edwina had chosen to run.

But, really, what choice had she? Raised in the

lap of luxury without a care beyond what to wear to the next ball, Edwina barely knew how to survive. Oh, certainly she had skills—dancing, flirting, performing parlor tricks like finding water with willow sticks or playing the piano blindfolded—but that hardly put food on the table. Other than her meager sewing income—which Pru augmented with sales from their vegetable garden and the occasional household position that came her way—the only thing that had kept them going through the last hard years was hope. But after five years of the excesses of the Reconstruction, that was gone, too. Now all that remained of her past was a weed-choked cotton plantation sold for back taxes, her father's watch, and a graveyard full of new markers.

The South she loved was no more. She had realized that the day Pru had been spat upon by a white man just because of her dark skin, while she, a white woman, had been vilified for sharing blood with a woman of color.

No, she wasn't running away. She just had no reason to stay.

As they neared their room at the end of the landing, the door swung open and the freckled boy darted out. "All set up, ma'ams. You need anything, just yell over the banister to Yancey." Then he was off at a run down the hall.

"Set up" meant tattered linens were stacked on the unmade beds in each of the two bedrooms opening off the sitting area, and a pitcher of cold water sat on the bureau. Edwina peered down into its murky depths. "Is this the water we're not supposed to drink?"

"I'll stick with brandy," Lucinda muttered, carrying her valise into the bedroom on the left.

Maddie stopped beside the pitcher, took a look, and shuddered. "It looks used. How vexing."

"I wonder what's wrong with it?" This whole water thing confused Edwina. "With a creek running right through the middle of town and all those waterfalls streaming down the slopes, how could the water be so bad?"

"Probably the mine," Pru said as she hung her coat on a hook beside the door. "They often use harsh chemicals to leach gold or silver from the raw ore. If it seeps back into the ground, it can taint the entire water table."

Edwina turned to stare at her. "How do you know these things?"

"I read."

"About mining practices?" Edwina shouldn't have been surprised. Her sister took in information like a starving person gobbled up food. But mining practices? "Why would you read about mining practices?"

"Why wouldn't I?" As she spoke, Pru set herself to rights, straightening her sleeves, brushing her skirts, running a hand over her tightly pinned hair. "I'm only guessing, of course. But since the mine is upriver from the town, and I did see some sluices and a thick canvas pipe running down from one of those waterfalls to what I assume is a concentrator, I can only deduce the water is being used to leach out unwanted chemicals." She paused in thought, one long, graceful finger gently tapping her full lower lip. "Or maybe it's for a water cannon. I'll have to check."

"Oh, please do!" Shaking her head, Edwina walked into the bedroom she was to share with Pru.

An hour later, their valises were unpacked, their beds made, and they were as refreshed as four women could be, sharing one pitcher of cold water between them.

"We're famished," Lucinda announced, walking into the sitting room with her valise in her hand and Maddie on her heels. "Shall we brave the cooking in this wretched place and go down to the dining room?"

"Dare we?" Edwina asked.

Pru straightened her collar and checked her buttons. "I'm willing."

"Excellent." Swinging open the door, Lucinda motioned the other ladies into the hallway, stepped out after them, and locked the door. "And while we eat," she said, following them down the stairs, "Edwina can tell us all about her new husband, and Maddie can tell us about her errant husband, and Pru can tell us what she hopes to do with all that astounding book learning."

And perhaps while we're at it, Edwina added silently, *you'll tell us what you have in that valise you guard like stolen treasure.*

TWO

*O*h, *drat!*
Filled with foreboding, Edwina picked up the note bearing her name that someone had shoved beneath the door while they had been choking down a barely edible dinner in the dining room below. She had a fair idea who had left it there. While the other three ladies filed past her into the sitting area, she forced herself to open it.

The familiar script. This time, only six words:
Eight o'clock outside the hotel. Brodie.

"What is it?" Pru asked, moving on toward their bedroom.

"Not bad news, I hope." With a deep sigh, Maddie plopped into one of the worn wingbacks by the flyspecked window. "I deplore bad news."

"Do you, Pollyanna?" Shooting her a look of amusement, Lucinda sank gracefully into the other chair. "How odd."

Maddie's cheerful optimism was the antithesis of Lucinda's cynical outlook, and the two women had enlivened their dismal meal with gentle banter. Lucinda had accused Maddie of having

41

her head so far above the clouds she couldn't see the rain falling on her feet. Maddie had retaliated by asking if Lucinda was a misplaced Scot.

But now, seeing the stricken expression on Edwina's face, Lucinda's smile faded. "What's wrong?"

Edwina gripped the note in a tight fist as if she had the man himself by the scruff of his neck. "He's here! And he expects me to meet him outside the hotel tomorrow morning. *Tomorrow!*" Apparently the washout hadn't damaged the road enough to make it impassable.

Maddie turned to Lucinda. "I'm assuming she means her husband."

Edwina had told them about Declan Brodie and his four children, and her growing reservations about marrying a stranger. Maddie had tried to reassure her by explaining that arranged marriages were not uncommon in Britain. "Although mine wasn't, of course. Ours was a love match."

"And see how well that turned out," Lucinda had remarked, adding, "Married or not, men are as steadfast as a loose woman's virtue."

"What should I do?" Edwina now asked her new friends.

"Run," Lucinda advised.

"Meet him," Maddie countered. "He deserves at least that."

"Pack." Moving to the wardrobe in their bedroom, Pru pulled out her carpetbag and set it on

42

the bed. She began packing garments inside.

Edwina studied the note again, thoughts jumbling in her mind. "Perhaps he just wants to talk. Pay his respects. Perhaps he doesn't intend to actually *leave* tomorrow." She looked hopefully at the two women seated by the window. "That sounds reasonable, doesn't it?"

Lucinda shrugged.

"What does he say exactly?" Maddie asked.

She told them. "Twelve hours. That's all I have left." Too restless to sit, she began pacing the small sitting area.

"It could be a grand adventure." To sweet Maddie, every cloud was woven with golden threads and sprinkled with diamonds. "This marriage might very well be all you've ever dreamed."

"Surely you don't believe that, Maddie," Lucinda challenged. The worldly New Yorker had made it clear what she thought about marriage and men. Though she seldom spoke about herself —and when she did, offered little information— it was obvious she held both the wedded state and the male gender in low regard. "Have you ever seen a truly happy couple?"

"Angus and I might have been, had he ever stayed around long enough for us to get to know one another."

"Or you might have been utterly miserable. Two letters in five years. The man should be shot."

"Maybe he was. Maybe that's why he hasn't written." Maddie sent Lucinda a worried look. "Surely I would have been notified if he had been, don't you think? I wouldn't want him to be dead."

Too distracted to attend their conversation, Edwina wandered into the bedroom and plopped down on the bed beside Pru's valise. She needed her sister's steady calmness now. She needed to hear that everything would be all right, even if it was a lie.

"Why is he in such a hurry?" she complained. "He could have waited a few more days."

Pru looked at her.

From the other room, Maddie called, "Perhaps he can't wait any longer to meet his lovely bride," which elicited a chuckle from Lucinda.

Realizing any words spoken in the bedroom could be easily heard by the two women watching through the open door into the sitting area, Edwina shot them a scolding look. "We can hear and see you."

"We can see and hear you, too," Lucinda responded gaily. "Although it would help if you spoke up a touch."

Edwina flopped back across the ratty counterpane. "Such haste is unseemly. I'm not a cow to be herded around. I'm a gently bred lady."

"You're a nitwit," her sister muttered. "That's why we're here."

"Nonetheless, I deserve better. I *had* better."

44

"You've been married before?" Maddie called.

Lucinda's muttered response was just loud enough to carry into the bedroom. "And she's doing it a second time?"

"Yes, I was, and he was such a sweet boy." Edwina stared up at the ceiling and tried to picture Shelly's face as he had appeared nine years ago on their wedding day. Both scarcely seventeen and oh, so foolish. "He looked so handsome in his sword and sash."

"One does get pulled in by the uniform," Maddie mused. "Angus is with the Tenth Hussars. Assuming he's still alive."

Barely listening, Edwina let her thoughts drift back to those early days, when hope and southern pride had flowed through the South like summer wine until they'd all become drunk on Confed-erate patriotism.

It had been a summer wedding. They'd held it in the garden under the wisteria arbor. Bees had droned in the flower beds, and the air had been heady with the scent of sweet alyssum and dianthus and stocks.

Then had come the wedding night, and the realization that she had made a terrible mistake in marrying a childhood friend who was more like a brother than a sweetheart. After that one fumbling, awkward night—the memory of which still gave Edwina the shivers—poor Shelly had marched off in his smart gray uniform, only to return four months later, minus a leg.

"What happened to him?" Maddie asked.

"Gangrene." Edwina didn't want to think of those last horrid weeks—day after day watching him waste away—the suffering, the stench, the awful emptiness in his eyes. "It near broke my heart."

Pru snapped the wrinkles out of a skirt with such vigor it sounded like the crack of a whip in the small room. "You only married that poor boy because he was your friend," she reminded Edwina. "He had no one else to wave him off to war, and you felt sorry for him."

"Maybe I shouldn't have married him, Pru. But I loved him." Tears welled up—for herself, for Shelly, for all the lost dreams. "Why did everything have to change? I wish that wretched war had never happened."

Pru paused in her packing to look at her.

"Except for the slavery thing," Edwina amended with a half-hearted wave of one hand. "Naturally I wanted that to stop."

"We English ended that nasty practice years ago, thank heavens."

"After," Lucinda pointed out to the English-woman, "you introduced that nasty practice here."

"No matter how it ended," Pru cut in, "on behalf of freed slaves everywhere, I just thank the Lord it's over."

"On behalf of Yankees everywhere," Lucinda quipped, "you're welcome."

"Ha!" Sitting up, Edwina glared at her sister, still piqued by her callous, if true, remarks about Shelly. "You were never a slave, Pru, and don't pretend you were."

"My mother was."

"And our father was a slave to her." Edwina saw her sister's face tighten and knew she'd misspoken. Despite their friendship with Lucinda and Maddie, Pru still insisted they not discuss their shared father. Anger seeping away, Edwina put her hand on her sister's arm. "Please, Pru, let's not get into that again. The war's been over for five years. There's even a man of color in the Congress. Can't we finally put slavery to rest?"

"Half color. And Mr. Revels was never a slave." Pausing in her folding, Pru looked at the far wall, her expression troubled. "I try. But then I see all those bewildered Negroes wandering through the towns we pass, and I get angry all over again. They can't read or write, Edwina. They have no training to start new lives. Someone should help them—do something."

Edwina studied her sister, feeling that pang of sympathy warring with her impatience. Freed slaves weren't the only ones left bereft and bewildered. The South had been utterly destroyed. Thousands upon thousands had died. What more could be done to right that terrible wrong? Kill thousands more? "Here's an idea, then," she suggested. "Let's go back to Rose Hill, dig up my grandfather's bones, and stomp the stuffings out of them. Will that make you feel better?"

Pru bit back a smile and resumed packing. "It might."

"Sounds a bit drastic," Maddie called. "Even the Scots don't dig up their dead."

Flopping back again, Edwina watched lacy cobwebs on the stained ceiling swing to and fro in a gentle draft, and felt such a sense of despair it seemed to clog her throat. "I just want to put it all behind me," she said in a wobbly voice. "All that pain and death and destruction. I don't want to think about all those new graves. Is that so wrong? To want to start over?"

"No, love. It isn't." Sinking onto the edge of the bed beside her, Pru reached out and patted Edwina's hand. "I'm just not sure marrying a man you never met is the way to go about it."

"I agree," Lucinda called. "Men will always break your heart."

"Sad, but true," Maddie put in. "And if you do marry a stranger, sometimes getting to know him better will only lead to impossible hopes and expectations they are unable or unwilling to fulfill."

"Well, what choice did I have?" Edwina complained, sitting up again. "A Klansman or a carpetbagger. It seems all the men were either married, so defeated they couldn't go on, or so angry they wouldn't let the killing end. I can't

48

live like that any longer. I won't."

Pru resumed packing. "Eldridge Blankenship was unmarried, and was neither Klansman nor carpetbagger. He would have made a fine husband."

"Or a beaver," Edwina argued, earning a laugh from Lucinda. "Did you see those teeth? Besides, he wanted children."

Another subject they hadn't broached with their new friends, so Pru didn't respond.

But Maddie's curiosity was aroused. Tipping her head to study Edwina through the open door, she asked, "You don't want children?"

Edwina shrugged.

"How do you plan to stop them from coming?"

"There are ways," Lucinda said before Edwina had to admit she was hoping to talk her groom into abstinence. "A man named Charles Goodyear has invented a rubber sheath that fits over—"

"Lucinda Hathaway!" Prudence gave her a look that would have done her name proud. "I cannot believe you would discuss such a thing!"

"We're none of us virgins," Lucinda pointed out. "Including you, I'd guess, since you're experienced enough to know what I'm talking about."

Surprised, Edwina turned to her sister, expecting an immediate denial. But Pru didn't meet her gaze, although her caramel-colored skin did seem to darken a bit.

"Fits over what?" Maddie persisted.

Lucinda rolled her eyes. "For someone with an arts background you have a somewhat limited imagination, don't you, dear?"

"I'm a photographer, not a—my word! You're talking about French letters, aren't you? They're made of *rubber?* I thought they were made of linen or silk or animal intestines."

"Intestines? Good Lord. You Scots truly are backward."

"I'm English, Lucinda, as well you know."

"Be that as it may, rubber sheaths have been around for at least a decade. Apparently neither you nor your *Scottish* husband has ever used one."

"There was no need."

"No need? You mean you didn't—"

"Of course we did," Maddie cut. "Many times. Often in the same day. But contraception wasn't an issue. I wanted children. Very much."

Edwina gaped at her two friends, amazed that they could so blithely discuss such taboo subjects as consummation and conception. They seemed so confident and assured. So experienced. "I wish I could be more like you two," she said wistfully. "Say whatever you want. Travel where and when the mood strikes. Follow your dreams wherever they take you, instead of just being someone's wife."

"Oh, being a wife isn't so bad," Maddie allowed. "I rather liked it. Until he dumped me on his family and left. Ghastly man, that earl."

"Earl?" Lucinda sounded shocked. "You were married to an earl?"

"His father is the earl. Angus is only third in line, which was why he was in the military, of course."

"Edwina, you wouldn't last two minutes on your own," Pru said, responding to her earlier remark. "You can't even cook."

"Who cooks?" Maddie said airily. "I'm sure your new husband will be delighted with you, Edwina, whether you can cook or not. Angus didn't seem to mind that I couldn't cook. But then we rarely left the bedroom. When he bothered to come see me, that is."

The next morning at ten minutes after eight o'clock, Edwina stepped out of the Heartbreak Creek Hotel into such bright, glaring sunlight it made her head pound even worse than it had throughout the night. Raising a hand to shade her eyes, she looked around, wrinkling her nose at the smell of the horse droppings in the street and the stale reek of whiskey and tobacco smoke drifting out of the open door of the Red Eye Saloon next door.

Other than the distant thudding of machinery up at the mine, the town seemed deader than it had when they'd arrived the previous day—no gawkers peering through the greasy windows of the saloon, no wagons lumbering down the muddy street, and no unsmiling man resembling that tiny tintype waiting outside the hotel.

"So where is he?" she groused, squinting down the boardwalk. "It's after eight. He should be here by now." After spending a near-sleepless night dreading this meeting, she now found herself churning with impatience for it to be over. Rather like the terrified anticipation felons facing a firing squad must feel. "It's rude to keep a lady waiting. A *wife* waiting."

What if he never comes? What if the money runs out and we're stranded in this nasty little town forever?

A sharp breeze, crisp with spring's promise even though snow still capped the peaks above the mine, cut through Edwina's thin coat and made her shiver. Beside her, Pru patted and smoothed and checked her buttons with annoying predictability.

"Stop fidgeting, Pru," she snapped. "It's giving me a headache."

"Poor dear."

The lack of sympathy in Pru's tone fueled Edwina's pique. "And another thing." She met her sister's bland look with a warning glare. "If you refer to yourself as my maid again I will cause such a ruckus it'll make your hair curl."

"My hair is already curled."

"I mean it, Prudence."

52

"In a bad mood, are we?"

Realizing she was sounding like a petulant child, Edwina let go a deep sigh and along with it, most of her anger. "I wish Maddie and Lucinda were here. Maybe I can hire on as Maddie's photography assistant. Or as Lucinda's personal seamstress. I should have thought to ask."

"No matter. You're married." Pru straightened her bonnet after a sudden gust almost snatched it from her head. "And we decided to let them sleep, remember? Besides, we said our good-byes last night."

"I know. But still . . ." Edwina would have liked having them there for support. Maddie's eternal good cheer might have kept her spirits up, even as Lucinda's innate pragmatism would have reminded her that she'd made her choice and had best get on with it. "This waiting is fraying my nerves."

What if he misrepresented himself? What if he's an ogre? A toothless, squint-eyed, wife-beating ogre?

Blinking back the sting of tears, she stared down at her tightly clasped hands. Thank God she had insisted on the two-month waiting period so they could get to know each other before doing . . . *that*. Perhaps she should extend it to three. Yes, three would do nicely. That way, if he didn't work out, she would have time to come up with another plan before he insisted on exercising his husbandly duties. Her skin prickled at the thought.

"I don't think you'll have to wait much longer."

Edwina looked up to see her sister staring fixedly past her shoulder. "Is it him?"

"He," Pru corrected absently. "And yes, I think so."

When Edwina started to turn, Pru grabbed her arm. "Don't look. You'll appear too anxious."

She *was* anxious. She was tired, anxious, and terrified. "Well?" she prodded impatiently. "What does he look like? Is he presentable? Clean, at least? I never trust those tintypes."

"He's . . . ah . . . presentable. And bigger."

Edwina resisted the urge to burst into nervous giggles. "I should hope so. That tintype is smaller than my watch."

This was insane. The whole idea was insane. What was she thinking to marry a complete stranger, some backwoods mountain-man rancher type?

What if he's wearing animal skins?

"What is he doing?" she asked, trying to keep the quaver from her voice. "Has he seen us? Is he coming this way? Is my bonnet straight?"

"Stop fussing," Pru hissed. "He's talking to someone. No, wait. Now he's walking toward us. Compose yourself."

Edwina told herself not to look, but found her head turning anyway. A quick glance, then she faced forward again, a sense of relief coursing through her. A well-dressed man, wearing a smart bowler hat and finely tailored suit. She'd only had a glimpse, but he had seemed presentable. Older than she'd expected, perhaps. And rounder, and a bit hairier with that flaring mustache, but presentable, nonetheless. A benign man. Easily managed. She let out a deep exhale. *Thank you, Lord.* "He'll do," she whispered to Pru with a happy grin. "He won't be any trouble at all."

Her sister reared back to gape at her. "You're jesting."

"No, truly, Pru." She patted her sister's gloved hand in reassurance. "I have a good feeling about this. As soon as I convince him to shave off that silly mustache he'll be quite the thing."

"Mustache?" Pru started to laugh. "Oh, dear."

Edwina's smile faded. "Oh, dear, what?" She tensed as footfalls approached from behind.

A deep voice said, "Morning, ma'am," and the man in the tailored suit and bowler hat stepped around them and on down the boardwalk.

Edwina's shoulders slumped. "Drat. Where the dickens is he?"

Then she saw Pru's head tilt up, then higher still, and suddenly she felt an ominous presence behind her. It was all she could do to turn slowly, and then all she could do not to shriek out loud.

He was huge, bristly-jawed, scowling, and not presentable at all. He didn't even do them the courtesy of removing his dusty Stetson when addressing her, and—*merciful heavens*—was that a gun in his belt?

"Edwina Ladoux Brodie?" he asked in a deep voice every bit as welcoming as his stern features.

"Gwaugh," Edwina garbled, caught between "Good God" and "What?"

The man's dark gaze flicked between the sisters, paused briefly on Pru's scarred wrist, then settled on Edwina. "Is one of you Ed—"

"Yes!" Edwina managed, having finally found her voice. "I'm her—she—Edwina Ladoux, that is. Brodie." She lifted a shaky hand toward Pru. "And this is my—"

"Traveling companion," Pru cut in, with a nod of her head. "Prudence Lincoln."

The man frowned at Pru for a moment, then swung his attention back to Edwina. It was oppressive, the way he looked at her. Intrusive and rude.

Realizing she had twisted the strings of her reticule so tightly around her wrist that her fingers had gone numb, Edwina didn't offer her hand but simply stood there, her heart drumming so hard she thought she might faint.

Surely this great hulking lump wasn't her husband. He looked nothing like the tintype. Well, perhaps a bit. But only because both men had dark hair and eyes, and neither seemed capable of smiling.

The man in the tintype was certainly more

properly dressed in a banded drover shirt and a dark coat.

This man wore a battered sheepskin jacket over an unbleached work shirt and worn denims, and instead of being clean-shaven wore a three-day growth of dark beard on his scowling, square-jawed face. Plus, he looked older. Well, not so much *older,* as less young, or perhaps just tired. And those eyes—

Edwina abruptly lost her train of thought when she realized he had been scrutinizing her just as thoroughly as she had been scrutinizing him. Except he didn't even try to hide the blatant assessment, his studied gaze moving boldly down to her smart, although well-worn kid slippers, then up over her also worn, but still quite fashionable gabardine traveling cloak, and finally rising to the drawn silk spoon bonnet she had dressed up with jaunty rosettes and peacock plumes to disguise the fact that it was five years out of date. It seemed to hold his attention for an extended time, and to Edwina's experienced eye he didn't look particularly pleased with what he saw.

"I wasn't expecting two," he muttered, tearing his gaze from her hat to scowl at Pru.

Edwina stiffened, although despite her height and even if she had risen on tiptoe, she still wouldn't have reached past his chin. "I shall go nowhere without my—"

"Traveling companion," Pru cut in.

Edwina glared at her.

Pru smiled sweetly back.

Two women walked by, shooting speculative glances from beneath the brims of their cottage bonnets at the man glaring down at them. Farm women, Edwina guessed, eyeing their faded calico dresses and scuffed boots. Sturdy, practical farm women. She wondered if they spoke English. An insane urge to run after them and ask almost sent her into hysterical laughter. It was bizarre. Comical, really. Then she glanced up at the man towering over her and amusement faded. Obviously he didn't share her appreciation of the absurd, judging by the tense line of his mouth and the disapproving glint in his dark brown eyes.

He mumbled something, scratched at his bristly jaw, then sighed. "Come along then." And without waiting for a response, he turned and started down the boardwalk.

Edwina gaped at his broad back. "I beg your pardon!"

"Oh, dear," Pru muttered.

He stopped and swung back.

"Come along where?" Edwina demanded.

"To the wagon." He waved a big hand in the direction he'd been headed. "By the mercantile. It's already loaded." Turning, he commenced walking. Or clumping. The man's stride was twice Edwina's, and with his full weight coming

58

down on the narrow sloped heels of his boots, each footfall sounded like a hammer blow on the wooden boardwalk.

"What's the rush?" she called, bringing him to a stop once again. She had hoped they might chat for a moment. Perhaps step into the hotel dining room for a cup of tea. *Something* to mark their first meeting.

This time, he at least had the good grace to retrace his steps, but when he stopped before her, Edwina wished he hadn't. Without even trying to mask his impatience, he snapped, "The washout and a busted wheel have already cost me an extra day. I need to get back. Now."

For what? A pig sticking?

"What about our things?" Pru asked. "We have only two bags."

"Where?"

"In the hotel. I'll have the bellboy bring them down." And before Edwina could stop her, Pru darted into the lobby.

Battling panic, Edwina stood rooted where her sister had abandoned her. Unable to meet that piercing gaze, she studied the boardwalk, listened to him breathe, blinked at his astoundingly large boots.

Tension built until the weight of it filled Edwina's mind and drove a burst of words out of her mouth. "I have friends," she said in a rush. "In the hotel. I must say good-bye." Then before he could respond, she whirled and fled into the hotel after her sister.

Pru was nowhere in sight. But instead of pounding up the stairs in search of her, Edwina veered toward the clerk at the front desk, desperate for some reassurance about the man waiting outside. What if her husband was a known desperado or murderous villain intent on carving out their hearts as soon as they reached the edge of town? What if the reason he had to advertise for a new wife was because he had murdered his last one?

Reaching the desk, she glanced back, then stiffened when she saw that her husband had moved inside the doorway where he now stood, arms crossed over his chest, watching her.

Heart thudding against her ribs, Edwina motioned the clerk closer. "Do you know that man, Mr. Yancey?" she whispered, tipping her head in the lump's direction. "The one by the front door. No, don't gawk!"

The clerk peered past Edwina's shoulder. "You mean Big Bob?"

"Big Bob?" *Who the dickens is Big Bob?*

"Everybody in these parts knows Big Bob."

Not Declan Brodie? Had her husband sent this lummox in his stead? Hope soared. "You're sure," she pressed. "The big man by the door."

Oh, please, oh, please.

"Yep. Big Bob. Highline Ranch. That's him."

Not my husband. Not Declan Brodie. Edwina

60

almost sagged in her relief. But euphoria abruptly died as suspicion took its place. "Is he a dependable man? Honorable?" *Will we be safe traveling with him?* was what she wanted to ask but was afraid to alert her hulking escort to her fears.

Mr. Yancey scratched at his bald scalp. "Well, yeah. I suppose. He was the sheriff, after all. Before the trouble, that is."

Trouble? She looked back at Big Bob—what an absurd name—and found him still watching her, those dark eyes gleaming like two chips of wet flint in his sun-browned face.

"Wait a minute," the clerk blurted out, reclaiming her attention. "You're *that* Mrs. Brodie!" Tilting his head to peer around Edwina, he waved to Big Bob.

Big Bob didn't wave back.

"You're the new missus." The clerk grinned happily, showing gaps in his rust-stained teeth. Edwina had noticed such dental discolorations on several other locals and deduced the water in Heartbreak Creek must be as ghastly as the conductor had said. She resisted the impulse to rub a gloved finger across her own front teeth.

She was about to question the clerk further when Pru came down the stairs, trailed by the freckled bellboy tottering under the weight of their two carpetbags. On his heels came Maddie and Lucinda, who stopped beside the front counter to stare at the man waiting by the front door.

"Is that your husband?" Maddie whispered in a voice low enough for Edwina and Pru to hear, but hopefully not Big Bob.

"God help her if it is," Lucinda murmured.

Panting, the boy let the bags drop beside Edwina, then stood back with an expectant look, rather like that of a spaniel after laying a fresh kill at his master's feet. Edwina turned her own expectant look toward Big Bob. She was down to so few coins she was reluctant to part with a one if she didn't have to.

After a long hesitation, and with a scowl of irritation that didn't bode well for the long ride to the ranch, Big Bob came forward. Ignoring the four women staring at him, he reached into his trouser pocket, pulled out a coin, and held it out.

Grinning, the boy snatched it up. Before he could dart away, the dark-haired man rested his hand on the youngster's thin shoulder.

"Why aren't you in school, son?"

"It's closed, sir."

"Closed?"

"It's always closed on Saturday, sir."

Big Bob shot a surprised glance at Mr. Yancey. "It's Saturday?"

The clerk showed rusty teeth and nodded. "All day."

"Hell. I'm *two* days late." And with an accusing look at Edwina, as if the delay and his own inability to keep track of it were somehow her

62

fault, he snatched up the carpetbags and headed toward the door. "Come on. We're burning daylight."

Edwina stared after him, thoughts of escape racing through her mind. Then Pru's hand pressed against her shoulder blades, shoving her through the door and onto the boardwalk.

"You poor thing," Lucinda muttered, stepping out behind them.

"Oh, I don't think so," Maddie argued. "I think your husband is rather handsome. And big, like Angus."

"He's not my husband," Edwina said over her shoulder.

Pru stopped pushing. "He's not?"

Edwina repressed a giggle. "That's Big Bob." She drew out the name, adding a flourish, like a barker at a county fair announcing the prize hog. "Apparently he was sent to fetch us." Seeing Pru's frown, she quickly added, "But don't fret. The clerk said he was once a sheriff, so we'll be fine. I think."

Taking advantage of her sister's befuddlement, Edwina turned to give hugs to Maddie and Lucinda. "I shall miss you," she said, fighting tears.

Lucinda blushed and looked away, obviously uncomfortable with emotional displays.

"Not for long," Maddie announced. "Since we're staying. We decided last night."

"Staying?" Edwina reared back. "Here? In Heartbreak Creek?"

"Only for a while," Lucinda warned, even though she was smiling, too.

Edwina glanced at Pru, saw a reflection of her own happy confusion in her sister's expression. "But why?" she asked, turning back to her friends.

"Why not?" Maddie grinned and looked around, her eyes alight with excitement. "This is the perfect place to start my photographic expedition. The real West. And this way, if we stay together, rather than traveling on alone, we'll both be safer."

"And also," Lucinda added, with a nod toward the tall figure heading down the boardwalk, "if this foolish proxy marriage of yours doesn't work out, we'll be close by to spirit you away."

THREE

Patience was not something Edwina had in abundance. And boredom only depleted it further. Granted, as the wagon rolled out of Heartbreak Creek and into the wooded canyons, the lovely mountain scenery had kept her distracted for several miles. But moving along as slowly as they did, she had ample time to peruse the road ahead, which greatly diminished any anticipation she might have harbored about what lay around the next bend.

Trees. Then more trees. Occasionally even a tree with actual leaves, instead of varying lengths and shades of green to blue-green needles. And so many cones of all differing shapes and lengths . . . my, it fair boggled her mind. For an hour, anyway.

Then there were rocks of all sizes and composition to draw her attention—from giant boulders to tiny shards of glittering quartz to stones as black as pitch. Back home, there was more dirt than rocks. In fact, large rocks—as opposed to tossing-size rocks—were so scarce her grandfather had had to import quarry stone to build the entrance pillars. So at first, Edwina had found such an endless display of stones and rocks and boulders quite interesting. But then . . .

Well, really. They were only rocks. She doubted even her sister's prodigious intellect could be challenged by a rock for very long. *If* Prudence was even awake.

Swiveling on the front seat, Edwina glared down at her sister, dozing on a blanket-covered bed of straw, cushioned by soft sacks of flour and sugar, while *she*—the one who had spent a sleepless night worrying—bounced around on a hard wooden seat next to a giant mute. *Honestly.*

For the next hour, Edwina amused herself watching birds flit through the high branches. But riding with her head at such an upward angle put a crick in her neck, and since the birds flew away well before the wagon drew near enough for her to be able to identify them, that pastime soon lost its appeal as well. The high point of the first ten miles was the sighting of a deer, which quickly bounded into the brush at their approach.

Then more of the same. Trees. Rocks. Flies perching on the horses' rumps. Boredom grew and patience shrank. Until finally, after being tossed about atop the poorly sprung seat for over three hours in utter silence, Edwina could bear no more.

"How did you get your name?" she asked in near desperation. "Big Bob is . . . unusual." Surely his parents wouldn't have named him that.

He turned his head and frowned at her.

Edwina frowned back, unable to decide what lay behind that flat stare. Amusement? Interest? Nothing?

"Well," he finally said, facing the road again. "I'm big."

Edwina gasped. "Are you? I hadn't noticed."

No response. Perhaps he believed her. Perhaps he was deaf. Perhaps he was such a dimwit he couldn't recognize sarcasm.

Aspens were interesting, she decided a while later. Wind blowing through their leaves created such a lovely watery sound, like a rushing stream or trickling brook, which might have been enjoyable to listen to had she not needed to relieve herself. But rather than mention that to the lump, she squirmed in silence, repeatedly checking the watch pinned inside the pocket of her coat, convinced they would surely stop soon.

Forty-five minutes later, she turned to the man beside her and said, "Stop the wagon."

He reared back. "What?"

"I have to get out."

"But—"

"Now. I have need of privacy. Now. This minute."

"Oh."

Without waiting for the wagon to roll to a full stop, Edwina poked Pru awake, waved her to follow, then leaped to the ground and dashed into the brush.

"He's a cretin," she muttered to her sister a few moments later as they put their skirts to rights. "Dumber than wet mud. A giant mute with the brains of a flea and the personality of a pound of rancid lard. He's so—"

"Hush," Pru whispered, fighting laughter. "He'll hear you."

"I don't care. I don't want to ride anymore. I don't want to sit by that man another minute." She turned to Pru with a pleading look. "If I walk back to Heartbreak Creek, will you come with me?"

"No. Now let's return to the wagon before a bear finds us."

"A bear?"

Their journey resumed.

The sun arced, then started its slow westward slide behind the tall trees crowding the rocky road. Shadows lengthened and the air grew cooler.

Pru hummed softly in the back and Edwina sat stonily in front. The mute coughed once, proof that he was still alive, but other than the clopping of the horses' hooves and the steady jangle of harness chains, all was quiet.

It was driving Edwina insane.

"Tell me about my husband," she said, thinking if someone didn't speak soon she might burst into song. Or tears. Or throw herself beneath the horses' hooves.

Big Bob flicked the reins on the matched bay geldings' rumps. Flies scattered, circled, then resettled. "What do you want to know?"

He had big hands, she noticed. As expected in a man his size. Yet they were surprisingly elegant, with wide palms and long blunt-tipped fingers. Rather beat-up and callused, and the little finger of his left hand had apparently been broken in the past, and had healed crookedly with an outward bend. It looked oddly vulnerable on such a strong hand. Edwina mused that in an easier life, had Big Bob the brains and imagination, he might have been a stonemason or even a sculptor.

Realizing he was looking at her, still waiting for an answer, she blurted out the first thing that came to mind. "Is he a good man?"

The question seemed to surprise him. Facing forward again, he stared past the horses' ears and gave it some thought—such a great deal of thought, Edwina feared again for the quickness of his mind. But then, he'd already demonstrated an inability to keep track of the days of the week, so she shouldn't have been surprised.

"He tries to be," he finally said.

Don't we all. "Is he handsome?" A ridiculous question, but she was becoming irritated with his terse responses and hoped the absurdity of it might shock some life into that stony expression.

It worked. He actually rocked back on the seat as if trying to distance himself from the idea. Or her. "I don't know about that," he muttered, studying the trees beside the road as if they were of sudden keen interest.

Edwina watched color inch up his thick neck and across his bristly jaw. A blush? His sun-browned skin was only a shade or two lighter than Pru's, so it was hard to tell. But the tips of his ears were decidedly red, which told her the question had confounded him. Intrigued, she pressed harder. "Has he a sense of humor?"

"Never thought about it."

No surprise there. "Is he a wise man?" She appreciated a fine mind. She spoke three languages, herself—if one counted a smattering of church Latin and garbled French patois—and she could add four columns of numbers in her head. But Pru was the smart one. She had read every volume in the library at Rose Hill.

Back when they had books. And a library to put them in.

"He's made a mistake or two," Big Bob allowed.

Edwina didn't doubt it, if her husband was forced to advertise in a catalog to get a woman. Which didn't say much for her, she thought glumly, since she had responded to it. "Have you known him long?"

"All my life."

"Do you think we're well suited?"

He shot her a quick, surprised glance. "Time will tell, I guess."

Not much of an answer. A feeling of hopelessness swept through her. What had at first appeared an acceptable way out of an untenable situation now seemed a series of terrible mistakes—from answering that matrimonial advertisement, to the proxy marriage and accepting Mr. Brodie's travel money, to climbing into the wagon that morning. But every time she came to the conclusion that she should have done things differently, the same tired question arose—like what? What else could she have done?

Back home there were few employment opportunities and dismal matrimonial prospects, and racial resentment on both sides had been nearing the breaking point. There had already been riots and lynchings and night riders creating havoc. She and Pru had both been threatened. They had to escape while they could and before something dreadful happened. And since they had no money and no family left, and the only thing of value Edwina had was herself, what presented a better chance of a fresh start somewhere else than offering herself up as a mail-order bride?

From the fat to the fire. Edwina sighed. Maybe she was worrying for nothing. Maybe her husband was the honest, upstanding man his letter indicated he was. Maybe he would be all she had hoped.

She glanced at the taciturn man seated beside her. For all his disapproving looks and high-handed ways and rough manners, he seemed a sensible, straightforward man. She doubted he would work for a complete fool or someone he couldn't hold in some small respect.

"Do you like him?" she asked.

His big shoulders rose and fell on a shrug. "Most of the time."

"And the rest of the time?"

Another long pause. "He's impatient," he admitted finally. "Some might say stubborn, but I think that's a bit harsh. And not much of a talker."

"Like you."

The corner of his mouth quirked. He turned his head and looked at her, his gaze so focused Edwina felt skewered. "Exactly like me." And as she watched, the quirk widened into a wicked grin.

Mercy sakes.

Edwina almost tipped up her heels in astonishment. No rust-stained teeth for Big Bob. No missing teeth, either. She stared, so captivated by those dark, mocking eyes it was a moment before his words sank in.

Realization hit with a thud. Heat rushed into her face. *You idiot!* she railed inwardly. *You utter ninny! How could you not have known?*

Under his amused regard, rational thought deserted her. It was several moments before she was able to muster sufficient wits to form a sentence. "It occurs to me, sir," she said through stiff lips, "that I haven't asked your full name."

"No, you haven't. But then, it's only been . . . what? Six hours?"

Sarcasm? Edwina narrowed her eyes. Perhaps the lump wasn't so slow, after all.

He touched his left index finger to the brim of his hat. "Declan Brodie, ma'am." He put the emphasis on the first syllable—Deck-lan. "*Robert* Declan Brodie. But some folks call me Big Bob."

Her husband. *Good Lord.* She truly was the nitwit Pru said she was.

Pru! Whipping around, Edwina scowled at her half sister who grinned back at her from her nest of burlap sacks and blankets in the back of the wagon. "You knew," she accused.

Pru nodded, her dark brown eyes alight with laughter.

"How long?"

"About ten miles. I can't believe you're just figuring it out."

She turned back to glare at her husband—*her husband, for heaven's sake.* "Why didn't you say something? Tell me who you were?"

"I thought you knew."

"Knew what? That you had a pseudonym? Why would I think *Big Bob* was Declan Brodie?"

"Who'd you think I was?"

Some nincompoop sent to fetch us, she almost shrieked in his face. Then realizing she was about to make a fool of herself—again—Edwina took a deep breath. By the time she slowly released it, she had regained her composure. Somewhat.

"I am not calling you by that ridiculous name. Big Bob. It's absurd." Blithely, she brushed a chaff of straw from her skirt. "Sounds like a character in a dime novel. Hardly dignified." Clasping her hands in her lap, she stared down the road. "I shall call you Mr. Brodie." *You great hulking lump.*

"*Mr.* Brodie. I like that. Sounds respectful."

She didn't look his way, but could hear the laughter in his voice. It was an odd voice, low and rich and . . . rumbly. Perhaps it was damaged. Perhaps in a fit of pique, some poor woman he had pushed beyond the limits of sanity had tried to choke the life out of him. She smiled, imagining it.

"I don't much like Edwina, either," he added after a pause.

"Oh?" She turned with raised brows. "And why not?"

"Sounds like something a shoat would say."

"Shoat?"

"Baby hog." His gaze slid over her in a way that made Edwina's skin quiver and her temper flare. "And since you don't look much like a hog, maybe you've got another name we could use?"

Edwina was too provoked to respond. No one had ever criticized her name. Admittedly, it was a horrid name, but . . . *a hog?*

"No? Well, we could call you Ed, I guess. Short and simple. Ed."

"My middle name is Pricilla," she informed him coldly. A name she liked even less, since it had been her mother's, but at least it was more feminine than Ed.

"Pricilla." He said it thoughtfully, as if testing the name for suitability. "Prissy. Miss Priss. Yeah. That'll work."

Edwina stared silently ahead, ignoring Pru's muffled snorts of laughter.

It wasn't until the last rays of the setting sun backlit the western ridges like a distant fire and the air had grown so cold Edwina was shivering in her thin coat that she spoke again. Turning wearily to her husband—that scoundrel—she asked through numb lips, "How much longer?"

"Not long." He nodded toward the jagged silhouette of a rise in the road ahead. "Soon as

74

we top that ridge, we'll stop for the night."

Stop for the night? Surely that didn't mean what Edwina suspected. Dreading the answer, she forced herself to ask, "Is your farm that near?"

"It's not a farm. It's a ranch. And no, it's still a ways."

She waited for him to offer further enlightenment. He didn't.

"Then exactly how much longer will it take to reach your . . . *ranch?*"

"With the late start"—he paused to send her an accusing look—"and the washout, it'll take longer. If all goes well"—another pointed glance, this one more of a warning than an accusation— "we should get there by noon tomorrow."

Tomorrow! She looked around for a hotel, boardinghouse, dwelling of some kind. There was nothing but woods, then more woods. "What about tonight? Where will we sleep?"

"You ladies will sleep in the wagon. I'll sleep under it."

He said it like that was the most reasonable statement in the world. As if sleeping outdoors, in the woods, in the cold, in their clothes and in the presence of a strange man was as natural for two gently reared southern ladies as taking the next breath.

Edwina clapped her hands over her mouth but couldn't stop the laughter from coming. And coming.

• • •

Declan didn't consider himself a humorless man. He liked a joke now and again and had even participated in a prank or two in his time. Granted, things had been a bit dire of late, with cattle prices dropping and water holes drying up and four rambunctious children to raise, but he hadn't forgotten how to smile, no matter what his friend Thomas Redstone said. He'd even managed to maintain his good humor and not let his dismay show when he first saw his bride that morning on the boardwalk outside the Heartbreak Creek Hotel.

Definitely not the sturdy farm woman he'd envisioned, but a bedraggled, rail-thin beauty in a ridiculous hat, who appeared every bit as shocked and disappointed in him as he was in her.

It had been an awkward meeting. The entire day had been awkward. And now, after it was too late to back out of this proxy marriage short of a time-and-money-wasting annulment that would leave some slick-haired lawyer richer and him poorer, he was finding that in addition to being nothing like the woman he had bargained for, his new wife was also clearly unstable. Nobody with good sense ever laughed this long for no reason on purpose.

"Mr. Brodie," the mulatto woman, Prudence Lincoln, said at his shoulder. "I think we'd better stop."

He eyed his bride, who was muttering behind her hands and rocking to and fro on the seat beside him. "What's wrong with her?"

"I think she . . . ah, swallowed a bug."

Hell. Transferring the leathers to his left hand, he reached back with his right to pound her back.

Prudence Lincoln grabbed his arm. "I don't think you should do that, sir," she said, her eyes round in her light brown face. "That is to say, I think she's coughed it out already."

Relieved, he withdrew his arm and faced forward again.

His wife continued to rock and mutter.

"But I still think we should stop. Sir."

Hiding his impatience, Declan looked around. Seeing that they had pulled alongside a small clearing with a tiny creek running through it, he reined in the team. He glanced at his wife and was relieved to see she was no longer hiding her face and had recovered somewhat. "How's this?"

She turned her head and gave him an odd, glassy-eyed smile. "Oh, this is delightful. Perfect. Everything I could have dreamed." She started to say more, but her traveling companion gripped her shoulder, and not gently, he noted.

"This will be fine, Mr. Brodie," Prudence Lincoln said. "This'll be just fine."

Declan couldn't help but notice the mulatto was a beautiful woman. And judging by that lively sparkle in her brown eyes, a smart woman, too.

But he saw kindness there, as well, and obvious concern for his odd little wife. So he nodded and turned the team. He was tired of sitting, too.

After pulling off the road, he unhitched the horses, rubbed them down with a scrap of burlap, then led them to the creek. Once they'd taken their fill, he staked them so they could graze and went back to the wagon.

The women, who were engaged in a tense, whispered conversation, abruptly fell quiet when he drew near and watched in silence as he moved boxes and sacks and kegs of sundry ranch supplies to the front of the wagon so they would have more room in back. Gathering the blankets he'd brought from home, he held them out.

They snatched them up and immediately set to work, fluffing hay so vigorously they were soon coughing on dust and speckled with chaff.

Shaking his head, Declan went to find firewood. The sun was almost down and the air was cooling fast. If he didn't hurry, it would be too dark to hunt. Moving quickly, he gathered enough wood to last through the night, piled it in the middle of the clearing close to the wagon but well away from overhanging tree limbs, then arranged flat rocks in a crude fire ring. That completed, he returned to the wagon.

As he pulled his shotgun from beneath the seat and slipped a handful of shot shells into his pocket, he watched the women work on their cozy little nest, a bit aggravated that he was expected to do all the camp chores by himself when there were two able-bodied women on hand to help. If this was an indication of things to come, it didn't bode well.

"Think you'll need all five of those blankets?" he asked tersely, thinking of his own cold bed on the ground.

His wife turned to look at him. A moment later, a wad of coarse, straw-specked wool landed against his chest. "Will that be enough?" she asked through lips as tight as a tailor's stitch.

Apparently, it would have to be. Ignoring the apologetic smile Prudence Lincoln sent his way, he tossed the blanket under the wagon and straightened to face his wife's backside as she bent over to flick errant bits of straw from her blanket.

It was a nice butt, despite her thinness. Pear-shaped, with a gentle upward curve to a trim waist. And nice ankles showing beneath the hiked-up hem of her skirt, too, although the boots that encased them were far too flimsy. A snake could easily bite through that fine leather and—

Suddenly aware that Prudence Lincoln was looking at him, he averted his eyes. "I'll be back soon."

"What?" His wife bolted upright so fast her frilly bonnet slid down over her forehead. Shoving it back, she said in that high-pitched voice he was learning to dread, "And just where do you think you're going?"

Irritation peaked, spreading along his frayed nerves in a warm rush, awakening old resentments of half-forgotten arguments with another woman in another time. Struggling to rein in his temper, he hooked a thumb toward the junipers and pinyons crowding the clearing. "I *think* I'm going into those woods. To get supper. That okay with you?"

"Supper?" Her gaze dropped to the gun in his hand, then back up to meet his. She had pretty eyes. Blue and full of life. They didn't hide much. And what they were showing him now was that she was scared.

Hell. This just got worse and worse. A loon, a shrew, and now a coward. If she wasn't so easy to look at, she'd be entirely useless. "You'll be all right," he assured her. "I won't be far."

"You promise?"

He nodded, both surprised by her sudden child-like trust and annoyed at her clinging. If she had been the sturdy farm woman he'd contracted for, instead of dwelling on her fears she would be getting the fire going and setting coffee on to boil. The thought of it made his stomach rumble. "There are sacks of cornmeal and coffee up front," he offered, hopefully.

His wife blinked at him.

The mulatto filled the lengthening silence with

a rush of words, "Thank you, sir. That'll be just fine. We'll come up with something, don't you worry. The pans and utensils are up front, too?"

"In the leather pouch."

"Thank you, sir."

His wife continued to blink.

Prudence Lincoln smiled thinly.

"Well, I'll be off then. Shout if you need me." With a lingering glance at the unfilled coffeepot sitting on the front bench, he turned toward the woods.

When he returned forty-five minutes later, smoke coiled above the crackling fire, the smell of coffee drifted in the cool air, and Prudence Lincoln was turning johnnycakes on a skillet over the fire.

He quickened his step.

Hearing him approach, she looked up, smiling when she saw the grouse and two squirrels dangling from his hand.

He dropped the dressed carcasses on a rock near the fire. "It's not much. But it'll do."

"It'll be plenty, sir. Thank you."

He glanced over at his wife, who sat huddled on a stump near the flames, using the end of a blanket to shield her eyes from the smoke. She didn't speak or look his way.

Miss Lincoln pulled a rag from her skirt pocket and wiped her hands.

Only one was scarred, he saw. A pattern of paler

skin spread over the back of her right hand and up her wrist. A burn scar. Maybe a scald.

"You want me to panfry those, Mr. Brodie? Or I could rustle up a spit and roast them over the fire if you'd prefer."

He looked over at his wife, wondering why she wasn't tending their meal, and found her studying him through eyes that were red-rimmed and teary. He turned back to Prudence. "Panfry, if it's not too much trouble."

With a nod, she set to work quartering the carcasses.

Declan put the shotgun back under the seat and went to check on the horses. When he returned, his wife had disappeared and the smell of frying meat and onions made his stomach rumble again.

"Hope you don't mind," Prudence said as he hunkered beside the fire to dig a tin cup out of the pouch. "I took an onion from the sack up front."

"I don't mind." With his kerchief wrapped around the handle of the coffeepot, he poured, then returned the pot to the coals. Cradling the cup in both hands to warm his fingers, he breathed in the welcome scent of coffee and took a sip. Hot and strong. Like he liked it. He gave Prudence a nod.

She smiled and flipped over a squirrel hindquarter in the skillet.

A gentle breeze rustled through the piney boughs, adding to the musical babble of the creek and the occasional snort from the horses. Overhead, the first stars glittered like tiny pinpricks in the domed sky, and off to the east, backlighting tall spruce and firs, an early crescent moon struggled to clear the mountain peaks. It promised to be a cold night.

Declan took another swallow of coffee and looked around, wondering where his wife was. "She asleep or run off already?" He said it with a smile, but in truth, he wouldn't have been that upset if she'd made her escape. She wouldn't be the first woman to run out on him.

"She's getting water."

So she wasn't completely useless. He watched Prudence Lincoln bustle around the fire, stirring this, turning that, and wondered again why his wife wasn't doing it. He frowned at the shadows along the creek, thinking if she didn't show up soon, he'd have to go after her before she got lost. Or scared up a bear. He smirked, picturing Miss Priss's reaction to that.

"She called you her traveling companion," he said after a moment. "That a new way of saying slave?"

The dark-skinned woman snapped upright, her brown eyes flashing with anger, the spoon clutched in her hand like a weapon. "I am not a slave, Mr. Brodie. Never have been, never will be."

He met her anger with a wry smile. "Then why you doing for her like you are?"

They stared at each other for a moment. Then the anger faded from her eyes. Setting the spoon on a rock, she wiped her hands on that rag again and studied him. The glow of the fire highlighted the arc of her cheekbones and the fullness of her lips and put an orange sheen in her dark eyes.

He thought again how pretty she was and wondered why someone with her looks and brains would align herself with such an impractical, flighty woman as his wife.

A night owl called out, startling her. She glanced up at the trees, then at the creek, and finally back down at Declan. He could see she was picking her words with care. "You have to understand, Mr. Brodie. Edwina is . . . inexperienced."

"At what?"

She waved a graceful hand in a gesture that encompassed him, the campsite, the dark shadows looming just beyond the firelight. "All this. She's led a sheltered life. Until the war, anyway. But these last few years have been difficult. She's worked very hard to keep us going."

"Doing what?"

"Sewing." She gave a bright smile Declan didn't altogether trust.

"Sewing."

Prudence nodded. "She's an excellent seamstress."

"She sews. While you do everything else."

"Well . . . yes."

Declan felt the beginning of a headache. "Can she at least cook?"

"Well . . ."

"Christ."

"But I'll teach her."

Declan watched the rag twist in her fingers and felt his temper unravel. "Lady, I've already got enough kids. I don't need another."

"She'll be fine, Mr. Brodie. It's just that all this is very new to her. If you'll just be patient—"

"Patient?" Declan shot to his feet. "I've got four children to corral, three thousand cattle to round up and cull and brand, a barn in need of a new roof, and more chores than I can tend in three lifetimes!" He flung the dregs of his cup into the flames, loosening a burst of sputtering, hissing steam. "I don't have the time, or money, or patience for patience!"

She took a step back, her eyes round and fearful. "What do you plan on doing?"

"Why, I'll . . . I'll just . . . Damnit to hell!" What could he do? He still needed help around the ranch. He still needed a mother for his children. He'd already spent a small fortune getting the woman out here.

Christ. Redstone had the right of it. A man who bought a horse without riding it first shouldn't be surprised when he's thrown.

Yanking off his Stetson, Declan raked a hand through his hair, then slapped the hat back on.

He rubbed the back of his neck and sighed, knowing he should be yelling at his wife rather than this woman. "How about we send her back and you stay on?" he offered.

She almost smiled. "You thinking to marry me now, Mr. Brodie?"

"Hell, no. I've already got one wife too many. But I'll pay you."

"To do what?"

"Cook. Clean. Ride herd on my kids. Tend a garden."

"Pay me how? You just said you have no money."

"Shares on the cattle."

The smile broke into a chuckle. "I need cattle like you need another wife, Mr. Brodie. No, you strive for patience and give me time to train her."

The headache spread, settling in his temples with an insistent throb. His damn wife had tricked him, made him think she was up to the job. Hell, his kids would probably run her off in a week. He thought of the grief that prankster Joe Bill would put her through and took some gratification in picturing that. "How long?" He was already past his thirty-third birthday. He didn't have that many years left.

"Haven't you agreed on a three-month trial period?"

Three? He thought it was two. Not that it mattered. The woman would never be what he expected and needed.

"If in three months she hasn't come around," Prudence went on when he didn't answer, "then you can send her packing."

"And you'll stay?" he asked hopefully.

"It'll go faster than you think," she hedged. "Edwina is smart. Just give her a chance."

She didn't look smart, Declan thought, glancing past Prudence Lincoln's shoulder to see his wife struggle up from the creek, her back bowed from the weight of the overfilled pail hanging from both hands. With every step, the bucket banged against her knees, sloshing water onto her hems and over those dainty leather boots. Pitiful. His youngest son could do better.

"Give her time, Mr. Brodie. She'll figure it out."

"She better."

Supper was a silent affair, the tension thick enough to chew. The only redeeming thing about it was how tasty it was. If Prudence Lincoln could teach his wife to cook this good, things might work out, after all.

After wiping his plate clean with the last johnnycake, Declan set it on a rock by the fire, still hungry and wishing he'd bagged another grouse. He looked over at Miss Priss, perched on her stump and pecking at a drumstick like a baby bird, and resisted the urge to say something about wasting food.

At least she'd be an easy keeper, he thought glumly. And she was easy on the eyes . . . or would be, if she ever smiled. So far all she'd given him were smirks, grimaces, and looks of shock and disdain. Not that he particularly cared. A woman's smile could be a dangerous thing, laden with enough deceit and cunning to mask the blackness in her heart. Yet, as he watched his wife listlessly shove food around on her plate, he had to wonder if she had the fortitude for subterfuge. She seemed a hot-tempered, emotional sort, and not disciplined enough to hide what she was thinking. Or maybe he was just more watchful now and not so easily fooled.

Hunger overriding manners, he nodded toward the untouched grouse breast on her plate. "You going to eat that?"

She gave him another of those shocked looks.

"No?" When she still didn't respond, he reached over and plucked it from her plate. "Thanks," he mumbled through a big bite of succulent grouse meat.

She opened her mouth, closed it, then found her voice. "I cannot believe you actually took food from—"

"So, Mr. Brodie," Prudence Lincoln blurted out, cutting her off. "Tell us about your children."

Declan looked from one to the other, amused. An odd pair, these two. Connected in a way he didn't understand.

"Four, you said?" Prudence Lincoln's fixed smile started to falter.

Popping the last bite of meat into his mouth, Declan wiped his fingers on his trousers and nodded. "Three boys and a girl."

"My. How lovely. How long have they been without a mother, sir, if you don't mind my asking."

All their lives. "Four years."

"That's too bad. Losing a parent is so hard on children."

You don't know the half of it, Declan thought and tried to think of a way to change the subject. But before he could, Miss Priss chimed in, her blue eyes narrowed in suspicion.

"How did she die? Your wife."

Heat rose in his neck. "Arapahos." And before they could question him further, he rose. "I've got to check on the horses."

Edwina watched her husband's big form disappear into the shadows, then turned to Pru. "Well, that's odd. What do you make of that?"

"Make of what?" Prudence began gathering dirty plates and utensils and dropping them into the empty water bucket. "He doesn't want to talk about a sad time that obviously still upsets him. Nothing odd in that."

"But he didn't look sad or upset. He looked furious."

"Probably at you for pressing him about it." Picking up the bucket, Pru held it out. "You going to wash these, or shall I?"

"I'm not going back down there. It's dark. There could be bears."

"And if we leave dirty dishes around the campsite, they may come up here while we're sleeping."

"Up here?"

"I'll do it," a deep voice said, startling Edwina so badly she almost fell off the stump. Heart thumping, she watched her husband walk into the light. He looked calm, the anger she had glimpsed earlier no longer there. But she had seen the sudden flash that had sparked in his dark eyes and had brought his lips tight against his teeth. She recognized fury when she saw it. And having seen it in her husband, and knowing the strength in his sturdy frame and big hands, she now felt a new fear take root in her mind.

FOUR

Edwina hardly slept that night, in part because she was listening for bears, or shivering with the cold, or coughing out errant bits of hay. But mostly because of the sounds that came from beneath the wagon.

Groaning, yawning, tossing, turning. It sounded like an alligator wrestling match. And when he wasn't doing that, he was snoring. Not as loudly as her father, who could shake the rafters when he got his rhythm going, but just audible enough that she could hear it through the blankets, hay, and slats of the wagon if she lay very quietly and listened. Which she did, just to make sure he was still down there and not wandering about doing God knows what or leering down at her over the side rails of the wagon.

The night seemed endless.

Which is why she was so shocked when she opened gritty eyes to glaring sunlight—when only a moment ago it had been the middle of the night—and saw Declan Brodie leering down at her over the side rails.

"Waugh," she said, lurching upright and almost knocking a tin cup out of his hand. "W-What are you doing?"

He shifted the cup to his left hand, shook coffee off his fingers, then wiped them on his thigh. As he straightened, his gaze swept over her wrinkled dress, then up to pause on her hair. "Rough night?"

She lifted a hand to feel a tangled mess of straw and pins and knotted hair. *Drat.* She would never get a comb through it. Letting her hand fall back into her lap, she sent him a bleary-eyed glare. "You snore."

"So do you." He held out the cup.

"I do not." She eyed the cup, wondering if he had already drunk from it, then realized she was so desperate for something to thaw the chill she

91

didn't care. "Where's Pru?" she asked, clutching the warm cup in icy hands.

"At the creek."

She studied him as she sipped, noticing things she had missed the day before. Tiny crow tracks spreading from the corners of his eyes toward his temples. A white scar disappearing into the dark stubble above his top lip, another cutting through his left eyebrow. Sable brown eyes so deeply set his long lashes almost touched his brows. Wisps of dark, curling hair hanging below his dusty hat to the back of his collarless shirt.

He looked wide awake and entirely too cheerful, which aggravated her no end. "Do you sleep in that hat?" she asked, irritably.

"Not usually."

"Maybe you're bald and trying to hide it."

He shrugged.

"Are you?"

"Would it matter?"

And they say women are vain. "I suppose not."

He pushed away from the rails. "Best get up. We leave in five minutes." Turning, he walked toward the front of the wagon and the horses that Edwina was surprised to see were already hitched.

"What about breakfast?" she called after his retreating figure.

"You missed it. Five minutes."

Fifteen minutes later, she was back on her perch beside her husband, gnawing on a strip of jerky as tough and tasty as a shoe sole, while Pru knelt behind her, trying to comb the tangles and straw out of her hair.

It was giving her a neck ache, all the pulling and jerking. Her scalp felt like it was on fire. "Ouch!" she cried when a particularly hard yank made her bite her tongue. "What are you using? A pitchfork?"

"Be still," Pru scolded. "If you had put on a scarf like I told you, we wouldn't have such a mess to deal with."

"I did put on a scarf. It came undone." Edwina winced at another painful tug. "I ought to just cut it all off."

Her husband glanced over, his dark gaze moving down to where the ends of her hair brushed the back of the wagon seat. "Don't."

She blinked in surprise. That was the first word he had spoken since telling her she had five minutes to get ready to leave.

"When the horses' tails get tangled," he said, "we use lard to straighten them out."

Edwina frowned at the horse rumps bobbing in front of the wagon. "That explains the flies," she muttered.

He made a snorting noise, and she looked over to find him grinning at her. Not that wicked smile of yesterday, or the smirk that tilted up one corner of his wide mouth, but a real tooth-showing grin that carried no menace or mockery, just friendly amusement. It changed his stern face into something altogether different, and she couldn't help but smile back.

"We wash it after," he assured her. "Several times, if need be."

"My. All that for a horse."

"Hair's important."

She made a point of glancing at his hat. "Especially to those who might be losing it?"

"Or those with a lot of flies on their rumps."

Laughter burst out of her. For a moment she forgot her reservations about this man and her fears about the course she had set for herself. "I see you do have a sense of humor, Mr. Brodie," she said, with a chuckle.

His gaze dropped to her mouth, then abruptly shifted away. He popped the reins, urging the horses to pick up their pace, and in the time it took for a smile to fade, Edwina felt the space between them become unbridgeable once more.

"There," Pru said, a few minutes later, putting an end to her torture. "Lets get it pinned up and your bonnet back on before the wind tangles it all over again."

That accomplished, Pru yawned, muttered something about not getting much sleep because of Edwina's thrashing around, and settled back in her cozy nest.

Edwina sat quietly as the miles rolled by and the land changed. Forest gave way to rocky ridges, then long sloping hills covered with tufts of grass, the tops of which were burned brown by winter frost, even as fresh green shoots pushed up through the tightly woven roots clinging to the earth. The horizon broadened, stretching from one peak to another below a vast open sky dotted with puffs of cloud as white and wispy as the cotton lint that had blown across the fields during picking time at Rose Hill.

Tipping her head back to watch a hawk float by, Edwina took a deep, weary breath, drawing in air that smelled of damp earth and horses and the campfire smoke that clung to the jacket of the man beside her.

Her husband.

The man with whom she had promised to share the rest of her life.

A shiver of unease ran along her nerves, and turning her head, she studied this man she barely knew, as if his strong profile, with its bold nose and square jaw and fiercely scowling brow, might give her the reassurance she needed.

He might have been a handsome man, she realized, had he allowed more gentleness and humor into his expression. She wondered if he had always been so grimly unapproachable or if something had happened to make him that way. She wondered why he had stopped being a sheriff, and what the "troubles" were that the hotel clerk had alluded to, and why he had taken a stranger to wife rather than one of the sturdy farm women in town. A complicated man, Declan Brodie was, she decided, and she wondered if she would have the time or courage to figure him out.

"Tell me about the children," she said after a while.

Startled out of his brooding thoughts, he shot her a quick glance before facing forward again. "Might be best if you found out for yourself."

He must have realized how ominous that sounded, because he added hastily, "They're good kids. At heart. But they've had no one riding herd on them for the last four years, so they've grown a little wild."

"They've had you."

He shook his head. "I try. But I've got my hands full keeping the ranch going and food on the table. They need a mother."

Four uncontrollable children, a struggling ranch out in the middle of nowhere, and a husband who was a stranger and gone all the time. Could it be any worse?

Yes. She could be back home, fearing to sit on her porch after dark, and wondering if there would be money for lamp oil or food on the table next week.

Movement behind her, then her sister's voice at her shoulder. "What are their ages?"

"The oldest is Robert Junior, but he prefers R.D. Going on thirteen and big for his age. Doesn't talk much, but he's a hard worker and has eyes like an eagle."

"They're yellow?" Edwina asked, earning a poke from Pru.

That quirk of a smile. "They're sharp. Makes him a good hunter. Joe Bill is nine, and most like his mother in temperament and looks. He took her passing hard and may show some resentment toward you at first. He's also a trickster, so keep an eye on him."

He flicked the reins and sighed. "Then there's Lucas. He's a year behind Joe Bill, and smart as a whip. He was always a happy child, but after his mother . . . well, now he's mostly off in his own world, reading or drawing or taking things apart, then putting them back together. He's no trouble at all, although sometimes I think it might be better if he was."

"Your daughter is the youngest?"

"Brin." For the first time, his expression relaxed a bit and something almost resembling a smile softened the grave lines of his face. "She'll be seven late next month, and she's already so pretty it'll take your breath away." Then the almost-smile faded on another long sigh. "I should probably warn you, though. She's got some irregular ways, having lived most of her life without a woman to guide her."

"Irregular ways?" Pru, having risen on her knees to hear them better, gripped the backrest for balance as the wagon lurched and bounced over the rocky road. "What does that mean exactly?"

"You'll see. I'm hoping between the two of you, you'll be able to smooth out some of her rough edges."

Grand, Edwina thought. A stoic, a trickster, a recluse, and a little girl with "irregular" ways. She could scarcely wait. "How soon until we reach your ranch?" she asked, dread settling like a stone in her stomach. Or perhaps that was the jerky.

"We've been on ranch land for the past hour." His mouth tight, he nodded toward the road ahead where it dwindled to a narrow, precarious track clinging to the mountain on one side and dropping into thin air on the other. "Once we clear Satan's Backbone, we'll be able to see the house."

And everything else, Edwina thought. The view must be astounding, with no trees or mountains to block the horizon. She leaned forward in anticipation. "Why was it named Satan's Backbone?"

When he didn't answer, she glanced over to find him staring fixedly ahead, his expression grim. The fingers of his right hand held the reins so tightly the veins stood out. His left hand was wrapped around the brake lever in a death grip.

Edwina shifted on the bench, trying to see ahead.

"Be still!" he barked. "You'll startle the animals!"

Confused, Edwina glanced at the horses, who were plodding steadily along, heads down, ears relaxed, showing no concern whatsoever.

Not so the man beside her. He was coiled tight as a spring, his fiercely concentrated gaze never leaving the road ahead.

Beginning to feel uneasy, Edwina glanced back at Pru, who shrugged to show she was confused by his odd behavior as well.

The track narrowed, crowding so close to the rocky wall rising on the left that once or twice the front wheel hub scraped against a protruding rock. But on the right there was nothing but air. Then the road curved to the east, and suddenly the sky opened above them and the land spread below, stretching for unbroken miles across a lush green valley ringed by tall timber that rose up steep slopes to distant white-capped peaks. It was magnificent. Breathtaking. Looking down over the side of the wagon at the thousand-foot drop-off was almost like flying.

"Oh, Pru," she said excitedly, twisting on the bench. "Have you ever seen such a thing?"

"Don't!" A big hand clamped over her arm.

Startled by the curt command, Edwina looked at her husband. His jaw was rigid, his face pale. There was almost a look of terror in his eyes.

Edwina tried to tug free of his bruising hold. "You're hurting—"

"Be still, damnit! Both of you. We're almost clear."

A moment later, the wagon rolled past the

sheer bluff and back onto wider ground. Boulders edged the drop-off, then brush, and finally tall trees that blocked the endless views as well.

He released her arm and sat back, his wide chest rising and falling on a deep breath. His color returned until a flush darkened his stubbled cheeks.

And finally Edwina understood. "Are you afraid of heights, Mr. Brodie?"

"No." He wiped a broad palm down his thigh. "I'm afraid of falling off of them." He shot her a look. "As anyone with sense should be." And before she could respond to that barb, he nodded past her shoulder. "There's the house."

It wasn't one house, she realized, peering through the gauntlet of trees as they started down the long slope into the grassy valley, but two identical single-peaked log structures standing side by side and connected by an enclosed breezeway with a broad front porch. As they rolled closer and the trees thinned so she could make out more details, Edwina's feeling of dread intensified.

Pru's hand gripped her shoulder—in reassurance or apprehension, Edwina wasn't sure which.

There was no yard, no trees, not a single shrub to screen the stone foundation. And seeing the house perched so starkly atop the rocky ground, all sturdy practicality, without grace or beauty or softening touches, made Edwina realize in a way she never had before that she had truly left her other life behind forever.

Declan reined in as Rusty charged the horses and children tore out the kitchen door like calves on stampede. He did a quick count, came up one short, then saw Lucas hanging back in the shadows of the porch.

He let out a deep breath and let go of the anxiety that always gripped him when he returned home after being away for a while. Not that he doubted Thomas Redstone wouldn't watch over his children as vigilantly as he would have, but with all the Indian troubles lately, and rebel renegades still prowling about, he never felt completely reassured until he saw all four faces grinning up at him. "The house is still standing, I see. Rusty, quiet!"

"Joe Bill tried to burn it down," Brin shouted over the dog's barks.

At least he thought that was Brin beneath the dirt, and her brother's clothes, and R.D.'s old slouch hat that bent the tips of her ears.

R.D. thumped his younger brother's head. "Luckily Thomas smelled the smoke."

"It was an accident," Joe Bill defended.

"Like Sand Creek was an accident," Thomas Redstone said, coming around the side of the house. "You are late."

"There was a washout at Damnation Creek."

101

Declan frowned at the rifle in Thomas's hand and the tall bay he was leading by a braided bosal halter. "You leaving already?"

Thomas's gaze flicked to the two women staring wide-eyed from the wagon, paused for a heartbeat on Prudence Lincoln, then swung back to Declan. Even though his face showed nothing, Declan could see the laughter in his stone black eyes. "A man who raises pigeons in his tipi should not invite in a hawk."

"Or a bull snake," Declan countered.

Thomas grinned, his white teeth a shocking contrast to his dark ruddy skin. "You have enough wild savages running around, *nesene'*. You do not need another." Turning to the children gathered beside the wagon, he said, "*Ne'aahtove eho*. And no fires." After they nodded, he swung up on his horse and, with a nod to Declan, reined the bay around and kicked it into a lope toward the creek.

"Mercy sakes," his wife said. "Who was that?"

"Thomas Redstone." Declan wrapped the reins around the brake handle. "Lost his band at Summit Springs, so now we're his family."

"He's Indian?" Pru asked.

"Cheyenne. Mostly." Declan watched the ex–Dog Soldier melt into the thicket along the creek and wished Thomas had stayed a while longer. He could have used his help to distract the women while he broke the news of their new mother to his children. Moving stiffly, he climbed down

102

from the driver's box. As soon as he touched ground, children came at him from all sides—Brin tattling on Joe Bill, Joe Bill tattling back on Brin, R.D. trying to tell him about a cougar he'd seen on a ridge behind the creek. Only Lucas remained silent, all of his attention fixed on the women in the wagon.

"Go on, now. Leave a man in peace to stretch his legs." Declan tried to sound gruff, even though he was gratified by their warm reception.

"Who's that lady?" Brin stared in fascination at Miss Priss's bonnet. "And what's that on her head?"

"Never you mind." He waved them toward the building on the left. "Get on into the house. I'll be there directly to talk to you."

"But we're hungry," Brin complained. "Thomas didn't feed us nothing but some roots and berries out of his parfleche bag."

"Pemmican." Joe Bill made a face. "Smelled like R.D.'s boots."

"Better than your feet."

Declan gave Brin a gentle nudge. "Go. I'll bring food when I come."

"But—"

"Now."

As his children headed toward their sleeping quarters, Declan grabbed the bags and helped the women from the wagon, anticipating some scathing comments about his unruly children or his home. He knew the place was a bit rough and rustic compared to some grand two-story southern plantation mansion, but it was sturdy and warm and he'd built it with his own hands, and he was proud of it, no matter what they said.

Surprisingly, they said nothing—good or bad—but filed silently after him as he carried their carpetbags not toward the parlor entry but to the working end of the dwelling that housed a kitchen and eating area on the ground floor, and a spacious master bedroom in the loft above.

After Lucas was born eight years ago, he'd added the second structure with a connecting breezeway to provide separate sleeping quarters for the children. A year later, Sally had insisted on enclosing the breezeway and adding a front porch so they would have a nice entry and a sit-down parlor in case anyone dropped by, which no one ever did. Now he used the enclosed area between the two buildings mostly for storage.

After waiting inside the kitchen doorway for the women to pass through, he kicked the door closed and looked around, his sense of frustration rising again.

The room was a mess and smelled like burned something—hair?—Joe Bill's "accident" no doubt, judging by the puddles of water on the floor and the charred rag in the sink. It also appeared that Brin had tried her hand at cooking—a hopeful sign, despite the stack of dirty dishes on the counter and the flour dusting the floor and the broken eggs dripping yolk off the edge of the table. At least she was considering a more feminine role than that of army scout or buffalo hunter.

With a sigh, he turned toward the staircase rising along the west wall and over the door into the parlor. "You'll take the loft," he explained as he carried their bags up to the open mezzanine that overlooked the first level. "I'll move my things out later."

Prudence Lincoln started up the stairs behind him. "And where will you sleep, Mr. Brodie?"

"In the parlor."

Miss Priss paused on the bottom step and looked around. "There's a parlor?"

"Between the two buildings." Ducking to clear the beam across the landing, he walked past the oversized bed he'd built to accommodate his height and dumped the bags on the floor beside the wardrobe he'd also built. He waited until both women entered the open room, then nodded toward the six-foot partition against the inside wall. "There's a hip tub and wash bowl and necessary behind that screen. I'll bring up water later. Anything else?"

Miss Priss unpinned her bonnet and set it on the night table beside the bed, then turned a slow circle as she took in the room.

Declan looked around, too, trying to see it

through her eyes. Sun-bleached calico curtains hanging listlessly over the tall window on the peaked wall. Dusty books stacked in one corner, an overflowing basket of soiled clothing in another. A faded floor runner with a tattered edge beside the rumpled bed. It was a mess, just like downstairs.

But that's why he needed her, damnit. How was he to keep a house going, meals cooked, washing done, a garden tended, and ride herd on four young children while managing a sixty-thousand-acre spread and three thousand head of cattle, with only a twelve-year-old boy, an ex-preacher who was drunk most of the time, and a crippled handyman to help him?

Bracing himself for criticism, Declan planted his hands on his hips and glared at his wife, waiting for the complaints to begin.

Spinning slowly to a stop, she finally met his gaze. She looked perplexed. "Where did you get this furniture?"

"I built it."

"All of it?"

He nodded and waited for her to say something bad about it.

Instead, she smiled. "It's nice. I like it."

Declan was so thrown off balance by that comment he didn't know what to say.

"I like the sturdy simplicity of it." She ran her hand over the six-inch-diameter log foot rail, then slowly up the corner post. "With the warm, natural color of the wood showing through."

Declan watched her fingers move over the pine he had oiled to a satiny sheen, and for one shocking moment he could have sworn he felt the stroke of that hand on his back.

"I'm so tired of dark, fussy, ornate European furniture." Letting her hand fall to her side, she looked at him in a way she hadn't before. "I like this much better."

Battling a sudden overwhelming feeling of confinement, although he wasn't sure why, Declan crossed to the stairs. "I'll bring water after I talk to the children. And clean up the mess they left," he added as an afterthought, then was irritated that he had. Tending the house was her job now. She might as well get used to it.

"Don't you worry about cleaning up, Mr. Brodie," Prudence Lincoln called after him. "We'll take care of the kitchen and rustle up something to eat, too. You go do what you've got to do."

As soon as the door beneath the stairs into the parlor closed, Pru turned to Edwina with a scolding look. "What was that about?"

"What was what about?"

"You were toying with him," Pru accused. "Rubbing up against his furniture and saying how much you like it."

"But I do like it. Come over here and feel the

finish and—" Pru's words suddenly sank in, and Edwina gaped at her sister in shock. "Rubbing? I was not rubbing on anything! What a nasty thing to say!"

Prudence regarded her through narrowed eyes. "You weren't flirting with him?"

"Heavens no! I'm struggling to find ways to hold the man at arm's length, not lure him closer. Why would you think such a thing?"

Pru relaxed her truculent stance. She gave Edwina a wry smile and shook her head. "For all that you're a widow and were the biggest flirt in the parish, you really don't know that much about men, do you?"

"And you do?" Peeved to be accused of something she hadn't done, and by a person who *supposedly* had even less actual experience in such matters than she had, Edwina added testily, "I wasn't flirting! And I do prefer this furniture to that dark, heavily carved style Mother so favored. Anyone would, considering."

Pru raised her hands in a gesture of surrender. "All right. Sorry I misspoke. I'm just concerned." She started down the stairs.

Edwina stomped after her. "Concerned about Declan Brodie? Ha!"

"He's a good man, Edwina," Pru said over her shoulder. "I think you should give him a chance."

Edwina was about to issue another retort when she glanced over the banister and down into the kitchen. The fight went out of her. "Lord, what a mess. Looks like marauding monkeys came through."

"Nothing a little scrubbing won't fix." Crossing to the cook stove, Pru lifted two faded aprons from a peg, tossed one to Edwina and tied the other around her waist. She looked around, spotted a frayed broom and battered dustpan in the corner, and handed them to Edwina. "You sweep and I'll come behind you with a mop. We'll be finished in no time."

While Edwina swept the eggshells, flour, and unidentifiable chunks from the plank floor, Pru set about mopping up the puddles by the sink.

"What do you think of the children?" Edwina asked, bending to sweep a pile of debris into the dustpan.

"I think he's right. They need a mother."

"They were so filthy I couldn't even tell which one was the girl."

"The tattler with the gray eyes, I think. Unless she was the one hiding in the doorway." Having dealt with the wet floor, Pru stoked the fire in the cook stove, then dug out the makings for corn biscuits. "The tall one must be the oldest, R.D., and the blond with the singed bangs had to be Joe Bill."

Edwina found a waste barrel by a door leading out the back of the house to a fenced garden area and beyond that, a big, rambling barn. She emptied the dustpan, propped it with the broom in the corner, and went to help Pru, who was working the pump lever at the sink. "I'll wash the dishes, if you find us something to eat. I'm famished."

Soon the smell of onions and frying fatback filled the kitchen.

Edwina scrubbed listlessly as she stared out the window above the sink at the wagon track stretching down the valley. That sense of isolation and alienation tugged at her again. Was this what her life was to be from now on? Endless chores, a lonely marriage to an unapproachable man, raising another woman's children, and staring out of this small window, hoping to see a visitor come down that road?

"Pru," she said in sudden panic. "Promise me you won't leave."

"I'll have to someday."

"Don't be silly." When her sister didn't respond, Edwina turned and watched her spoon cornmeal batter into a muffin tin, then slip it into the oven. "You know you can stay here as long as you want, Pru."

"And if I don't want?" Without meeting Edwina's eyes, Pru pulled several cans from an open shelf, then rummaged in a drawer for a way to open them. "What if I want to do something on my own?"

Dread uncoiled in Edwina's chest, rising to

constrict the muscles in her throat. "Like what?"

Working at the cans with a knife, Pru managed to get them open enough to pour the contents—beans—into the skillet of onions and fatback. "Maybe I'll teach. Start a school for freedmen and women."

Edwina stared at her, dread building to heart-thudding panic. What would she do if Pru left her? How would she survive without the sister she had depended on for all of her life?

And how would Pru survive without her? To be a woman alone was risky enough. But to be a beautiful mulatto woman, who was neither white nor Negro, left Pru prey to both races. "But, Pru," she argued weakly, her mind still unable to grasp what her sister had said. "Where would you go? How could you be on your own and be safe?"

"I'm not helpless. I can take care of myself." She sent Edwina a chiding smile. "I've been watching over you all this time, haven't I?"

Edwina started to point out that she watched over Pru, too, which was one of the reasons they were out here in the back of beyond in the first place. But Pru would only laugh. Her sister didn't see the danger posed by the drunken gangs in Crappo Town or the white night riders. Pru thought if she didn't cause a ruckus and kept her head down, trouble would pass her by.

But Edwina knew different. She had heard the talk and seen the resentment in the eyes that followed Pru. And the hunger. Pru was a beautiful woman of mixed blood—an unforgivable thing to some. She was also better educated than most white men and carried herself with a quiet dignity that roused spite and envy—in whites and blacks.

That girl doesn't know her place. She's uppity. She needs to be taught a lesson, and if Edwina doesn't do it, someone else will.

It was sickening. Edwina's instinct was to lash back, show them such evil talk didn't matter, brazen it out. But she didn't dare. She wasn't about to risk her sister's life, or her own, just to stay in a place that held no meaning for them anymore. There had to be a better way, a better life waiting for them somewhere.

Was this it? Here on this lonely ranch with this unruly family and awkward man? Edwina didn't know. But for now, at least, she and Pru were safe. It was a start. But if Pru left her, it would all be for nothing.

"I worry about you, Pru. And about me. What if I made a terrible mistake?"

After stirring molasses, a can of tomatoes, and a big pinch of ground mustard into the beans, Pru wiped her hands on her apron and turned to face Edwina with a smile that was both sad and determined.

"And what if you haven't? It's obvious this family needs you."

Edwina gave a broken laugh. "It's you they need. Not me."

"Then make them need you." Pru must have seen the tears Edwina was trying so hard to hold back. Blinking against her own, she walked over and put her arms around her. "And how could they not grow to love you, little sister? You're sweet, kindhearted, fiercely loyal, smart—"

"Stop," Edwina said, laughing in spite of herself. "You're making me sound like a spaniel." Putting some space between them, she swiped at her cheeks and put on a wobbly smile. "Just promise me you'll stay until I get my feet under me. Otherwise, I'm going with you, I swear it."

"I promise." Still gripping her shoulders, Pru gave Edwina a hard look. "But you must promise me that you'll give this marriage a chance."

Edwina sighed. "He doesn't even like me, Pru. You've seen the way he looks at me."

"Then make him like you."

"How?"

"By being more likeable. And maybe rubbing up on something other than his furniture."

"Pru!"

Her sister met her outrage with a laugh. "Go on, now." She gave Edwina a gentle shove toward the door. "Call your family to lunch. I think I saw

113

a triangle dinner bell hanging beside the door when we came in."

Shaking her head at her sister's audacity, Edwina turned toward the door just as it opened and her new family trooped in.

And they didn't look happy.

FIVE

As Declan ushered his pouting children into the kitchen, he was greeted with the delicious smell of fried pork, onions, and baking muffins. His dour mood immediately lightened.

The place was clean, too, he saw, looking around. And the women were smiling in welcome. At least one of them was; his wife looked as if she'd been crying. He hoped it was because of the onions. He didn't need another scene after what he'd just gone through.

R.D. and Lucas had taken the news of their new mother well enough. R.D. asked if she was a better cook than Chick, the ranch hand who now did most of the cooking. Lucas just looked at him in silence, that same, sad look on his thin face. As expected, Joe Bill had strenuously insisted he already had a mother and didn't need another one—a tired refrain. Even after four years, the boy still wouldn't accept that his mother was dead. Brin had simply echoed whatever Joe Bill said, except at a shout and with tears.

"Children," he said now, putting on his best smile while gripping Brin's and Joe Bill's shoulders in warning. "This is the new ma I told you about."

Brin tipped her head back to frown up at him through the dark tangled curls poking out beneath her tattered slouch hat. "Which one?"

"The one with the light hair."

"I like the chocolate one better. What's wrong with her hand? Why is it different colors?"

"She's not chocolate," Joe Bill argued. "She's butterscotch."

"She's Prudence Lincoln," Declan cut in, feeling his control of the situation already start to unravel. "And she's not chocolate or butter-scotch. She's Negro. And the other lady," he went on before they could make any more unmannerly remarks, "is your ma."

"I ain't calling her ma," Joe Bill said. "I already got a ma."

"Joe Bill—"

"I ain't calling her ma, neither," Brin seconded, crossing her arms over her thin chest. "I don't like her."

"Brin—"

This time his wife cut him off. "Then you may call me Edwina or Pricilla." She stalked forward with that combative look Declan had come to recognize. "Or Mother, or Mrs. Brodie, or

115

Queen Victoria. I don't care which, as long as you do it with respect."

The children inched closer to his side as she stopped and studied each of them in turn. "I will not tolerate poor manners or unkind remarks directed at me, or my . . . friend, Miss Lincoln. Is that clear?"

Without waiting for them to respond, she lifted her gaze to Declan and smiled. It wasn't a friendly smile. "And I'm sure your father will back me up on that," she added, "since he has paid dearly in time and money to get me here, and is doubtless indisposed to making the long trip back to Heartbreak Creek today."

A threat? Declan scowled at her, unsure how to respond and wondering where his cowardly, complaining wife had gone. Maybe his children did need to be chastised for their rude remarks, but they were *his* children, and *he* should be the one to do it. But before he could point that out, Prudence Lincoln stepped into the breach with another of her overly bright smiles.

"Please, please, come sit down everyone. The corn muffins are just about ready."

Magic words, as far as his children were concerned. The test of wills instantly forgotten, they scrambled into chairs around the table.

It was a tense meal, although that didn't seem to put a damper on his children's appetites, Declan noticed. Brin's complaint that Thomas had fed them nothing but pemmican must have been right. He wondered why Chick hadn't fed them as he usually did, then realized he hadn't seen either Chick or his other ranch hand, Amos, since he'd gotten back.

"Where's Chick?" he asked.

"Joe Bill burned his leg," R.D. said through a mouthful of beans. "Trying to make smoke signals. Went to cut a new one."

"It was just laying there in the barn," Joe Bill defended. "How was I to know it was his leg?"

Declan was wondering what else Joe Bill might have burned other than his front hair and Chick's leg when he caught the looks of horror on the ladies' faces. "Chick McElroy," he explained. "Cooks and helps out some. Lost his leg to snakebite and now wears a peg leg." Turning back to his eldest, he asked, "Amos with him?"

R.D. shook his head. "Drunk. Tried to baptize Thomas."

Joe Bill laughed out loud, spewing bits of corn-meal onto the table. "Uncle Thomas baptized him instead, ain't that right, R.D.?"

Brin hooted and waved her spoon, slinging beans on Prudence Lincoln's apron. "You shoulda seen it, Pa! Amos kept hollering and sputtering every time Thomas shoved his head under. Looked like a giant fish the way he flopped around."

Declan stared morosely at his plate rather than

face the looks of disgust he was sure the ladies were aiming at him and his children. Not that they didn't deserve it, but he was too weary to deal with his children's behavior or his wife's complaints right then. He still had a wagon to unload, horses to unhitch, and three days of chores that had piled up while he was gone.

He sighed and spooned more beans onto his plate. Since that odd moment in the bedroom when Miss Priss had given him a friendly smile instead of her usual condescending smirk, he'd been hoping things might yet work out. But ten minutes in his children's company had likely shot that hope to hell. Finishing off his beans, Declan reached for the last corn muffin. At least the food was good.

After the merriment over the river scene died down, when Declan was thinking the rest of the meal might pass without further incident, his wife finally chose to speak. "Are you enjoying your meal, children?"

"Oh, dear," Prudence Lincoln muttered.

Declan looked up.

As did the children, eyeing their new ma with expressions of belligerence, laced with distrust and a trace of wariness. Smart kids.

"I hope so," Miss Priss went on in a friendly tone. "As it will be your last in this house. Unless . . ." Letting the word hang like an executioner's ax, she paused to take a dainty bite of muffin, set it back on her plate, dabbed at her mouth with a napkin—where had she found a napkin?—then looked up with that terrifying smile. ". . . you improve your table manners."

Silence. The children looked at one another, then at Declan. He saw expectation in their eyes and knew they were waiting for him to do something to show he was solidly in their camp and ready to send this usurper fleeing. He wasn't surprised his children and Miss Priss would butt heads; he just hadn't thought it would happen so soon.

"Pa . . . ?"

Chewing slowly so as not to aggravate the headache thudding behind his temples, Declan looked at his daughter's bean-smeared face. "Yes, Brin?"

"She can't do that, can she? Starve us?"

Declan shifted his gaze to his wife's determined face and realized how thoroughly he had under-estimated this woman. She was definitely not a coward. He admired that, even though it rankled that she had forced this little showdown without giving him prior warning. "Apparently, she can."

"That's not fair!" Joe Bill slapped his spoon onto the table so hard beans flew up to catch on the crinkled ends of his singed blond hair. "Pa, tell her!"

"I have no intention of starving you," Miss Priss said calmly. "You will be fed as you deserve." That smile again. "Slops in the barn."

"Slops?" Joe Bill looked at Declan. "Pa!"

Brin turned to Lucas, who sat beside her, watching the exchange in silence. "What's slops?"

"Pig food."

"Pig food? Pa!"

With a sigh, Declan stepped reluctantly into the fray, hoping to hell he was picking the right side. "Act like a pig, eat like a pig."

"Pa!"

Then things really got loud, and everyone started shouting at once, and the pounding in Declan's head built to a deafening thud against the inside of his skull, until finally with a bellow of exhaustion and frustration, he shot to his feet. "Enough, damnit! You sound like a pack of wild dogs!"

Stunned silence.

Hands on hips, he scowled down at the slack-jawed faces gaping up at him. "You children shame me with your mean-spirited bickering. I raised you better than that. And you"—he glared down the length of the table at his wife—"you're supposed to bring order to my home, not chaos!"

His wife opened her mouth, but Declan cut her off before she could speak. "You're right. They need better manners. And schooling, and what-ever else you can teach them. I'm not sure this is the way to go about it, but I'll back you up . . . to a point. I'll send them to the barn if you say so.

I'll even take them to the woodshed if need be. But don't you raise a hand against them, or belittle them, or turn them against one another. And don't come crying to me if it all blows up in your face. I've got no time for it. You started it, you finish it. I've got a ranch to run." And turning on his heel, he stalked from the room.

Edwina's sense of triumph lasted until the door closed behind him and Brin wailed, "But I don't wanna eat pig food!" and burst into tears.

Joe Bill sent Edwina a look that promised retribution. "Now see what you did."

R.D. reached over and patted his little sister's shoulder. "Quit crying, Brin. It'll be all right." Rising, he took Brin's hand and motioned to his brothers. "Come on. We got to help Pa unload the wagon."

With a final knife-edged glare at Edwina, Joe Bill followed his older brother and little sister out. Lucas, bringing up the rear, paused to give Edwina a puzzled look, then trailed after them.

As soon as the door closed, Pru pushed herself to her feet. "That went beautifully."

"Do you think so?" Edwina had her doubts. If it went so beautifully, why did she feel like casting up her lunch?

"No. I don't know." Pru gathered spoons and plates. "Something must be done. Those children are in desperate need of guidance."

"You don't think I can give it?"

Pru chuckled. "Oh, I'm sure you can."

Rising, Edwina carried a pile of dirty plates to the sink. Resting her hands on the counter, she looked out the window to see R.D. disappear with a sack of potatoes into what she guessed was a cool room or root cellar beneath the house. "You think I was too harsh with them?"

Memories burst into her mind—the switch rising and falling, blood flecks on the rug, her big sister's arms holding her while she wept. A prickle ran through her. Then she thought of her husband's warning not to raise her hand against his children, and the prickle became a shudder of disgust. "He thinks I was. But I would never use a cane on them, Pru."

"I know that."

"I'm not like my mother."

"No, you aren't." Her sister's arm slid around her shoulder. "And you never could be, dearest."

As always, her sister's reassuring words and gentle touch drove the suffocating memories back into the shadows. It frightened Edwina how much she needed that touch still, and how terrifyingly alone she would feel if—when—Pru took it away. Had she truly become that weak and dependent? Angry with that notion because she feared there was truth in it, she pulled away from her sister's grip.

"But something has to be done, Pru. It's not fair

to us or the children to allow such behavior to go on."

"You're right." Pru began scraping the plates.

"Then why are you upset?"

"I'm not upset. I'm worried." After dumping the food scraps into the slop bucket by the back door, Pru pulled a rag from the sink and began wiping down the counter. "I fear you've got a battle on your hands. Mannering these children won't be easy. Things will probably get a great deal worse before they get better."

Edwina thought of Declan's warning about Joe Bill being a trickster, and the boy's hard glare before he left. She didn't doubt that even now the battle lines were being drawn.

"Declan stood up for me, though." And Edwina was still a bit surprised that he had. "At least there's that."

Pru stopped wiping and looked at her, a smile teasing her lips. "Declan? When did you start using his given name?"

"What else should I call him?" Feeling heat in her cheeks, Edwina turned away to finish clearing the table. "*Mr.* Brodie sounds so . . . subservient . . . so docile."

Pru laughed out loud. "Docile? You?"

Edwina paused, a sudden mental image capturing her mind. Her husband, standing in the doorway with his children, his damp hair tumbling over his furrowed brow . . . lots of hair, as dark and glossy as that Indian fellow's, except with a slight wave, rather than stick straight. She bit back a smile. *That rascal.*

Shaking the image away, she turned back to her task. "And you should quit 'sir'-ing him all the time, Prudence. It sounds too—"

"Subservient?"

"Oh, hush. Or I'll tell the children the pig food was all your idea."

By suppertime, Edwina had come up with her "mannering" strategy; simple and direct, easily understood, and with only a few rules to follow. To encourage cooperation, she helped Pru prepare a sumptuous stew with items gleaned from the now fully stocked root cellar below the kitchen, and as a further inducement, they baked three loaves of bread and a rhubarb cobbler. To make sure the message reached them, Edwina set the loaves to cool in the open window above the sink so that the tantalizing aroma of freshly baked bread could drift on the warm afternoon breeze.

"I hope you know what you're doing," Pru said as Edwina set beside each plate a folded napkin with a crocheted edge, part of a stash of musty-smelling linens she had found in the back of a china cabinet built into the staircase wall. "You can't go at them with everything at once."

"I don't intend to." Edwina surveyed the table—cups, plates, tableware, napkins—everything in place. Satisfied, she positioned the slop bucket, which she had thoroughly washed just in case, in full sight on the counter by the sink. "Today we're only concentrating on table manners."

"Only." Pru sighed.

"Are we ready?"

"As we'll ever be."

The inducements apparently worked. When Edwina stepped out onto the front stoop to ring the bell, she found her new family already converging on the house like carnivores drawn to a fresh kill. A disturbing thought. But she held fast to her position blocking the doorway, hands clasped at her waist, a smile of welcome masking her steely resolve.

Unable to get past her, they stopped before the stoop, staring at her in restless confusion.

Edwina noted two new faces in the group—the ranch workers, no doubt. "I hope everyone is hungry," she said cheerfully. "We have a wonderful dinner prepared, as I know all of you have worked hard this afternoon."

Faces relaxed somewhat. Except for Declan's, whose dark eyes narrowed in suspicion. Already, the man knew her too well.

"If you don't mind," she went on pleasantly, "there's just one teensy little thing I'd like to ask of you before you go in."

The children shifted impatiently. The newcomers—a limping, wheat-thatched, freckled young man who she assumed was Chick, and a bleary-eyed middle-aged man with a look of defeat, who was probably Amos—regarded her with befuddlement.

After pausing to be sure she had everyone's full attention, Edwina said, "Wash. Faces, necks, hands front and back. I left soap and toweling beside the trough out back."

For a moment, there was so little reaction she wondered if she had only thought the words, rather than spoken them aloud. Then Brin—whom Edwina recognized by her short stature and the tattered slouch hat that almost covered her eyes —held up a hand and said, "Both hands? I only use this one."

How does one wash only one hand? "Both," Edwina answered, trying not to smile. The child was certainly a character, irregular ways and all.

"Seems a waste."

Other mouths opened, but before arguments erupted, Declan waved his offspring toward the trough outside the barn. A moment of resistance, more milling, then the children filed past, mumbling and glaring at Edwina.

"You, too." Declan motioned to the two new-comers. With a considering look at Edwina, he turned to follow them.

"Oh, and one more thing," Edwina said to his broad back.

He stopped and turned, his expression showing impatience.

"No hats at the table, please. If losing hair is a problem, I will be glad to loan you a scarf to prevent it from falling into the food."

He blinked. Then understanding dawned. Edwina wasn't sure how she knew that, or knew that he was amused—there was little change in his usual stern expression—yet the laughter was there, hiding behind his expressive eyes. Perhaps she was getting to know him better, too.

"And the flies?" he asked, deadpan.

Masking her own amusement with an off-hand gesture, Edwina said, "Since I doubt you have fresh mint, I'll hang cotton balls at the window."

"Try mountain elder. I think there's some blooming by the creek."

"Why, thank you so much for the kind suggestion. Perhaps I'll stroll down there later."

"Watch for cats if you do. R.D. said he saw a big one on the ridge." He must have seen her confusion. "Big cats," he clarified. "I don't know what they call them in your part of the country—cougars, pumas, mountain lions, whatever. This one is full grown. If you see it, don't run or it'll get you for sure."

"Lions? You have lions?"

"Sometimes." Looking pleased to have shaken her composure, he flashed that startling grin and continued on around the side of the house.

Stepping back inside, Edwina closed the door, giving it an extra tug to make sure the latch fell.

Round one to Declan. Yet, despite her unease over lurking mountain lions, she couldn't help but smile in anticipation of her next battle with her clever husband.

"Don't start ladling the stew into the tureen," she instructed Pru, who was adding final seasonings to the big pot on the stove. "Wait until they're seated, so they can see what they'll be missing if they don't cooperate."

"You're mean."

"I'm determined. Here they come."

She had just taken her position in the chair at the foot of the table, smile in place, hands folded in her lap, when her damp-faced family trooped in the back door.

While the children scrambled into their seats, Declan introduced the women to his workers, Chick McElroy and Amos Hicks. Then pointing the stammering, red-faced gentlemen to empty chairs, he hung his and Brin's hats on hooks by the door, and took his place at the head of the table opposite Edwina.

As soon as everyone had settled and all eyes were pinned on Prudence as she spooned stew into a chipped porcelain tureen, Edwina said, "Before we begin, children, there are a couple of things we need to address." She said it in a friendly way but wasn't that surprised that the young faces turning toward her didn't return her smile.

Undaunted, she pressed on. "First of all, your

father"—she paused to direct an especially bright smile at Declan, who watched her warily from the other end of the table—"has asked that I not turn you one against the other, which I assume also means I should not favor one over the other. Is that right, Mr. Brodie?"

A pause, as if sensing a trap, then a slight dip of his head, which sent that errant lock of glossy black hair sliding down over his forehead. Edwina watched him absently reach up to push it out of his eyes, and realized again the man had the loveliest hair, and the biggest hands, and a way of looking at a person that almost made her feel—

"Go on."

Jolted out of her momentary lapse, Edwina cleared her throat, then acknowledged his reluctant nod with a gracious one of her own. "Therefore, children, be advised that when a rule is broken by one of you, the consequences will fall on all of you."

Brin leaned toward Lucas. "What's consequences?"

"Punishments," Lucas whispered back.

Smart boy, Lucas.

"That's not fair," Joe Bill muttered.

"What rules?" R.D. asked.

"They're quite simple, really." Edwina counted off on her fingers: "Chew with your mouth closed. Don't speak when your mouth is full. Don't gobble your food or slurp your soup. No shouting, kicking, arguing, cursing, hitting, belching, shoving, or hats at the table. Keep your napkin—that's that folded piece of cloth beside your plate—in your lap when it's not in use, and whenever possible, use your utensils rather than your fingers."

Brin leaned toward Lucas again. "What's utensils?"

"Eating things. Knives, forks, spoons, and suchlike."

Brin sat back. "I'm not allowed to use knives," she told Edwina. "Pa consequenced me after I cut Joe Bill."

Edwina choked, then clumsily covered it with a cough. "Then we will see that your food is cut into bite-sized portions until your punishment is lifted."

"What if you're eating peas?" Joe Bill looked to his brothers for support. "The only way to get them in your spoon is to push them with your finger, right? What do we do then?"

"Push with the flat side of your knife, instead of your finger."

"I'm not allowed to use knives," Brin said again.

"What about corn on the cob?" This time it was R.D. "Can we eat that with our hands?"

"And chicken legs!" Brin shouted, joining happily in the game.

Declan sat back in his chair, one arm hooked over the backrest, apparently unconcerned by the torment his children were dishing to their new stepmother.

Edwina's facial muscles started to quiver with the effort of maintaining her smile. "We will address each question as the circumstance arises. But for now, let's just concentrate on the rules I have mentioned."

"What rules?"

She refrained from shouting them out as she laboriously counted them off again. "And because this is new to you," she added, "you will be given two chances."

"Would that be two chances each?" R.D. asked. "Or two total?"

"Total."

"So if Joe Bill burps, it's okay the first time? But the second time we all got to eat slops?"

Edwina pressed fingertips to a sudden tic that had developed in her right eyebrow. "Exactly."

"What if he can't help it?" R.D. frowned at his younger brother. "He's a mouth breather, you know."

What a surprise. "We will take that into con-sideration." Then before they could dream up further challenges, she added with an edge of desperation, "Now, who would like to say grace?"

"Grace!" Brin shouted. "I said it first! I win!"

Ignoring the muffled laughter coming from the direction of the stove, Edwina narrowed her eyes at the man watching from the other end of the table—was that a smirk? "Mr. Brodie, perhaps you will lead us in a blessing?"

The smirk faded. "Amos, you do it. You're the preacher here."

Amos Hicks pressed back in his chair, a look of panic on his face. "N-N-No—I-I—"

"I'll do it," Chick McElroy offered with a grin that revealed chipped front teeth. "My grandpa was a Baptist."

"Excellent. Thank you so much, Mr. McElroy. Children, if you will bow your heads, please."

After an extended period of squirming and throat clearing, Chick began in a voice worthy of any pulpit, "O Lord, before you send us wretched sinners and Godless heathens into the fiery pit of hell to burn forever in the crackling flames of eternal damnation, we ask that—"

"Pa," Brin cried, eyes round with terror, "I don't wanna go!"

"Me, neither!"

"What's a heathen?"

Pandemonium erupted.

Edwina slumped back in defeat. While Declan struggled to calm his sons and reassure his frantic daughter, she pressed a hand to her brow and wondered why she ever thought she could bring the grace of good manners to this household. This wasn't her family. These weren't her children, and Declan wasn't her husband. Not really. And if they chose to live like wild beasts, it was certainly no reflection on her. She didn't even have to stay if she didn't want to. She could always go back to

Heartbreak Creek with Pru and teach Negroes to read. A fine idea. Yes, that's exactly what she should do. She would start packing tonight.

"Mr. McElroy." Her sister's calm voice cut through Edwina's dismal thoughts and the children's raised voices. "If you wouldn't mind finishing up, sir? Dinner is getting cold."

Instant quiet. Cherubic faces all around.

How did Pru do that?

"Chick," Declan prodded, with a warning look. "And this time without the fire and brimstone."

"Oh. Yes, sir. Well . . . let's see. Bless this food, amen. How's that?"

"Fine. Now serve the damn stew."

"Pa said a cuss word," Brin crowed. "He has to eat slops!"

Edwina closed her eyes as pandemonium broke out again. Her first supper in her new home with her new family. A total failure.

If she hadn't been laughing so hard, she might have wept.

SIX

Except for Rusty, no one ate slops. At least as far as Declan could tell; he and Amos had left well before dawn and had been too busy clearing a rockslide from a water hole to go back to the house for lunch.

After a long morning digging in rocky soil, they were settling in the shade of a scraggly juniper to dine on cold beans and jerky when R.D. rode up, his saddlebags bulging with food the women had prepared. Grateful and pleased, Declan gobbled down panfried chicken, fresh corn muffins, two hard-boiled eggs, and dried peaches. Not a bad lunch. Maybe this wife thing would work out after all, as long as the mulatto stayed.

After R.D. left, he and Amos continued working through the afternoon moving rocks. When they finally got the water flowing again—such as it was—the sun was slipping behind Swallow Peak, and the air was cooling fast. Bone tired, they mounted up and headed home.

The Milky Way was a misty band across a cloudless indigo sky by the time they splashed through the creek. As they reined toward the barn, Declan noted the house was quiet and dark except for the faint glow of a single lamp in the kitchen wing. He sighed. Another meal missed. Rotating the kinks out of his knotted shoulders, he drew in a deep breath that smelled of wood smoke and sage. Even with only a cold supper and a lumpy settee awaiting him, he was glad to be home.

After tending the horses and turning them out, they crossed to the back door, the crunch of their boots on the rocky ground sounding unnaturally loud in the stillness of the night. He stepped onto the stoop and pulled open the door, then froze, startled by the sight of his wife sitting in a chair by the stove, sewing on something.

She looked up, eyes wide. Then seeing who it was, her expression softened into a hesitant smile. "I was starting to worry."

About what? Him?

Setting her sewing aside, she rose and motioned them in. "Come sit. You, too, Mr. Hicks. I've kept supper warm."

Suddenly Declan was conscious of how dirty he was, and how pretty she looked in the lamplight. He wondered if she'd been waiting up for him and if so, why? Then he forgot the question when she pulled two overflowing plates from the oven, and the smell of roasted beef, and mashed potatoes, and collards with bacon sang to his empty stomach.

Amos nudged him from behind.

"We need to wash," Declan muttered, and turned to shove the old preacher back across the stoop.

When they returned a few minutes later, their plates were waiting on the table and his wife was back in her chair, sewing. He hung his hat on a peg beside the door, sent Amos a look telling him to do the same, then took his chair at the end of the table. They wolfed down the food.

She glanced up from her sewing every now and then, but said nothing.

Just as well. He wouldn't have taken the time

to respond. The meal was that good. He wondered if she had cooked it or if she had left it to the mulatto. "Where's Miss Lincoln?" he asked between bites.

She gave that half smile again, her eyes reflecting back the lamplight like tiny twin fires. "Asleep. She's had a hard day."

He motioned with his fork. "Doing all this?"

"The garden. Pru loves to dig in the dirt."

Did that mean his wife cooked this fine meal? There was hope yet.

"And to supervise me, of course."

Hope faded.

She went back to her sewing, taking small precise stitches, her fingers nimble and quick. He had a sudden image of those same fingers stroking the foot rail of his bed, and felt again that odd rush of heat along his back.

Uneasy with where his thoughts had wandered, he steered his mind to a safer subject. "The children help out today?" He'd told R.D. to work with Chick in the foaling pen—some of the mares were getting close—but the three younger children were to stay available in case they were needed.

"With Pru? Yes."

"Not you?"

She bit off the thread, then folded the cloth. It appeared to be a dress, but seemed too small. Maybe an apron. Women loved their aprons.

When she looked up again, her lips were

pursed—either in disapproval or to hold back a grin.

Declan guessed a grin. For all her shortcomings, the woman dearly loved to smile. And laugh. At him, mostly. Not being a big laugher himself, it was a bit disconcerting. Although in truth, he didn't mind being smiled at now and then, even though he didn't entirely trust it.

"When they were with me," she said, her eyes dancing in the wavering light, "they mostly tried to look up my skirts."

Declan stopped chewing. "They what?"

Before she could answer, Amos's fork clattered to his empty tin plate. Shoving back his chair, he abruptly rose, muttered, "Th-Thanks, ma'am," and fled the room.

Declan sat, nonplussed, watching Miss Priss clear away Amos's plate and fork. After setting them in the sink, she turned to face him, leaning back with her elbows bent behind her, her hands gripping the edge of the counter. The pose stretched the fabric of her dress tight across her breasts, flattening them in such a way Declan saw they were fuller than he had thought. He found himself waiting for one of those tiny pearl buttons to slip free.

"Apparently," she went on, jerking him back on track, "between that ghastly blessing at dinner, and Joe Bill's wild imagination, they're convinced I have a devil tail."

"A devil tail?" He managed not to smile.

"I don't think they like me very much." She said it offhandedly, as if it didn't matter, but he heard a contradiction in her voice.

"It's not you," he assured her and hoped it wasn't a lie. "It's the idea of you. Give them time." He felt a momentary regret that he hadn't prepared his children better for a new ma, then shrugged it off, telling himself she hadn't helped the situation by throwing all those rules at them first thing.

"I would have fixed more had I known you'd be so hungry."

He looked down, realized he had eaten everything on his plate, and set down his fork. Yet he was reluctant to leave, and he wasn't sure why. Maybe just trying to put off another back-cramping night on that lumpy settee Sally had insisted they buy for the parlor.

Or maybe there was another reason.

Silence spread through the room to the rhythmic tick of the stove as it cooled. He folded and refolded his unused napkin and set it beside his plate, wondering why he didn't get up and leave. He was glad she didn't feel the need to chatter all the time, but was also bothered by it since he didn't know what she was thinking, or if she was waiting for him to speak—about what, he had no idea. He'd never been that comfortable around women—except for the obvious, of course, but that didn't require talking. In social situations, he mostly felt big and awkward, not sure what he was supposed to say or what was expected of him. During his years with Sally, those awkward moments had stretched into long silences that had eventually grown into indifference so thick it had formed a wall between them. He wondered if that would happen with this wife, too, and if he would come to a point when he might try harder to keep that wall from forming.

"I cleaned the parlor today."

He nodded, relieved to have the silence over. "That's nice."

"I removed the saddle. Hope you don't mind."

"There was a saddle in there?"

"Two, in fact. And saddlebags. I had R.D. take them to the barn."

She had a nice voice when she wasn't preaching or passing out rules. Soft and musical, dragging out the words in more syllables than were there, finishing on a higher note at the ends of her sentences. It kept him listening, pulled him closer to hear more.

"It's a lovely room," she went on. "But that settee is much too small for a man your size."

He watched her, neither agreeing nor disagreeing, wondering if this was an invitation to return to his own bed. Maybe with her. The idea made the muscles across his chest tighten and his breathing go shallow. His mind said it wouldn't be wise—they hardly knew each other—it was too soon.

But his body said maybe not.

He took a sip of water and cursed himself for not visiting Rosemarie when he was in town.

"Mr. McElroy found two spare mattresses in the bunkhouse," she said. "We aired them out. He and R.D. made a platform with boards and kegs they found in the barn, and I found linens in the cabinet by the stairs. It's a bit makeshift, but with the mattresses pushed together, it should at least be wide enough. I think you'll be more comfortable."

Not knowing whether to be relieved or disappointed that he wouldn't be back in his own bed, Declan nodded his thanks.

"Will you be gone tomorrow as well?" she asked.

"Mostly. Roundup's starting."

"I see."

He cleared his throat and shifted in the chair. "I might need R.D. and Joe Bill, but I'll leave Chick to watch over the house."

"Perhaps I can help."

She must have seen his skeptical look. "I'm a good rider," she insisted. "I had the most beautiful plantation walking horse you ever saw."

Gaited horses were useless in mountains. But instead of pointing that out, he said, "Send lunch. That way Amos won't have to stop to fix it."

She smiled like that was the finest idea she'd heard all day. "Lovely."

He wondered why she was being so agreeable all of a sudden and where the prickly hothead he'd married had gone. Not that he minded; a biddable woman was a rare and wondrous thing . . . or so he'd heard. He'd never met any, except for whores, but they were paid to be agreeable so that didn't count. And this woman was definitely not a whore. Pity, that. Pushing back his chair, he rose.

"Will you be wanting breakfast before you leave?"

He hesitated, his hand resting on the back of the chair. "It'll be early."

"You should eat something."

"I'll grab some jerky."

She had come away from the counter and was leaning across the table to pick up his plate and fork. The motion opened a gap where she'd loosened her collar, and Declan caught a glimpse of creamy flesh. Again, he had to force himself to look away.

She carried his dishes to the sink, wiped the counter with a rag, then faced him as she dried her hands. "I'm sorry we overslept and didn't fix you something this morning. You must have been very quiet."

He was. So quiet he'd heard every sound coming from the open loft over the kitchen. A snore, a sigh, the rustle of bedcovers. Sounds that seemed alien and out of place in the dawn stillness of his house—sounds that reminded him he was no longer alone—that he was married to the woman upstairs in his bed, and if he let her, she would change his life forever. "You probably couldn't hear me over your snoring."

She stopped drying. "I do not snore."

"Must have been the mulatto, then."

Anger flared in her eyes. She slapped the rag onto the counter with such violence, Declan blinked in surprise. "Don't call her that," she snapped, taking a step toward him. "Or nigra, or darky, or girl, or nigger, or half-blood, or any of the other hateful names people throw around so easily. She's more than the color of her skin or the amount of white blood in her veins. She's a person and my friend. Call her Prudence or Miss Lincoln."

Declan felt the heat of shame rise in his neck. She was right and he knew better. He'd had similar conversations with his children about Thomas Redstone's mixed blood. "I'll remember that." Feeling foolish, he walked to the parlor door and opened it. "Good night, then."

"Good night, Declan."

He pulled the door closed behind him, then stood there, shrouded in shadow, breathing in the scents of furniture wax, musty bedding, and that faint flowery smell from the packets of dried flowers Sally used to slip between the folds of the good linens.

Declan. A two-syllable word she managed to make into three.

He tensed as footfalls approached his door. Lamplight showed in the gap by the floor, then quickly faded as she started up the stairs, the hollow thump of her heels on the treads marking her progress. Then overhead, the creak of the floorboards as she crossed the bedroom. A different creak when the wardrobe door opened and closed. A moment later, softer footfalls as she crossed barefoot to the screened water closet.

Then silence. Yet he remained frozen in darkness, his imagination detailing every movement. Her long, graceful fingers unbuttoning the tiny pearl buttons one by one. The dress sliding away. Did she wear a corset? He couldn't remember if he'd felt one when he'd lifted her down from the wagon the day before. She had no need of it— she was so slim his hands had almost spanned her tiny waist.

He looked up when he heard a soft thump on the floor above him, and pictured those round breasts swinging free as she bent to step out of her petticoats, then rising firm and high when she lifted her arms to unpin her long, shiny hair.

Did she sleep in a thick flannel gown like Sally had? Or something frilly and sheer?

More footfalls toward the bed. A muffled sigh, then silence again.

Disgusted with his own foolishness, Declan turned away, his body tight and his mind rattled by his wild imaginings. After stripping off his clothes, he flopped back on his put-together bed and stared up at the ceiling, his fingers laced behind his head.

What the hell was wrong with him?

He should have stopped in to see Rosemarie when he was in town. Now there was a woman a man could understand. Sweet, quiet, and accommodating in all the right ways. And the only things she required in return were a nice ride and two dollars. The perfect woman.

Then why was he lying here in the dark with his John Thomas pointing at a different woman, and his mind in total confusion?

"Well, I did what you said," Edwina railed the next morning as she marched after Pru to gather eggs and feed the chickens in the pen beside the barn.

It was early. Dew still clung to the sparse grass, dampening the hems of her skirt. The sun shone brightly. Birds sang. It was a beautiful day. She was furious.

"I was all smiles and sweetness and nice as you please. For what? Ha!" She waved the grain bucket for emphasis, slinging a spray of corn and breadcrumbs, which immediately brought the dog in to clean them up.

"Sweetness." Swinging open the gate, Pru waited for Edwina to come through, then latched it behind her. "I can't even picture it."

Pru opened the door to the coop, then stepped back as chickens spilled into the sunlight, squawking and darting in circles as if their tail feathers were on fire. As soon as Edwina started tossing grain and breadcrumbs, they settled down to business.

"The man's hopeless, Pru. A stone-faced mute. Maybe he's damaged."

"He didn't compliment the meal? Or notice how clean the kitchen was?" Pru's voice grew muffled as she moved deeper into the shadowed coop, checking the nests for eggs. "He didn't say any-thing to you?"

Edwina peppered a beetle headed toward her with grain, then quickly looked away when a chicken began pecking at it. "He said I could send lunch but I couldn't chase cows."

"Send lunch where? And why would you want to chase cows?"

"It sounds fun."

Pru muttered something Edwina didn't catch.

"He also said I snored," Edwina added. "Which I don't. And he stared at my chest a lot. The man hardly said fifty words the whole time."

Pru's head appeared in the doorway of the coop. "He stared at your chest?"

"I know." Edwina sighed and looked down at her less-than-voluptuous bosom. "At least he didn't laugh."

But Pru did. "You silly thing. Your bosom is

fine. You just need to eat. You're too skinny."
Taking a deep breath, she ducked back inside.

"Is that how you got your big bosom? By overeating?" Edwina hated being called skinny. Or "Stick" as Shelly had once referred to her.

"That's my fine African blood," Pru called from inside.

"Then you must have a lot of it in your fanny," Edwina muttered.

"I heard that."

"I just wished it poked out some," Edwina said, tossing another handful of grain. "Remember how Lucinda's poked out? Her bosom looked so grand in that lovely silk dress."

Pru stepped hastily out of the coop, exhaled in a rush, and took several deep breaths. "Whalebone corset. And I cannot believe we're discussing Lucinda Hathaway's breasts. Here." She thrust the filled egg basket at Edwina and began shaking dust and feathers and straw from her skirts. "That coop is nasty. Next time you're going in."

"We should make the children do it."

"And end up with an egg fight on our hands?" Having put her skirts to rights, Pru retrieved her basket, patted her hair, and checked her shoes. "The last thing we should put into those children's hands is raw eggs, especially after what you did yesterday."

Edwina smiled in spite of herself, picturing Joe Bill's face when she'd cracked that egg over his head for trying to look up her skirts. "It worked, didn't it?"

"Those children are incorrigible. And you're not much better."

After dumping the last of the grain, Edwina followed her sister out the gate and latched it behind her. With her arm looped through Pru's, they walked across the yard. "Oh, they're not so bad. I like Brin. She's got spirit. And Lucas is sweet, although I wish he would talk more so I could get to know him better. He seems so lost."

"Just be watchful," Pru warned as she opened the back door. "No telling what mischief they'll think up next."

Mischief wasn't the word for it, Edwina realized a moment later when they entered the kitchen door. More like total destruction. A devastating blow that left her numbed with shock and despair.

Surprisingly, it didn't come from Joe Bill, the prankster, or Brin, the curious meddler. But from Lucas—shy, sweet Lucas.

Her heart seemed to shrivel in her chest when she saw the countless pieces strewn across the kitchen table. Pieces of her watch. The Waltham Bond Street watch with the push-button time set and the initials CW engraved on the back. Her father's watch. The only thing she had left of him. "Oh, Lucas, no!" Shoving past Pru, she rushed toward the table. "What have you done?"

The boy shrank back, his eyes round in his small

147

face. "Joe Bill said it was all right. That I could take it apart. Didn't you, Joe Bill?"

Only then did Edwina see the other boy standing by the parlor door. "You!" Fury engulfed her, sent her charging toward him.

Joe Bill ducked into the parlor.

Edwina tore after him. "Why would you do such a thing? That was my father's watch!"

Joe Bill wrestled frantically with the latch on the door onto the porch, finally getting it open just before Edwina reached him.

"You little dickens!" she cried, racing after him down the porch steps. "You come back here!"

He ran around the side of the house. She pounded after him, cleared the corner at a dead run, and plowed face-first into a tall, solid body that smelled of horses and alfalfa and sweating male. As she stumbled back a strong hand grabbed her shoulder to steady her. "What the hell's going on?"

"She's crazy, Pa," Joe Bill cried, twisting in the grip of Declan's other hand. "She hit me in the head with an egg and started screaming like—"

"That was yesterday, you little schemer," Edwina shouted back. "And the next time you lift my skirts, it'll be *two* eggs I crack over your head!"

"Quiet!"

The combatants glared at each other across Declan's broad chest, their breaths coming in short, quick gasps.

"What's going on?" Declan demanded, scowling down at them from beneath his wide-brimmed hat.

"She's crazy, Pa. Like one of Chick's demons. Look under her skirt. You'll see."

"Oh, for mercy's sake!" Jerking her shoulder free of Declan's grip, Edwina whirled around, flipped up the back of her skirts, and waggled her bloomer-clad bottom. "There! Do you see a tail? No!" Letting her skirts drop, she turned back to meet her husband's astonished face. "Satisfied?"

"I, ah—"

"It could be curled up, Pa. Check her drawers."

Edwina gasped.

"Joe Bill!" Declan gave the boy's shoulder a rough shake. "There's no devil tail, and that's the end of it!" He scowled down at his son, his face flushed either from anger or embarrassment. Edwina decided on anger and shot Joe Bill a triumphant smile. Which quickly faded when Declan rounded on her. "And no more egg throwing, you hear? You're supposed to be the adult here. He acts up, send him to me. Understand?" He waited for her reluctant nod, then turned and waited for Joe Bill to give his.

"All right, then." Releasing Joe Bill's shoulder, he planted both hands at his waist, his long fingers splayed across the thick leather belt he seemed to favor over braces. Without shoulder strap supports, his denim trousers rode low on his hips, and

Edwina suspected a good yank would pull them—

"Now what did he do this time?"

Mortified, Edwina jerked her gaze from his belt area. "They broke my watch."

"I wasn't me, Pa. It was Lucas took it apart."

Edwina shook a finger at him. "And who said it was all right for him to do that?"

After a few futile attempts to exonerate himself, Joe Bill reluctantly admitted he had told Lucas that if he wanted to see how a clock worked, there was one on the loft night table he could take apart.

"Which he did," Edwina added, feeling again the despair of losing a beloved treasure. "And now it's in pieces all over the kitchen table."

"I'll have Lucas put it back together," Declan said.

Joe Bill shook his head. "He tried, Pa. It won't go. He thinks some parts are missing."

Edwina blinked hard at the ground, tears blurring the memory of bending over her father's body, pulling the watch from his vest pocket, and trying desperately to wipe off the blood.

"We'll get another, then."

"You can't. It was my father's."

There was a long pause. Then Declan turned to his son. "Go to the woodshed."

Edwina's gaze flew up. She glanced from her husband's set face to Joe Bill's frightened one. Guessing what Declan intended to do, she grabbed his arm. "No, wait. What are you doing?"

"He needs to be punished."

"By whipping him?"

Declan looked down at her, his dark brows drawn low over his eyes. "Then what do you want me to do?"

"Certainly not hit him. He's just a boy."

"A boy who purposely destroyed something that wasn't his."

Realizing she still held his arm, she pulled her hand away. "Will hitting him bring it back?"

Muttering under his breath, Declan took off his hat, dragged his fingers through his hair, then put the hat back on. He spread his palms in frustration. "Then what do you want, Ed? Just tell me and I'll do it."

Edwina looked at Joe Bill, saw the tears the boy was struggling bravely to hold back, and she felt the terrible fears of her childhood crowd her mind. "Apologize," she said to the boy. "Tell me you're sorry and you won't do it again."

"I-I'm sorry. I won't do it again." His hazel eyes darted to his father's stern face. "I promise, Pa."

Declan glanced at his son, then at Edwina. His expression showed doubt and confusion. And maybe relief. "That's it? That's all you want?"

Realizing that if she gave in too easily she might appear weak, Edwina quickly improvised, asking if there were stalls in the barn, and if so, how many were currently in use.

"With the mares foaling, most of them are."

"Who cleans them out?"

"Chick."

"For the next two weeks, Joe Bill will do it."

Rocked by the injustice of it, Joe Bill cried, "All by myself?"

Ignoring him, Edwina said to Declan, "And he'll also keep the water buckets and troughs full, tend the chickens every morning and your horse every night."

"That's not fair!"

"You'd rather go to the woodshed?" his father asked.

"But what about Lucas? He's the one who broke it."

"Don't you worry about Lucas," Edwina told the sputtering boy. "He'll get what's coming to him. Besides, if I were you, Joe Bill, I'd be more concerned about that nasty rooster who guards the henhouse."

"Pa!"

"Meanwhile," she continued loudly over his plaintive objections, "I believe there are some stalls that need your attention."

After Joe Bill disappeared toward the barn, muttering and stomping hard to show how unfair he thought it all was, Declan said, "You thrive on this, don't you?"

"On what?"

"Crisis. Chaos. Confrontation."

Stung that he thought she actually *enjoyed*

punishing children, Edwina responded a bit more sharply than she intended. "I'm only doing what needs to be done. Which I wouldn't have to do if *you* had done what you were supposed to do in the first place."

"I have a ranch to run," he reminded her.

"Then go do it." *You great lump.* "I've got another *crisis* to manage with one of *your* children."

"Okay, then," he said cheerfully. "Adios." And unbelievably, he turned his back on her and started toward the wagon and team waiting in the yard, loaded with shovels and picks and a dozing Amos Hicks.

Anger ignited, consuming any lingering reservations she might have had. Confrontation? Ha! She'd give him a confrontation. "One more thing," she called after him.

He swung back. "What now? I should have been gone an hour ago."

Anger bolstered by his surly impatience, Edwina stalked forward, stopping when her skirts brushed the toes of his boots. She glared up at him, letting him see the resolve in her eyes. "If you ever take a strap, a cane, a switch, a whip, or anything else to these children, Declan, I will come at you with a pitchfork, I swear to God."

He reared back, his dark eyes round with surprise . . . and maybe anger. "You're threatening me?"

"I am."

"Over my own children?"

"Children you have put into my care. And I will never countenance the beating of a child. Not even by a parent. *Especially* by a parent."

"The hell you say."

He stared at her so hard and for so long Edwina began to doubt the wisdom of coming at him head-on. She probably should have taken a subtler approach, maybe put on a show of meekness like Pru might have done. Although as hardheaded as Declan seemed to be, that might have sailed right past him.

In either case, this was too important to chance on misunderstandings. This was something she would never back down on. This was something she had endured as a child, and she was determined no boy or girl in her care would ever suffer as she and Pru had.

"I mean it, Declan."

She watched the anger fade from his eyes, replaced by something she couldn't define. "Well, hell," he finally muttered. "Joe Bill has the right of it. You really are crazy, Ed." And shaking his head, he turned and walked toward the wagon.

Edwina frowned after him, not sure what to think. That was twice he'd called her Ed. Not as bad as the pig-sounding Ed-wee-na, or as hated as Pricilla, or as demeaning as Miss Priss.

Ed. A man's name.

"Ed," she said aloud, liking the sound of it.

Bold. Strong. A woman of consequence. Bemused, she turned back to the house. She just hoped he wasn't calling her that because of her un-pointy chest.

SEVEN

Edwina's talk with Lucas promised to be much harder because by the time she returned to the house her anger had faded into weary disgust, which definitely took the edge off her determination to exact retribution for the hurt the boys had so carelessly dealt her.

Punishing them wouldn't bring her father's watch back.

But how could she *not* punish them? What would that teach them?

Her mother's voice shrieked through her mind, each word punctuated by the crack of the cane across her back. "I. Am. Doing. This. For. Your. Own. Good." Edwina felt her gorge rise and forcefully blocked the sounds and images from her mind. This wasn't the same. She wasn't enjoying it, no matter what Declan thought.

Opening the kitchen door, she stepped inside to find Pru's dark head bent beside Lucas's light brown one, as they carefully gathered the watch parts and put them in a small tin. Lucas's quick glance told Edwina he might have been crying.

She hoped not. She knew the boy had no meanness in him. He was just a curious and troubled boy who kept his mind occupied by figuring out how things worked so he had no space left in his head for the bad things.

She had done the same, but had used music instead of puzzles. Not because she liked the sound of it, but because if she pounded the piano keys long enough and hard enough she could shut out the terror, and the despair, and the sound of her mother's voice.

Music and Pru had saved her.

Now she had a chance to save this little boy. From what, she didn't know. She just sensed he was hurting and needed someone to make it stop.

"Lucas," she said.

He looked up, his eyes puffy and worried. Before she could say anything more, he blurted out in a rush, "I just wanted to see how the gears worked. That's all. I didn't mean to break it." Moisture gathered in his soft brown eyes, eyes a shade lighter than his father's but just as expressive.

Edwina eased down into the chair beside him, turning slightly so she could face him. She wanted to reach out and comfort him but doubted he would welcome her touch. Not yet. Maybe not ever.

"I know you didn't, Lucas."

He swiped a sleeve over his runny nose.

"Did Pa take Joe Bill to the woodshed?"

"No."

"Is he gonna take me?"

"No." Edwina felt the burn of righteous anger in her throat. "Has he ever taken either of you to the woodshed?"

Lucas shook his head, sending a flop of sun-tipped hair sliding down his forehead. Another similarity to his father. "He took R.D. once when he caught him fooling with matches in the barn. R.D. said it was the scariest thing ever. Not the whipping, but that Pa was so mad."

Edwina let out a breath she wasn't aware she'd been holding. She couldn't have stayed with a man who was brutal to his children. But a whipping over something as dangerous as playing with matches in a barn filled with straw and hay? That she could understand, and excuse.

Unsure how to handle this, Edwina looked over Lucas's bent head at Pru, hoping for answers.

But her sister shrugged and shook her head, then rose from the table. "Think I'll see if we've got a ham hanging in the cool room downstairs."

After she left, Edwina sat for a moment, drumming her fingers on the table. Then she rose, went into the parlor, dug out a piece of writing paper and a stub of pencil from a bookcase drawer she had cleaned out the day before, and returned to the kitchen. Placing them on the table, she took her seat again. "Joe Bill's punishment is to clean out the stalls, fill the troughs, and tend the chickens and his father's horse for two weeks. What do you think yours should be?"

"I don't know. I could help him, I guess."

"He also said he was sorry and he would never do it again."

"I can say that if you want."

"Go ahead."

He did.

She nodded her acceptance of the apology, then pushed the paper and pencil toward him. "Now write it. Twenty-five times."

She sat quietly until he finished the task. Then she looked over his childish scrawl, nodded, and set the paper aside. "Now tell me why you're sorry."

"I broke your watch."

"Perhaps. We'll see once you have it back together. What else?"

When his face showed confusion, she helped him. "You let someone else talk you into doing what you knew was wrong. Isn't that so?"

He looked away, a flush turning the ears that showed beneath the uneven cut of his light brown hair a bright strawberry red. "I guess."

"You're smart, Lucas. Smart enough to decide for yourself what's right and wrong. So from now on, I expect you to do that. If you're ever in doubt about what that is, ask me or Miss Lincoln or your father. Understand?"

He nodded.

"Good." And wanting this to be over before she burst into tears of sympathy, Edwina quickly meted out his punishment: for the next two weeks he was to weed and water the garden, feed the barn cats, set and clear the table, and sweep the kitchen every night.

He accepted it with a quavery "Yes, ma'am."

Edwina felt a bit quavery herself. And like a veritable tyrant. At the rate she was passing out chores, if either of the other two children required punishment, she and Pru would have nothing left to do but lounge on the porch all day, tatting doilies and sipping mint tea.

Lucas took to his chores without complaint. Joe Bill didn't. But Edwina graciously ignored the rude looks he directed her way, and other than a lingering wariness between her and Declan, the incident passed and the house soon settled into a pleasant, although busy routine.

April ended with a hailstorm that left a new dusting of snow on the valley and four chickens dead. Edwina cooked them that night all by herself, including gutting and plucking them—which was absolutely the most disgusting thing she had ever done—rounding out the meal with mashed potatoes, turnip greens, and the last of the carrots in the bin under the house. No one except Pru seemed to appreciate her efforts, but Edwina thought it was delicious.

As the days stretched into May, dawn came

earlier and dusk came later. By the end of the first week, roundup was in full swing, and with the two older boys helping their father and Amos gather cattle, the house seemed quieter and emptier. Taking advantage of their absence, Edwina and Pru did a thorough cleaning of both structures. The removal from the children's quarters of several years' accumulation of grime and clutter took longer than it should have, since Brin carried half of every load they took to the burn pile back into the house, insisting each item was too valuable to throw away.

Late each morning of that busy roundup week, Edwina would ask Chick McElroy to saddle a horse for her, and with her saddlebags loaded with foodstuffs, she rode out toward the swirling cloud of dust that marked the entrance to the box canyon where the men held the cattle.

It was one of Edwina's favorite chores. She loved riding, and hadn't had a chance to do so since she'd sold their ancient mare and buggy to meet the tax bill on Rose Hill the previous year.

But that was then. Today, she had a fine horse beneath her, and astounding vistas all around, and air so cool and crisp and thin it sometimes left her breathless. Happily she rode along, enjoying the solitude and marveling at this wild and lonely country that was so different from the place where she'd spent all of her life.

Back home, wisteria, and forsythia, and spindly

snowball bushes would be in full bloom. Orange day lilies would be crowding the fence of the resting place, and wide-faced caladiums would be peeking around the raised stone vaults beneath the drooping limbs of ancient oaks and stately cypress.

How she missed it. Not the South as it was now but before the war. The tea parties, and country dances, and sweaty-faced boys. Frogs and crickets adding their voices to the music drifting up from the slave cabins down by the bayou. Hot, sultry, magnolia-scented nights when she sat on the floor next to her window, her arms folded on the sill, listening to the Negroes sing and wishing she could escape her fine plantation home and be down there in those clapboard cabins with Pru, laughing and catching lightning bugs in a jar.

Gone forever.

Breathing deep to dispel those sad thoughts, Edwina looked around at this valley that might be her home for the rest of her life. It was a savage place. The very boldness and scope of it shouted a constant reminder that frail humans would never be more than visitors here, easily defeated by a harsh climate, hungry predators, and the inflexibility of rocky peaks and stone-walled canyons that even rushing water couldn't wear away.

Savage, yet beautiful in a way that made her heart race and her spirit soar. Challenging.

Untainted. A world apart from what she'd left behind.

Instead of azaleas and camellias, she saw bright yellow sunflowers, tall pines and pinyons, and blue-tinted junipers. Rolling, open hills, wooded canyons filled with birdsong, high ridges where only a few stunted trees curled in the wind beneath a sky so crisp and blue it hurt her eyes.

It might not have the gentle allure of the bayou country back home, but it was seductive, nonetheless. She might find a place for herself here.

She heard the cattle long before she reached them. A huge, bawling, milling throng of restless animals that kicked up so much dust it soon coated Edwina's throat and left grit in her eyes. Cutting a wide berth, she angled upwind toward the wagon parked beneath a triangular canvas canopy tied to three scraggly pine trees.

As she approached, two smaller figures ran ahead of two others toward the wagon. By the time she reined in, R.D. and Joe Bill were waiting to help unload the saddlebags, while Declan and Amos washed in a metal bowl perched on a stump beside the wagon. Branding and castrating was stinky, dirty, noisy work, and the water in the bowl was a reddish black when they finished, yet neither man looked particularly clean.

Declan nodded in greeting, then hunkered on his heels in the shade while Edwina unwrapped the food. She was just starting to fill the plates when Joe Bill called his father's attention to a rider coming in from the west.

"Tell who it is?" he asked his oldest son.

Lifting a hand to shade his eyes, R.D. squinted at the figure for a moment, then dropped his arm and grinned at his father. "Thomas." His grin was wide and toothy, like his father's. And even though he still had to grow into his nose and fill out through the jaw, he would be a handsome man someday. Also, like his father.

Declan went to meet Thomas Redstone. The Cheyenne dismounted and they spoke for a moment, then still deep in conversation, they walked slowly back to the wagon.

This was only the second time Edwina had seen Thomas, so she didn't know what to read in his stern, sharply angled face when they walked up. But Declan looked worried. Edwina smiled in welcome.

"*Haaahe*," Thomas said with a nod, taking a seat on the ground beside the front wagon wheel. He was dressed as he'd been before—a topknot with a feather attached and the rest of his long black hair hanging loose except for two small braids at his temples—a blue army jacket worn as a sleeveless vest over a faded pullover shirt with long sleeves and an open front placket—open-hipped leggings, rather than trousers, covering his legs down to knee-high, fringed leather moccasins

—and a long rectangular length of soft leather hanging past his knees, front and back, held in place by a thick belt with a bone or antler buckle.

She had read about Cheyenne Dog Soldiers and how they proved their fierceness in battle by staking themselves to the ground with a lance or knife driven through that length of leather, then defending to the death the patch of ground on which they stood. Thomas Redstone looked the part.

He had swarthy skin, a broad forehead and high cheekbones, and eyes as dark and hard as chips of coal. And although he moved with measured deliberation and wasn't as physically imposing as Declan, he radiated such restrained energy it seemed to hum in the air around him.

Uneasy under his stare, Edwina filled a plate and held it out.

He didn't take it, but continued to study her, his gaze unwavering.

Edwina stared back, sensing he was testing her somehow, and if she looked away first she would lose. A gust of wind swept through, peppering them with grit and snapping the canvas overhead until the ropes binding it to the trees groaned. Her wrist began to wobble with the strain of holding out the filled plate, but she didn't look away.

"Nia'ish." With a barely perceptible nod, he took the plate from her hand and settled back against the wheel. The encounter had lasted mere

seconds but had left Edwina feeling light-headed and shivery. It was an effort to keep her hand from shaking when she filled another plate and passed it to Declan.

He took it with a nod of thanks and sank onto his heels near Thomas, his hat pushed back on his head. "Come to eat? Or help."

Thomas shrugged. "One follows the other."

They ate in silence, as they did every day when Edwina brought lunch. Which always surprised her. Put three women and two girls together and the chatter would have been constant. But these five seemed to have nothing to say, despite the fact that they hadn't seen Thomas Redstone for over two weeks.

Men. They were hopeless.

"Lucas spoke today," she announced, both to break the lengthy silence and to show Thomas Redstone she wasn't intimidated by his presence.

Declan looked up, cheeks bunching as he chewed. "Did he?"

She watched his Adam's apple bob up and down as he swallowed, and saw that he needed a shave, and the black stubble of his beard shadowed his thick neck almost down to the shaded hollow at the base of his—

" 'Bout what?" Declan prodded.

To cover her lapse, Edwina dabbed at her mouth with her napkin. She had brought a half dozen with her, but it seemed hers was the only one in use. "Worms. The ones that leave tiny holes in the radishes."

Declan forked up another bite of sliced roast beef. "Work ashes into the dirt before you plant." More chewing. Swallowing. Muscles moving under the sun-browned skin. His neck was surprisingly long, she realized. Not disproportionately so, of course, but with a nice slope down to those wide shoulders.

Realizing her mind was wandering again, Edwina reined it in. "And beetles. He spoke a lot about beetles. He even drew several on a scrap of paper and told me more than I ever wanted to know about dung beetles, and borers, and weevils, and grub worms and suchlike. He shows quite an interest in insects. And drawing. He's an accomplished drawer. Artist."

She knew she was babbling. But with Declan looking at her that way, and Thomas Redstone's dark eyes boring into her like one of Lucas's pine beetles, it was difficult to concentrate on what she was saying. "The point is, he's talking."

"He's been talking since he was two," Declan said.

"Not to me."

"You weren't even here when he was two," Joe Bill reminded her in a churlish tone. "Our real mother was here then."

Declan turned his head and looked at him.

Edwina didn't see any change in his expression,

but apparently Joe Bill did. He bent over his plate, a flush blossoming across his cheeks.

Hoping to lighten the tension, Edwina smiled at Thomas Redstone. "Will you be coming back to the house for supper this evening, Mr. Redstone?"

He gave it long consideration. "The dark-skinned woman will be there?" he finally asked.

His deep voice carried as much expression as his face—which was none—but those dark, intense eyes conveyed a message that roused all of Edwina's protective instincts. "Are you referring to Miss Lincoln?"

He didn't respond but continued to look at her until eventually his silence and the manners that had been beaten into her with a willow cane compelled Edwina to speak. "Yes. She'll be there."

"Then I will come," he said solemnly. "I want to know her." And he punctuated that announcement with a sudden and astonishing white-toothed grin that completely changed his face.

Goodness gracious. He's as handsome as Declan. Then on the heels of that thought came one even more shocking. Wants "to *know* her"? Did he mean in the biblical sense? *Oh, my Lord.* Edwina didn't know whether to be amused or horrified. Thomas Redstone was after Pru.

As soon as his wife rode off, Declan sent the boys and Amos to drive the next batch of calves to be branded into the brush enclosure they'd built against the canyon wall, then he turned to Thomas. "How do you know it was Lone Tree who burned out the Cox place?" Just saying the Arapaho's name made Declan so furious he could hardly think.

"He makes no secret of it. Colonel Carr's Pawnee scouts killed his father and a son at Summit Springs last summer. He seeks revenge."

"I had nothing to do with that."

"You are white. All white men look the same to a man who is wrong in the head."

Too restless to sit, Declan paced under the sagging canopy. "Lone Tree was at Summit Springs? I thought they were all killed or captured."

"He had gone hunting and was not in the encampment when the blue coats came. He feels shame that he was not there to protect his family."

The Dog Soldier leaned back against the wagon wheel, his forearms outstretched across his bent knees. In his right hand he held a spent and distorted fifty-caliber bullet that he rolled back and forth between his thumb and forefinger. "It is a hard thing to lose a child."

Declan had seen him do that many times and guessed his friend was thinking about his own family, which had been lost years ago when that same bullet had plowed through his wife's back and into his infant son's chest. Thomas intended to find the trapper who had fired it and shove the bullet into his beating heart.

Declan resumed pacing. He wished he had it in him to do the same to Lone Tree. Not just because he suspected the Indian had killed his wife, Sally, but because by killing her, the renegade Arapaho had also robbed Declan's children of their mother. Even though Sally had abandoned them, she loved her children and they loved her. She didn't deserve the death that had befallen her.

"Lone Tree's anger festered through the winter," Thomas went on. "Now he gathers other angry warriors and vows to kill any whites and Pawnee he can find." Thomas tipped his head back against the wheel and gave Declan that hard, fixed stare, reminding him that even though they shared a bond, there would always be barriers between them. "It is a common story, *hovahe*. One told many times around the campfires of the Cheyenne."

Declan didn't want to be pulled into that old fight, so he stayed on track. "Summit Springs is closer to Nebraska than these mountains. Why would he come this far west?"

"For you."

"Me?" Declan stopped pacing. "Just because I put him in jail once?"

"Because he has a fear of closed places, and you locked him in one and watched him howl like an animal."

"I had no choice, Thomas. He almost beat a man to death." Even so, and because of his own aversion to high places, when Declan had seen the

Arapaho's irrational behavior, he had gone against the judge's ruling and had released him early. No man should have to suffer that kind of fear.

"Better for his honor to kill him."

"Hell." Declan stalked the length of the canopy and back again, his mind racing so fast he couldn't slow it down enough to think clearly.

Locking up Lone Tree had been one of his last acts as sheriff in Heartbreak Creek. A week after the Indian's release, Sally had run off, and within days, the rumors had started. It was only after the trooper brought news of finding the charred bodies of his wife and her lover, Luther "Slick" Caven, that the whispering had stopped. But by then, the damage had been done.

"And also because while he was in your jail," Thomas added, "a flash flood washed out his village. His wife and daughter drowned."

"And that's my fault, too?"

Thomas shrugged. "Because of you, he was not there to protect them."

"Another weak excuse." Declan stopped pacing and idly watched a hawk float by, wingtips pivoting to guide its silent flight above the rocky ground. "Is it just me he's after? Or my children, too?"

"He will take from you all that he can."

Declan looked at Thomas. "Do you think he was the one who did that to Sally? I was never sure." Even now he remembered his sick feeling when

170

the trooper handed him Sally's broken locket and bloody dress.

"He says no. But he had lived among whites long enough to learn how to lie."

Son of a bitch! Declan stared blindly down the valley that cradled his ranch—his home. Did he have to leave it to keep his children safe? He would, of course. He would do whatever he had to do to protect them. He just needed to figure out the best way to accomplish that.

Hearing a shout, he turned to see Joe Bill waving. His son pantomimed that the calves were penned and ready, and for Declan to come.

Declan waved back that he understood, but couldn't make himself move. What did cows—or the ranch—or all his struggles to make a good life out here really amount to when a madman was stalking his family?

"Maybe he will take your new wife, instead," Thomas said after a long pause. "She has a strong heart. She would not die as easy as the other one and Lone Tree would like that."

An image of Ed flashed through Declan's mind, her blue eyes snapping fire, her chin jutting as she threatened to come at him with a pitchfork if he raised a hand to his own children. Fierce, crazy, courageous Ed. No, she wouldn't die easy.

Thomas rose. He slipped the bullet back into the small pouch hanging on a strip of leather around his neck, then tucked the pouch beneath the placket of his shirt. "I will help you, my white brother. I will stand beside you against Lone Tree. But then my debt to you is paid."

Declan sighed and shook his head. "There is no debt, Thomas. You owe me nothing. Never have, never will."

"I owe you my life."

Declan regarded his friend, barely recognizing in him the same violent, crazed drunk he'd pulled from beneath a pile of brawlers in the Red Eye Saloon five years ago.

It had been a dark time for Thomas. A confused mixed breed caught between white and red and belonging to neither, he had watched his tribe head for extinction and the land he loved being eaten up one acre at a time by an endless flood of settlers, and he had no longer understood the world or his place in it. So he had taken his wife and young son into the mountains where they had lived a peaceful, solitary life until a trapper's bullet had ended it.

Afire with grief and rage, Thomas had joined up with Black Kettle's band, where he had earned his place as a Dog Soldier and had fought hard to protect his tribe and their way of life.

But the whites kept coming.

And the People kept retreating.

And the grief never went away.

Until finally, the only solace Thomas could find was in a bottle.

That's how Declan had found him, under that pile of thrashing bodies in the saloon in Heartbreak Creek. Being the sheriff at that time, he had done his duty and had locked Thomas in jail for thirty days.

Hatred had kept the battered warrior alive. Hatred for the world he no longer fit into or understood—hatred for Declan for locking him up and depriving him of his alcohol—and especially, hatred for the trapper who had killed his family. Eventually the alcohol left his body. The rage didn't. But by the time Thomas's monthlong sentence ended, he and Declan had formed a wary friendship, which was tested a year later when Declan's dark time came.

So to Declan's way of thinking, he and Thomas had saved each other.

"There is no debt," he said again, then smiled. "But if it will make you feel better, I'll let you watch my back until Lone Tree is stopped."

Thomas nodded solemnly. "*Nia'ish*, my white brother. Your goodness is as ever flowing as the great waters."

Declan laughed. "And your compliments are as lasting as buffalo chips in the rain."

Grinning, Thomas rested a hand on Declan's shoulder. "Come," he said, steering him toward the makeshift corral where Amos and the boys waited. "We will finish torturing your cattle, then we will ride to your tipi for a fine meal. And on the way, you will tell me about the dark-skinned woman."

"Have your eye on her, do you?"

"She is a fine-looking woman."

"And a hell of a cook."

"Ho! That is a good thing, *nesene'*, because your new woman needs to eat. She is too skinny."

"Maybe. But she's mean, and with my kids to contend with, that counts for a lot."

Thomas nodded sagely. "*Nehetome.* I know this to be true."

EIGHT

T hose were his exact words, Pru. 'I want to know her.' " Edwina mimicked Thomas Redstone's deep, monotone voice. "That can only mean one thing."

Pru shot her a look of exasperation in the mirror over the washstand in the water closet. "It can mean several things. Don't make a simple statement into something it's not. Can you spare any more pins?"

Edwina pulled a pin from her twist, passed it over, and watched her sister struggle for the umpteenth time to force the unruly curls at the back of her neck into her tightly wound bun.

Pru sighed. "This is hopeless. I should wear a scarf."

"It's fine. And anyway, what does it matter? He's just an Indian."

Her sister whipped toward her. "And what's wrong with being an Indian, might I ask?"

Delighted to have pierced her sister's calm façade, Edwina smiled sweetly. "Why, nothing at all. Except that he speaks a different language, lives in a house made of animal skins, has hair longer than yours, and wears trousers that don't even cover his . . . upper legs."

"They don't?"

Having finally gained Pru's full attention, Edwina happily expounded. "I saw it with my own eyes. When he walked up, I could actually see the muscles move in his"—she leaned closer to whisper—"fanny."

Pru reared back to blink at her. "You saw his fanny?"

"His hip, anyway. Both sides. Right here." Edwina poked at her own hip, which was discreetly covered by drawers, two petticoats, a gabardine skirt, and a calico apron that was only marginally tattered. "I tell you, Pru, I was horrified. Utterly horrified."

"Horrified" might be an exaggeration. More like shocked. So much so that she had scarcely been able to look away. "He had very nice muscles," she added, wondering if Declan's would move and bunch and stretch in the same way, and if the skin there would be a paler hue than the sun-browned shade of his face and that shadowed V where his neck met the open collar of his shirt and where occasionally a few very black stray hairs would—

"How odd," Pru mused, interrupting her imaginings. "I didn't notice that before. Well, no matter." One last pat on her hair, and she turned and headed toward the stairs. "It's getting late. We'd best finish supper."

"You just keep an eye on him," Edwina warned, coming down behind her. "It's apparent he has designs on you."

"Oh, pshaw." Pausing at the foot of the stairs, Pru cocked her head toward the voices beyond the back door.

"Lucas!" Brin shouted from the backyard. "Pa brought Thomas!"

"Mercy." Suddenly all aflutter, Pru rushed across the kitchen. "They're here already and I haven't even put the rolls in."

By the time Declan, the children, and their guest came through the back door—freshly washed and hatless—the table was set with an extra place, coffee was boiling, roast beef, potatoes, and vegetables were waiting to be served, and the rolls were browned to perfection.

As had become their habit, Amos Hicks and Chick McElroy didn't join them, preferring to take their meals in their cozy bunkhouse because—as Brin put it—all Edwina's rules "gave them the shivers." Which was fine with Edwina since it was difficult for her not to shiver, herself, whenever she was downwind of the odoriferous ranch hands.

Luckily Declan had higher standards of cleanliness and regularly made use of the oversized washtub in the laundry shed—or so Brin had informed her with a look of deep disgust. Which relieved Edwina's mind, since she couldn't imagine how difficult it would be for a man Declan's size to fit into the delicate hip bath in the water closet off the bedroom. Not that she'd been trying to imagine it, of course. Idle curiosity. Nothing more. Which was surely the same reason her sister's gaze fastened on Thomas Redstone's open-hipped leggings as he took his place at the table.

Other than Brin's prattle about the new barn kitties, and Joe Bill's recounting of a hawk he'd seen fly by with a snake in its talons, it was a strangely silent meal. Thomas Redstone stared at Pru, Pru stared at her plate, and Declan divided his stares between Edwina and his talkative daughter. Joe Bill and R.D. were too intent on gobbling their food to even look up, and Lucas focused on carving mountains with gravy waterfalls in his mashed potatoes.

Edwina found it fascinating. A family of near-mutes. She should write a book. Maybe Maddie could document it with photographs.

It wasn't until the edge had dulled on their

enormous appetites and Thomas was into his third serving of roast beef that Declan spoke. "I was right, wasn't I?"

Thomas glanced at Pru. "Yes. She is a fine cook."

Pru must have seen Edwina bristle. "Actually," she cut in, speaking for the first time since the meal had begun, "Edwina prepared the meal."

Declan's gaze shifted to Edwina. "She did?"

It was a bit insulting that he sounded so surprised, but Edwina remembered her manners and smiled graciously.

"I thought you said she couldn't cook," Joe Bill said.

"Apparently I was wrong." The smile Declan sent her took some of the sting out of Joe Bill's rude remark. "It's good, Ed. Really good."

Edwina nodded her thanks and dabbed at her mouth with her napkin to hide the smile of pleasure she wasn't able to hold back. How odd that kind words from her own husband would make her blush like a schoolgirl.

Turning his attention back to Thomas, Declan said, "There's an old cougar prowling the ridge up behind the creek. Already got two calves. Keep an eye out when you're coming and going."

Thomas tipped his head toward R.D. "*Voaxaa'e* will get him."

Brin tried to repeat the word but got tangled up in the vowels. "What does that mean, Thomas?"

"It means eagle. Because your brother sees far and true."

R.D. grinned through a mouth full of string beans. "That's me. Eagle Eye Brodie."

"My turn!" Brin shouted. "What am I?"

Thomas thought for a moment. "You are *neske'esta*. One who chatters like a chipmunk."

"A chipmunk! I love chipmunks!" Bouncing in delight at this new game, Brin demanded that he name Joe Bill.

Thomas didn't have to think long for this one. "He is *okom*, the wily coyote. The trickster."

Joe Bill preened, apparently taking that as a compliment.

"Do Lucas!"

Thomas turned to the boy watching him with wide, intelligent eyes. "Lucas is like our brother the raccoon, *matseskome*, because of his quick hands and curious mind."

Looking pleased, Lucas ducked his head, hiding his blush behind that flop of light brown hair.

The children delighted in trying out their names, laughing at each other's garbled attempts at pronunciation.

"And Miss Lincoln?" Edwina asked, watching Thomas closely. If he truly had designs on her sister, this would be the telling moment. If he tried to flatter her, Pru would level him with her steely stare. If he insulted her or said something untoward about her mixed blood or Negro status,

Edwina would cut him down like the dog he was.

Thomas sat back, both palms resting on his thighs. A smile teased the corners of his wide mouth. "She is *eho'nehevehohtse*. One who leaves wolf tracks."

Well, that made no sense whatsoever. Edwina glanced at Pru, waiting for her to say something. But her sister just sat there like a ninny, so Edwina felt compelled to jump in. "That doesn't sound very nice."

Thomas continued to study Pru. Edwina could tell by her sister's rigid stillness that Pru was as uncomfortable under that probing gaze as she had been. "The People honor the wolf for his wisdom," he explained in his flat voice. "For a woman to leave tracks of the wolf means she can outsmart men. Some men, anyway," he added, his eyes crinkling at the corners.

Declan made a small noise at the other end of the table. Edwina glanced at him, saw he was fighting laughter, and gave him a reproving look. "Well, she is brilliant," she defended. "You're certainly right about that."

Thomas nodded. "And perhaps soon she will be *heme'oono* as well."

This time Declan couldn't restrain his amusement. "And how do you say 'one who moves fast like antelope'?"

Edwina looked at him in surprise. "You speak his language?"

"A word here and there." His grin bespoke mischief.

Suddenly uneasy with where this might be headed, and sensing unspoken messages passing between the two men, Edwina broke in before it went too far. "And what would my Indian name be?"

The warrior turned his head and regarded her for so long with those dark, assessing eyes Edwina wished she hadn't asked. "You are *ma'hahko'e*," he finally said. "Because you are fierce and protective and speak what is in your mind."

Fierce. Protective. Edwina smiled, liking that. "*Ma-ha-ko-e*. And what does that mean, Mr. Redstone?"

"Badger."

As roundup wound down over the next few days, the Cheyenne warrior became a regular face at the supper table. Edwina found it vastly entertaining to watch Thomas watch Pru, and Pru's unsuccessful struggle not to watch him back. But it also troubled her, not knowing where this attraction would lead, and how her sister would reconcile her confused feelings for the handsome Indian and her deep desire to go back to Heartbreak Creek and start a school for displaced Negroes.

It had become obvious to Edwina why teaching was Pru's passion; she was quite good at it. By the second week after their arrival, she had begun staying at the kitchen table after the evening meal so she could teach letters to Brin, and help Joe Bill and Lucas with their reading and numbers. R.D. was already a fair reader and had a head for numbers—learned no doubt by keeping the cattle tally for his father.

Edwina, although not as gifted a teacher as Pru, helped after she finished the dishes, and felt a parent's pride that the younger three were quick learners, if somewhat lazy . . . except for Lucas. He soaked up anything they could teach him and was soon helping Brin.

Most evenings, while she cleaned the kitchen and Pru instructed the children, Declan excused himself to attend his endless chores. But once Thomas became a regular guest, after they had eaten and before he retired to his cot in the tack room off the barn, he and Declan would carry their coffee to the porch and talk in quiet, deep tones as the light faded from the western sky. Edwina suspected they drank more than coffee out there but made no mention of it. However, as the week wore on, instead of going onto the porch or to his cot, Thomas began to linger in the kitchen, watching Pru and listening to the children's halting recitations with great interest.

Edwina found it curious, and one night as she and her sister prepared for bed, she mentioned it. "Do you think Thomas can read, Pru? The way he hangs about when the lessons are in progress makes me wonder."

"I've wondered, too. Do you think it would be rude to ask?"

"No, but would you feel comfortable working with him? You seem a bit awkward around him."

"I don't know what you're talking about," Pru retorted, ducking behind the water closet screen.

"Then you'll ask him?" Edwina pressed.

Pru didn't answer.

But the next night she mentioned to Thomas that since he spoke English so well, did he also know how to read it? Ever tactful, Pru was.

Thomas shook his head. "When I was a boy, missionaries came to our tribe to convert us 'heathen savages' to your Christian God. They also taught letters and numbers to any who would come to their tipi to learn. Only a few children did." He smiled crookedly. "To avoid chores, I think."

"Were you one of them?" Pru asked.

"Sometimes."

"So you know your letters?"

He lifted one shoulder in a shrug. "A few. But I do not know how to make them into words. The People do not talk in letters. We use pictures and symbols."

"Letters are symbols, too," Pru explained. "They stand for the sounds we use to form the words we speak. Would you like for me to show you?"

Thomas studied her across the table. "It is important to you that I know this?"

"It should be important to you," Pru hedged. "A man who can't read and write is more easily fooled into putting his mark on papers he doesn't understand."

"Like the white man's treaties?"

Pru gave a rueful smile. "Sadly so."

"Then you will teach me this, Prudence," Thomas announced in his solemn way. "So that someday I can offer my own treaties to the White Father in Washington."

Thus, the crowd around the table grew, for without Thomas to keep him company on the porch, Declan moved inside as well, taking his place at the end of the table where he made notations in his tally book and studied his catalogs and seed pamphlets.

Edwina cherished those evenings. Sitting in the warm kitchen while she worked on the dress she was sewing for Brin's upcoming birthday—listening to Pru's gentle voice as she helped the children and Thomas—stealing glances at the man at the other end of the table. There was a sense of connection she hadn't felt in a long time. She almost felt part of a family again.

And sometimes he would look up, his dark gaze fastening on hers, and for a moment, strange, sharp currents would move between them, and Edwina would sit frozen, unable to look away, her nerves tingling with a hot surge of emotion that left her confused, and tense, and . . . confused.

Then he would look back down at whatever he was reading and she would be able to breathe again and her scattered thoughts would settle once more. But if he smiled . . .

Oh, that smile.

The weather turned wet and blustery as roundup week drew to a close. The cattle not marked for sale were loosened into the hills to fatten on summer grass, while the culls were held back to be driven into Heartbreak Creek. Jubal Parker, a nearby rancher—nearby meaning only thirteen miles away—sent a couple of ranch hands over with fifty-two more head to add to Declan's herd so they could all be driven into town together. Once there, they would be auctioned to cattle buyers, then herded to the junction fives miles east of town to be loaded onto railroad stock cars bound for Omaha and Kansas City.

Apparently this year Declan had decided to take the whole family with him to Heartbreak Creek. Only Chick and Rusty would remain behind to tend the milk cow, the chickens, and the mares with their new foals. He didn't seem to mind. His leg made riding difficult, and sitting in the wagon with the ladies and children for the long trip apparently had as little appeal for him as it did for Edwina. The man seemed to smell worse every day.

Concerned for his health, as well as that of anyone in his vicinity, Edwina gave him a piece of toweling, a bar of strong soap, and instructions to make use of them during their absence. "And do wash those clothes while you're at it," she had suggested firmly. "Or I will."

The night before they were to leave, a warm wind swept down the valley, breaking up the clouds and promising good weather for the cattle drive into Heartbreak Creek. That evening after supper, pretending to give in to the children's urging, although Edwina suspected it had been his intent all along, Declan promised if the sale went as he hoped, they would stay in town for an extra couple of days.

Edwina could scarcely contain herself.

"Won't it be grand to see Maddie and Lucinda again?" she asked Pru the next morning as she slipped last-minute items into the valise they would take. "And shop! Look." She held out a handful of coins. "Isn't Declan generous? He said to get whatever we wanted." Carefully slipping the coins into her coin purse, she snapped it closed and dropped it into her reticule. "I'm thinking of getting ribbons for Brin. And I need thread and cloth for new aprons. Perhaps a book for Lucas. And Joe Bill and R.D. could use new shirts. What will you shop for?"

Pru laughed. "I think you've already spent more than you have there."

"Then I shall simply ask for more."

"And be indebted to him?"

186

Feeling the beginnings of a blush, Edwina busied herself folding a skirt into the valise. "He should provide for us. He's my husband, after all."

"Is he?"

Ignoring that, Edwina swung the valise off the bed. "Come on. We're running late, and you know how Declan hates to wait."

The cattle, Declan's sixty-seven plus Parker's fifty-two, herded by the three boys, Parker's two hands, Thomas, and Amos Hicks, had already left. Declan would follow with the ladies and Brin in the buckboard, which was already loaded with extra water, blankets, slickers and coats, three baskets of food Pru and Edwina had prepared, and enough rifles and ammunition to hold off an army.

"Expecting trouble?" Edwina asked when Declan lifted her into the driver's box and she saw the weaponry stacked under the bench seat.

"You never know," he answered evasively.

It was barely dawn when they finally rolled out of the yard, Rusty yapping at the horses' heels and Chick waving them off.

This time they took a lower route through the valley, avoiding Satan's Backbone, the high, narrow track that had so bothered Declan when they'd come through in April, so it was all new scenery to Edwina. And just as beautiful, but in a different way. With spring grass coming in, herds of elk grazed the rolling hills, while deer stayed close to the brushy border along the winding creek, browsing on leaves and twigs. Occasionally they spotted a bear, but always at a distance, and once, up high on a rocky slope, they saw a small herd of buff-colored sheep.

For the first few miles Brin chattered excitedly. Then as the morning stretched on, yawns began to overcome her, and Pru made a bed with the blankets Declan had sent and suggested she rest for a while. Soon the two of them were dozing peacefully as the wagon rolled along within sight of the cattle, but not close enough to be bothered by their dust.

Edwina glanced at her husband, thinking how different this trip was from the one they'd taken out of Heartbreak Creek less than a month before. He wasn't so frightening to her now. And the future didn't look quite so dark. And she didn't feel as out of her element as she had then.

Was it she who had changed so much? Or had he become less disapproving and more approachable?

Lifting her face to the chill morning air, she breathed in the tangy scent of junipers and pines and early spring wildflowers. "It's a beautiful morning," she said in a low voice, so as not to awaken the sleepers.

"It is." Declan turned his head and looked at her, that infrequent smile teasing his mouth. "And you're looking right pretty, yourself, Ed."

Definitely less disapproving. She smiled back, enjoying this side of her husband. With so many people in and out of the house, and with Declan gone so much of the time, moments alone with him had been few and far between.

He must have felt the same way. Shooting a glance at the pair sleeping in the back of the wagon, he motioned for her to come nearer.

Curious, Edwina leaned over until her shoulder almost brushed his.

"Closer."

She inched across the wooden seat until her arm rested against his. "What?" she whispered.

Instead of answering, he tipped his head to the side so his hat cleared her bonnet, and pressed his lips to hers.

Startled, Edwina froze. His heat engulfed her. She smelled horses. Tasted coffee. Felt the scrape of whiskers and the whisper of warm breath against her cheek.

After what seemed like forever, yet much too soon, her husband drew back. "Well," he said with a deep sigh. "Finally." His grin was broad and dazzling as he turned back to the road.

Finally, indeed.

Edwina had been kissed before. Heavens, she'd been married before. But none of the ardent kisses of her childhood swains, or even the awkward kisses Shelly had given her, caused quite the ruckus inside her chest that Declan's did. Why?

What was different? Or had she just been rattled by the suddenness of it?

She needed to know.

"Do that again," she ordered. And closing her eyes, she puckered her lips and lifted her face.

A burst of soft laughter fanned her cheeks.

Startled, she opened her eyes and drew back to find her husband struggling to hold his merriment in check. "What?" she asked, feeling a rush of heat into her face. *Lord, he must think me an utter ninny.*

"You confound me, Ed," he said, shaking his head. "You keep me off balance and stumbling around like a starving dog in a butcher shop. I never know what you're going to say or do next."

Not sure how to take that but unwilling to let him see her confusion, she tried to brazen it out with a bright smile and a nonchalant wave of her hand. "Well, you are somewhat dense," she said blithely. "As I recall, when we first met, you were struggling to keep track of the days of the week."

She might have said more, but suddenly his free arm came around her shoulders and pulled her tight against his side.

He kissed her again. And this kiss wasn't as tentative or tender as the one before. And it lasted longer. And it awakened tingles inside her that were a yard away from where their mouths touched.

"Oh," she said in a breathless voice when he finally released her.

"Oh?"

"Oh, my." She struggled to pull air into her fluttery lungs. "That was much better."

Which sent him into silent laughter again.

They rode without speaking for a time. Edwina wondered if he would kiss her again, and if he did, should she allow it, and decided she would. But he didn't, which was strangely disappointing. So using the excuse of brushing a pine needle from her skirt, she inched back to her side of the seat, then cast about in her addled mind for something to say that would show she was as unmoved by the kiss as he appeared to be. "The clerk at the hotel said you were once the sheriff in Heartbreak Creek."

He nodded. "For almost three years. 'Sixty-three to 'sixty-six. Brin was born there."

"Why did you quit?"

His expression hardened. He didn't answer.

"Is that when you bought the ranch?"

"I bought the ranch before I was sheriff."

"You did? When?"

"In 'fifty-eight, the year R.D. was born. You sure ask a lot of questions."

"But why did you take on the role of sheriff when you had a ranch?"

She thought he wasn't going to answer. When he finally did, his voice was as flat and expressionless as Thomas's, and his features had lost animation as effectively as if a mask had dropped over his face. "My wife wanted to live in town. She needed more . . . people around her."

Edwina studied him, hoping he would say more. When it became apparent he had said all he was going to, she tried a different subject. After glancing back to be sure there were no listeners, she leaned toward him to whisper. "Brin reminds me daily that her birthday is coming up. Have you planned anything yet?"

His brows rose. "Planned anything?"

"A celebration of some sort. A gathering."

"A gathering?"

Realizing he had no idea what she was talking about, she tried another tack. "Gifts, then. Have you gotten her a gift?"

"I, ah . . ."

"You haven't. Oh, Declan." She sighed. "You must get her something while we're in town."

"Okay. Sure." A pause. "Like what?"

Dense as granite. "You decide. Any other birthdays coming up?"

He thought for a moment. "R.D.'s is next month. Or is that Lucas? I'll check the family Bible when we get back. I think it's R.D., though."

"I'm sewing her a dress."

That look of befuddlement again. "A dress? For Brin? Why?"

"In case you haven't noticed, Declan, Brin is a girl. And girls need dresses."

"Why?"

"Because they're girls!" *Lord.*

He stared down the road in thought. "But where would she wear it?"

"Wherever she wants." Striving for patience, she added in a low voice, "The point is, Declan, girls need dresses because they're frilly and feminine, and because pretty things make girls feel pretty."

"I doubt it'll work that way with Brin." And he went on to tell her of his daughter's lifelong ambition to be a buffalo hunter, or an army scout, or a mountain trapper. "In fact, I don't think she's ever had a real dress."

Edwina was aghast. "Didn't her mother ever dress her in one?"

That shuttered look again. "Her mother left when she was two."

Left? An odd way of saying died or passed on. Edwina studied him as an awful thought bounced through her mind. What if the woman wasn't dead? What if she was out there somewhere?

If so, then Edwina's marriage to Declan wouldn't even be real.

Which meant she wouldn't have to wait another two months, or bother with an annulment. She could leave any time she wanted.

That realization unleashed a cyclone of panic inside her chest. "I thought your first wife died," she forced herself to say, wondering why the

193

thought of leaving would create such sudden anxiety.

"She did. After she left."

Edwina waited, but that was all he seemed willing to say.

And she didn't probe any further.

NINE

Heartbreak Creek seemed even deader than it had during their last visit, probably because it was Sunday afternoon and people were home with their families. Without the distant pounding of mine machinery, the town was eerily quiet. Even the ravens hunched in lethargic silence in the tall firs.

"I'm hungry, Pa," Brin complained. "When can we eat?"

"What happened to all that food Ed and Miss Lincoln packed?"

"You ate it. Can I get out? I'm tired of sitting."

"Soon." A block farther, he pulled up outside the hotel and set the brake. "I'll see if they're serving supper," he said, hopping down. When he returned a few minutes later, Maddie and Lucinda were right behind him.

"Edwina! Prudence!" they called, rushing to the wagon, hardly waiting for Edwina and Pru to step down before gathering around them.

194

"We have missed you terribly!" Maddie said, hugging each in turn. "And we have such wonderful news! How long will you be in town? Are you staying here? Oh, I'm so delighted to see you."

Lucinda refrained from gushing, although her green eyes were alight with joy. "Please come in, ladies. We were just planning supper. Will you join us?" Her gaze flicked to Brin, gawking over the side rails, then to Declan, who was climbing back into the wagon. "You're all welcome, of course."

Edwina gave her husband a questioning look.

He picked up the reins and released the brake. "I need to check on the cattle. If the boys haven't eaten, I'll bring them back if it's not too late."

"It won't be too late," Maddie assured him. "I'll make sure there's plenty of food for whenever you can get here." She leaned toward Edwina to add in a dramatic whisper, "I share quarters with the new owner, you see." Seeing Edwina's look of shock, she laughed. "It's Lucinda! She bought the hotel! Can you credit that?"

Edwina gaped from one grinning face to the other. "When? Why?"

Still laughing, Maddie shooed them toward the double doors. "Come in and see the miracles she's wrought, and we'll tell you all about it."

"Don't forget your bag," Declan called as Edwina started across the boardwalk. Reaching over the seat, he lifted the valise from the wagon bed.

Edwina took it from his grip. "You won't be long?"

"A couple of hours. By dark at the latest."

Nodding, Edwina glanced at Brin, who had scrambled onto the bench beside her father. "Would you like to stay with me, Brin?"

"Heck, no."

Declan frowned at his daughter. He started to speak, but not wanting a scene in front of the others, Edwina cut in. "We'll see you later, then." And refusing to let her stepdaughter's rejection ruin her joy in visiting with her friends again, she pasted on a bright smile and followed Pru inside.

Miracles indeed. Fresh paint instead of peeling wallpaper, clean windowpanes, polished wood-work, sparkling sconces, and not a single cobweb on the chandelier gracing the lobby. If she hadn't recognized the old man wearing the tailored suit and showing stained teeth who was watching them from behind the front desk, she might not have known it was Mr. Yancey and this was the same hotel she had stayed in a month ago.

"Oh, Lucinda. Everything looks so grand."

Maddie beamed proudly. "That's what I tell her, but she still insists there's more to do."

"Hardly grand," Lucinda scoffed, although Edwina detected a note of pride in her voice. "But at least it's clean. And once the fabric for the new drapes comes in and the carpets arrive, it'll be much better. We're also redoing each room, but that will take a while. Everything has to be shipped in, and with the railroads threatening a new route, things are a bit muddled. Here, let me send up your bag in case you want to freshen up. Billy?"

The same freckle-faced boy who had been here before rushed over. But this time, instead of patched overalls and unruly auburn hair, he wore a smart uniform with gold braces and brass buttons, and a fresh haircut. After directing him to carry the valise to the room next to the Presidential Suite, Lucinda said, "So, how do you like my new enterprise, Pru?"

"I'm most impressed. I can see you've worked very hard."

Edwina nodded in agreement, thinking Lucinda must have had a fortune hidden inside that carpet-bag she had guarded so vigilantly. "But why here in Heartbreak Creek?"

"Why not? I have to be from somewhere, don't I? Besides," she added, one corner of her wide mouth tipping up in a crooked smile, "if I can convince the railroad to reroute through Heart-break Creek, this dismal little town might become quite prosperous once again."

Edwina grinned. "Which will make you pros-perous as well?"

"Exactly."

"Reroute?" Pru asked.

As Lucinda led them into the dining room, she

explained that washouts were a common problem along the current route, and if the tracks came through Heartbreak Creek instead, the railroad wouldn't have to redo the trestle and culverts every spring. "But you've tasted the water," she added with a shake of her head. "So you can see why the railroad might be hesitant to come through this area." Stopping beside a window with a lovely view of the mountains, she directed them to a cozy table topped with a spotless cloth and a vase of fragrant spring lilacs. "Will this do?"

"It's perfect," Edwina said.

As they took their seats, a young woman still in her teen years and wearing a starched white apron over a serviceable black dress rushed over. "Hidy, ma'ams," she said in a breathless voice. "What'll you have?"

"Miriam," Lucinda said softly.

"Oh. Sorry." Clearing her throat, the woman put on a wobbly smile, dipped a half curtsy, and said, "How may I serve you today, ladies?"

Lucinda nodded approval and asked Miriam to bring a plate of assorted cheeses and fruit, and tea for each. After the woman dashed off, Lucinda gave an apologetic smile. "We're still in training. But at least with the town offering such limited employment opportunities, we should have plenty of workers to fill our needs. Now where was I?"

"The water," Pru supplied, no doubt being the only one, other than Lucinda and the railroad engineers, who had any interest or understanding of the water requirements of steam locomotives.

"Ah, yes. Our nasty water." And launching into a lengthy description of the damage harsh minerals can do to locomotives and tenders, Lucinda explained how she was trying to convince the mine owners to stop using the water cannon to blast the ore loose, since that also dissolved other minerals, which were then washed down into the stream that serviced Heartbreak Creek. "That's why our water is so hard," she concluded. "It leaves a film on everything, which is quite harmful to the steam engines."

Pru nodded sagely.

Maddie stared dreamily out the window.

Edwina fought to stay awake.

"But even knowing that," Lucinda went on, "with production down and the water cannon being the most efficient way to break out the ore, the owners are naturally reluctant to start a new extraction method at this point."

"Naturally," Edwina agreed, her eyes watering from the effort of holding back a yawn.

Luckily Miriam arrived then, wheeling a delicate wicker cart laden with fruit, cheese and crackers, and a lovely china tea set.

Edwina had grown up with the tradition of an afternoon repast, although at Rose Hill they had served chicory coffee instead of tea and brandied fruit compote rather than canned fruit. And as she watched Lucinda load their plates with thin wedges of cheese and sliced canned peaches and shortbread crackers, she realized how much she missed these little niceties, and the companionship of other women, and the ritual and grace of a lovely afternoon tea.

"Now, Edwina," Maddie began once they were all served, "do tell Lucinda and me how it fares at your husband's ranch. What is he like? Is he handsome? I was so hoping to meet him."

"Handsome?" Edwina dabbed her napkin to her lips to hide a smile. "You tell me. You've seen him. Twice, in fact." At Maddie's look of surprise, she laughed. "Big Bob is my husband. Robert Declan Brodie, although he prefers Declan."

"Oh, my," Lucinda murmured.

"I knew it!" Maddie crowed, shaking a cracker at Lucinda. "Didn't I tell you? The moment I saw him in the hotel lobby I said, 'Luce, there's something about that man. He's definitely no one's underling.' Didn't I say that?"

"You did."

Grinning in triumph, Maddie turned back to Edwina. "Well? Is he nice? Does he treat you well? He seemed rather severe."

"He can be," Edwina admitted, nodding to Lucinda's offer of more tea. "But that's just his way. And yes, he treats me well. But the children . . ." She sighed. "They've been rather a challenge, to say the least."

"Oh, they're coming around," Pru said. "Remember, they've been years without a mother."

"Yes, we heard the gossip," Maddie said.

"Oh?" Edwina set down her teacup. "What gossip?"

"Nothing of consequence." Motioning for Miriam to clear their plates, Lucinda waited until the young woman left before she spoke again. "But apparently your husband's first wife was a bit flighty."

"Flighty?"

Maddie leaned forward to whisper, "They say she was involved with another man. A gambler."

"Now, Maddie, we don't know that for certain," Lucinda admonished gently.

Edwina blinked in disbelief. Declan's wife was an adulteress? What kind of fool had the woman been to prefer another man over Declan?

"There was quite the to-do when she disappeared," Maddie continued over Lucinda's halfhearted objections. "Some said your husband threw her out in a jealous rage. Others said she ran off with her gambler fellow. A few were even convinced that Mr. Brodie had killed her."

"Killed her?" Edwina shrank from the idea, a hand pressed to her throat. Not Declan, a man who could hardly discipline his own children.

"He didn't, of course," Lucinda said hastily, sending Maddie a reproving glare. "An Indian war party killed both her and her gambler. A patrol from the fort found them, and . . . well, it was definitely Indians."

Edwina scarcely heard as everything suddenly fell into place—all the shuttered looks, the barriers he had thrown up, the distrustful glances. It all made sense now. It wasn't because of her but because of his first wife.

A sharp sense of relief rushed through her, and with it came a swell of sympathy for a man vilely maligned. Poor Declan. How unfair. No wonder he held himself aloof.

"It's only gossip," Lucinda said. "Hardly worth mentioning. And I wouldn't have, except . . ." A look passed between Lucinda and Maddie that immediately set off warning bells in Edwina's mind.

"Except that what?"

"Well . . . there's to be a gathering tomorrow evening. A shivaree for a newly married couple. The whole town is invited." When Lucinda hesitated, as if debating whether to continue, Maddie jumped in.

"It's that horrid Alice Waltham. A wretched, nasty woman. She was a close friend of your husband's first wife, and she insists there's more to the events of her disappearance than has been told."

"Really?" Pru shoved her plate away, her normally bland expression tight with anger. "Like what?" Having been the brunt of gossip and the viciousness of evil people who despised all Negroes, she had little tolerance for cruelty.

"She's convinced Mr. Brodie killed his wife. Stupid woman." Lucinda waved the notion aside. "Of course, no one really believes that drivel. But if you and your husband attend the shivaree tomorrow, you should be prepared for some sort of confrontation."

Pru shrugged. "Then we won't go."

"Oh, yes we will," Edwina snapped. "I refuse to be run off by some viper-tongued prevaricator. Besides, if we don't attend, it might appear we believe her nonsense. No, we're definitely going."

Pru sighed. "Oh, dear."

Knowing how difficult such situations were for her sister, Edwina tamped down her anger. No need for Pru to get caught up in something that might spill over into a personal attack because of her mixed blood. It had happened too many times in the past. "You needn't go if you would rather not, Pru. I'll have Declan there to make sure I don't get myself into too much trouble. Besides, no telling how late this shivaree will last, and we really shouldn't leave the children on their own for long. You know the mischief they can get into."

Pru crossed her arms over her chest. *Stubborn woman.*

"Unless, of course," Edwina added, struck by a

brilliant idea, "Declan asks Thomas to watch them. Then you needn't stay with the children. Although"—she put on a thoughtful face—"the last time he did, Joe Bill almost burned down the house. Oh, I don't know. Perhaps you should stay, after all, just to help Thomas. Or not. It's up to you." Sometimes she was so clever she amazed herself.

"Fine. I'll stay," Pru said ungraciously. "But don't think it has anything to do with your manipulations."

"Heavens, of course not. I know exactly why you're staying."

Looking distressed by the sudden downturn in a lovely afternoon, Maddie rushed into the breach. "I'm so looking forward to it. I've never been to a shivaree and I'm anxious to get tintypes for my portfolio, assuming the photographic supplies I ordered from E. and H. T. Anthony arrive in time."

Relieved to move on to a less charged subject, Edwina asked how her photography expedition was going. Maddie happily told them, and within a few moments good cheer was restored, as if the subject of Declan Brodie's first wife had never come up.

"And guess what?" Maddie clapped her hands in childlike delight. "I'm having a special wagon built with its own dark tent so I'll be able to develop tintypes as I tour. Isn't that exciting?"

"She'll be quite the gypsy," Lucinda said with

a fond smile. "I shall be distraught here without her."

"Oh, don't be absurd, Luce. You have so many town projects in the fire you won't even know I'm gone."

"What town projects?" Pru asked.

"More than I can handle, I fear."

"Might there be room for a school for displaced Negroes?" Pru asked. "I saw several freedmen and -women when we were here before."

"We could make room. And perhaps open it to Chinese workers, as well, if the railroad lays a new line through town."

And so the tension was forgotten and the afternoon passed in delightful conversation—Pru talking about her dream of teaching, Edwina recounting her disgust at cleaning and preparing her first chicken, Lucinda telling how they'd ordered a bell for the little church steeple, and Maddie describing her first encounter with a buffalo skinner who didn't want his photograph taken. Edwina was having such a grand time she didn't even notice it had gotten dark until the tromp of boots through the lobby and Brin's loud voice told her the family had arrived.

Lucinda closed the dining room to outsiders and had the men push several tables together so they could all eat at one long table, including Amos, Thomas, and the Parker ranch hands. It was a lovely meal and reminded Edwina of the big Sunday gatherings on the shaded lawn at Rose

Hill, when the smell of magnolia blossoms mingled with the delicious aromas of roasting sausages, boiled crabs, and shrimp gumbo, and distant laugher and music drifted on the warm breeze rising up from the bayou.

While talk went on around them, Edwina turned to Declan, seated on her right. "How did the cattle sale go?" They were a bit crowded, but she was left-handed—another reason for Mother to bring out the cane—so they didn't bang elbows. Yet she was acutely aware of him beside her—his bigness, his silence, the way his hand dwarfed his fork. Long fingers, nicked and scarred, dusted with dark hair. So different from hers.

"Not as well as I'd hoped, but well enough."

"Well enough to stay another day?"

He glanced over, a troubled look in his dark eyes. "Is that what you want?"

"I'd like to, yes."

That shutter came down. "Whatever," he said and looked away.

Remembering what he'd said earlier about his wife, and all the nasty gossip she'd heard about his first marriage, she felt a sudden need to reassure him. "It's just that I haven't had a chance to shop yet. Have you?"

"Shop?"

She leaned over until her face was inches from his shoulder. "For Brin," she whispered. "Haven't you gotten her anything yet?"

"Ah . . ."

"You haven't."

She drew in an exasperated breath, and suddenly her senses exploded with the essence of Declan, his heat, the smell of soap, horses . . . him. Her body instantly reacted—her heartbeat quickening, her skin tingling, her thoughts scattering like some addlepated adolescent sneaking her first kiss under the pawpaw tree. Rattled, she pulled back, straightened the napkin in her lap, sipped from her glass. Once her nerves settled, she cleared her throat and said, "And there's a gathering tomorrow evening. A shivaree."

"For the Hamiltons."

"You know them?"

"Tom took over as sheriff after I left. Good man."

Edwina watched him take a bite of roasted pork and wondered how the sight of a man chewing his food could be so fascinating. And swallowing. Mercy, the things it did to his throat.

"Heard they were moving to New Mexico Territory."

She smiled vaguely, having forgotten what they were talking about.

He studied her through dark eyes softened by lamplight. "I'm guessing you want to go to this shivaree."

"Would you mind? Pru said she would watch over the children."

"I don't dance. Fair warning."

"I do dance," she shot back. "Fair warning to you." Grinning, she popped a piece of biscuit into her mouth.

"Threatening me again?"

"Perish the thought. A big man like you?"

And there it was, the smile she'd been hoping for. And with it came that same strange, shivery, quivery reaction she'd felt when he'd kissed her. It startled her to realize how much she was actually beginning to like her stern-faced, unapproachable husband.

"You're doing it again." The low rumble of his voice seemed to vibrate in the air around her.

"Doing what?"

Instead of answering, he pushed his empty plate away and turned to Lucinda at the end of the table. "Do you have a room I could rent?"

Edwina almost dropped her fork. Reacting was one thing. Acting on it was an entirely different thing altogether. Heat rushed into her face. She couldn't catch her breath and the urge to flee almost overwhelmed her.

"A room? Certainly," Lucinda said. "How many would you like?"

"Just one for Edwina and Miss Lincoln."

What? Edwina blinked, her mind swirling in confusion. "But what about you?" she blurted out. Then horrified by what she'd said, she quickly added, "And the children? And"—unable to recall a single name, she waved vaguely in the direction of the men staring at her from the far end of the table—"And them?"

The Indian fellow was grinning, his gaze darting from Declan to Edwina and back to Declan again. "Ho," he said softly.

Declan shifted in his chair. "I've made other arrangements for the family."

Other arrangements? What other arrangements? "But . . . ?" Edwina stared at him, the unfinished thought hanging in the air. Arrangements where? And why weren't she and Pru included? Weren't they part of the family, too?

But before Edwina could ask him that, Lucinda said, "We have plenty of rooms available, Mr. Brodie. Take as many as you need. As my guests, of course."

Realizing her mistake, Edwina felt more heat rise in her cheeks, embarrassed that in her ignorance of her husband's financial situation, she might have put Declan on the spot.

"I appreciate the offer, ma'am. But I had a house here once. If it's still usable, we'll stay there."

And before Edwina could question him further, he pushed back his chair and rose. Immediately, the other men followed suit. "Thank you, ma'am, for this fine meal. Now if you'll excuse us, Miss Hathaway, ladies, we have horses to tend and children to get situated."

"Of course, Mr. Brodie."

"Good night, then." And without a backward

glance, he ushered his children and the other men from the room.

To Edwina, it felt like a slap in the face.

As soon as the door closed behind them, she threw her napkin down beside her plate with enough vigor to rattle her teacup. "Can you believe that? He all but said he didn't want anything to do with us, didn't he, Pru? 'I've made other arrangements for the family,' " she mimicked. "What are we, barnyard animals?"

"Now, Edwina," Pru began.

Lucinda cut her off. "It did seem rather odd—"

"See, Pru!"

"—especially after the way he stared at you throughout the meal."

Edwina blinked. Then discounted the notion. "Ha!" She'd been sitting right beside him and had noticed no such thing. "If he looked at me at all, it was probably with disapproval. I gutted a chicken, for heaven's sake! What more do I have to do?"

"Chicken gutting always worked for me," Lucinda quipped.

"As I recall," Maddie said with a smile, that dreamy look in her eyes, "Angus reacted rather well to something sheer. Maybe a touch of lace here and there. Nothing too revealing, of course."

"It's me." Battling an urge to weep, Edwina planted her elbows on the table and dropped her head into her hands. "Men have never found me attractive. Probably because I'm not pointy."

"Pointy?"

"Here we go," Pru murmured.

"Well, look." Dropping her hands, Edwina puffed out her meager bosom. "What man would be attracted to a woman who looks like a boy?"

Lucinda started to laugh, then stifled it when Maddie sent her a stern look. "You don't look like a boy, dear."

"Shelly thought so. He said I looked like a stick."

"He would," Pru muttered.

Edwina glared at her half sister. "What's that supposed to mean?"

Before Pru could answer, Maddie hastily cut in. "Oh, I'm certain Shelly found you attractive. I'm sure he loved you to distraction."

"Oh, Lord." Edwina dropped her head into her hands again. She didn't have to look up to feel the glances pass between the others. Dimly she heard the scrape of chairs and knew they were coming to console her. The flat-bosomed, unalluring, pitiful creature that she was.

"After all," Maddie crooned, taking Declan's chair and slipping an arm around Edwina's shoulder, "he did take you to wife, didn't he?"

Edwina sniffed behind her hands. "More or less."

A pause. "Either he did or he didn't, dear."

"Or tried and couldn't," Lucinda added from her left.

"Or found me so unattractive, he got it over

with as soon as he could." Unable to hold back the tears, Edwina grabbed her napkin and pressed it to her leaking eyes. "What am I doing wrong?" she wailed. "Why don't men want me? First Shelly, and now Declan. What's wrong with me?"

"It isn't you," Pru said, her tone more angry than sympathetic. "It's them."

Edwina laughed brokenly. "Of course it is. One man could hardly consummate our marriage and the other won't even try. It must be them."

"You mean . . . you and Mr. Brodie haven't . . ."

"I insisted on a three-month delay so we could get to know one another. So, no, Maddie, we haven't. Which is just fine with me, I assure you."

"You don't want to consummate your marriage?"

"Why would I?" Edwina blew her nose, wadded the napkin into a ball, and tucked it beside her plate. "It was awful with Shelly, and I'm in no rush to repeat the experience. Although it would be nice to know Declan actually *wanted* to . . . you know . . . even if he couldn't."

"You're priceless." With a sigh, Lucinda rose and began scraping the plates. "You don't want him to take you to bed, but you do want him to want to take you to bed. What are you going to do when he finally does?"

Irritated by the condescending tone, Edwina swiped the back of her hand across her eyes, took a deep breath, and hiked her chin. "I am not a coward, Lucinda. I will do my duty."

"Your duty." Lucinda began stacking the dirty dishes.

Muttering under her breath, Pru rose and joined her.

Maddie continued to pat Edwina's shoulder. "You must have had a ghastly experience with your first husband, dear. I'm so sorry. For all his shortcomings, at least Angus did that right."

"It wasn't Shelly's fault. I just wasn't that attractive to him, I guess."

"Oh, for Lord's sake!" Dishes clattered back to the table as Pru whirled, hands planted on her hips. "This is ridiculous. I promised Shelly I wouldn't say anything, but I cannot allow you to do this a moment longer."

"Do what?"

"Blame yourself." Pru took a deep breath, then said in a rush, "The reason you weren't attractive to Shelly is because you weren't a man!"

Silence. Then Maddie's soft whisper. "Does that mean—"

"I wondered," Lucinda said thoughtfully. "With a name like Shelly, one would."

Edwina blinked at her sister, trying to make sense of her words. "You mean . . . Shelly . . ."

"Was a weak sister, yes!" Pru threw her hands up in exasperation. "Didn't you ever wonder at his close friendship with Frederick?"

Edwina rocked back. "Frederick, too?"

"How does that work, I wonder?" Maddie asked

Lucinda. "Two men. Together. How would they go about that?"

"Maddie, please!"

"It's a natural curiosity."

"Save it for later."

Edwina continued to stare at her sister, shock and disbelief swelling into such a sense of betrayal she thought she might vomit. "Why didn't you tell me, Pru?" she demanded in a wobbly voice. "Why didn't Shelly tell me? Why would you let me marry a man who didn't love me?"

"He did love you." Looking as if she might cry, too, Pru sank into the chair Lucinda had vacated. She took Edwina's hand in both of hers. "Just not in the way a man loves a woman."

Edwina felt fury build as memories flashed through her mind. The ceremony, the toasts, the forced smiles and sly looks. Had everyone known but her?

Shelly had seemed so desperate to have her, but without the joy or tenderness she had expected. It had been an awkward, almost frantic coupling. And afterward, tears. For both of them. Hers, from regret and shame and embarrassment. His, she had assumed, from disappointment or because he would be marching off to war in just a few hours.

Damn him. Damn Pru. Why hadn't they told her? Said something? Acid burned in her throat. *All those years.* "You let me think it was me."

"I'm sorry."

Emotion swirled in her mind. How could they do that to her? She wanted to scream and claw her chest open so the pain could get out. All those years wasted in regret and self-doubt. All those years thinking there was something wrong with her. *Damn them.*

She jerked her hand free of her sister's grip. "You should have told me, Pru." She wanted to slap her. Hurt her back. "You let me believe it was all my fault when it wasn't. Why would you do that to me? Why?" She watched tears fill her sister's eyes, slide down to fall in fat drops on the tablecloth, and was glad her sister was in pain, too.

"I thought that deep down you knew. You loved him. He loved you. I thought it would be enough."

"You were wrong."

"I know. I'm so sorry."

"Oh stop, please," Maddie cried, her own face wet with tears. "You mustn't do this to each other. Prudence, tell her you're sorry. Edwina, say you forgive her."

"Hush, Maddie," Lucinda snapped. "This is a good thing."

Edwina reared back to glare at her. "Good?"

"Yes. Because now you have no need to fear your new husband."

"I don't fear Declan."

"Oh?" Leaning down, Lucinda planted her hands on the table across from the other three ladies. She leveled her green gaze at Edwina.

"Then why haven't you allowed him into your bed? Why are you insisting on this silly three-month waiting period? Why are you just pretending to be a wife, rather than actually being one?" She straightened and let her hands fall to her sides. "You're afraid, that's why. You think making love to Declan will be as disappointing and awkward as making love to Shelly was."

Maddie nodded thoughtfully. "That makes sense. If Angus hadn't been so arduous and skilled and—"

"Please, Maddie. Not now."

"Sorry." The petite Englishwoman gave Edwina's shoulder a quick hug. "But she's right, Edwina. This is a good thing. Because now you can open yourself to your husband without regret or fear."

"A lamentable choice of words," Lucinda muttered.

Maddie ignored the comment. "You do want to, don't you, Edwina? Open yourself to Declan? Because I can assure you in the right man's hands, you will have no regrets or disappointments."

Edwina felt heat rush into her face just thinking about it. "And what about him? What if he's the one disappointed?"

"Then we shall just have to make sure he isn't." Maddie laughed in delight. "Oh this will be such fun! By the end of the shivaree tomorrow night, I promise you, dear Edwina, your handsome bull of a husband will be pawing at the dirt to get at you."

"Gads." Lucinda gave a mock shudder. "You're supposed to be encouraging her, Maddie, not scaring the stuffings out of her."

Considering Declan's size, it was a rather frightful image, Edwina thought. But interesting . . .

"How is your head?"

Looking over from the fence rail he'd been leaning on, Declan saw Thomas walking toward him. Sneaking would be more like it. Despite his solid build, the man's tread made as much noise as a mouse tiptoeing across a feather quilt.

"What's wrong with my head?"

Thomas stopped beside him. His teeth flashed white in the faint moonlight. "If she had a war ax, it would be stuck in it."

Declan snorted. Turning back, he crossed his arms along the top rail of the paddock and watched the horses root in their piles of hay for the tastiest leaves. "Nothing new in that."

"Ho. Then I am sorry, *nesene'*. It is not good when a man must share his tipi with a woman he does not like."

"Who said I didn't like her?"

Continuing as if Declan hadn't spoken, Thomas added, "But it is probably best. She is too skinny. A man needs something to hold on to on long, cold nights."

"She's not too skinny." In fact, Declan thought Ed might have gained a pound or two. Either that, or she was less pinch-faced and anxious than when she'd first come. Until tonight, that is, when he had botched everything with that "family" comment. He'd known he was in trouble the minute he saw her face. Ed wasn't much for hiding her emotions. But he'd thought she would be pleased to stay and visit with her friends. And anyway, he hadn't known the condition of the house then and didn't want her thinking she had to spend half the night cleaning it up.

Still. He probably could have handled it better. *Hell.*

Down the road, a single window glowed in Jeb Kendal's small log house. Another light bobbed past as a carriage rolled by, its harness chains jangling in rhythm to trotting hoofbeats. From across the creek came the distant plinking of a piano, barely heard over the rush of water. All reminders that he was back in town.

Memories pricked at him. Unhappy memories.

He should have stayed at the ranch and sent the men on without him.

Pulling the bullet from the pouch tied around his neck, Thomas leaned his forearms across the rail and idly played the bit of lead through his fingers. "This wife is not like the other," he said after a long silence.

Declan studied the Indian's moon-sculpted

profile, remembering that the warrior had shown little liking for Sally. And even though Thomas was right, and Ed was nothing like Sally, it irritated Declan to hear his dead wife judged by a man who scarcely knew her. "She was a good mother, Thomas."

"And wife? Was she a good wife as well?"

Declan looked away, anger flashing through him; anger laced with pity and regret and guilt. "It wasn't all her fault. I wasn't that good a husband back then."

Beside him, the spent bullet rolled and turned. He could hear it, the gentle scrape of the metal against the roughness of Thomas's fingers.

"And now?" Thomas asked.

Declan stared into the darkness. *Now I'm not a husband at all.*

When he got no answer, Thomas dropped the bullet back into the pouch beneath his shirt. "Will you go to the gathering tomorrow?"

"The shivaree?" Declan shrugged. "Maybe. Ed wants to."

"Then I will watch over your children."

"Miss Lincoln already said she would watch over them."

"Then I will watch Miss Lincoln watch over them. They will all be safe with me. Lone Tree will not harm them."

Declan had forgotten about Lone Tree. Ed had been taking up so much of his mind he hadn't thought of anything else. "I appreciate that, Thomas."

They stood in silence as the breeze rose, cutting through Declan's cotton shirt. He thought of Ed, and of kissing her, then her asking him to do it again. What woman did such a thing? *Much better,* she'd said. He smiled. He'd like to show her *much better.* With a sigh, he pushed away from the fence. "She's got me running in circles," he admitted to Thomas as they walked toward the house. "I can hardly keep up with her."

Thomas chuckled. "Do you need *matoho* to bring you courage?"

"Peyote?" Declan shuddered. "No. Never." The one time Thomas had talked him into chewing the cactus buttons, Declan had vomited like a drunken mule skinner before sinking into nightmarish dreams for hours.

"Then I will pray to the Great Spirit to guide you."

"Hell, while you're at it, ask him to get me through this dance I let her talk me into."

"Ask your own God, *ma'hahe.* Mine does not work miracles."

TEN

By morning, Edwina had found her balance again, which was odd, since she had hardly slept at all. Judging by the tossing and turning on the other side of the bed, Pru didn't sleep much, either.

The night had seemed interminable. But Edwina had made good use of her sleeplessness, browbeating herself for the first hour or two before moving on to self-pity, then righteous anger, and finally trying to figure out what she should do next.

By the time dawn turned the mountaintops pink, Pru had fallen into a fitful sleep, and Edwina was seated at the little table by the window making her lists.

She thrived on making lists. They always brought order to her mind. Just the act of arranging items in a neat row on a blank piece of paper made her feel more in control. But these lists brought little peace.

The first was a catalog of all the things she wanted to say to Pru—how hurt and betrayed she felt, how wrong Pru had been to withhold from her the truth about Shelly, and how furious she was that her sister had let that lie go on for so long. She wrote furiously, scratched out, rewrote. Then once she had poured her anger onto the paper, she read it over, nodded in satisfaction, then wadded it up and tossed it into the wastebasket.

Next came a shopping list. Shopping lists were her favorite. They were happy lists and always made her feel better even if she never bought the items she wrote down. Once she'd completed it, she folded it and slipped it into the pocket of her skirt.

Which left, finally, the hardest of all. Declan's list. That one took a great deal of thought, and by the time it joined the shopping list in her pocket, Pru was waking up.

They dressed without speaking, continuing the chill silence that had sent them to the separate sides of their shared bed hours ago. Last night the hurt and anger had still been too raw to put into words. But now . . .

Now Edwina was mostly sick of the whole thing. At some point between the browbeating and righteous anger, she had realized that Pru was right. Deep down she had known about Shelly. Not the mechanics of the thing—that was far beyond her comprehension and experience—how *did* they go about it?—but she had always known Shelly hadn't loved her in *that* way. He had never looked at her in the same avid manner other boys did. He had never tried to steal a kiss, or accidentally brush against her breast, or let his hands wander where they shouldn't. She had sensed, even then, that something was lacking.

But she hadn't cared and had married him anyway because he was her escape. Shelly would never hurt her, or raise his hand against her, or belittle her—well, other than that hurtful "stick" comment. He was her friend and companion. So when he had proposed—for whatever reason—she had ignored the doubts, and in her typically impulsive, desperately naïve way, had donned her blinders and leaped from the fat into the fire.

But no more. She was wiser now. Less fearful. And after a night of soul-searching, she had decided it was time to clear the air.

Starting with Pru.

But it was hard. It was still difficult for Edwina to accept that her beloved childhood friend and adored half sister had knowingly sent her into a union that was destined to end in disappointment and bitterness.

That betrayal changed things, created a subtle shift within Edwina's mind, as if the foundation of all her perceptions and beliefs and expectations had been skewed just enough to open a gap in her trust. Did Pru and Shelly think she couldn't bear the truth? That she would never find out? What was truth and what was illusion? She no longer trusted herself to know.

But she would no longer tolerate deceit. From Pru. Or herself.

So as the sky brightened beyond the window, Edwina constructed a new foundation. One grounded in absolute honesty. Without subterfuge, misconceptions, and half-truths. She would dare to open her eyes and see the world as it was, not as she wished it to be. She would put the past behind her—including Shelly, Rose Hill, her mother, and the haunting memories of all that was lost—and become a newer, stronger, wiser Edwina, ready to embrace the endless possibilities of a better future.

Of course she would. Then she would restore the South, end famine, and secure the vote for women. Ha!

It was nearing time to meet Maddie and Lucinda for breakfast prior to their shopping excursion when Edwina finally broke the silence that had lingered in the air like the odor of last night's fish.

"Pru," she said, as her sister started for the door. "I need to say something to you."

Pru turned, her dark eyes troubled, her mouth set in a defensive line.

Edwina tried to reassure her with a smile, but the muscles beneath her skin felt stiff. "You were right. Deep down, I think I knew about Shelly. I just didn't want to face it."

Relief softened Pru's frown. "I should have told you."

"Yes, you should have. It was cruel to let me think it was my fault." This time Edwina's smile succeeded. "But I forgive you. You're my sister. I'll always forgive you. No"—she held up a hand as Pru started toward her, her eyes brimming—"Stay away. Don't even look at me. If you do, I'll start crying, and after a sleepless night my eyes are puffy enough."

Pru hugged her anyway, and they both shed tears. But there was still that space between them, and Edwina feared something had been lost.

"I'm so sorry," Pru said, dabbing a hanky at her dripping nose. "I—"

"Hush." Edwina didn't want to talk. She didn't want to think. She just wanted it over. "Hurry or we'll miss breakfast. I'm famished."

Shopping in Heartbreak Creek was beyond dismal. The one shop that catered to women mostly catered to women who catered to men. The millinery shop catered more to sturdy farm women, although Edwina did find a lovely scarf she insisted on getting for Pru. She also managed to locate a book for Lucas on watch repair at the Fix-It Shop, but so far, nothing suitable for Brin's seventh birthday. They were headed into their last hope, Bagley's Mercantile, Feed, and Mining Supplies, when Edwina almost slammed into Declan as he came out the door.

"Whoa," he said, grabbing her elbow to steady her. Odd how a simple touch on her arm could cause such havoc inside her chest. As soon as she regained her balance, he released her to tip his hat at the women crowded behind her. "Morning, ladies."

225

After exchanging greetings, the other three went into the store.

Edwina hesitated, wondering if now would be a good time to discuss with her husband the list she'd made.

He looked especially handsome today, she thought, and wondered if that was a new shirt. It must have been; the fold creases still showed down the front. And he'd shaved. And had a trim. Even his boots were polished.

Realizing he was studying her as intensely as she had been studying him, she made a show of craning her neck to see past him into the store, where she saw her three friends gathered at the counter, exchanging words with the proprietor. Unpleasant words, it seemed. Leave it to Lucinda.

"Are the children with you?"

"No."

Uneasy under that probing stare, she looked down, noticing for the first time a package the size of a hatbox tucked under his arm. "What's that?"

"Something for Brin."

"May I see?"

"Nope."

"Why not?" Wrapped packages always brought out the child in Edwina.

"It's a surprise."

"Not for me. And what if I get the same thing?"

"You won't."

Voices rose from inside. Even Maddie's. Edwina

looked past him again to see both Lucinda and Maddie in battle stance, arms akimbo, chins thrust forward. She should go see what was happening.

"Do they have dolls in there?" she asked, instead.

"Dolls?"

"I thought I might get one for Brin. When Pru and I were cleaning out the children's quarters, we noticed she didn't have one."

"She did at one time, I think. But as I recall, she and Joe Bill tied it to a stake and burned it."

"I wonder who thought that one up," Edwina murmured.

Seeing movement behind him, she looked past his broad shoulder to see Lucinda and Maddie stomping furiously toward the door, trailed by Pru, who clutched her reticule so tightly it was a wadded ball, even though her expression appeared serene and untroubled.

Edwina wasn't fooled. She recognized that look as the armor Pru donned when she was upset and trying not to show it.

"What a nitwit," Lucinda snapped. "I cannot believe in this day and age, and after all this country has gone through, there are still people who think that way."

"What happened?" Edwina asked, edging protectively toward Pru.

"It's not important," Pru murmured.

"It most certainly is! That man will rue the

day he crossed Lucinda Hathaway. I can make or break his stinking little store. And I will."

Declan's calm voice cut into Lucinda's tirade. "What did he do?"

"There were samples of taffy on the counter," Maddie said, her voice vibrating with indignation. " 'Take one,' he said. 'No charge.' So we did. But when Pru reached for hers, he slapped her hand away and said 'It's not for niggers.' "

"Maddie, please," Pru said. "These things happen."

Sadly, they did. And often enough that Edwina had finally given in to Pru's entreaties to ignore the cruelties rather than cause a scene. It had happened less frequently since they'd left the South, but that didn't make it hurt any less.

Shifting Brin's parcel to his left side, Declan started inside.

Pru caught his arm. "Please, Mr. Brodie. Don't do anything. It's just words. That's all. Not worth making a fuss over."

Declan showed his teeth in a smile that was anything but reassuring. "I won't make a fuss, Miss Lincoln. Now if you ladies are through shopping, why don't you head back to the hotel while I have a word here with Cal."

Nodding in approval, Lucinda looped her arm through Pru's and steered her down the boardwalk. Maddie glanced at Edwina, but Edwina shook her head as she watched her husband go inside. "I'll be along. I need to talk to Declan for a minute."

"Back already, Big Bob?" the bucktoothed proprietor said when he saw Declan heading toward him. "Well, hello there," he added, when Edwina came to stand at her husband's side. "This the new missus? Hidy, ma'am. Cal Bagley, at your service. What can I do for you folks today?"

"You can—" Edwina began before Declan's hand on her shoulder cut her off.

"I'll handle this, Ed," he said in a low tone.

"But she's—"

"I'll handle this." This time his tone carried warning and his grip tightened in emphasis. "Wait outside." He faced the shopkeeper again. "I think there's been a misunderstanding, Cal. Those ladies who were just in here said you refused to serve one of them."

Bagley nodded. "The nigger."

Edwina started forward again, then stopped abruptly when Declan turned and looked at her. He didn't speak. Just looked. But his expression was one she had never seen on his face before, and it sent a shiver up her back. She retreated a step, then another. "I'll wait outside," she mumbled, then whirled and fled the shop.

But she didn't go far, and as soon as the door closed behind her, she edged back, positioning herself so she could watch them through the front window.

There wasn't much to see. Declan did most of the talking. Cal Bagley did most of the nodding. By the time her husband turned and waved her back inside, the shopkeeper was sweating like a field hand and wearing a sickly grin.

As she approached the counter, Declan looked around and asked the shopkeeper if he had any dolls in the store.

"Dolls?"

"My wife wants to buy one for Brin."

"A doll? For Brin? What for?" A nervous laugh that quickly faded. "Bottom shelf." He waved them toward the back wall. "Or I have another jackknife like the one she broke last Christmas."

Astonished, Edwina looked back over her shoulder at Declan as they headed toward the rear of the store. "You let a six-year-old have a knife?"

"Just get the doll," he muttered, using his bulk to herd her down the aisle.

"How many stitches did Joe Bill end up needing?" Cal Bagley called after them. "Must have been half a dozen."

Declan didn't answer.

There were only two forlorn rag dolls that must have been gathering dust on the shelf for over a year. Edwina picked the less faded and went on to select a shirt for each of the boys. After Declan paid, they finally made their escape, Declan loaded with her parcels as well as his.

"What a nasty little man," Edwina muttered, trying to keep up with her husband's long stride.

"He's just a wad of hair with teeth stuck in it. Harmless."

"Tell Pru that."

He glanced over at her from beneath the brim of his hat. "You seem more upset than she was. You're protective of her, aren't you?"

Edwina shrugged. "She's very dear to me. Can we slow down?"

He did, and after a moment Edwina was able to catch her breath. As they neared the hotel, she slowed even more and finally stopped. "Is there someplace we could talk, Declan? Somewhere other than the hotel?"

"Talk about what? If this is about me running you out of the store—"

"How about over there?" she cut in, pointing across the street to a bench outside an empty storefront with a giant tooth painted across the cracked window.

With ill-concealed reluctance, he led her through a maze of horse droppings, then up onto the opposite boardwalk. Once she and the parcels were settled on the bench, he leaned a shoulder against a post supporting the overhang and thrust his hands into the back pockets of his trousers . . . an action that pulled the shirt so tight across his chest the top button of his collar slipped loose to expose a sprinkle of dark hair.

Edwina thought of Shelly's hairless chest and looked away.

For a moment, neither spoke. Then he said, "If this is about that comment last night . . ." He let the sentence hang.

Not wanting to make it easy, she simply raised her brows and waited.

"It's a small house," he went on when she didn't speak. "Hardly room for the kids, much less Thomas and the other men."

She continued to smile and wait.

"Besides, I didn't know what shape it would be in. As it was, took us over an hour to clear out the mouse nests and spiderwebs." When that still got no response, he pulled his hand from his back pocket, rubbed a knuckle under his jaw where the barber had nicked him, and sighed. "You're part of the family, Ed. You and Miss Lincoln, both. I didn't mean to make you think you weren't."

Not much of an apology, but then, he was a man. "Thank you, Declan."

With a look of relief, he straightened from the post.

"And now," she said, "there are some things I need to discuss with you, if I may."

He groaned. Not aloud, but she knew him well enough now to hear what he didn't say almost as clearly as what he did. Settling back against the post, he folded his arms over his chest, crossed one ankle over the other and waited.

Now that she had his attention, nerves almost overcame her. But this was important, so she took a deep breath, exhaled, and jumped in. "My first marriage was a failure. I blamed myself for that, convinced the reason my husband couldn't love me properly was because he found me unattractive. Which apparently, he did, but not in the way I thought."

There. That wasn't so hard. Although judging by her husband's expression, she might not have explained it as well as she should.

She took another breath. This time when she exhaled, she felt a bit steadier. "But that's all in the past," she went on. "I'm wiser now. My expectations are more realistic. So I've decided to put aside my doubts and give this marriage a real chance."

"Doubts about what?"

"You . . . know."

His expression said he didn't.

She cleared her throat. "Consummation."

"Consummation?"

"What I mean is—"

"I know what it means, Ed."

"Well then." She shifted on the bench and tried to ignore the unladylike sweat dampening her gloves. "Toward that end, and before we . . . you know . . ."

"Commence consummation?"

"Yes, that." She smoothed a wrinkle on her

skirt. "I'm hoping you might answer a few questions for me. Just to be certain we're compatible, of course."

"Of course."

His tone brought her head up. "Don't you laugh at me, Declan. This is serious."

"I can see that. Ask your questions."

"There are only a few." Pulling from her skirt pocket the list and a stub of pencil, she spread the paper on her knees, careful not to smudge the script with her rampant perspiration. With pencil poised, she read off item number one. "Do you have feelings for anyone else, man or woman?"

"Feelings?"

"Amorous feelings."

He straightened off the post. "For a man? Is this a joke?"

She glanced up, saw the thunder in his eyes, and felt more perspiration gather under the brim of her black horsehair bonnet. "Well, no. But I've seen how close you are to Thomas and—"

"Good God."

"I'll mark that as a 'No.'" Which she did with a shaky x. Now for a hard one. Putting on a bland smile, as if it wasn't the most audacious question she had ever put to a man, she asked, "Are you attracted to me?"

He blinked.

"I know I'm rather thin. And my, um, attributes are not as fulsome as one might hope, but—"

Deep laughter cut her off.

"Please, Declan. Don't make this harder for me than it already is."

He sobered. "Your attributes are fine, Ed."

She let her shoulders relax. "You're sure? Truly?"

He gave it some thought. "I guess to be truly sure I'd have to see them first." And the wretched man actually *looked* at her breasts as if expecting her to expose them for his perusal.

Restraining the urge to kick him in the shin, she breathed through her nose and strove for serenity. "I think not."

"Perhaps later, then."

What? Later? Later when?

"Do you find *me* attractive?" he asked.

Forcing her thoughts away from all the lurid imaginings the word "later" had conjured, she made a shaky offhand gesture. "When you smile, perhaps. You have a lovely smile, Declan. You should use it more often."

"I'll remember that." He relaxed back against the post.

A cool gust of manure-scented air swept over them. The follow-me-boys streamers hanging from her hat fluttered and stuck to her damp neck. "Number three. Do you want children?"

"I better, since I have four."

"What I mean is, do you want *more* children. With me. Us. Together." She waited, her cheeks burning, the pencil stub poised.

Again, he didn't answer. When she looked up to see why, she found his amused expression had been replaced by something else, something she couldn't define.

"I'm guessing you don't," he finally said.

"Well, no."

"I see."

It saddened her to watch that shutter come down again. "No, Declan, I don't think you do." She had hoped to avoid telling him this, but he had a right to know the truth, and if this marriage was to work, there must be no secrets between them. "The thing is, I'm fairly certain madness runs in our family."

He didn't seem surprised, which was a little insulting.

She pressed on anyway. "And although I love children and would have liked to have my own, I don't want to pass down tainted blood."

"Who's mad?"

"My cousin Tremont for one. He's partial to ball gowns. Aunt Queenie giggles constantly, and another cousin carries a stuffed cat with him wherever he goes. And perhaps my mother." Then because she didn't want to discuss the cruelties of her childhood, she quickly moved on. "One last question and we're done. It's not really a question, I guess. More like a request. A stipulation, if you will. Or perhaps a—"

"Just say it, Ed."

She looked down at her hands and was surprised to see she had crumpled the paper into a twisted mess. She tried to smooth it out, smudged the writing, and gave up. This was the most difficult to say, but it was important that she make herself very clear and that he understand this was not something open to discussion. Lifting her head, she met his gaze without wavering. "You mustn't hit me, Declan. Ever."

"Hit you?" He shoved away from the post.

Sensing an outburst, she hurried on. "I don't know—nor do I want to know—what happened in your first marriage. But if you raise your hand against me, Declan, I'll leave you and never look back. I swear it."

For a moment he stood stock-still. Then with a sudden sharp inhale, he seemed to expand, grow taller, swell up like a dog raising its hackles. "You think I hurt my wife? That's why she left?"

"I-I don't know, Declan. I'm just saying—"

"I hear what you're saying! Damnit, Ed!" He spun away, took two steps, then whirled back. "Yes, she left because of me," he said savagely. "But not because I hit her. I would never hit a woman!"

"Even if she was unfaithful?"

An ugly look came over his face. "I see your friends have been carrying tales." He bent over her, hands planted low on his belt, his lips pulled back from his teeth. "Well, here's a new one. One that hasn't made the rounds yet. One

I'm sure your friends will delight in passing along. I knew my wife was seeing another man. I knew she was leaving me. Hell, I gave her money to do it." He straightened. "Any other questions?"

"Why?"

"Why the money? So she wouldn't take the children with her."

"No, why did she leave you?"

The question sent him back a step. "Hell if I know. She cared for him. He cared for her."

"And you didn't."

"I never hit her, Ed. Ever."

Edwina knew there were other ways a man could hurt a woman besides using his fists. But she had already learned more than she wanted to about the sad state of Declan's first marriage, so she didn't press it.

"Now I have a question for you," he said.

Edwina nodded.

"Was your husband the one who hurt you?"

"Shelly? No. Shelly would never hurt me."

"Then why are you afraid of me?"

"I'm not afraid of you." And wouldn't admit it if she were.

"No? Then what?"

She was sweating like a racehorse now, and every word out of her mouth seemed to leave her breathless, no matter how much air she gulped in. "It . . . the . . . you know . . . didn't go well with my first husband."

"Consummation?"

She nodded, her cheeks burning. Never in her deepest nightmares had she ever thought to discuss such a thing with a man.

"And you're thinking it'll be the same with me?"

She shrugged. "Perhaps. I don't know."

He laughed out loud. Not in derision but in genuine amusement that such a thing could even be possible. "Trust me, Ed. You'll like it."

So arrogant. Yet she liked that. She liked that he wasn't tentative or unsure as Shelly had been. She liked that he found her attractive despite her lack of attributes. And she especially liked to hear him laugh.

"If you say so," she said demurely.

Which made him laugh again. "You are by far the most confounding woman I have ever come across. You done with your list?"

"For now."

"Good." Pulling from his pocket a small wad of tissue, he thrust it toward her. "I got this in the ladies' store. Thought you might want to wear it to the shivaree you're forcing me to take you to."

The ladies' store that catered to men? With some trepidation, Edwina took the packet from his grip. Opening the tissue, she found a long white satin ribbon embroidered with an intricate ivy design in gold thread, dotted with clusters of tiny white beads. "Why, Declan, this is beautiful. You got this for me?"

"No, I got it for Thomas, but he decided to wear a war bonnet instead."

A laugh burst from her. "You'll never forgive me for that comment, will you?" Bemused, she played the sleek ribbon through her fingers. "This is lovely." And it was. Delicate and feminine and not at all what one might expect from such a shop.

"You said females liked pretty things."

She smiled up at him, surprised that he remembered their conversation on the long wagon ride into town. "I have just the dress to wear this with. Thank you."

"You like it?"

"I do. Very much."

"Show me. Stand up."

Heat rushed into her cheeks. She glanced around, but the boardwalk was deserted except for two old men playing checkers outside the assay office at the other end of the street. Feeling scandalized, but deliciously so, she slowly rose from the bench.

He came forward to meet her, stopping when they stood less than a foot apart and her forehead was level with his chin. Which put her vision in line with the faint pulse that fluttered in the hollow at the base of his throat and the crisp dark hairs that showed in the vee of his shirt that was gaping just enough that she could almost—

"Kiss me, Ed."

Her gaze flew up. "K-Kiss you? Here? Now?" She glanced at the men bent over the checkerboard, then back to his smiling mouth, where the tips of white teeth showed behind lips that moved to form a word she scarcely heard until it was repeated again louder.

"Now, Ed."

"But someone will see us."

"Then they'll have something to gossip about, won't they? Kiss me."

She stared at his lips. Dare she? Perhaps a quick "thank you" kiss. That's all. No more.

Astounded by her own audacity, she rose on tiptoe, lifted her face, and pressed her mouth to his. It was startling and electrifying and—

Shocked, she jerked back. "Was that . . . did you just put your tongue in my mouth?"

Laughter rumbled out on a rush of warm breath that fluttered her eyelashes and tickled her cheek. She smelled coffee. Barber's talc. Declan.

Imaginings of "later" suddenly filled her mind.

She stepped back, her knees wobbling beneath her. It was too much. Too fast. She felt so off balance and out of breath she thought if she didn't sit down, she might faint.

Instead, she fled. "Pru and I will see you later," she called back as she hopped off the boardwalk and into the street, barely missing a well-seasoned pile of droppings. "Eight o'clock sharp in the lobby."

She refrained from running. But just as she reached the boardwalk on the other side of the street, she paused and glanced back.

He was standing where she'd left him, his weight on one hip, his hands low on his hips. Watching her. And smiling.

Which made her smile.

ELEVEN

By eight o'clock, Edwina had received enough instruction to fill a book. How to flirt. How to charm. How to bring Declan to his knees in quivering lust. A horrifying image. Maddie's, of course. For a proper Englishwoman, she had a rather unfettered imagination. No doubt the artist in her. Angus must have been a cold stick, indeed, to walk away from such a lovely and lively woman.

But it wasn't lust Edwina wanted to inspire. And she certainly didn't need instruction in flirting; that was something at which she heartily excelled. Instead, her apprehensions all centered on what came *after* the flirting. That "later" part Declan had alluded to.

And yet . . .

Sometimes when she looked at her husband, or

242

when he looked at her, the air all around them seemed to grow so thin she felt like she was floating above the ground in a whirlwind of confused emotion and tingling nerves and unformed wants. That was the part she didn't understand. The part that both terrified her and pulled her closer, until sometimes just standing beside Declan made her chest hurt and her throat so tight she could scarcely swallow.

It was absurd, really. She was far too old for such adolescent foolishness. She had certainly never felt that with Shelly or any of her other youthful beaux. And it didn't seem entirely proper that she should feel it so strongly for Declan, who was almost a stranger despite being her husband.

And yet, sometimes when she looked at him . . .

"He's here," Lucinda said from the window, jarring Edwina's thoughts back on track. "And looking quite smart. Are you ready?"

For what? But if there was one thing Edwina Ladoux Brodie did especially well, it was masking her fears behind a pleasant smile, which she did now. "Yes, I'm ready."

"Put this on."

Standing patiently, she allowed Maddie to drape her shoulders with Lucinda's merino shawl with its delicate fringe—which they had all decided was the perfect complement to her cornflower blue dress with the white trim and scalloped hem—which was the perfect complement to the ribbon Declan had given her—which had taken an hour and three pairs of hands to weave through the elaborate curls gathered at the back of her neck.

She took a deep breath and let it out, wishing Pru was still there. But Thomas had come by an hour earlier to take her to Declan's house to watch the children, which had sent her reserved sister into such heights of delight she had almost dithered. Edwina wondered if she'd recovered enough yet to utter a word to her stoic escort.

"You don't think he'll mind taking all of us?" Maddie asked, throwing a short caped jacket over her own shoulders. "I would hate to intrude."

"You're dying to intrude," Lucinda argued, waving them into the hallway. "You can't wait to see his face when he sees Edwina."

In better times, Edwina had worn gowns of lace and satin and brocade. She had adorned herself with costly jewels, rather than a single tiny garnet ring that had once belonged to her grandmother. She had walked down elegant staircases under fine crystal chandeliers that shimmered with the glittering light of dozens of candles. Yet now, as she descended the uncarpeted staircase of the rustic Heartbreak Creek Hotel, dressed in an out-dated frock and a borrowed shawl and wearing a simple ribbon in her hair, she felt as shaky and breathless as a debutant headed to her first ball.

Declan stood in the lobby, hat in hand, looking broad and solid in his slightly worn black suit and stiff shirt with its high, banded collar that fit too snugly around his thick neck. She couldn't see his expression because he was looking down at the long fingers playing over the brim of the Stetson he was gripping in both hands. His dark, damp hair caught the light from the sconces, showing glints of red and gold and deep shiny black, and already it was starting to slide down over his forehead as it dried. He muttered something, then shifted his weight from one foot to the other and sighed so deeply she could hear his exhale from the top landing.

My husband, she thought.

The idea of that—of him—of his not knowing how to dance but still taking her to this shivaree —made her smile.

"Good evening, Declan," she called to him.

His head came up. For a moment, he went utterly still. Then as she started down toward him, his lips parted on a deep breath. He didn't smile, nor did his expression betray his thoughts, but she saw his big hands tighten on the hat brim until the edge curled in his fingers.

"Ed," he said.

That's all. Just Ed. But hearing it spoken in his deep voice, and feeling the impact of that dark, unwavering stare made her feel more beautiful than she ever had.

• • •

It was like herding turtles, Declan decided, as he steered the women down the boardwalk at such a leisurely pace he had to clench his jaw to keep from yelling at them to "git along now" like he did with laggard calves.

It was also disconcerting the way people looked at them as they sashayed by. Declan "Big Bob" Brodie—the notorious ex-sheriff who had banished his wife to a horrible death at the hands of savages—ushering three beauties dressed in their Sunday best to the social event of the spring.

He was in high cotton, for sure. And hated every minute of it.

Glowering at a drunk gawking at the women from an alleyway, he wondered why he had let Ed push him into this. He wasn't a dancer, didn't dare drink with three women to nursemaid, and even though they were still a block away, he could already sense the whispers and speculations and sly glances headed their way. *Hell.*

He ran a finger between his sweating neck and his too-tight collar and wished he'd sent the boys into town to sell the cattle without him.

In an effort to stave off impatience, he studied the women walking ahead of him. Ed was the prettiest, even from the back, and especially in that blue dress that matched her lively eyes and with his ribbon wound through her glossy light brown curls. He had debated buying it and had hesitated giving it to her, not sure what she would make of it. But now he was glad he had. Whether it was the ribbon, or the dress, or her own vibrant self, she looked extra pretty this evening.

They were all lookers. Well-featured women, with trim waists and straight backs and rounded hips that moved side to side with each measured step. Ed's moved more than the others, probably because her back was longest. Or maybe because she had a perkier stride, coming off her heel with a little bounce before she stepped forward onto her other foot. No toe-dragger, his Ed, but a woman who led with her chin, like she was pushing against an invisible barrier and was chomping at the bit to get through it.

His Ed. When had he started thinking of her as "his"?

A voice called his name, and he turned to see Emmet Gebbers angling across the street toward him, his sad-eyed wife clinging to his arm and struggling to keep up.

Emmet was both the banker and the mayor of Heartbreak Creek. He and Mrs. Gebbers had always treated Declan fairly, even when all the talk started. Probably because they had lost two sons in the war and still carried that grief in their eyes. Slowing from his turtle pace to a full stop, Declan touched two fingertips to the brim of his hat. "Mrs. Gebbers. Emmet."

Emmet puffed up like he did whenever he was

around Declan, as if that might lessen the substantial gap in their heights. "Declan."

Mrs. Gebbers gave him that soft smile that had probably marked her as a beauty thirty years earlier. Now she just looked tired and a little broken. "Mr. Brodie," she murmured.

The other three women turned back, smiling expectantly at the newcomers. Declan introduced them to the elderly couple, then watched Ed hook them with her smile and reel them in with a healthy dose of southern charm. He almost laughed, wondering if they would be quite so taken with his gracious, soft-spoken wife if they knew she had threatened him with a pitchfork.

After a few pleasantries about the fine weather and the shivaree they were attending, they continued on together, the four women in the lead, the men following along in their wake. Aware of Emmet beside him, Declan tried not to watch Ed's butt too much.

"Glad you're here, Declan," the older man said after they'd walked a stretch. The banker-mayor was one of the few who used his given name rather than Big Bob, which Declan appreciated. "With Tom Hamilton leaving, we're out a sheriff."

The collar seemed to tighten around Declan's neck.

"You interested?"

"No."

"I know things were a little rough when you

248

left," Emmet rushed on. "But most folks have put all that behind them. Water under the bridge."

Declan didn't respond.

"You were a good lawman, Declan. And if the railroads decide to reroute through Heartbreak Creek, we'll need a good lawman again."

Declan watched the sway of Ed's hips and thought about Sally, and the ugliness of the past, and wondered how his hot-spirited wife would have reacted to some of the things that had been said about him back then—and some of the things that might yet be said about him tonight. "I'm a rancher now, Emmet."

"You were a sheriff, too."

"I've got kids. A new life." *A new wife.*

"Think about it. That's all I ask. And I'm not the only one asking. Aaron Krigbaum—you remember him, he owns the mine—he's concerned, too. With the ore giving out, he's having to let men go, and they're starting to grumble. He'd like someone around to keep an eye on them so they don't damage any equipment on their way out."

Declan barely remembered Krigbaum. When he'd been sheriff before, the mine had been a lot busier and Krigbaum had stayed pretty much either up at the mine office or at home. The Krigbaums weren't a particularly social couple.

"Just think about it," Emmet pressed.

"All right. But don't hold your breath."

The party was already in full swing when they arrived. Not the usual old-fashioned shivaree with all the noise and revelry of a rowdy send-off for the newly wedded couple, but more like a combination good-bye gathering and wedding dinner, with food and music and dancing, as well as punch for the ladies and enough free-flowing whiskey behind the smithy's shop to keep the men from running off home the first chance they got. The music was lively, the musicians more enthusiastic than talented. The piano player and his piano had been brought down from the Red Eye Saloon and were joined by a fiddler, a harmonica player with a tambourine, a man with a washboard, and another who beat a tempo on a collection of overturned buckets. More noise than tune, but everyone seemed to enjoy it.

It didn't take long for their group to attract notice. Even as Declan herded the ladies toward the food table, glances were shifting from him to Ed and whispers were starting. He was accustomed to it, but he regretted that he hadn't warned his wife that not everybody would be in a welcoming mood. Especially Alice Waltham, who was marching toward them, her mouth pursed so tight it looked like a drawstring pouch.

Hoping to shield Ed, Declan stepped forward.

But Lucinda Hathaway and the Englishwoman flew past him like swooping hawks. "Why, Alice Waltham!" Lucinda Hathaway cried, hooking the other woman's pudgy arm and neatly spinning her around and away from Ed. "What a beautiful dress!"

"French, I'll warrant." Maddie Wallace took her other arm. "I'm so parched, aren't you? Do let's have some punch, and you can tell us which fashion house you favor. New York or Paris? I do so hope you'll let me take your photograph for my collection." And before Alice seemed aware of it, they had steered her halfway across the room.

Which opened the path to all the men who'd been eyeing Ed.

And that's when Declan's real misery started.

It rankled that even with him standing guard, every man still on his feet thought he had a right to ask his wife to dance. And it rankled even more that his wife seemed so delighted to accept. In morose silence he watched her charm the townsfolk who had been so quick to think the worst of him a few years ago. *People. Hell.*

After an hour of kicking up her heels, she finally came back to him, her face flushed, her curls coming loose and sticking damply to the back of her slender neck, and her blue eyes dancing with life.

"Oh, Declan," she said breathlessly, grabbing his forearm with both hands. "Isn't it grand? I declare, if it got any better I'd have to hire someone to help me enjoy it. My feet are in agony."

"We can go if you'd like," he offered hopefully.

"Don't be silly. You haven't danced with me yet."

"I don't dance."

Her grin turned wicked. "You will."

"I won't."

"Stubborn as a blue-nose mule." She looked past him, then stiffened, her nails biting through his suit and shirt and into his arm. "Oh, no!"

"What?" He jerked around, half expecting to see a war party bearing down on them. "What's wrong?"

"He's coming over here."

"Who?"

"That stinky man." Suddenly all aflutter, she grabbed his other arm and yanked him around to face her. "Quick. Dance with me."

"I told you I don't dance."

"You have to! He smells horrid. And look." Releasing his arms, she thrust her hands into his face. The gloved palms were damp and grimy and smelled faintly of . . . wet dog? "He's filthy. Now hurry before he gets here."

"I don't dance."

"Pretend, for mercy's sake!" Grabbing his right hand, she slapped it onto her left hip, then gripped his left hand in her right, and thrust it out as far as her shorter arm would allow. "Just stand there and sway. Dancing isn't that complicated."

He looked down at her, trapped by those blue

252

eyes and the feel of her hip beneath his hand. "I know."

"What?" She drew back. "You know?"

"I do." And before she could cut loose at him, he wrapped his right arm around her back and pulled her so close he could smell her flowery scent and feel the heat of her body from his belt buckle to his chest. "Hold on," he said and, grinning down into her surprised face, took the first step.

And suddenly Edwina was flying in a whirling, sweeping waltz, around and around, dip and turn, until she felt like her feet were floating above the ground, and all that bound her to the earth was his strong arm around her waist and his dark eyes smiling down at her.

It was heaven. It was the best of the past come alive again. It was youth and joy. It was wonderful.

When the music finally slowed, she settled back to the earth, breathless and grinning and wishing it could go on forever.

"You said you couldn't dance," she accused as she struggled to catch her breath.

"No, I said I *didn't* dance."

"Why not?"

"I look like a circus bear."

"You silly man. You're anything but a circus bear."

Some of the amusement left his eyes as he looked around. "I doubt they think so."

She pivoted to follow his gaze and saw the faces staring back at them. Some in envy. Some in derision. Most in amusement.

"I don't like making a spectacle of myself," he muttered, a red stain inching up his neck. "Or you."

She couldn't help but laugh. "Oh, Declan, sometimes you're so sweet I could just eat you up with a spoon." And to prove it, she rose on tiptoe and planted a quick kiss on his cheek, which brought a chuckle from the nearest gawkers, and a deeper flush to his face. Turning, she waved past the staring townspeople to the piano player and the ragtag musicians gathered around him. "Another waltz," she called gaily. "I want to dance with my husband."

"You're pushing your luck."

She laughed. "But, Declan, it's so much fun."

He wasn't sure if she meant dancing was so much fun or goading him into doing it was. Either way, he couldn't resist the teasing challenge in her lively blue eyes. At that moment, he would do near anything she wanted.

"I warned you," he murmured against her rose-scented hair. And anchoring her in his arms, they danced. Around and around, clearing the other dancers out of their way with their exuberance, bobbing and dipping and twirling to the rhythmic clapping of the watchers. Until she was panting, and even Declan was out of breath.

Until all the gawking faces were forgotten, and it was just the two of them holding on to each other as they twirled around and around.

Until a scream cut through the magic, and a blood-drenched man with a wooden leg and an arrow sticking out of his back staggered into the light and collapsed at their feet.

Declan stumbled to a stop, instinctively clutching Ed tight to his chest.

Then a man shouted, "Good God, that's Chick! Indians got Chick!"

And instantly Declan's experience snapped him into action. Spinning Ed around, he pointed her toward Lucinda and Maddie. "Go to the hotel. Lock the door and don't open it to anyone but me or Thomas."

"What about Pru and the children?"

"I'll get them. Go. Now!"

Bending over Chick, he began issuing orders. "Send for Doc Boyce," he told one man. "You," he said to another. "Get the women out of here. Hamilton, have the men who can shoot get rifles and meet outside the bank. The rest of you, barricade yourselves inside until we know what's going on."

People scattered in a rush. Shouts echoed along the canyon walls. Horses ran past, buggy wheels kicking up dust.

Doc ran up, his black satchel in his hand. Shoving Declan aside, he rolled Chick onto his side and cut open the shirt to reveal that the arrow had passed through Chick's back to emerge just under his collarbone in front. Both wounds were starting to clot, which Declan took as a good sign.

"Chick," he said, trying to distract the boy from what Doc was doing. "What happened? Who did this?"

"L-Left me for d-dead." The cowboy's voice was a wobbly rasp. His eyes rolled in their sockets. "Tore up the p-place. Looking for you. Oh!" His body twisted, his spine arching as Doc probed the entrance wound on his back. "Sweet Jesus, take me now!"

"Quit whining," Doc ordered. "You're not dying. You," he called to two men grabbing food off the table, "stop stuffing your faces and come carry this man to my office."

"Who?" Declan prodded as the men came to lift Chick to his feet. "Who was looking for me?"

"T-Tall. Busted nose. A-Arapaho. Holy Christ that hurts!"

Lone Tree.

Heart pounding, Declan shot to his feet. He spun, looking for a horse, didn't see one, and started to run.

Edwina stopped pacing and stared at the closed door, willing it to fly open and for Declan and Pru and the children to come bursting inside.

It didn't.

She resumed pacing. "They should be here by now, shouldn't they? It's been hours."

"It's been less than fifty minutes," Lucinda reminded her, looking serene and composed in her chair opposite Maddie by the window, the only sign of her agitation being the way her fingers traced and retraced the seam on the grip of the tiny four-barreled pepperbox pistol resting in her lap.

"I should have gone to his house to help with the children."

"You don't know where his house is," Maddie pointed out.

"I could have asked."

"He told you to come here." Lucinda's tone was edged with impatience. "And here is where he'll come when all is safe."

"I'm sure everything is fine," Maddie soothed. "But I do wish you'd stop waving that huge pistol about, Edwina. It isn't loaded, is it?"

"Of course it's loaded. What good would it do if it weren't loaded?" As soon as the words were out, Edwina wanted them back. Stopping mid-stride, she gave Maddie an apologetic look. "I'm sorry, Maddie. I didn't mean to snap at you. I'm just so worried."

"I know, dear."

Edwina counted fifteen steps to the far wall, turned, and counted fifteen steps back. *Two more laps and I'm going after them, by God.*

"I prefer scatterguns myself," Maddie said. "Angus took me grouse hunting once. I didn't hit anything, of course. Well, really, how could I? They're so pretty."

Edwina made another circuit, then paused to check the day clock on the bureau. Two more minutes gone.

"He was an excellent shot, though. As a soldier should be, I suppose. He was a Rifleman with the Royal Green Jackets of the Light Division. A forward rider, which is very dangerous. Then he transferred to the Tenth Hussars. They're cavalry and have the loveliest blue uniforms. I believe they use sabers as well as guns. Perhaps I should order one to keep in my gypsy wagon."

"A soldier?" Lucinda quipped.

Maddie's laugh sounded a bit forced. "A scatter-gun. What do you think, Edwina?"

Edwina thought she might scream.

Lucinda sighed. "Oh, do stop pacing, Edwina. This carpet is new and I'd hate to see a path worn in it so soon."

Edwina opened her mouth to argue, then froze when she heard a footstep in the hall. She leaped into motion, following the plan they had made. Frantically waving for silence, she motioned for Maddie and her umbrella to take a position on one side of the door, while Lucinda took the other, pistol at the ready. She moved to stand in front of it, the pistol clutched in her hand.

They waited.

Visions of creeping Indians filled Edwina's mind. More footsteps. Muffled voices.

Edwina's heart pounded so loud she almost missed the knock. Thumbing back the hammer of her father's Colt Army pistol, she rested her finger alongside the trigger guard, then nodded to Maddie to open the door.

As soon as she turned the knob, people burst into the room, almost knocking her off her feet. Declan, Pru, the children, and three other men crowding the hallway.

"Ed?" Declan shouted, shoving past the others.

"Here." On shaky legs, Edwina moved forward.

Relief flashed across his face, then faded when his gaze dropped to the pistol aimed at his chest. His hand shot out. In a single motion, he grabbed the barrel, shoved it toward the ceiling, and jerked the gun from her grip. "Good God." Then he saw the palm pistol in Lucinda's hand and the umbrella still clutched in Maddie's, and said it again.

Laughing and crying, Edwina bobbed up and down, trying to hug one elusive child, then Pru, then another child, then Pru again, until finally Declan pulled her to him. "Are you all right?"

She blinked up at him, steadied by the strong hands gripping her shoulders, wanting to hug him, shake him, burrow into his chest and be safe forever. "Y-Yes."

"Then why are you crying?" Brin asked at her elbow.

Swiping the back of her hand over her watering eyes, Edwina smiled down into the dirty face that stole a little more of her heart every day. "Because Pru is safe, and you and your brothers are safe, and your papa is safe and because I was so worried that—"

"Got anything to eat?" Joe Bill cut in. "Pa said he would bring something back, but he didn't, and my stomach is starting to suck on my backbone."

It was late. Thanks to the Hathaway woman, his children had been fed and were now settled in a three-room suite, the boys in one bedroom, Ed and Prudence and Brin in the other, while Amos sat guard in the connecting sitting room, his rifle loaded and ready.

It was past midnight when Declan returned to relieve him. After assuring him that Chick would recover, he sent him downstairs to join the Parker ranch hands who were watching the entrances to the hotel, then locked the door behind him.

This suite had no balcony, but Declan made certain the sitting room window was securely locked, then pushed back the curtains. No moon, and only a few stars. Maybe that was good. Maybe not.

Not wanting to make himself an easy target in a lit room, he turned down the lamp as far as it would go, which left just enough light for him to see what he was doing. Then positioning one of the chairs so he could see both the window and the door, he settled in to wait out the night, one rifle resting across the armrests, another propped against the windowsill, and two handguns loaded and ready on the chair table. With a weary sigh, he rotated the kinks out of his neck and shoulders.

He'd been gone most of the evening, walking through the town with Tom Hamilton—the new groom and soon-to-be ex-sheriff—making sure shooters were on the roofs behind the storefronts and lookouts were posted at strategic points in and out of town.

No one knew what to expect, or if the raid at his ranch had been an isolated incident or the beginning of a full Indian uprising. Tom had telegraphed the sheriff in Thomsonville, the nearest town, and Fort Lasswell, which was a day away, but neither place had reported problems. So for now, all they could do was be ready for anything. Hopefully, when Thomas came back from his scouting foray, they would know what they were up against. Then maybe Declan could figure out what to do next.

He didn't want the sheriff's job, but he couldn't take the family home to the ranch as long as Lone Tree was running loose. They wouldn't be safe out there so far from help. Assuming he had a home to go back to. Chick had said they'd torn up the place, which probably meant they'd slaughtered what they could and burned what was left. He'd know how bad it was when Thomas got back. But he sure hated the waiting.

Beyond the window, stars disappeared one by one as a cloud bank moved over the peaks. The air felt heavy and tasted of rain. Small, sharp bursts of light flashed between the clouds.

Slumping back, he stretched out his legs and wiggled his toes, smiling at the faint soreness along the bottoms of his feet.

Dancing. How many years since he'd done that?

Sally had been a tiny little thing and, because of their height difference, hadn't liked dancing with him. Said it was like being dragged around by a carnival bear.

But Ed didn't seem to mind. In fact, if her grin was any indication, she actually enjoyed dancing with him. But then, his energetic wife seemed to find enjoyment in most everything. And she never went at anything in half measures, either, whether she was threatening him with a pitchfork, or trying to manner his unruly kids, or dancing under the stars in a crusty little mining town. It drew people in, those high spirits. As if her exuberance might rub off on a person if he stood close enough, making him feel a little less lonely, a little less weary, a little less burdened. It worked that way with him, anyway. He just hoped those high spirits extended into the bedroom. Now that would be a treat, for sure. He smiled, thinking about it.

"What are you grinning about?" a voice whispered.

He almost jumped from the chair. Jerking the rifle up, he whipped around to see a ghostly white figure floating toward him. "Ed?"

"I didn't hear you come in."

Christamighty. Letting out an explosive breath, he slumped back into the chair. "You scared the bejesus out of me."

"Oh, I doubt that. I suspect you have plenty bejesus left."

As she drew closer into the faint lamplight, he saw she wore a white robe that didn't reach to her ankles and her feet were bare. Her hair was loose, hanging in dark waves down her front, hiding from his wandering gaze those attributes she was so worried about. Just thinking about them perked him up. "What are you doing up so late?" he asked her.

"Looking for paper." She sank into the chair across from his, fluffing out the robe and carefully arranging it so that everything of interest was discreetly covered. "I wanted to make a list."

He propped the rifle against the side of his chair, then settled back into the cushions. Her face was a pale oval in the dim light. He couldn't read her expression. "What kind of list?"

"I have questions. But now that you're back, I'll just ask you."

Not liking the sound of that, he tried to head her off. "Save it for morning. You should get some rest."

"Who is Lone Tree?"

Hell. Thunder thumped in the distance, a single, muffled sound, like a shoe dropping on the floor above. "Who said anything about Lone Tree?"

"Pru. She heard you and Thomas talking. Why is he after you?"

"I put him in jail once."

"Why?"

"For fighting." He could feel her impatience, heard it in the rhythmic tap of her fingers on the arm of her chair, and knew she would keep at him until she heard it all. "He has an aversion to closed spaces. I didn't know that when I locked him in his cell." Having his own demons to contend with, Declan would have devised a more humane punishment had he known. "He went a little crazy." More than a little crazy. Wild. Like an animal. Howling. Pounding on the walls until his hands bled. Crouching in the corner, shivering and weeping and wetting himself. Declan had never seen anything like it. He just prayed nothing like that ever happened to him. "He wouldn't eat or drink. Didn't sleep."

"What happened?"

"The circuit judge sentenced him to ten days. When I saw how hard it was on him, I shortened it to five. But he didn't come out the same as he went in. During those five days, something broke in his head. He blames me for it."

More lightning. Thunder. Wind rattling the windowpane like a cat trying to get in. He thought of Lone Tree out there waiting for his chance and hoped the rain would keep him hunkered down for the night.

"So now he wants revenge?"

Declan nodded. "But it should be the other way around. I think he's the one who killed my wife."

A sound escaped her. A sigh of sympathy, maybe—for him or Sally—he wasn't sure which. But she didn't speak, and for that he was grateful. It didn't seem right talking to Ed about his first wife. Maybe because his feelings about Sally—their life together, his guilt, her death—were so confused he still hadn't sorted them out.

"Are the children in danger?"

"I'll protect them. And you. I swear it."

"I know." She smiled. He couldn't see it, but he heard it in her voice. Felt it like a hand against his cheek. "I trust you, Declan."

Hearing that, something cracked inside him, a tiny fissure that spread through him so fast it reached every part of him in an instant.

He almost went to her then. Desperate to be inside her. Now. Here on the soft carpet with her eyes wide open, so he could see into her mind when he took her, and hear her say his name, and feel her spirit wrap so tight around him the ghosts of the past couldn't find a way in.

Instead, he turned to the window and the darkness beyond, where thunder rumbled, and rain danced against the glass, and a wet, red dawn spilled like blood over the bared teeth of the peaks.

Later.

Lone Tree didn't come that night. Or the next day.

But Thomas did. And he brought more bad news than good.

Declan's house was still standing. The barn had been set afire, but the roof had burned first, then caved, allowing enough rain in to keep the rest of the structure from burning completely. The milk cow and chickens were dead. The supplies in the cold cellar had either been taken or destroyed. Cattle had been run through the kitchen door, then slaughtered when they tried to escape out the back. In addition to the damage they caused, the house had been ransacked.

It could have been worse.

But not for Jubal Parker. He and his wife were dead, their house reduced to a smoldering framework, their livestock slaughtered.

The message was clear: Lone Tree wanted Declan home. That's why he had left his house standing, so that he would have something to come back to. And when he did, the Indian would be there waiting. Which left Declan with no choice but to take the sheriff's job and stay in town where his family would be safe.

Hell and damnation.

TWELVE

The next morning, after arranging for the ladies and the two younger children to continue staying at the hotel, Declan, the oldest boys, Thomas, Amos, and the Parker ranch hands moved into Declan's house on Elderberry Creek and started the renovations necessary to make it livable. He didn't expect it to take long with so many able hands to share the task, especially when several townspeople pitched in, too. Others donated pieces of furniture and kitchen supplies, and Emmet Gebbers arranged through the bank for building materials so Declan could add on a room for the boys and convert the small carriage house into a usable stable. Even Cal Bagley, apparently anxious to show Declan there were no hard feelings, helped out by forking up a box of foodstuffs to fill the pantry.

Meanwhile, Edwina and Maddie put their talents to work making quilts out of the discarded curtains from the hotel and patching old linens to use as bedding. Pru helped in the hotel kitchen and with supplies donated by

Lucinda provided hearty meals for all of them.

Thank goodness for kind friends and generous neighbors.

Throughout the busy week, Declan insisted to anyone who came by that he was only taking the sheriff job temporarily, and as soon as the Indian issue was settled, he'd go back to ranching. Nobody seemed to believe him. Edwina was gratified by the outpouring of support, and although her husband tolerated the help with good grace, she sensed he hated to accept charity, especially from people who had been so quick to misjudge him in the past.

Only a few continued to hold him in suspicion, the most flagrant being Alice Waltham. Her animosity even carried over to Edwina, as the "usurper" of her friend's children. Despite the woman's determination to spread gossip wherever she could, most of the townspeople took little note of it, so Edwina held on to her temper and continued to smile and pretend it didn't matter. But she resolved that as soon as the family settled into the refurbished house, she would confront the woman and set her straight about Declan.

On a cool, overcast morning several days after the shivaree, Tom Hamilton and his new wife left to catch the train to Santa Fe, and that afternoon, in the back room of the sheriff's office, Mayor Gebbers swore Declan in as Heartbreak Creek's new "temporary" lawman.

The first thing Declan did after pinning on the badge was to name Thomas his "temporary" deputy. The second was to wire Fort Lasswell and ask what they intended to do about the Indian unrest in the area.

"Inquiries," he told Thomas with a sly grin, "always sound more official when there's a title attached to the inquirer's name."

An hour later, word came that Lieutenant Haywood Guthrie and a dozen mounted troopers would be arriving in Heartbreak Creek in a couple of days to assess the situation.

"Now maybe we'll catch the bastard and I can get back to ranching," Declan muttered to Thomas as they left the telegraph office and headed down the boardwalk.

"An hour as sheriff, and already you talk of leaving," Thomas observed.

"I didn't ask for the job."

"And yet you took it."

"As did you."

Thomas turned his head and looked at him, his expression bland. "I said I would stay until Lone Tree is stopped. If this piece of metal on my shirt will make that easier, then I will wear it. If," he added with a wry smile, "your fine white friends let me."

"If they want me as sheriff, they'll let you."

Even though Declan expected a few raised brows over his naming an Indian his deputy, he hoped that since Thomas had become such a frequent sight around town, it wouldn't cause too big a stir. It probably helped that Thomas had started dressing in real trousers, rather than a breechcloth and open-hipped leggings, and had traded his fringed leather war shirt for a cowboy work shirt with a banded collar. He still wore his front braids, but now pulled back with the rest of his long hair and tied with a leather thong from which hung his eagle feather. Thomas referred to his new look as being "whitewashed." Even so, he cut quite a figure, and Declan had seen more than one woman eyeing him as he walked by.

"You will go with the blue coats to your ranch?" Thomas asked now as they headed back to the office.

"I need to see what's left and check on the stock."

"You will take the women and your children with you?"

"The oldest two. Miss Lincoln will stay here with Brin and Lucas." Declan shot the Cheyenne an amused look. "Which probably means you'll be staying, too."

"As deputy, it is my duty to stay when the sheriff leaves."

"Sure it is."

Two ladies came out of the mercantile. They nodded politely, their gazes flicking between the two men, then going wide when Thomas flashed his startling grin. Another thing that boosted his acceptance. Having no wish to stop and chat, Declan touched the brim of his hat and walked on.

"And your wife? Will she be staying, too?"

A wagon rolled by, kicking up tiny breaths of dust behind the wheels. Declan gave the driver a nod even though he couldn't remember his name. Henson? Hendrick? A miner. Son with a squint. "She said there were some clothes she needed to get. And she wants to see if there's anything left we can use to fix this place up." He hoped that would be enough explanation for Thomas because that was all he was going to say.

Things with Ed became more confused every day. Which kept him thinking about her more than he should. And looking forward to her trips to the house to supervise him and see how the work was going. And wanting her in his bed.

She amused him. Kept him wondering. And ever since she'd mentioned consummation—did anyone even use that word anymore?—getting her under him was all he could think about. Hopefully, once he got her away from her friends and all the people who seemed to be crowding into their lives, they could address that issue again.

In private. In his oversized bed. With just enough moonlight streaming through the tall window to see those attributes she'd brought to his attention.

Later. Everything seemed to be waiting for later.

• • •

"You sure you don't mind staying behind?" Edwina asked as she buckled the strap on her valise.

The soldiers had arrived yesterday evening, and Declan had insisted they leave for the ranch this morning. She expected him to come pounding on the door any minute. The man had the patience of a five-year-old. A really big, really handsome five-year-old. Smiling, she pinned on her bonnet.

"Whatever," Pru said.

Confused by the tone of disinterest, Edwina studied her sister's form, silhouetted against the pink dawn as she stared out the hotel window. Throughout the bustle of trying to get the house ready, she had seen little of Pru, other than in the evenings when they were both too exhausted to do more than wash, change into their nightclothes, and fall into bed. Yet now, she sensed a widening of that awkward space that had lingered between them ever since Pru had told her about Shelly's proclivities.

"It should be no more than three days. And Thomas promised to take Brin and Lucas fishing every day, so you won't have to watch them constantly."

Turning back into the room, Pru tightened the sash on her robe with a quick, sharp jerk. "It doesn't matter."

Edwina frowned. Instead of being delighted that

she would have time with Thomas, Pru seemed unhappy at the prospect. Edgy. Almost angry.

"Why are you upset?"

"I'm not upset."

"Is it Thomas? Has he done something?"

Pru straightened the lamp on the table by the wingback, then went to stand at the window again.

"I thought you liked Thomas."

Her sister didn't respond.

"He certainly seems taken with you."

"Is he?" The tone was mocking.

Which confused Edwina even more. "I think so. Don't you?"

Pru gave a harsh, sharp bark of laughter and whipped around, her eyes snapping fire. "And what about this?" In a gesture so sudden and unexpected it sent Edwina back a step, she jerked aside the lapel of her robe to expose the fine web of pale scars that marred the darker skin across her right shoulder and down beneath the crocheted neckline of her gown. "Do you think if he saw this he would still be *taken?* I doubt it." Yanking the robe closed, she faced the window again, her back stiff, her arms folded tightly across her waist. "How could he?"

It was a moment before Edwina could respond. They never spoke of Pru's scars. Just seeing them made Edwina recoil. Not in disgust, but guilt. It was her fault her sister had been burned. It was her fault the jug of milk had spilled. But when

Pru had rushed in to take the blame as she so often did, Mama had whirled on her, the pot of scalding water clutched in her hand.

In the back of her mind, Edwina could still hear Pru's screams and her mother's shouts of fury. She could still feel the damp grit cutting into her palms and knees as she'd crawled across the wet floor toward her sister even as the blows had rained down on her back and head.

Mentally jerking her mind back from those horrid memories, she tried to keep her voice even. "Pru, it doesn't matter. You're a beautiful—"

Pru whirled on her, that beauty contorted into a snarling mask. "Of course it matters! It's always mattered! Every time I look in the mirror, it matters!"

"Pru, please . . . don't do this." *To yourself. To Thomas. To me.* Edwina felt like she was suffocating under the guilt of what she'd caused.

"Do what? Face the truth?" Pru swept a hand down her robed chest. "That no man could look at this and not be repulsed?"

"You're being unfair."

"Unfair!" Lifting her face to the ceiling, Pru laughed bitterly. "And what do you know about fair and unfair? You, who have everything."

Edwina flinched at her sister's words. Then indignation overcame shock. "Everything, Pru?" She marched toward her sister, chin jutting, hands fisted at her sides. "A mother who beat me? A father who allowed it? Two brothers dead before their time, and a husband who could hardly bear to touch me? Is that the *everything* you mean?"

"You have white skin. In this world that *is* everything."

"Good Lord! Is that what this is about? The color of my skin?"

"Yes. No." With a choked sound, Pru dropped her face into her hands. "I don't know."

Edwina's anger faded into confusion. What was really going on?

Thoroughly at a loss and not sure what else to do, she reached out and rested her hand on Pru's shoulder. "Pru?"

Beneath her palm, she felt the hitch in her sister's breathing and knew she was crying, and that scared her. Pru almost never cried. "What's wrong?"

The answer was a long time in coming. And when Pru finally spoke, there was a tone of hopelessness in her voice that Edwina had never heard before. "I just wanted . . . I hoped they wouldn't matter."

They? "You mean your scars? You think your scars will make a difference to Thomas?"

"They make a difference to me. Because of Thomas."

Edwina pulled her hand from her sister's shoulder, shocked that Pru would have these doubts, much less voice them. Her beautiful, brilliant, capable sister had always seemed impervious to the little insecurities and worries that plagued Edwina. Another illusion shattered.

With a sniffle, Pru dabbed at her eyes with the cuff of her robe. "I know. I'm being silly."

"Not at all." Edwina understood now why her sister was upset. She had fears about her own scars, which were minor in comparison to Pru's. "Have you seen Thomas's chest?"

"Of course not. Have you?"

"No, but he's a Cheyenne Dog Soldier, isn't he? Surely he participated in that Indian sun dance ceremony." Edwina shuddered, just thinking about it . . . piercing their chests with sticks attached by leather strips to a pole, then hanging there until the weight of their own bodies ripped their flesh free. She'd read it could take days. "The scarring would be immense, I'd think. So why would he be repulsed by yours?"

"They repulse me. Why not him?" Pru fussed with her robe and retied the sash. "Just the thought of him seeing . . . I couldn't bear it."

Ah . . . vanity. Edwina understood it well, having suffered her fair share of that vice and all the fears that came along with it. How gratifying to know that her perfect sister had her worries, too. "I know what you mean," she murmured in sympathy. "I was worried about my flat bosom, too. But when I asked Declan about it, he said it didn't matter."

Pru looked up. "You discussed your bosom with Mr. Brodie?"

"Of course I did. If it was going to upset him that they weren't pointy, I needed to know before we . . . you know."

Pru clapped a hand over her mouth.

"Oh, don't be a prude." Waving an airy hand, Edwina walked back to the bed and the valise waiting on top of it. "Just talk to Thomas. I think you'll find the scars will make no difference to him whatsoever."

Pru took her hand away. But her eyes still showed her shock. "Mercy. I could never be so bold."

Footsteps sounded in the hall. Heavy footsteps, from a big man.

Edwina picked up her valise. She studied her sister. "You're right. He's probably not worth it."

"I didn't say that."

"No? Then you admit he is worth it?"

"I didn't say that, either."

Edwina reached the door just as a knock sounded. "Good-bye, Pru. I'll see you in a few days." She turned the knob, then paused to send her sister a teasing grin. "And hopefully when I return we'll both have news to share."

They traveled fast, everyone on horseback except for Edwina and Amos, who rode in the wagon. Unloaded, the ill-sprung buckboard bounced over the rocky road, and Edwina had to grip the arm rail tightly to maintain her balance. Hopefully on the way back it would ride easier, loaded down with items salvaged from the ransacked ranch house. If not, she was determined to ride horseback, rather than spend another day tossed about in this bone-jarring conveyance.

When they crossed Satan's Backbone, the sun hung high overhead and as soon as they cleared the trees and rolled into the home valley, the sickly sweet stench of putrefying flesh rose on the warming air. Edwina swallowed hard and pressed a handkerchief to her nose and mouth, but it didn't help much. Except for dark-winged shadows circling in the sky, the ranch buildings stood stark and lifeless on the horizon . . . until they drew closer. Then as they approached, more shadows flew up from the bloated, half-eaten carcasses of arrow-riddled cattle, and gore-spattered coyotes slinked into the brush.

Declan rode on ahead of the soldiers, his expression grim.

Suddenly dizzy, Edwina closed her eyes as her mind spun back to the night the Yankees came through Rose Hill, leaving death in their wake.

Gunshots, screams. Black, greasy smoke coating her throat, burning in her eyes. Mama laughing as blood dripped down the steps. *Oh, Daddy.*

She pressed her lips tight to keep from gagging. "Ed? Ed, are you all right?"

Startled, Edwina opened her eyes to see that they'd stopped and Declan was standing beside the wagon, frowning up at her. Air rushed out of her. She sagged in relief. "Y-Yes. It's just the smell."

His fingers dug into her waist as he lifted her out of the wagon. The pain of it restored her balance, and by the time her toes touched the ground she was able to push those hated memories to the back of her mind.

"It'll get worse before it gets better," he said, watching two troopers lean into ropes as they dragged what was left of the milk cow away from the house. "We'll have to burn them. But once the smoke clears, it won't be so bad." He turned to Amos. "Help the boys collect the dead chickens, then load the wagon with firewood and take it to where the troopers are stacking the carcasses. I'd like to get the worst of it done by dark."

Amos nodded and walked toward the soot-streaked barn.

Lifting her valise from the back of the wagon, Declan motioned her toward the house. "Luckily, Lieutenant Guthrie and his men are helping. I don't know how we would have cleaned this up without them."

As they walked across the yard, Edwina felt again that odd sense of being pulled back into the past. Like Rose Hill, Declan's house had been spared the torch, but the wanton, purposeless destruction seemed almost worse. More than an insult. A violation.

The kitchen door gaped open, hanging by one hinge. The parlor door was out in the yard. All that remained of the settee and several other pieces of furniture was a half-burned pile of upholstery and splintered wood. As they walked past it, a gust of wind sent a tuft of singed cotton racing across the ground like a scurrying rodent.

"The kitchen is a mess." Declan stepped ahead of her over the threshold. "But Thomas said they didn't do much to the loft, so it's usable."

Edwina felt like weeping. Shards of broken crockery littered the floor. Cabinet doors were torn off. All the lovely linens had been pulled from the cabinet under the stairs and ripped to shreds. The table and chairs were no more than scraps of broken wood and the cook stove had been tipped on its side. Even canned goods had been attacked, their contents spattered across the counters and floor where the decaying food and cow dung drew swarms of flies that droned and circled in the fetid air.

She touched her husband's arm. "Declan, I'm so sorry." She had been here only a few weeks, but this house had begun to feel like home. Her home. How much worse it must be for the man who had labored to build it.

"I'll send the boys to help you after they move the firewood." He looked around, then his gaze found hers. "We'll fix this, Ed. I promise."

She forced a smile. "I know." She lifted her arms to unpin her bonnet, then froze at a scrabbling sound from one of the lower cabinets.

Declan heard it, too. "Probably a rat. Stay back." Pulling her behind him, he picked up a busted chair leg and advanced toward the cabinet.

The scrabbling became a whimper, then a whine. A filthy canine face appeared in the opening.

Declan lowered the chair leg. "Rusty?"

The dog, his coat matted and caked, crept tentatively from the cabinet. Then recognizing Declan, he lunged forward, whining and barking and flinging flour and bits of food from his furiously wagging tail.

Setting down her valise, Declan dropped to his knee amidst the broken crockery of his ruined kitchen and let the ecstatic dog lick his chin.

A simple thing. But it brought tears to Edwina's eyes. And as she watched the enthusiastic reunion between her husband and his dog, she knew that despite the destruction of their home, this family would be all right. Together they would clean what they could and rebuild the rest.

They would persevere.

Swiping away her tears, she rolled up her cuffs and set to work.

The afternoon passed in a haze of rage for Declan. The years he'd spent carving out a home in this wilderness, the endless backbreaking work. For nothing. *Christ*. He wanted to shout his fury into the coiling smoke that hung in the still air from the burning carcasses of his cattle.

It could have been worse, he told himself. But still, it was bad.

The well was fouled with dead chickens and had been used as a latrine. Until they could dig a new one, they would have to lug water from the creek and boil it for cooking and drinking. The barn they could repair, although not anytime soon. The house was salvageable, and by dusk, through the efforts of Ed, Amos, and the boys, the kitchen was fairly clean: the broken crockery gone, the smashed furniture carted to the burn pile, the food and dung scraped off the counters and floor. Luckily, most of the flies and stink had departed with the decaying food and manure. Declan righted the stove, boarded over the broken window to deter varmints, and re-hung the front and back doors. The cabinet doors would have to wait.

The loft wasn't so bad. Even though the log furniture had been defaced with war axes, and the window broken, the bedding was usable and the water closet appeared to be untouched.

It was dark when they finally stopped for the day, exhausted, filthy, and hungry. Luckily Ed had insisted they bring two boxes of canned goods from town, one of which Declan traded to the lieutenant for a share of the small buck a trooper had shot. Since he hadn't had time to check out the cook stove, Declan built a fire outside and they cooked their supper under the fading sky and upwind of the burning cattle carcasses.

It was a quiet meal. Even the boys were subdued, although they managed to pack away a substantial amount of food before turning their attention to working the crust out of Rusty's matted coat. Declan didn't eat much—the reek of rotting meat and singed fur pretty much dampened his appetite. Ed just picked at her food, her head nodding between bites.

Declan studied her across the campfire, admiring the way the flickering light played across her features, highlighting the rise in her top lip, the curve of her cheekbones, shining up through her long eyelashes to cast dark, spiky shadows under her brow. She was so weary she could scarcely keep her eyes open. He smiled, watching her try.

She'd worked like a demon all afternoon. Toting and carrying and sweeping and bossing Amos and the boys around like a regular tyrant. Guthrie's sergeant could take a lesson.

He watched her eyes drift closed and stay closed. "Ed."

When she didn't respond, he said it again, louder, which brought her drooping head up with a jerk.

"Go to bed."

She looked blankly at him, her gaze unfocused. "What?"

"I had Amos carry up wash water. Go on before it gets cold."

"But . . ." She glanced over at the darkened house, then back.

"R.D. and Joe Bill will walk with you." Declan would have done it himself, but he didn't trust himself not to climb into bed with her. She was obviously too tired for that. And he was too tired to do it right. Later.

"Boys, take Ed to the house."

R.D. folded his knife and rose.

"It's just over there," Joe Bill argued. "She can't get lost."

"Shut up and get up," R.D. ordered, jabbing a toe into his little brother's butt. "I'm tired."

"But where we going to sleep?"

"I left your bedrolls on the porch," Declan said. "We'll clean up the rest of the house tomorrow. Ed, wake up."

It took her a moment to get her bearings. With R.D.'s help, she got to her feet, then wobbled until she found her balance. A big yawn, a slurred "G'night, Declan," and she turned toward the house, steps dragging, shoulders slumped with weariness.

He watched her cross the yard, looking small and fragile between his rangy sons, and something soft and gentle whispered through his mind—not so much a thought, but a feeling—one he hadn't felt in so long he scarcely recognized it. Hope.

"Newly married?"

Startled from his fanciful notions, he looked over to see Lieutenant Guthrie settling onto the log Ed had vacated.

"Just over a month."

"Thought so." Guthrie pulled out a small tobacco pouch. After biting off a chunk, he jerked the drawstring closed and returned the pouch to his pocket. He chewed for a moment, then said, "She's got the look."

"The look?"

More chewing. The bulge in the soldier's cheek grew as spit softened the tobacco. "Like you could hand her a buffalo chip and tell her it was a biscuit and she'd believe you, just because you said so."

That image, interesting though it was, combined with the lingering stench of decaying meat soured Declan's stomach even more.

Guthrie rolled the tobacco to the other side of his mouth and commenced working it from that angle. "Southern, I'm guessing."

Declan nodded.

"My wife was southern. Scared of everything. Redskins, snakes, bugs, you name it." The soldier stared into the flames, squinting as the breeze gusted and sent smoke swirling into his face. "Went on a two-week patrol. When I got back, she was gone. Just up and left. Didn't have the heart for this country, I guess. Not like yours."

Declan felt an absurd swell of pride, as if his wife's courage was his doing. It bothered him, though, that this rough soldier had seen Ed's worth so quickly, when he was just now figuring it out.

A log shifted, sent sparks bursting into the air like frenzied fireflies. Declan eyed the man across the fire, thinking Guthrie looked a decade older than most junior officers he'd met. "Been a lieutenant long?"

"This time? Almost two years. Time before that, five." He gave a lopsided grin that showed tobacco-stained teeth. "Attitude unbecoming. It's the German in me. No tolerance for rank stupidity."

They sat in silence as the fire burned down from blue flames to red coals. Down the valley, a pack of coyotes howled their displeasure at the loss of their easy pickings. Off to the east, the cattle smoldered below a veil of smoke that cast a brownish haze over the rising moon.

"My thanks to you and your men for helping out today," Declan said after a while.

Guthrie nodded and sent a stream of tobacco juice into the coals where it hissed and sizzled into steam. "Seen a lot of Indian raids in my time. Some worse than others." He studied Declan, his cheek bunching as he chewed, his eyes reflecting the orange of the dying fire. "This one seems personal."

"It is." Declan explained about Lone Tree, his stint in jail, and the Arapaho's intent to kill him and his kin to salve his damaged honor. "Until he's stopped, I can't stay here and put my family at risk."

"We're to scout the Parker place," the soldier reminded him.

"All you'll find there is charred wood and two new graves."

"So I hear." Guthrie scratched his chin where an old scar showed pale in the dark stubble of his beard. "I guess, since there's nothing left to draw the Indians back to their place, I could leave some men here."

"I'd appreciate that."

"So ordered." Bracing his hands on his knees, the lieutenant pushed himself to his feet. "You want, I'll have my men dig you a new well. No telling what all those redskins dropped in there."

"Thanks."

"We leave at first light. Back the day after." He spit into the fire pit, nodded to Declan, then turned and walked into the darkness.

THIRTEEN

Declan sat for a moment longer, then rose and stretched the kinks out of his back. The moon had risen above the bands of smoke that hung in the air, and in the silvered light he could see the tents of the troopers lined up not far from the creek and a string of horses tied between two tall pines.

After pissing into the fire, he kicked dirt over what coals still lingered, then headed to the house, wondering where he'd sleep. What remained of the splintered settee had been added to the cattle pyre. He'd brought no bedroll, hoping he would be sleeping in his own bed, and anything left in the barn had burned. *Hell.*

He checked on the boys, found them sprawled on the porch, Rusty between them, all three snoring. Stepping over them, he picked up the saddlebags he'd left on the porch earlier and went inside.

Moonlight lit his way through the ransacked parlor and into the kitchen. He stopped at the foot of the stairs and listened. No sound from the loft. But he pictured her as she'd been that morning last month on the way to the ranch when he'd awakened her with a cup of coffee . . . curled on her side, clothes rumpled, straw tangled in her hair. He smiled, remembering how cantankerous she'd been, and wondered if she would be as upset with him now if he went up there and woke her up.

The idea of it made his heart thump in his chest. *Now's not the time,* he reminded himself. She was tired. He was tired. It would be better for both of them later.

He started up the stairs anyway, telling himself he was just checking that she was okay and to see if there was any water left so he could wash.

Moonlight shone through the shredded curtains on the broken loft window, sending long silvery tentacles across the plank floor to drape the bed in pale light and rounded shadow. She had kicked off the covers and was curled on the dark side of the bed, facing toward the door. She lay as he had pictured her, on her side, hands tucked under her cheek, knees drawn up. Except this time, instead of a rumpled dress, she wore a white gown that covered all but her hands and toes. Her braid had come loose and hair spilled over the pillow in soft waves and tangled curls. She breathed the deep, measured breaths of deep sleep.

He stood beside the bed, wondering at the impact this woman had already made on his life. He hadn't intended that. He'd just wanted a simple, uncomplicated woman to help with the chores and ride herd on his children. Not a companion, not even a lover, and especially not someone who befuddled him and made him laugh.

Instead, he got Edwina Ladoux. Miss Priss.

His Ed.

A sudden need to touch her almost overwhelmed him, and he had to clench his fist to keep from slipping his hand under that hem and running his fingers up her thigh. He wanted to taste her skin and feel her heat around him. He wanted to climb in beside her and wrap her hair around his hands and whisper in her ear that "later" had come.

Christ. He was acting like a green kid.

Turning away in disgust, he almost tripped over a mound of skirts and petticoats piled on the floor. He gathered them up and laid them over the foot rail, then without looking toward the bed, continued into the water closet.

Another petticoat. Hairpins. An underthing so sheer it hardly made a lump on the floor. He stared down at it, his heart thumping again.

Slowly he bent and picked it up.

Silky. Soft. Her scent still clung to it—something sweet and flowery. Roses, maybe. It looked ridiculously incongruous in his big hand and weighed no more than a breath. Carefully, he hung it on a hook, hung the petticoat beside it, then stood frowning. They looked alien to him, hanging where his clothing had always hung, in the room he alone had used for the last four years. A sudden and disquieting thought arose in his mind that this was no longer his space, his room, his house. He was the intruder here. The one who didn't fit.

The hip tub still held her bathwater, cool now and mostly clear except for a thin soap residue floating on top. Dropping his hat on top of the saddlebags, he stripped and stepped in. He found a small bar of soap in a dish on the lip of the tub and dipped it in the water. As he lathered up, he realized the flowery scent came from the soap. Definitely roses. He used it anyway, needing to rid himself of the taint of putrid meat.

When he finished, he climbed out and dried off. Digging shirt and trousers from his saddlebags, he quickly pulled them on, hoping that being fully dressed would calm the turbulent thoughts circling in his head. After kicking his dirty clothes into the corner, he put on his hat, picked up his saddlebags and boots, and stepped barefoot around the screen.

Ed hadn't moved. Her breathing hadn't changed. The need to touch was still there, and this time, he couldn't make himself walk away.

Defeated, he set down the boots and saddlebags, hung his hat on the bedpost, and gently pulled the quilt over her, making sure it covered her to her neck. Then with a weary sigh, he lowered himself on top of it, stretched out, and closed his eyes.

Edwina awoke to a shout, then the thump of boots on the stairs.

With a gasp, she lurched upright and reached for the covers, then shrieked when she grabbed a hand instead.

Declan, sprawled fully clothed on top of the quilt, blinked up at her. "Huh?"

Still trembling with fright, she punched his shoulder. "You scared the dickens out of me, you big lump! What are you doing in here?"

He rubbed a hand over his face, then let it fall back to the quilt. "What?"

A voice shouted up the staircase. "Pa? You up there?" Joe Bill.

Edwina jerked the covers higher and glared at her husband. "Tell him you're not." Then realizing what she'd said, she clapped a hand over his mouth and yelled, "He's not up here. Go away."

"Then where is he?"

"I don't know. Go away."

Muttering. Retreating footsteps.

She yanked her hand away, flung hair out of her eyes, and looked down to catch Declan in the middle of a yawn, his lids dropping.

She shoved at him.

His eyes opened, wandered for a moment, then focused on hers. He grinned sleepily up at her. "Ed."

"Get up!"

The grin spread. "I am up." He lifted his head to look down the long length of his body. "See?"

On reflex, she did, then jerked her gaze back to

his. Up, indeed. She punched him again. "What are you doing in my bed?"

"It's my bed. It's where I sleep."

"No, it isn't. You slept here? Tell me you didn't sleep here. All night?" And she hadn't even noticed?

"The settee is busted and I didn't bring a bedroll. Now stop hitting me and kiss me good morning."

"Why didn't you bring a bedroll?"

"I didn't think I'd need one." That drowsy grin again.

Edwina's mouth opened, but before she could think of anything to say, Joe Bill's voice came up the stairs.

"Pa! I know you're up there. I heard you talking."

Edwina sent her husband a warning look.

He yawned.

"The soldiers want to talk to you, Pa. You coming down, or not?"

"Okay, okay," he yelled. With a deep sigh, he sat up and set his bare feet on the floor. "Tell them I'll be there in a minute." Scratching his head with one hand, he bent to pull a sock from his saddlebag with the other.

"I knew you were up there." More muttering. Footfalls, cut off by the bang of the kitchen door Declan had just re-hung.

"Well, I hope you're satisfied," Edwina hissed at her husband's back.

293

"Satisfied?" Declan shoved his foot into a boot, paused, then shook his head. "Not hardly." He resumed shoving and tugging.

"What were you doing in here?"

"Sleeping."

She watched muscles flex beneath his stretched shirt as he worked on the other boot, still shocked that they had slept in the same bed and she hadn't even noticed. Had he touched her? Done something to her while she was sleeping? The notion sent a shiver of . . . something . . . through her that made her nerves quiver and jump in odd places.

"Did you . . ." The thought faded away when he rose to his feet, distracting her with all his yawning and stretching and scratching. He seemed especially tall this morning. Bigger than usual. Her gaze swept up the back of his long, sturdy legs, over his wrinkled shirt to the big hands ruffling through his dark unruly hair until it poked out every which way.

Had those hands been on her? She had always been a sound sleeper, but surely she would have known if they had.

Dropping those suspect hands, he began tucking in his shirt. "Did I what?"

It took her a second to remember. "Did you . . . do anything?"

"About what?"

"You know."

He frowned back at her over his shoulder.

She brushed a tangle of hair out of her eyes and pulled the covers higher. "While I was sleeping. Did you . . . you know."

Befuddlement gave way to laughter. He finished tucking in his shirt, then turned, leaned over, and planted his fists on the mattress beside her. "Are you asking if I commenced consummation while you were sleeping?"

Edwina pressed back against the log headboard. Rattled by his nearness, she checked for dirt under the nails of the hand not holding the covers to her chin. "I'm a sound sleeper."

"So you don't know if I did this?" He reached under the covers and put his hand around her ankle.

She tried to pull it back.

He moved his hand up her calf.

"Stop that."

"You don't remember this?" Above her knee now, his palm roughened by calluses, his fingers almost spanning her leg. "Or this?"

So distracted was she by what his hand was doing, she didn't see his head come down until his mouth pressed against hers. She froze, her pulse hammering in her temples, her skin tingling where his beard stubble raked gently against her chin, then along her jaw as he brushed his lips across her cheek to her temple. Why did he smell like roses?

Under the covers, his hand slid higher.

She thought she should tell him to stop but her throat wouldn't work.

"Trust me, Ed," he whispered into her ear. "You'll remember." Then with a gentle pat on her bare fanny, he straightened, lifted his hat from the bedpost, and settled it on his head. "Later, wife. That's a promise."

Then grinning, he turned, ducked under the beam over the landing, and clumped down the stairs.

Still smiling, Declan stepped out the kitchen door, pleased to note that during the night the wind had risen to clear away most of the stink. There were still tiny wisps of smoke curling above the blackened pile where the carcasses had been, but the huge mound had been reduced to a fraction of its original size, and what smoke hung in the air smelled of wood smoke, not charred meat.

"Morning, Sergeant," he called as Guthrie's next in command left the group of soldiers standing with Amos around a small cook fire and walked toward him. "The lieutenant already gone?"

"Yes, sir. About two hours ago."

Sergeant Quinlan was a tall man with a head as hairless as a cannonball. To counter that lack, he cultivated an impressive mustache that he coated with pine resin and sheep tallow to keep the ends curled tight as a pig's tail. Joe Bill, having a keen interest in facial hair since he couldn't grow any yet, had related all the particulars over supper. Declan wondered how the man could work his rifle without getting tangled up in the lever.

As the sergeant approached, Declan stepped off the kitchen stoop to meet him. "Got any coffee over there?"

"Yes, sir, we do. Your man just started a new pot."

"Had breakfast yet?"

"Yes, sir. And please thank your wife for the bacon she sent over last night. The men sure appreciated it."

As they walked toward the campfire, Quinlan said, "The lieutenant left orders my men were to dig you a new well. After you get your coffee, maybe you'll show us where, so we can get started."

There weren't a lot of options, Declan decided, a half hour later, as he stood by the old well and looked around. They could dig up-flow of the old well, he guessed, and hope the fouled water didn't backwash into the new well. Or he could move higher up, but that would put it farther from the house, which would be a problem in freezing weather.

"You might find water up there," Quinlan offered, nodding toward a stand of aspen about fifty yards up the slope that rose on the west side of the house. "Where you find aspen, you usually find water."

"We tried up there. But whatever seam is feeding those aspen must split off somewhere between here and there. We couldn't find it."

"Wait up, gentlemen," a cheery voice called.

Declan turned to see Ed coming toward them, holding a cup in one hand and pinning a wide-brimmed straw bonnet to her head with the other. The crisp morning breeze sent untied streamers fluttering out behind her like flocking birds and molded her skirt tight around her hips and legs.

Long legs. Smooth and firm. A butt as warm and soft as a new foal's belly. His hand closed tight at the memory.

"Good morning, Sergeant. Isn't it a grand day?"

"Yes, ma'am, it is."

"What are you doing out so early?" Declan asked as she stopped beside him. He'd expected her to start on the parlor this morning.

"I've come to help. Hold this while I secure my hat. The wind is atrocious today." Thrusting the cup into his hands, she lifted her arms.

He watched how the motion pulled the fabric of her dress tight across her breasts and wondered how he was going to make it until later.

"There now," she said, once she'd re-pinned and retied. She retrieved the cup, took a sip, then licked coffee off her top lip. "Joe Bill should be here with the sticks in just a moment, then we can get started."

"At what?" Declan knew she was a hard worker,

but surely she didn't intend to dig beside the men.

She looked up at him from beneath the floppy brim of her hat. "Amos said you were digging a new well."

"I am."

"Where?"

"I haven't decided yet."

"Exactly. Which is why I'm here." She must have seen his confusion. "I find water. It's one of my few talents." She smiled reassuringly at the sergeant. "And I'm very good at it, even if I do say so myself."

Declan frowned. There was a reason it was called water "witching." It was unnatural. Illogical. On a par with rainmaking and hair restorers and evangelical swooning. He'd thought Ed too smart for such foolishness.

"You're a douser?" the sergeant asked.

"I am."

Declan snorted. "It's bunkum."

"It most certainly is not. And I'll prove it." She nodded past his shoulder. "Here comes Joe Bill. You'll see."

"Will these do?" Joe Bill held out several slim switches as he approached Ed. "It's the best I could find."

Ed took them from his grip. "They're forked?"

"All but the one. And I skinned the forked ends like you said."

"You're sure they're willow wood?"

Joe Bill muttered something.

"Excellent." Ed chose two from the bunch, studied them closely—for what, Declan had no idea—then made a final selection. "Prepare to be amazed, gentlemen." Gripping the forked ends in her bare hands, she turned her wrists until her knuckles faced up, her thumbs out, and the stick was pointed halfway between earth and sky. Then she commenced marching.

And marching. Back and forth, back and forth, her brow furrowed in concentration, her steps measured and slow.

"I told you she's crazy, Pa."

Declan didn't respond, but he was beginning to agree.

"I saw a douser once in Missouri," Quinlan said as they watched Ed work her way slowly up the slope in a crisscross pattern like a hound coursing for a scent. "Don't have the gift myself, and I damn sure can't explain it, but I saw it work with my own eyes."

"Crazy as Cooter Brown," Joe Bill said.

Halfway up the slope, Ed stopped, rotated her neck and shoulders, shook out her arms, then started again.

"You gotta make her stop, Pa. It's embarrassing."

Declan turned his head and looked at his son.

"Well, it is. She's even got you wearing perfume."

Declan frowned, then remembered the soap. He was wondering how to defend his manhood to his own son, when Ed yelled, "Found it!"

To Declan, "it" looked like every other patch of dirt within a hundred-mile radius.

But Ed was bobbing on her toes with excitement. "It's a big flow. Joe Bill, get that long switch without a fork, and I'll tell you how deep it is."

Muttering under his breath, Joe Bill went.

"What makes you think it's here?" Declan tried not to sound too skeptical. Yet if he was going to ask men to dig in this rocky soil, he'd like to have a reason for picking this spot other than that a stick told him to.

Ed rolled her blue eyes. "I declare you're the stubbornest man alive. Just stay here and watch what happens when I walk by." Moving about ten yards away, she gripped the forked stick like she had before, flat across her palms, knuckles pointing up, and walked slowly toward them.

Three yards out, the tip of the stick began to twitch. At one yard, the twitches became jerks, and when she reached Declan, it swung sharply down to point directly at the spot she had indicated. "See?" Letting go of one fork of the stick, she winced and rubbed her palm on her skirt.

"Well, if that don't beat all." Quinlan spoke in such a tone of deep admiration and respect Declan tried not to glower.

Ed grinned happily back. "Have I made you a believer, Sergeant?"

"You have, ma'am. You surely have. I'll get the men and we'll start digging." He walked back toward the campfire, barking orders as he went.

"What's wrong with your hand?" Declan asked.

She studied her palm. "Rubbed a bit. It happens if you grip too hard and the pull is strong."

"Let me see."

Taking her smaller hand in his, he traced a finger across the red welt cutting across her palm.

"That tickles," she said in an odd voice.

He looked up, found himself sinking into her eyes, and forced himself to let go. "How does it work?" He had watched her hands when the stick started twitching and moving, and he was convinced she hadn't shifted her grip or turned her wrist or done anything that he could see. Yet the stick had moved in her hands . . . apparently while she held it as tight as she could. It made no sense.

"It's magic," she said with that imp's grin.

"It's bunkum."

"You'll see."

Joe Bill returned with another willow switch. This one had only been cut on one end and was an entire twig, about three feet long, less than half an inch in diameter, and very limber. Like the forked sticks, the cut end had been scraped of bark.

She went to her starting point ten yards out and turned. "When I get closer, watch for the switch to start bobbing, then count each bounce."

Gripping the tip of the stripped end with the thumb and forefinger of her right hand, and bracing it with her left, she walked slowly forward. As she neared, the drooping end started to twitch. When the tip hung directly over the spot, it began to bounce up and down in a regular rhythm.

"Count," Ed said, her entire attention focused on the bobbing switch.

At twenty-two, the bouncing began to slow. By thirty, it had stopped altogether. Ed let out a deep breath and lowered the switch. "You should hit water somewhere between twenty and thirty feet." She pointed at the ground between her toes. "Right here."

They took turns digging. Those not working in the four-foot-wide hole cut saplings and carted rocks to line the sides. They'd dig a few feet, send up buckets of dirt, shore the walls with stone and wood, then dig some more. They hit a trickle at seven feet, another at twelve. After temporarily plugging the seams as best they could with stone, they kept digging. By dark they were down almost twenty feet and into gravel.

Declan called it a day.

They shared their campfire that night with the soldiers, dining on the last of the venison and beans, with Ed adding a cobbler made of canned peaches, dried plums, and lumps of dough to form the crust. The bottom was burned crisp, the top gooey, the insides too sweet. But the soldiers couldn't seem to get enough of it, which Declan could see pleased Ed.

She was in her element. A beautiful, fluttering butterfly in a field of drab blue flowers, flitting from man to man, thanking them for their hard work and charming them with her smile. He figured tomorrow they'd dig to China if she asked them. It made him uneasy, reawakened his doubts; he'd been through this before, had watched one wife drift away and had done little to stop it. He wasn't sure what he would do if he saw this woman doing the same thing.

But for now, he did nothing, just watched in silence as she made her rounds, pouring coffee into one man's cup, laughing at some comment made by another.

His mood went from glum to morose.

Then when he'd about convinced himself he wouldn't care if this one left him, too, she lifted her head and looked at him across the fire.

Her smile faltered, softened into something tentative and unsure. It took the breath out of him. And he knew then he would never let this wife drift away.

"Is that hot yet?" he asked Amos, nodding toward the four buckets of water heating on the fire.

The old preacher shrugged.

"Then take it to the loft. Have the boys help you."

Amos and his sons picked up the buckets and started toward the house. Edwina watched them for a moment, then looked back at Declan.

He saw it in the widening of her expressive eyes. Read it in that shy smile that reached all the way down to his thudding heart.

Later had come.

Edwina tried not to dither, but it was hard.

That look. *Mercy.* She felt like the last hen in the coop when the fox came for a visit. The man was eating her up with his eyes.

Ever since that morning when he'd patted her bare bottom—her *bare bottom,* for heaven's sake—and said "Later," she hadn't been able to get that word—along with all it portended—and the feel of his warm, rough hand sliding up her leg, out of her flustered mind. And now this look, his eyes gleaming with something she had certainly never seen in Shelly's.

Law's amercy. She didn't know whether to run shrieking through the sagebrush or burst into titters of nervous anticipation.

So she went to take her bath, instead.

Soon, she thought a few minutes later, as she scrubbed herself into a heady, rose-scented lather. Soon she would know what had been lacking in her first marriage, and what put that dreamy look

305

in Maddie's eyes whenever she spoke of Angus, and what her body seemed instinctively to crave whenever Declan was near. She paused in her scrubbing, assailed by doubts as old worries rose in her mind.

Resolutely, she pushed them down. She wouldn't give him a chance to have second thoughts or disappointments. She'd pounce like a chicken on a June bug as soon as he walked through that door. Go at him like a possum in a pea patch. Hang on those broad shoulders like a cheap two-dollar suit—*No, wait. Not cheap.* She didn't want to appear trashy or common.

But then again, Maddie had said men liked women to be somewhat forward. *Somewhat forward.* What the dickens did that mean? Surely he wouldn't expect her to take her clothes off and prance around *bare naked?* Just the thought of it gave her the shivers. But not necessarily *bad* shivers.

"It smells like a flower garden in here."

With a startled cry, Edwina clasped her hands over her chest and whipped around in a slosh of soapy water.

Declan stood beside the screen, that hungry look in his eyes.

"W-what are you doing?"

"Waiting my turn." His gaze dropped to the tub. "Unless you think there's room for both of us in there."

In this tub? Both of them? Naked?

Stepping forward, he began loosening the buttons on his shirt.

Edwina watched in astonishment as he undressed right there in front of her, the whole while rambling on about the well, and relating some amusing thing Sergeant Quinlan had said, and telling her to be watchful because R.D. had seen cougar sign again at the creek, and complimenting her on her fine peach cobbler.

She scarcely listened, entranced by the unveiling before her.

First the hat, then the shirt. Seeing that the stool was covered with her discarded clothing, he leaned against the wall for balance as he wrestled off one boot, then the other. Then he started on his trousers.

Edwina watched, knowing it wasn't proper but unable to look away.

The trousers slipped down his long legs.

Her mouth went dry. Her heart pounded beneath her crossed palms. A distant part of her mind couldn't believe she was sitting here watching a man undress in front of her.

It made her feel bold and a little bit nasty. And tingly. All over.

No wonder men enjoyed their peep shows so much.

He was magnificent. Perfectly proportioned despite his height. She had seen naked men before—well, *a* naked man. But Declan was so different from Shelly. So much more . . . male.

And still he talked, his voice receding into a distant, buzzing drone in her head, unmindful of the fact she had stopped listening, stopped breathing, and could only stare in heart-pounding anticipation as he started on his drawers.

She suppressed an insane urge to giggle. How did he even keep them up with such narrow hips?

Ah . . . that's how.

Definitely more than Shelly.

Only dimly aware that he was no longer speaking, she let her gaze drift up his long, sturdy body, and wondered how this perfect man could actually be her husband. The man with whom she would share her life. Her bed. Her body.

Her skinny, un-pointy "stick" of a body. *Oh, God.*

"You getting out or not?"

Her gaze met his. He was smiling, his head cocked to one side, his dark eyes glittering in the yellow lamplight.

"Oh, Declan," she wailed.

Then, clapping her hands to her face, she burst into tears.

Fourteen

Well, that's deflating, Declan thought, grabbing for his drawers.

He'd thought since she'd been married before, he wouldn't have to worry about shielding her delicate sensibilities. He hadn't expected her to be so upset by the sight of a man's naked body, even one as big and clumsy and oversized as his.

Christ. Now he'd scared her.

Feeling awkward and embarrassed and every bit the "big lump" she'd labeled him, he quickly pulled on his drawers. Then he stood there, wondering what he should do.

He didn't want to leave. If he did, that would be the end of it. And he wasn't ready to give up on this woman.

He hunkered beside the tub. "Ed, what's wrong?"

She sniffled behind her hands. "You wouldn't understand."

He tucked a damp curl behind her ear. "Try me."

"You're so beautiful."

Beautiful? What the hell did that mean?

Joe Bill was right. Ed was definitely crazy.

Lifting her head, she brushed away tears with the backs of her hands. "See? I knew you wouldn't understand." She began splashing sudsy water on her puffy eyes. "And I'm—*ow, that stings.*"

He handed her a towel. "And you're what?"

After blotting her eyes, she passed back the towel and wrapped her arms around her raised knees to hide her chest from his gaze. "Nervous."

"About what?"

"You know." She made an offhand gesture that spattered him with soapy water and gave him a brief glimpse of one round, rosy-tipped breast. "What if it really is me? What if it's as awful with you as it was with Shelly? What if—"

"It won't be."

"How do you know?"

"I'll make sure of it."

"How?"

"Just trust me, Ed." He showed his teeth in what he hoped was a reassuring smile. "I've done this before."

"I'll just bet you have."

"Now, Ed." Hoping to dull that edge in her voice, he reached out to give her a friendly pat. Then he froze, his hand hanging above her shoulder, unable to comprehend what his eyes were seeing.

Aware of her watching, he trailed his fingers down the long curve of her back and over the slight ridges of scar tissue that marred the smooth, warm skin. He still couldn't get his mind around it. "Who did this?"

She tried to change the subject.

He wouldn't let her.

"It's not important, Declan."

"It is to me." His voice sounded harsher than he intended, so he tried to soften it. "Tell me." A drop of water slid from the damp hair at her neck. He watched it run down the bumpy ridge of her spine, and thought there was nothing quite so perfect, or fragile, or lovely as a woman's bare back. Even one crisscrossed with scars. "Who beat you, Ed?"

Her ribs expanded, then contracted on a weary sigh. "My mother."

It was a minute before he could speak. "Why?"

"Most of the scars are from the time I spilled a jug of milk." She smiled sadly. "I got off easy. Pru was scalded."

Declan flinched at the words. "By your mother? On purpose?" He remembered the pale markings on the Negro woman's wrist, like the dark skin had been bleached of color. "Why would she do such a thing?"

"Pru tried to intervene. I tell myself it was an accident, that the pot slipped. Maybe it did." She shrugged, as if this atrocity, this brutality toward two children was of no consequence. "It was a long time ago."

Declan realized his hand was shaking and pulled it away. "How long?"

"I was six. Pru, seven. Can we not talk about this anymore?"

"Sure." Feeling slightly sick and not nearly as amorous as before, Declan stood. Taking a towel off a hook, he wrapped it over his drawers, then walked over to the cabinet where his shaving mug and straight razor rested.

He knew he should say something, but he was so furious he didn't trust himself not to start yelling. To calm the anger churning inside him, he lifted the leather strop hanging beside the cabinet and began to sharpen the blade of his razor.

Goddamn her. What kind of mother would do such a thing? And what kind of father would let her?

Behind him, he heard a sluice of water as Ed stood. The soft scrape of her foot when she stepped out. The rustle of cloth as she dried off. He focused on the razor, dragging it back and forth, back and forth, while he searched for words.

"I'll never hurt you, Ed," he said, without turning.

"I know."

"And I'm sorry that happened to you." He sensed movement and, lifting his head, saw her behind him, wrapped in a towel and gazing back at him in the small mirror over the cabinet. She looked so sad.

"They disgust you, don't they? My scars."

He released the strop. Watched it swing back and forth on its hook. Carefully set the razor beside the mug. Then he turned.

And in that moment of turning, everything

changed. As if he'd stepped out of himself and, looking back, saw all his finely wrought rationalizations and justifications as the poor crutches that they were.

This wasn't about needing someone to help with the chores and his children. Or about wanting a woman in his bed. Or using one woman to help him forget his guilt over another.

It was about ending the loneliness that seemed to choke off a little more of his hope every day. About letting go of doubt, and distrust, and the mistakes of the past.

And reaching for Ed.

The idea brought on such a swell of panic for a moment he couldn't take a full breath.

"There's nothing about you that disgusts me," he said. And because he was afraid to let her see the need and fear in his eyes, and reveal to her how completely she owned him, he took her face in his big, rough hands and kissed her with all the emotion and feeling he'd been trying so desperately to keep safely hidden.

And she kissed him back.

"Ed," he said, and tried to pull her towel away.

"No." Anchoring the cloth to her chest, she stepped back, a smile tugging at her lips. "Bathe first. I can see the dirt."

He started to argue with her but changed his mind when a new idea presented itself. "You can watch, if you'd like."

She hesitated, like she might even consider it, which started his heart thudding again. Then she shook her head. "I have to braid my hair."

"Leave it down."

"It'll be a mess in the morning."

"Then braid it after."

That imp's smile, even as color inched up her neck. "After . . . later?"

"Go. I'll be there in a minute."

She left the room. Fled, was more like it. Like she was shocked at her own self. Or him. He had no idea what went on in that head of hers.

Beautiful, she'd called him. Big Bob Brodie, the carnival bear. Beautiful. The notion made him smile. Definitely crazy.

He bathed in record time. Minutes later, hair dripping, and wearing a towel that didn't hide his eagerness for his wife, he stepped around the screen, smelling like a rose bouquet.

She was standing at the moonlit window in her white gown. When she heard him come in, she turned and walked over to stand on the opposite side of the bed. She held out her hand. "Will you use this?"

He stared at the small packet in her palm, not able to make it out in the shadowed moonlight. "What is it?"

"A rubber thing that prevents babies. I can't remember what it's called."

Declan was a little shocked that she even knew

about such things. "Where'd you get that?"

"Lucinda. Will you wear it?"

He'd rather not. Just getting the damn thing on was enough to quell a man's enthusiasm. And why would she want him to?

Then he remembered that conversation they'd had several days ago, when she'd told him about her mother's madness and her fear of passing down to her own children that tainted blood.

"Have you ever hit a child, Ed?"

Her hand dropped back to her side. "I hit Freddie Helmsworth when he called Pru a mean name. And my brothers a couple of times."

"I mean, as an adult. Have you even wanted to hit a child?"

"Many times. Your son, most recently. But I never would."

"Then why do you think you'd beat your own?"

She didn't respond.

So he pushed harder. "I don't think you have it in you. But if it ever came to that, I'd stop you. Like you stopped me from taking Joe Bill to the woodshed. That's what parents are supposed to do. Protect their children. Even from each other if need be."

He saw her stiffen and knew she'd heard the unspoken criticism. "Daddy didn't know."

How could he not? But Declan didn't say it. If she wanted to hold on to that illusion, he'd let her. She'd suffered enough betrayal.

"Just because your mother was crazy doesn't mean you'll be."

"Is that a risk you're willing to take?"

He would take any risk for this woman. But he wasn't going to admit that. Not yet. "Do you want children, Ed? If you don't, that's all right." Which was a lie. He liked children. He would be proud to have one with Ed's blue eyes, and her joy and energy and odd sense of humor. "But if we have children, I'll watch out for them. And you. Always."

She made a small sound. He didn't know what it was until he saw her reach up and wipe her fingers across her cheek. "Yes, I want children."

He let out a deep breath, not aware that he'd been holding it in. "Then put that thing down and let's get started." Whisking away his towel, he climbed under the quilt.

She didn't move. "You're sure, Declan? I know I'm not some sturdy farm—"

He had to laugh. "Christamighty, Ed! Will you just take off your gown and get over here?"

She jumped under the covers.

"You still have on your gown," he reminded her.

"Oh. Of course." Without lifting the quilt, she removed the gown, shoved it to the floor, then lay back, arms at her sides, covers to her chin.

He thought of her nervousness and her timid kisses, and the shock on her face when he undressed. "You're not a virgin, are you, Ed?"

"Certainly not."

"Good." Rolling toward her, he put his hand on her breast.

She almost bolted upright. Then lay stiffly back, her heart hammering beneath his hand. "Sorry."

"There's nothing to be afraid of."

"I know. You just startled me is all. Please continue."

She was wound as tight as a cheap watch. He could feel her trembling, feel the rapid rise and fall of her chest as she breathed. Trying to calm her, he stroked his fingertips across her cheek, then down her neck to her shoulders, taking his time, talking softly about how soft her skin was, how smooth, how beautiful she looked in the moonlight.

Gradually, she relaxed. When he touched her breasts again, she tensed, but he kept at it, slow and calm, until she gradually began to give.

"Didn't your first husband do this?"

Her breath caught. She arched into his touch. "No . . ."

He was glad. "You're so soft," he murmured, stroking her from breast to her hip and back again. "Like satin."

"I'm not very pointy."

"Yet, see how perfectly you fit into my hand."

He stroked lower, across her belly, then lower still. She moved restlessly, but in a way that encouraged him.

"Did he do this?" Declan whispered against her

317

mouth, as he slid his hand up the inside of her thigh.

A sound soughed past her lips. Her hips rose to his touch. "No."

Leaning up on one elbow, he looked down at her, trying to see her face in the moonlight, wanting to know if she still had barriers against him. "He should have."

"W-Why?"

"Because . . ." He kissed her mouth, her chin, her brows. Tasted the salt of her dried tears, smelled roses on her skin. "That's the way it works."

"The way wh-what works?"

Rising up, he positioned her beneath him. "This," he said, and slid inside . . .

. . . His wife.

. . . His Ed.

And it was grand.

Edwina awoke to bright sunlight and the smell of coffee. Opening her eyes, she almost cried out when she found Declan, fully clothed, sitting on the edge of the mattress, looking down at her. "W-what?"

"Don't worry." He smiled. "I put the cup out of flailing range so you won't douse me like you did before. Morning, Ed."

He leaned down and gave her a kiss on lips that were still slightly tender from all the other kisses he'd given her through the night. Tonight she would insist he shave. Or maybe she should shave him. In the tub. Together. Bare naked. It would be a tight fit, but they could improvise. Maybe do that thing where she gets on top and he—

"I owe you an apology."

Yanked from her pleasant thoughts, she blinked in confusion, then almost flung herself against him before she realized she wore nothing beneath the quilt. "Oh, no, Declan," she assured him. "You were wonderful. Magnificent. The whole thing was just . . . well . . . wonderful."

His smile broadened. "I'm gratified to hear it. You were pretty amazing, yourself. But what I'm apologizing for is calling your water witching 'bunkum.' "

Amazing? She smiled, pleased. "So now you believe it works?"

"I do." Bending, he retrieved her gown from the floor and tossed it to her. "Come to the window and see for yourself."

She hesitated, waiting for him to move away, but he continued to sit there, that hungry look back in his eyes. "You expect me to put this on with you watching?" Even though they had been unclothed all night and had done shocking and intimate things, it had been under cover of darkness. To expose herself to his scrutiny in glaring sunlight was too unsettling.

"I do. You owe me. Especially after the show you made me put on for you last evening."

319

"Declan!"

He laughed. "Don't 'Declan' me. I watched you watching me. Now I know how a fifty-cent whore feels on payday." He must have seen her shock, because he quickly added, "That's a good thing. Come see." Rising, he went to the window, where he stopped well back from the opening, one hand gripping the side frame as he looked out.

Edwina hurriedly pulled on her gown, then crossed toward him, watching for any stray bits of glass she might have missed when she'd swept up the day before. "We have water?"

"We do. Those seams we found yesterday opened up overnight. Now the water level is seven feet from the top and holding."

"No more bunkum?" she teased, stopping beside him.

"No more bunkum."

Edwina saw that a wall of stones now ringed the well. Blue-coated men were stacking more rocks around two upright log poles on either side, while other soldiers were digging a trench from the well toward the house. Hearing voices below the window, Edwina leaned out the opening to see what they were doing.

Declan yanked her back. "What are you doing? Are you crazy? You could fall."

His harsh tone shocked her, his expression even more. "Did you think I was going to jump?"

She said it lightly, confused by his overreaction.

He released her shoulder. "You could have fallen," he snapped. "Just stay back until I can board it up."

Then she remembered his reaction when they'd crossed Satan's Backbone. Regretting that she had worried him, she linked her arm through his. "I'm sorry. I forgot you were afraid of high places." Oddly, that small failing made him even more appealing to her. More human.

His scowl deepened. His lips pressed in a tight line. Aware that she had pricked that fragile male ego, she patted the arm she held. "I'm afraid of spiders," she said to reassure him. "Snakes will warn you. Even bees buzz to let you know they're there. But spiders just lurk around, waiting to drop down on your head, or shoulder, or back, or get in your shoe, or—"

"I'm concerned, that's all. So unless you can fly, stay away from the window." And putting an end to the subject, he pointed at the men erecting the log scaffold over the well. "For now, we'll hang a rope and bucket off that. But when we come back, I'll bury a line in the trench and put a pump in the kitchen so we'll have gravity-fed water without having to carry it from the well."

We. When. Edwina liked the sound of that. It spoke of a future. Of not being alone. Of working toward something, rather than away.

She looked up at her husband. They were

bound by deed now, as well as fact. What a foolish risk she had taken, signing those proxy papers without even knowing the man to whom she was binding herself. What if he had turned out to be like that small-minded Cal Bagley, or a glum, filthy prospector who would disappear into the hills for months at a time? Or a drinker, a gambler, a man who thought it his right to beat his wife?

She studied the stubborn line of Declan's jaw as he watched the men working below. He had an austere face, angular and uncompromising. Except when he smiled. Then all the armor fell away, and for a moment, she was able to glimpse the man beneath.

A strong, capable man. One with a gentle touch despite his great size. One who could probably tip over a wagon but was afraid of heights. One who seemed to accept her, despite her flaws.

Would he ever love her? Would she love him?

Ninny. She had loved Shelly, hadn't she? And look what that got her. Maybe love was just a fabrication of novelists. Or poets. Or an insecure woman's mind.

"We did the right thing, didn't we, Declan?"

"Digging the well?" he asked, still watching the men below.

She would have to add practical and unromantic to his list of attributes. "Rushing the waiting period. We still have two months to go."

He shot her a guarded look, then turned back to the window. It was several moments before he spoke. "Regrets, Ed?"

She was surprised by the curt tone. He didn't meet her gaze, but she saw the tension in the rigid set of his shoulders, in the hard line of his brows, and sensed she had touched a nerve.

"No. Worries, maybe. But not regrets."

Still, he wouldn't look at her. "Worries about what?"

"We're very different, you and I. I'm impulsive. You're not. I like to dance and play and laugh. You don't. It'll take some adjustment."

He didn't respond. Which was another thing that worried her. How was she to know what he was thinking if he didn't talk to her? "Do you have regrets, Declan?"

He took such a long time to answer she wondered if he even heard the question. "I didn't do right by my first wife," he finally said. "I want to do better this time." When at last he looked down at her, she saw the smile in his eyes. "And I did dance with you, remember."

Edwina let out a deep breath. "Yes, you did." It wasn't much of an answer, but for Declan, it said a great deal. And suddenly feeling almost giddy, as if this beautiful day were spinning away from her and if she didn't hurry she might miss something wonderful, she spun away from the window. "Do you like poke salet?" she said as she ducked behind the screen to get dressed. "One of the soldiers said he saw pokeweed down by the creek."

Declan muttered something.

"Don't worry," she called to reassure him. "I know to boil it first. Three times. Maybe I'll make another cobbler if there's enough sugar left."

"Sounds . . . tasty. Be sure to take one of the boys with you." A moment later, she heard him clump down the stairs.

When Edwina came out the kitchen door, Joe Bill was waiting with a sour expression on his face and a bucket dangling from his hand.

"Don't you know how to swim?"

"Of course I do." Stepping past him, she headed toward the creek.

He fell in beside her. "Pa said I was to keep you from drowning. But if you already know how to swim—"

"How old are you?" she cut in, glancing over at him. He was tall, his blond head past her chin, but gangly. She probably outweighed him by fifty pounds, more if her skirts were wet.

"Nearly ten."

"And you think if I fell in, you could pull me out? Really?" She let her tone indicate what she thought of the chances of that happening.

He rose like a trout to a mayfly. "I can toss R.D. and he's nearly three years older."

"Is he?" She gave him a skeptical look. "Nonetheless . . ."

"And I'm strong." Pushing up a shirtsleeve, he flexed his bicep into a lump the size of a mashed apricot. "See?"

"Impressive. But still . . . are you really sure you could save me?"

If he puffed up any more, he would pop his buttons. "I'm sure."

"Well . . . all right, then. I guess you can come along." *If only his father were this easy,* she thought, as they continued to the creek.

"Especially," Joe Bill added with a smirk, "since the creek's only three feet deep."

Cutting a wide berth around the army tents—and their freshly dug latrine—they went upstream several hundred yards before ducking into the brush. It was like stepping into a different world. Outside sound faded beneath the babble of the creek. Leaves rustled overhead. Birdsong filled the air as warblers and swallows and finches flitted through cottonwoods, salt willow, and mesquite. The air felt ten degrees cooler and smelled of damp earth and the yellow and blue wildflowers crowding the bank.

"Do you know what pokeweed looks like?" she asked as they picked their way along the rocks at the edge of the water.

"I know it's poisonous."

"Not if you boil it good, then steam it with fried

bacon and onion. Tastes just like spinach, only better. Here's some." Stopping beside a leggy plant with pointed green leaves and ripening berries, she checked it well, then said, "Only pick the youngest leaves, and none that are starting to turn red. And don't eat any of the berries."

"Thomas eats all kinds of berries."

"Not this kind. This kind will kill you."

"And you're fixing to feed it to us?"

"Just the leaves."

"I'm not eating any."

"Suit yourself."

They picked leaves until the bucket was half full, then moved on, hunting another plant. Dragonflies circled above the rushing water, catching the light on their long gossamer wings. A squirrel somewhere behind them chattered and fussed. Far in the distance, a cow that had escaped the war ax called out for her herd.

Edwina was reaching down to check a plant when an odd noise caught her attention—a snuffling, chuffing sound—coming from the brush on the other side of the water. She straightened and scanned the far bank.

Dappled sunlight. Bugs arcing in the air. A bird startled off a drooping willow branch.

The creek was moving fast and shallow here, barely a foot deep but wider than where they had come in. A person could cross and barely get his shoes wet. Or his moccasins.

She glanced at Joe Bill, who had squatted beside her to dig in the rocks with a stick, his chin resting on his bent knees.

"Joe Bill."

"Yeah?" he asked, without looking up.

"We need to go back."

Something in her voice brought his head up.

"Now," she whispered. "Go."

He rose, the stick still gripped in his hand. "What's wrong?"

She took a step back, then tensed when the sound came again. "Did you hear that?"

"Hear what?" he whispered, standing so close she could feel the heat of his breath through the cloth on her arm.

"In the bushes." She pointed across the water, then almost jumped out of her shoes when the sound came again. "There! You didn't hear that?"

Before he could answer, the leaves rippled and shook. Edwina grabbed at Joe Bill, her breath suspended, her heart pounding like a wild thing trapped beneath her ribs. "What is it?"

Low to the ground, something moved, so dappled with shadow and light she could hardly tell the color or shape. Then the leaves parted and a crouched figure appeared. Huge and furred, with yellow eyes and a gaping mouth that showed a curling pink tongue and long stained teeth.

"Cougar!" Joe Bill shrieked and whirled to scramble up the bank. "Pa! Pa!"

327

"No!" Edwina grabbed the back of his shirt. "Don't run!" She yanked him back so hard he toppled. "He said don't run!"

But it was too late.

The cougar bounded out of the brush, mouth open in a snarl.

Without thinking of anything except the boy sprawled helpless at her feet, Edwina charged to meet it, shrieking in terror and waving the pail over her head. *"Go away, go away, go away!"*

The cougar checked and made a yowling sound, one paw up, claws extended.

"Go away!" Edwina screamed, waving and rushing into the water.

The cougar crouched and edged back, ears flat, tail twitching.

"Ed, drop!" a voice shouted.

Edwina ducked.

A rifle cracked. She heard the whine of the bullet past her ear, the whump as it struck flesh, then a broken cry as a huge, heavy weight crashed into her back and drove her face-first into the water.

FIFTEEN

The weight lifted. Hands grabbed at her, flipped her over as if she were a rag doll.

"Ed! Jesus, are you all right?"

Coughing and spitting water and grit, Edwina fought to drag air into her lungs as a heavy hand pounded on her back. "D-Don't," she choked out. "Stop!"

He stopped. She felt herself lifted from the water in arms that held her so tight she could scarcely breathe. A moment later, he laid her out on the soft bank in a bed of wildflowers.

"Talk to me, Ed! Are you all right? Are you hurt?"

She blinked up at her husband's pale, worried face. "Joe B-Bill?"

"He's here. He's fine. Tell her you're fine."

Joe Bill came into view. Dirty, wet, spattered with blood. "I'm fine."

"You're bleeding."

"Cougar blood. It's all over you, too, and in your hair. It fell on you. Scared Pa half to death, didn't it, Pa? Never seen you move so fast."

She shifted her gaze to Declan. His face had regained some color, but his eyes still showed fear. "W-what happened? I heard a shot, then—"

"Pa got him! Right through the throat. Almost

blew off his head, didn't you, Pa!" Joe Bill glanced at the creek behind him, then at Edwina. His hazel eyes were round in his dirty face and seemed unnaturally bright. "Can't believe you charged him. You're crazy, you know that? Mad-dog crazy!"

"Joe Bill," his father warned.

"Well, she is. Did you see her, Pa? Did you see what she did?"

"I saw."

Edwina frowned up at the faces hovering over her. She was shivering and wet. She felt mauled and beat up and bruised, and was in no mood for Joe Bill's foolishness. But when she opened her mouth to tell him that, she realized Joe Bill was grinning. At her.

"Can you walk?" Declan asked.

"I think so." But her legs didn't seem to work right, and if not for Declan's strong arm around her, she would have crumbled back to the ground.

"Crazy as Cooter Brown," Joe Bill said, hovering at her side and getting in the way as Declan steadied her. "Going at a cougar with nothing but a pail of spinach. That's just plain crazy."

Edwina wasn't sure, but she thought she heard a note of pride in his voice. "It was poke salet." She felt dizzy and her heart was racing so fast she could scarcely get the words out. Leaning against her husband, she paused to look back at the dead cougar, terror still coursing through her.

It lay sprawled on the bank where Declan must have thrown it after he pulled it off her back. Its fur was matted with blood and plastered to ribs that showed through its mangy pelt. It looked a little sad lying there like a pile of trash. "I thought it would be bigger."

"It's big enough," Declan muttered.

"And old," Joe Bill chimed in, still crowding at her side. "Probably couldn't hunt anymore. That's why it came after us, right, Pa?"

"Maybe."

Joe Bill sprinted on ahead, calling back as he ran. "I gotta tell them how you went at a cougar with a pail. They're not going to believe it."

After she had washed away the cougar blood and changed clothes, Edwina suffered through the concerned comments and questions throughout the rest of the day, putting on a brave smile despite the soreness that grew more pronounced with each passing hour. But by suppertime, she was hobbling like an old lady.

"What you need is a hot bath," Declan advised—the most he'd said to her since they'd come back from the creek. She wasn't sure why he was so quiet, but it was just as well; she wasn't feeling that talkative, either.

Every time she thought of that snarling face coming toward her, she started to shake. What if she'd gotten Joe Bill killed? What if Declan hadn't come when he did?

"You finished?" Declan asked.

She looked down at the plate wobbling in her hands. It was still half full. She couldn't remember what it was, or how much she'd eaten, or if she'd eaten anything at all. *Rabbit stew.* An image flashed in her mind. Amos bustling around the campfire, filling the plate and handing it over. "It's delicious. I'm just not hungry."

Declan pulled the plate from her hands and set it on a rock beside the fire. "Come on then. The boys already carried up bathwater." He rose, holding out his arm for her to take.

She pulled herself up. Then, mindful of her manners, she thanked Amos for fixing supper, and the soldiers for working so hard, and the boys for carrying up the water.

Declan's sons were so engrossed in scraping the underside of the pelt a soldier had taken off the cougar, they barely looked up. The smell of the raw skin made her stomach roll. She paused to watch them, wanting to shake Joe Bill and hug him and tell him how glad she was that he was alive. Instead, she contented herself with brushing her fingertips over his blond hair, which earned her a scowl, then let Declan lead her toward the house.

Big, solid Declan. There in the nick of time. A series of "what ifs" rolled through her mind, but Edwina pushed them away.

Home, now. Safe.

That was all that mattered.

Grateful for her husband's presence, for the sturdy strength of his arm beneath hers, she tipped her head against his shoulder and tried to ignore the ache in her back and shoulders.

With each step, she felt a weakening of the taut control she had struggled to maintain throughout the day. Here in the dark, with no one but her husband to see, she winced at the pull of stiff muscles, bit off a gasp when her ankle turned on a rock and a shock of pain shot up her bruised back. She made it into the kitchen, but the stairs defeated her. Without a word, Declan scooped her up in his arms and carried her to the loft. Once in the water closet, he set her on her feet, then began undoing the long row of buttons down the front of her dress.

"I can do that," she said, uneasy with the idea of him undressing her. Then realizing how absurd that was after some of the things they'd done last night, she made only a weak protest—more out of disgust with her own helplessness than for modesty's sake. "You needn't bother."

"It's no bother." He slid the dress off her shoulders and down her arms, hung it on a hook, then began to untie the tabs on her petticoat.

She studied him through her lashes, a bit confused by his reticence.

Was he angry with her? Disappointed that she wasn't more stalwart?

The idea of that annoyed her. She couldn't help being battered and sore. In addition to having a huge animal crash into her, she'd fallen into a rocky creek bed. Her palms were scratched, her chin scraped, and she would probably have bruises from head to toe.

"Step out," he said, holding her arm so she could balance.

"Are you upset with me?" she asked when he turned to hang the petticoat beside her dress.

"No. Raise your arms."

When he bent to lift the hem of her chemise, she put a hand on his shoulder to stop him. "Then what's wrong, Declan? Why are you angry?"

He straightened, hands planted low on his waist, his lips compressed in that resistant way he had. For a moment she thought he wouldn't answer. Then, without looking at her, he said, "I shouldn't have let you go down there. I knew there had been a cougar hanging around. I thought with the soldiers there, it would have left, but . . ."

He thinks it's his fault? "Hush." She touched her hand to his mouth. "You're not to blame for this, Declan. Joe Bill and I are okay. The cougar is dead. It's over."

Warm air rushed past her fingers as he let out a deep breath. He nodded and she took her hand away. "Go," she said, softening the order with a smile. "I can do the rest."

He hesitated as if he intended to argue the

point, then turned and left the small room.

Edwina finished stripping, then stepped gingerly into the tub. Steam rose as she sank into the hot water, temporarily dimming the room as it fogged the glass chimney of the lamp bolted to the wall.

She slumped forward, wisps of hair hanging down to brush against the water. Tremors rippled over her shoulders and along her arms . . . as if the fear still trapped within her body sought release.

She never ever wanted to be that afraid again.

Declan stood at the broken window and listened to her cry. She made little noise. But he had lived with an emotional woman for ten years, and he knew what that occasional sniffle and muffled sound meant.

I could have lost her.

Turning from the window, he prowled the room but still couldn't outrun that thought. Eventually he stopped trying and sank down on the edge of the bed.

Pictures flashed through his mind. Ed, charging —his son scrambling to his feet—the cougar crouched, ready to spring.

Christ! He brought his clenched fist down hard on his thigh, using the pain to drive the image away.

I could have lost her. I could have lost my son.

That realization made his chest hurt so bad for a second he couldn't move. Then with a great, hitching breath, he sucked air into his lungs, and his heart resumed its furious rhythm and blood roared past his ears in a dizzying rush.

They could have died.

But they didn't.

They could be dead.

But they're not.

Clinging to that thought, he closed his eyes and waited for calmness. When it came, he unclenched his fists. Flattening his hands on his thighs, he stared out the broken window at the aspens twisting in the breeze.

He sat that way for a long time, his mind churning with images and memories and questions he couldn't answer. But one thought kept circling around and around, like a half-remembered melody or a phrase repeated like a chant. Until finally he could no longer ignore it.

He loved Ed. He loved his wife. And stupid bastard that he was, he almost had to lose her before he came to that realization.

Edwina felt much better after her soak. The shaking had stopped, the terror had faded into memory, and all that was left was a bone-deep weariness, a tub of cold water, and two very puffy eyes.

She added a dozen bruises to that list when she stepped out of the tub and saw how the hot water had brought out the colorful marks that her fall had left down the front of her body. She wished Pru were here to concoct a salve or a balm or plaster-something to speed the healing. Pru always knew just what she needed.

She smiled, thinking of all the news she had to share with her sister when she got back. She wondered if Pru would have equally momentous news to share in return.

Once she'd pulled on her gown, she turned out the lamp, then moving with a lot less pain since her bath, stepped around the screen.

Declan was sitting in the dark on the far side of the bed. He was facing away, so she couldn't see his face in the dim moonlight coming through the window, but she recognized that stiffness in his shoulders and back and knew he was fretting about something.

He had shocked her earlier with his outburst of guilt. How silly to blame himself. It had been her decision to go to the creek and her decision to allow Joe Bill to accompany her. If Declan hadn't come running, they might both be dead.

That harrowing thought awakened the fear again, and Edwina had to pause for a moment to catch her breath and let her nerves settle.

Declan must have heard her, because he twisted around, saw her standing beside the screen, and immediately rose. "Feel better?"

She nodded. "Much better. Thank you."

"Good."

They stood in awkward silence, the bed between them. Edwina looked down at it and thought of all that they'd done here last night, and resolved not to let unspoken words rise between them.

"You saved my life."

"You saved my son's."

She gave a broken laugh and felt new tears clutch at her throat. "If I'd thought at all, I wouldn't have been able to do it. I was just so . . . angry."

"You were brave."

"Pure hysteria. How could I have faced you if I'd let harm come to your son?"

"Ed." He started around the end of the bed. A moment later, his strong arms closed around her and pulled her against his body.

She was crying again, and wasn't sure why, and couldn't seem to stop the tears no matter how often she blotted her face against his shirt. She drew in his warmth, his scent, his strength. She listened to the beat of his heart. And for the first time in more years than she could count, she felt safe.

When she got herself in hand, she drew back just enough to be able to see his face. His beautiful, stern, beloved face. "But he's okay, isn't he? Joe Bill?"

"He's okay."

"We protected him. Just like you said. Just like parents are supposed to do."

"We did." His voice sounded gruff, but his

hands were gentle as he steered her toward the bed. He lifted the edge of the covers. "Hop in."

It was more of a crawl, she was so sore. "I'll be a good mother, I believe," she said as he pulled the covers over her. "When I think about how mad I got when the cougar went for Joe Bill . . ." She couldn't finish the thought.

He straightened. "You've got a temper, that's for sure."

"I fear you're right." She took a deep breath, let it out, and felt some of the tension go with it. "I must have looked a sight, shrieking and jumping up and down and waving that bucket like a shrimper's wife when the fleet comes in."

"It worked. Challenge a cat, back away from a bear."

"What are you doing?"

He hadn't moved away from the bed but continued to stand there, looking down at her. He faced the moonlit window now and she could see he was smiling. "Waiting for you to quit babbling and go to sleep."

She levered herself up onto her elbows. "You're not coming to bed?"

"You're sore, Ed. You need your rest."

"You're right. So quit nattering and get into bed so I can."

He hesitated, then started unbuttoning his shirt. "I should get paid for this."

"For getting in bed?"

"For putting on another show. But since you're my wife, I'll do it for free." Flinging the shirt aside, he plopped onto the mattress, tugged off his boots, then stood and began loosening his trousers.

She watched, a feeling of possession moving through her, tempered by astonishment that this man was truly her husband.

The ropes under the mattress groaned with his weight as he slid in beside her. She waited for him to settle, then rolled toward him, tucking in tight against him, with her arm across his chest so he couldn't get away. He smelled faintly of horses and camp smoke and sweat. Much better than roses, she thought, yawning.

He gently stroked her back. "Lieutenant Guthrie and the other troopers should be back soon. Then we'll go home."

"This is home."

He hesitated, then kissed the top of her head. When he spoke again, something in his voice told her he was smiling. "To Heartbreak Creek, then. Tomorrow. Next day at the latest."

"I'm glad. I miss Pru and the children. Although I hope we won't be staying in town too long. I don't want our teeth to turn brown."

She smiled, anticipating the look on her sister's face when she told her about the cougar. She should write a dime novel about it. Maybe make it into a theatrical production like that Buntline book, *Buffalo Bill, the King of Border Men.* She could star in it, herself. Have Joe Bill wear that nasty cougar skin he was so taken with.

She yawned. *Edwina Ladoux Brodie, Cougar Router.*

Her eyes closed. Beneath her ear, the sure, steady beat of her husband's heart lapped at her senses like water on stone as she drifted into deep, dreamless sleep.

When she awoke, Declan was gone and the sun was already high in a cloudless blue sky.

Yawning, she rolled over, then groaned at the pull of sore muscles and various scrapes and bruises. It all came back to her in a rush—the cougar, Joe Bill sprawled at her feet, her mad, shrieking charge with the upraised bucket. Now that the danger was past, she had to smile at the ridiculous picture she must have made, flinging poke salet greens from the swinging bucket and yelling at a huge snarling beast to "go away."

But it had worked, hadn't it? She'd held off the cougar until Declan had arrived to shoot the poor beast. Crazy-as-Cooter-Brown Edwina must have done something right.

Wincing, she sat up and swung her feet to the gritty floor. Voices drifted up to the window. Rising stiffly, she padded over and looked out to see that the other soldiers had returned and Lieutenant Guthrie was standing at the well with

Declan. As she watched, the lieutenant scooped a handful of water from the bucket sitting on the rim, tasted it, then he nodded to Declan.

Ha, Edwina smirked. Bunkum, indeed.

She dressed and went downstairs. Declan must have repaired the stove because a pot of coffee was simmering on top of it and a tin cup sat waiting on the table. After pouring a cup, she stepped out onto the kitchen stoop into a crisp, cloudless day.

"There she is!" Joe Bill left the group of soldiers gathered around the cook fire and ran toward her. Some of Guthrie's men, Edwina surmised, since she didn't recognize them as the troopers who had worked on the well.

"Tell them, Ed," Joe Bill ordered, showing a hodgepodge of gaps, baby teeth, and permanent teeth in a big grin. "Tell them how you ran off a cougar with a bucket. They don't believe me."

Rout one cougar, Edwina thought, wryly, and suddenly she's the hero of the hour. But she did have to allow that it was nice to have Joe Bill grin at her for a change, rather than send her his usual scowl or smirk.

"Good morning, gentlemen," she called, stepping off the stoop and crossing toward them. "How did it go at the Parker place?" Edwina had never met Jubal and Mildred Parker, but she hoped they had been given a proper burial. She wished she knew if they had kin somewhere that should be contacted. She would remind Declan to check when they returned to town.

"About what we expected, ma'am," a sandy-haired soldier said. "We put markers over their graves so folks coming by would know whose place it was."

"Tell them, Ed!"

"Yes, ma'am," prodded a freckled soldier with a bucktoothed grin. "The boy here says you beat off a cougar bare-handed."

And the legend grows. "Actually I was armed with a bucket of greens." Edwina sent a chiding smile toward her stepson. "Apparently cougars like poke salet no better than Joe Bill here."

"Kept yelling 'go away' like it was some sort of barn kitty instead of a killer cougar," Joe Bill elaborated. "Told you she was crazy."

"And thank God for it," Declan said, coming up behind her. "She's a terror, that's for sure. Morning, Ed," he added, leaning down to kiss her cheek like it was the most natural thing in the world. "Ready to dig through what's left and see if there's anything we can salvage?"

Edwina blinked up at him, taken aback by his casual demonstration of affection. Her father had never kissed her mother in front of others. Or probably in private, either, considering the state of their marriage. It was surprising, but nice, that Declan felt comfortable doing so.

She wondered how he would react if she threw

herself at his neck like she wanted to. She smiled, picturing it. Maybe he'd scoop her up in those strong arms and whisk her away to—

"I guess we could start in the loft."

"W-what?" Had he really said that? In front of everyone?

"See what you want to salvage from there, then check out the other rooms. What do you think?"

"Oh, yes, well . . . there might be a few things." She tried to cover her distraction by pretending to consider his question. In truth, the main thing she wanted from the house was that marvelous log bed. Surely Declan could plane out the hatchet marks left by the Indians. And the tub would be nice to have. And maybe that cabinet where he kept his shaving mug. She thought of the way he'd looked standing there in that towel—all golden skin and rounded muscle and that arrow of dark hair pointing down—

"Unless you are too sore."

Edwina almost choked.

Taking her hand, he studied the scratches on her palm, the bruise above her wrist. The frown on his brow told her he was thinking of practicalities rather than improprieties. "If so, we could stay another day if you want. Figure out what to take back when you're feeling better." He continued to stroke her hand, sending a tingle all the way up her arm.

Another day meant another night—away from

the crowded rooms and constant interruptions—just the two of them in that big bed, in the dark . . .

"I'm not that sore," she said in a shaky voice.

His expression changed, shifted into something that sent blood pumping through her veins. When his gaze dropped to her breasts, she felt an instant reaction in places she had no name for.

How did he do that? With just a look and a smile he had her mind in chaos and her body in turmoil. *Mercy,* she was almost sweating. It was shocking and embarrassing and . . . well, a little bit nasty.

But if they did stay another day . . . and night . . .

"I'll talk to Guthrie," Declan said. "Tell him we'll leave at first light tomorrow."

Edwina might have been mistaken, but it felt like the big hand holding hers might be sweating, too.

It took most of the rest of the day to pick through what items and furniture remained, decide what could be repaired, then load everything onto the wagon.

He and Ed agreed on everything but the bed. She wanted to bring the whole thing. He just wanted the mattress, patiently explaining to his wife that the log frame was too bulky, and would have to be taken apart to get down the stairs, and he'd never be able to get out the chop marks, and it would be easier to get more logs and build another frame.

Besides, he had plans for that bed as soon as it got dark.

They compromised.

He got to make love to his wife in it that night, and in the morning he would take it apart and load it in the wagon.

Not his best negotiation, but Ed was satisfied. Repeatedly.

As was he.

It was midmorning when he closed and bolted the kitchen door for what he hoped would be only a temporary absence. He had no choice but to go. Yet, as they rolled down into the valley, the idea of leaving the ranch carried the bitter taste of failure.

Ranching had been his dream all his life. Even though he'd been raised on a Missouri bottom-land farm by a second-generation farmer, he'd always dreamed of working cattle rather than dirt.

He understood farming. With his size and strength, he probably would have been good at it. But there was something about cutting up good grassland with a plow blade that had always seemed wrong to him.

So, when he was sixteen and his brothers were old enough to help Pa, he'd headed west. For three years he'd worked at different outfits, learning the land, the climate, the ways of cattle. By the time he'd reached his twentieth birthday, he'd met Sally, married her, and staked his claim to sixty thousand mountainous acres that he named Highline Ranch.

Over the next few years he'd driven feral cattle

up from Texas and across the plains. He'd fathered children, built a home, battled blizzards and drought, and been so busy chasing his dream across this long, grassy valley, he'd lost his wife somewhere along the way.

He wasn't going to lose this one, too. Even if he had to leave the ranch and live in a ramshackle mining town until he was too old to wear a sheriff's badge, he would do it to keep his family safe and his wife happy.

Although, he mused, studying Ed's forlorn expression as she twisted on the seat to look back at the house, this wife seemed almost as sad as he did to be leaving their home.

"So what should we do for Brin's birthday?" she asked after a while.

"Give her the presents we got her."

She gave him a look from beneath the brim of her bonnet. "I mean should we invite other children to the house? Girls her own age? I could make a piñata and fill it with candy. Pru could make a cake. She makes the most delicious buttercream frosting. Do you think Brin would like that?"

"The cake part."

"You don't think she would like having a birthday gathering?"

"Not if she had to wear that dress you made for her."

She muttered something he didn't catch, which was probably for the best. They rode in silence for a time, then she said, "How did you break your little finger?"

"Joe Bill."

"No! I'm shocked!"

He kindly overlooked the blatant sarcasm. "Actually it was my fault. I told him to close the door but forgot to remind him to wait until I got my hand out of it." He smiled down at her. "I think you've won him over."

She laughed—a soft, rippling sound that had a breathy quality, which made him think of other breathy sounds she made. In bed. In the dark.

"Rout one cougar and you're a hero forever. I wonder what heroic feat I'll have to perform to get R.D. to talk to me."

"Good luck. R.D.'s not much of a talker. Never has been."

"Like his father?"

"I talk plenty," he defended. "In fact, since you got here, Thomas can hardly be around me, I talk so much."

She laughed. "So many talents. Talking *and* peep shows. You should go on stage in New Orleans."

"Want to pull over and see how talented I can be?"

"Hush. Besides, I already know how talented you are."

"Not in daylight."

"My, look at those orange flowers. Aren't they lovely?"

Sixteen

It was late afternoon when they reached the confluence of Heartbreak Creek and the smaller, less foul Elderberry Creek, which ran behind the refurbished sheriff's house.

Edwina was so relieved, she almost wept. She felt like she'd been run through a wringer in a bag of rocks, she was so sore from bouncing around on the hard seat all day.

Pulling the team to a stop, Declan waited for Lieutenant Guthrie to come alongside the wagon.

"You're welcome to stay at our place, Lieutenant. The water's better and we've got a woman who can cook like nothing you ever ate. Two of them," he added quickly before Edwina could dredge up the energy to take offense.

"Appreciate that." Leaning over, Guthrie doused a weed with a stream of brown tobacco juice, saw Edwina's look of distaste, and muttered, "Excuse me, ma'am," as he straightened. "But I'm giving the men an overnight furlough, and they'll be wanting to cut the wolf loose." He gave Declan a meaningful look. "I'll try to keep them in line until we leave in the morning, but I hope you'll be lenient with them, Sheriff."

"No shooting or fighting," Declan warned, "and we'll get along fine."

Guthrie nodded. They said their good-byes, then the troopers turned north into town, and Declan reined the team east along the track that followed the creek, Amos and the boys bringing up the rear.

As soon as the wagon pulled into the yard, Thomas stepped onto the front porch. Brin and Lucas rushed out after him, but at a word from the Cheyenne, they stopped at the porch railing and watched with anxious faces as he continued past them down the steps. He was limping, Edwina noted.

He was also wearing his Indian attire again, complete with war shirt, leggings, topknot, and eagle feather. But no deputy's badge. A huge, dark bruise covered one side of his face and he cradled his rifle across one arm.

Edwina glanced around, wondering where Pru was.

After telling R.D. and Joe Bill to help Amos unload the wagon, Declan climbed down and went to meet him. Feeling a prickle of unease, Edwina remained in the driver's box and watched the two men talk in low, earnest tones.

Something was wrong. Something had happened.

She looked around again. Where was Pru?

Without waiting for help, she climbed down. But once on the ground, she was assailed by sudden dizziness, her heart beating so hard she could feel the thud of it against the walls of her chest.

Clinging to the wheel, she glanced at the

children on the porch, scanned the carriage house, the side yards. But still didn't see Pru.

Then Declan turned. And in that instant their gazes met, she knew with a certainty that almost buckled her knees.

Something terrible had happened.

No, a voice screamed inside her head. *Not Pru.*

Frantically she scanned the yard again, found Thomas looking back at her out of his black agate eyes, and wanted to rail at him for not keeping her safe, for letting something happen. "Where's Pru?" she called.

Instead of answering, he turned and limped through the side yard to the stables in the carriage house.

Declan walked toward her. She clutched at the wheel, felt the nicked edge of the metal rim dig into her hand, and shook her head, willing him to stop and go back. "No," she said.

But still he came, closer and closer, until he filled her vision and all she saw was the placket on his shirt with three white buttons.

"Ed, I'm sorry." He put his hands on her shoulders, to steady her or keep her from falling, she didn't know. "Pru was taken."

Taken? How was someone *taken?* She didn't know what that meant. "Is she—is she dead?"

"No. I don't know."

"What happened? Taken where? By who? I don't understand."

"By Lone Tree."

A buzzing began in her ears, growing so loud she heard only snatches of what he said next. "When?"

"Yesterday afternoon."

We should have been back then. But I made him stay. Because of her, Pru would suffer again. She almost staggered from the pain of it. Then she saw Thomas come around the house leading his horse, and her fury ignited, burning so hot it brought tears to her eyes. "Why didn't he stop them? Why didn't he save her?"

"He tried, Ed."

Shoving her husband aside, she ran toward Thomas.

He stopped and waited for her to come, his bruised face impassive, his eyes as flat and hard as chips of black stone.

She wanted to hit him, claw those eyes, scream her rage in his face.

"How could you let this happen, Thomas? How could you let them take her?"

Favoring his bad leg, he pulled himself up onto his horse's back. After sliding the rifle into a sling by his knee, he looked solemnly down at her. "I tell you this, Edwina Brodie. I will find *Eho'nehevehohtse.* I will bring her back. That is my promise." With a nod to Declan, he reined the horse toward the mountains and nudged it into a lope.

"He'll find her," Declan said from behind her.

Edwina turned on him, the fury still strong inside her, her thoughts so scattered nothing was making sense. "Why are you still here? Why aren't you going with him?"

"I can't leave you and the children." He put his hand on her shoulder.

She shrugged it away and started toward the stable. "Then I'll go."

He pulled her back. "You would only slow him down."

Without warning, acid rose in her throat. She doubled over, retching, but nothing came out. *Pru. Oh, God . . . Pru.*

Declan's arm came across her shoulders. She hadn't the strength to fight him, so she let him steer her toward the porch where the children watched. Lucas was pale as parchment. Brin was crying, tear tracks showing through the dirt on her face.

Not now. Don't cry in front of the children. Wait. Later she could curl up somewhere and give in to the fear. She would wail and weep and rage until her mind went numb and her throat grew hoarse. Then she could decide what to do next.

Wait. Just a few more steps.

"Thomas said Lucinda sent food from the hotel," Declan told her. "Let's get the children fed, then we can talk."

Talk? About what? What was there to say?

What could he possibly tell her that would make sense of this?

When they reached the porch steps, Brin launched herself at her father, Lucas close on her heels. Letting go of Edwina, Declan went down on one knee and took them into his arms, murmuring that they were safe now, he was here, everything would be fine.

Edwina looked away, the need to give in to her own tears like a fist in her throat. How could anything be fine again?

R.D. and Joe Bill came up behind them, and suddenly everyone was talking at once, and Brin was crying and Joe Bill and R.D. were wanting to saddle up and go after Thomas.

Edwina couldn't bear it and continued on past them, desperate to escape the noise and the pain and the fear that clawed at her insides.

Just a few more steps.

It was a quiet dinner. Edwina couldn't eat, but stared blankly down at the table, terror lodged like a stone in her chest. The children scarcely spoke, and Declan spent more time watching her than eating.

The part of her mind not steeped in fear wondered why she was sitting here before a plate full of food, safe and secure, while Pru—

God . . . Pru.

"Ed."

Through a blur of tears, she looked at Declan's

hard, unsmiling face with that furrow between his eyes.

"You have to eat something," he said.

She looked down at the food on her plate, not sure what it was, or how it had gotten there. Dutifully she picked up her fork. But her fingers couldn't seem to grip it, and the fork clattered against her plate, then slipped from her grip. Such a simple thing. But she couldn't do it. Couldn't make sense of anything. Couldn't stop shaking. "I c-can't—" she began, then clapped a hand over her mouth as a sudden hot wave of nausea churned in her throat.

"Boys, tend your chores. Take Brin with you."

Dimly she heard the scrape of chairs, footfalls fading down the hall. Propping her elbows beside her plate, she dropped her head into her hands.

Not yet. Later. Just a little while longer.

But the dam had already burst.

Declan watched her from his place at the end of the table. He hated to see her cry, but he was glad that her brittle control had finally snapped. He was surprised she'd held herself together this long. That glassy-eyed look had scared him. Like she'd moved to a place he couldn't reach, and if she kept drifting, she would disappear altogether.

He wanted to go over there and comfort her, but he wasn't sure how, or if she would even let him, so he kept his seat. "Ed," he said, finally.

Slowly she looked up.

There was a savage look in her eyes. A fury he hadn't expected. Yet beneath it, he saw the bewilderment of a stricken child.

"Why, Declan?" Her voice wobbled. Tremors shook her chin. Her eyes were seeping wounds in her pale, tear-streaked face. "Why won't you go after her?"

"And leave you and the children here alone?"

"Thomas is hurt. He could have stayed."

"Even hurt, he can go where I can't."

He watched her digest that. Then her shoulders sagged in resignation. "Yes. Thomas will find her. He'll bring her back. He promised."

Declan clamped his jaw against an unreasoning swell of resentment. He wanted to be the one to find Pru. He wanted to be the one to bring her back and wipe that stricken look from his wife's face.

"I can't leave you and the children unprotected," he said.

She looked toward the window. "I understand."

He wondered if she did. He wondered if she knew that her pain was eating a hole in his chest. "Ed, I'm sorry."

She didn't respond.

Talk to me, he wanted to shout at her. *Just talk to me.*

She didn't. And so they sat.

Gravy congealed on the plate before him. A fly

droned slow circles above the butter crock. Beyond the window, horses paced and whickered as the boys threw hay over the paddock fence.

"What happened?" she finally asked, breaking the long silence.

Declan hadn't been able to get many details from Thomas before he left, and Brin was still so upset she didn't want to talk about it, but he related what he knew. "They were fishing at the creek," he began. "Brin got bored, so she and Pru wandered a ways down the bank, hunting tadpoles. They were about fifty yards upstream when two Arapahos jumped out of the bushes and grabbed for Brin. Pru tried to stop them. Thomas heard her scream and came running, but it was two against one."

"That's how he got hurt?"

Declan nodded. "Took a knife in the leg and a rifle butt to his head. When he came to, Pru was gone."

"What about the children?"

"Jeb Kendal—you met him, that log place down from ours—he'd heard Pru's scream and had grabbed his rifle and was running toward the creek when the children came tearing out of the brush with an Indian on their tail. When the redskin saw Jeb, he ducked into the trees and the children ran to Jeb. He thought he heard a woman cry out, but wasn't sure. A minute later, Thomas staggered out of the brush. They searched, but no sign of Pru or the Indians."

She thought about that for a bit, then asked, "How do you know for certain it was Lone Tree?"

"Thomas recognized one of the braves as his kin."

"But you're not sure. It could be some other Indian."

Declan knew she was grasping at anything to keep hope alive. He didn't want to take that away from her. But he didn't want to lie to her, either. "He's certain. Same war paint, same renegade war party."

"I don't understand. It makes no sense that Lone Tree would take Pru. Does it make sense to you? Why would he do that?"

"I don't know, Ed." Declan sighed and shook his head. "Maybe since they'd missed Brin, they didn't want to go back empty-handed. Or maybe they'd seen Pru around the place and thought she was part of my family, and taking her was a way to get at me. Or maybe they took her for the hell of it. I don't know."

"What will they do to her?"

The question he dreaded. And one he couldn't answer . . . at least in a way that would give her comfort. So he told her what he'd told his children and hoped it would be enough. "Thomas will find her."

She turned toward the window again, her jaw so rigid he could see the twitch of a muscle in her cheek. "He'd better. He's her only hope now."

"Ed, I'm sorry. I wish—"

In a sudden, abrupt movement, she stood and began gathering the dirty dishes.

"I'll do that," he said, rising to his feet.

"No." Picking up a stack of plates, she carried them to the counter by the sink. "I need to do something. I can't sit and do nothing."

Implying he could.

"I would go if I could, Ed. You know that."

She didn't respond. Wouldn't even look at him.

Defeated, he turned and left the room.

He stayed away as long as he could, mucking out the stalls and nursing his guilt into a fine resentment. What did she expect him to do? Put his family at further risk? Hadn't he done that already by putting Lone Tree in jail in the first place? Did she think he didn't feel helpless, too?

Christ. Just the thought of that crazy bastard getting his hands on Pru made him want to snap the rake handle in his hands.

He knew what the man was capable of. He'd seen the bloody dress, the crushed locket. He'd heard all the grisly details from the trooper who had found the charred, twisted remains of the stage passengers. It sickened him to think of the terrible things that might be happening to Pru right now.

But it sickened him more how glad he was that it wasn't Ed suffering.

When he left the stalls, the house was dark, the children long in bed. He stopped in the yard and watched night birds loop and soar in the fading sky. On a high ridge, a coyote yodeled, and closer by, hidden in the trees behind the house, water trickling down Elderberry Creek murmured like aspens in the wind. The sound of it soothed him, calmed his frayed nerves. He stood until the last lamp up at the mine winked out, then went inside.

He paused in the kitchen and listened but heard no sound from the main bedroom. He doubted he would be welcome, but opened the door anyway. Just to check on her. Make sure she was all right.

The room was dark. But he saw her form silhouetted at the window, fully clothed. When he stepped inside, she turned but didn't speak.

Aware of her watching, he hung his hat on a peg, then looked around.

The room was crowded with boxes of items they'd salvaged from the ranch. He hadn't had a chance to put the bed together, so the mattress was on the floor, taking up most of what space was left. The smell of raw wood and whitewash and smoke-scented bedding hung in the still air.

It wasn't how he'd envisioned their first night together in the refurbished house. He should have taken them to the hotel. He should have done a lot of things.

She still watched from the window, her face in shadow, her arms folded.

He felt her censure. It eddied through the air between them, as palpable as a slap. It fed his own resentment, but none of the words he wanted to say could get past the clog of guilt in his throat.

"Pru is my sister."

Her voice was soft, the words barely more than a whisper. For a moment he thought he'd misheard. "Your sister?"

"Half sister. We have the same father."

He should have known. Pru's skin—not dark, but not white, either—that odd bond between the two women that he hadn't fully understood. Not sure how he was supposed to respond, or even how he felt about that, Declan remained silent as she walked over to the rocker beside the small coal stove.

"Pru didn't want me to tell anyone," she said as she lowered herself into the armless chair with a stiffness that told him she was still sore from the cougar attack. "She thought it brought shame to our father, that white and black shouldn't mix. But I was never ashamed of Pru. She was my salvation."

Declan moved over to sit on a crate on the other side of the unlit stove. Resting his hands on his thighs, he said, "Tell me about her."

So she did, her words halting and slow at first, but gathering momentum and emotion as she went along—how inseparable they'd been as children, running through the slave cabins, fishing in the

361

bayou, trading notes behind the back of the tutor her father had insisted teach both girls.

"And your mother?" Declan prodded when she fell silent. "How did she react to that?"

"She hated it. She hated Pru because her own daughter wasn't as smart or beautiful as a slave's daughter. She hated me because I loved Pru more than her. But mostly she hated Daddy." She sighed. A sad, forlorn sound. An echo of the wounded child still trapped inside her. "I think she beat us because she couldn't get at him."

She fell silent again. Declan sensed she was mulling through her memories and was content to wait until she felt like talking again.

"I know I depend on her too much," she admitted in a voice thick with tears. "We talked about it. She said that once I was settled here she would go out on her own. Maybe start a school for Negroes. Teach them to read. I want her to do that. I want to let her go so she can build her own life. I do. But not like this. Not like this, Declan."

Her voice was weaker now, and so broken he could hardly make out her words. "It's like something has been torn away, and there's this giant, empty place inside me. And I don't—I don't know how to fill it." She leaned forward, her hands pressed to her face, and even though he couldn't see her face in the shadows, he knew she was crying.

Unable to sit by any longer, he lifted her from

the chair, then sat in the rocker with her in his lap. Murmuring softly, he rocked her as he'd rocked Joe Bill the night he'd told him his mother was dead. Unlike his son, Ed didn't fight him but curled against him, her face tucked under his chin, and gave in to her grief.

After a while, his arms began to ache and his feet fell asleep. But he continued to hold her and rock her, his cheek pressed against the crown of her head. Eventually, the crying slowly faded into sharp, hitching breaths, and he knew she was done.

"I would fill that empty place if I could," he said against her hair.

She sniffled and blotted at her face. "You're too big."

He was heartened to hear that, knowing that if she could make a joke—weak though it was—she was going to be all right.

"Besides," she added, sniffling again, "you have your own place."

That he did. And it was going numb with her sitting on it so long. Hating to move her, but needing to get blood flowing through his legs again, he lifted her up and set her on her feet between his knees. Then he reached up and began unbuttoning her dress.

She didn't stop him.

"Tomorrow I'll sign up a new deputy. Lift your arms." When she did, he shoved the dress over her head, tossed it aside, and started in on the tabs on her underskirt. "And I'll move the boys into the hotel with you and Brin. Step out."

"The hotel?" Bracing a hand on his shoulder, she stepped out of the petticoat. "I thought we would be staying here now."

"It's safer at the hotel."

"You don't think we'll be safe here?"

"Not with me gone." He tossed the petticoat on top of her dress, then faced his last obstacle—a filmy underthing that molded so sweetly to her body, even in the dim light he could see the shiver and quiver of every breath she took.

"Gone? Gone where?"

"After Pru." He reached for the hem of her underthing.

Her hands stopped him, capturing his face and tilting up his head so she could see into his eyes. "You've changed your mind. Why?"

"It's what you want. What you need for me to do."

"I need for you to stay safe."

"You can't have it both ways, Ed. I can't stay safe here with you and go after Pru at the same time."

"Then I'll go with you."

"No."

"But—"

"You'll stay. Because that's what I need for you to do."

She looked so beautiful to him right then,

silvered by moonlight, her expressive eyes so raw with emotion he knew he was seeing her as few ever had. Unguarded. Unmasked. Open to him in a way she had never been.

Reaching up, he brushed a curl off her brow. "I couldn't entrust my children to anyone but you, Ed."

He thought she would cry again. Instead, she leaned down and kissed him. Not tentatively. But with a fierce urgency that went beyond sex or lust. A mark of possession. A branding. "I love you, Declan."

Something swelled inside him, something he couldn't contain, a burst of joy so intense it pressed against his ribs and his heart. Struck mute by the force of it, he couldn't speak, and so acted, instead. With shaking hands, he pulled the chemise up and off. And there they were, those round, perfect breasts that were just pointy enough. Lifting his hand, he brushed his fingertips across a puckered tip and heard her breathing change.

He hadn't meant to do this. He hadn't intended to take her to bed. But he had wanted to comfort her, and this was the best way he knew how.

And she didn't stop him.

So he set to work on one breast, then the other, until she was pushing against him and her hands were gripping his hair to keep him on task.

"You'll find her and bring her back." Her breath came short and fast.

"Yes," he said against her damp skin.

"And you'll stay safe."

"Yes." Sliding his hand down over her soft, smooth butt, he lifted her right leg over his left thigh.

"And you'll come back to me."

"Yes." He slipped his hand between her legs.

"Say it."

"I'll come back to you. Always."

Her fingers clutched at his hair, pulled him so close to her chest he could feel the vibration of her heart against his lips. "Declan," she cried.

And that was the end of the hunt.

For her, anyway.

That time.

Dawn was just breaking over the mountains when Declan took his family to the hotel. He had expected some resistance from Lucinda—not about bringing Ed and the children but about waking her up at such an early hour: Lucinda Hathaway didn't seem the kind of woman to keep country hours. But she rushed down, still in her robe, relieved they'd returned safely from the ranch and anxious for news of Pru.

When Declan said they'd heard nothing and that he was leaving to search for her and hoped the family could stay at the hotel, she immediately took charge. Giving a key and hurried instructions to Miriam, one of the hotel workers, she told the children to go with her upstairs, where Miriam would help them settle into the suite they were to share with Ed.

"I'm giving them the room at the end of the hall." She pressed a key in Ed's hand. "That'll be safest, I think. I can even post a man at the head of the stairs, if you'd like. From that vantage point he can see anyone coming up from the lobby or down from the roof."

"I'd appreciate that," Declan said.

City woman or not, Lucinda was smart as a whip, and Declan had no doubt she could keep things in hand. He suspected the pretty Yankee had some hard experience behind her, and unlike the head-in-the-clouds Englishwoman, Maddie, she would know what to do in a crisis. Ed had proven she could keep her head, too, but with four children to keep track of, and worry over Pru to distract her, she might not be as alert to her own safety as he needed her to be.

"I'll be back or send word as soon as I can. I sure thank you for—"

Lucinda cut him off with a wave of her hand. "Just do what you need to do, Mr. Brodie, and bring Pru home. Maddie and I will watch out for your family until you get back." Putting on a smile, she patted Ed's shoulder. "I'll go wake up Maddie and get dressed. Then we'll see to breakfast."

"Thank you, Lucinda. From both of us."

"You're welcome. Now go get Pru, Mr. Brodie." Turning, the small blond headed up the stairs.

Declan looked down at his wife's tense face. He could see she was torn—send him after her sister—keep him safe with her. They'd talked about it in bed—after, when their bodies were worn out, but their thoughts were too churned up to let them rest.

Stay. Go. I'm afraid, she'd said in that hour of hush just before dawn.

To ease her worries, he'd told her the decision was out of her hands and that he *had* to go—*needed* to go—because her sister was his sister now, and he wasn't leaving her out there on her own. Which was true.

She had wept then, wrapping her arms tight around him, her tears hot and salty on his tongue as he'd moved inside her one last time.

"I'll be careful," he said now, as he had so many other times during the night. "Guthrie is going with me, remember. We'll find her."

On the way in, he'd awakened Ed Church in the telegraph office and had him send a wire to the commander at Fort Lasswell, explaining the situation and asking if Guthrie's men could help him out a while longer.

Declan hadn't told the fort commander that Pru was half black or that the deputy who had gone after her was a mixed-breed Cheyenne Dog Soldier. Things were complicated enough as it was.

He got his answer back right away. Five days. Then Guthrie's patrol was to wire back for further orders. Not much, but it would help.

So now he waited, telegram with orders in hand, ready to hand it over to the lieutenant as soon as he came downstairs.

"I'll guard your children with my life," Ed said.

"You already have," he said. "And they're your children, too."

She shot him a wobbly smile. "What should we do about Brin's birthday?"

"Have it anyway. My gift for her is in the sheriff's office on top of the gun rack."

"I'd rather wait for you."

"She needs something to take her mind off Pru. You all do."

She sighed and fiddled with the loose ties on her bonnet. They lapsed into silence, that awkward, waiting kind of silence that comes just before a difficult parting, when all the good-byes have been said, and all the warnings and instructions have been issued, and there's nothing left to say.

Except Declan had a lot more he wanted to say. He just wasn't sure now was the time to do it. Telling a woman what she meant to you, then riding away from her seemed cowardly to him. Like dumping a load of rocks at her feet, saying, "Look what I got you," and leaving her to do something with it. It was a risk. She might surprise you.

Or it could end badly.

Besides, such last-minute declarations had a fatalistic sound to them—a hint of that "just in case something bad happens" desperation that would only feed her fears. Better to put on a brave show and let her think this parting was nothing to worry about, that he'd be back soon and everything was just fine.

"You have the note for Emmet Gebbers?" he asked her.

She patted the drawstring purse hanging off her wrist. "I'll go by the bank as soon as it opens."

"Buck Aldrich should make a good deputy. If he can't do it, tell Emmet to talk to his brother." Thrusting his hands in his trouser pockets, he watched an ant scurry an erratic path across the plank floor. "I've also left instructions in the note for Emmet to let you sign on my account there at the bank, just in case."

Her head whipped toward him. "In case of what?"

He put on a smile, mentally cursing himself for putting that look of fear back in her eyes. "In case you need money for that dress in the front window at the mercantile I've seen you eyeing."

She looked away. "As if I'd buy store-bought. Especially from that Cal Bagley." She wound the end of her bonnet tie around her finger, unrolled it, rolled it again. He could see her hands were shaking.

Then in a sudden, accusing, almost resentful

tone, she said, "I didn't want to love you. I certainly didn't expect to. It complicates everything."

"It does?"

"Of course it does. If you don't come back—"

"I'll come back." Seeing the beginnings of tears again, he blurted out the words he'd wanted to say days ago but had felt too awkward to voice. "I love you, too, Ed."

"Now he says it."

He bent down for a kiss, got a punch in the arm instead. Fighting a smile, he straightened. "I do love you." It was easier the second time.

"Honestly." She waved a hand in dismissal, almost smacking him in the face with her purse dangling from her wrist. "That doesn't count for much if you say it *after* someone says it to you first."

"It doesn't?"

"Of course not. It sounds forced and insincere." She straightened the brim of her bonnet he'd bent when he tried to kiss her, then laced her fingers at her waist in a grip tight enough to choke a rooster. "You'll have to do better when you get back."

"How about I do better right now? You have the room key Lucinda gave you, don't you?"

Her lips twitched. "Don't be nasty."

"I thought you liked when I was nasty."

"The point is, Declan, that before you go gallivanting off taking foolish risks, you think about me and the children and Amos and Chick and your dog and all the people in this town who love and depend on you."

The dog, too?

"We need for you to come back. With or without Pru."

His amusement faded when he saw her blinking hard. "I'll come back, Ed. Always."

"You'd better."

"I will."

"Now." When he didn't respond, she peered up at him, her eyes wet and red-rimmed. "Now would be a good time to say that you love me."

"I love you."

"I know. Now behave." Lifting a hand, she waggled her fingers at the two figures coming down the stairs. "Morning, Lieutenant Guthrie, Sergeant Quinlan. Declan's going with you. Isn't that grand?"

Lieutenant Guthrie read his new orders, muttered something unkind about the commander, then told Quinlan to roust out the men. "Boot to boot. Twenty minutes, outside the livery." Turning back to Declan, he asked, "Figure it's the same war party that hit your place and Parker's?"

"I do."

"Hell, Sheriff—sorry, ma'am—what'd you do to that Indian?"

"My duty."

"Well, now he's mine, damn it all—sorry again, ma'am. Let's get going then."

SEVENTEEN

The best way to catch up with Pru was to catch up with Thomas—no one knew this country as well as he did. That in mind, Declan led Guthrie and his men along the edge of the Ragged Mountains, past the gorge, then north into the Ruby Range and prime summer hunting grounds. After the Sand Creek Massacre six years ago, remnants of Thomas's old tribe had settled up there on an aspen and spruce bench bordering a fast-moving creek. Declan figured if Thomas had gone there first, maybe someone in the village would know where the warrior had headed from there.

It was hard going up steep trails and over occasional hard-crusted patches of icy snow. As they passed beneath the Raggeds, slabs of polished rock soared upward, ending in the jagged, sharp-edged silhouette that had earned the range its name, while below them, barely heard over the clatter of hooves on the rocky trail, the roar of Anthracite Creek through Dark Canyon sounded like a continuous roll of distant thunder.

Declan tried to keep his breathing even. The higher they climbed, the more often they had to stop to allow the horses to blow, and even Declan found his lungs pumping harder than usual in the thin air. But that could have been fear. He hated these high trails. Even so, with the cool weather, good forage for the horses where they camped, and plentiful game, they made good time.

Two days after leaving Heartbreak Creek they topped a low ridge above a narrow valley and saw an Indian encampment strung out along a shallow, rocky creek a quarter mile away.

Declan reined in. "How do you want to do this?" he asked Guthrie.

"I'm thinking." The lieutenant punctuated that with a stream of tobacco juice, then reached into the *sabretache* case hanging off his sword belt and pulled out a brass telescope. He peered through it at the village, then handed it to Declan. "Eleven tipis, less than two dozen horses. Mostly women and children. A poor group."

Hearing that, Declan was glad of the deer he'd shot earlier and strapped behind his saddle. With so many warriors lost in the Indian wars, he figured keeping a tribe fed would be a harder task than usual, and maybe the gift of fresh meat would be his entry into the village.

He scanned with the scope but didn't see Thomas's horse, which told him Lone Tree probably wasn't in the village, either. Yet he thought he recognized the markings on a tipi in the center of the encampment. After Sally had disappeared, he and Thomas had come through here and had spoken with an elder—Spotted

Horse, if he remembered right—and the old Cheyenne's tipi had carried the same galloping horse drawings as the one he saw now.

Sliding the telescope closed, he returned it to the lieutenant. "How about I go in alone?"

"How about you don't?" Guthrie dropped the scope back into his *sabretache* and rolled the wad of tobacco to his other cheek. "You get yourself killed and I'm back to second lieutenant. Again."

Declan tried not to let his frustration show. "Then why don't we all go partway so they'll see you and know you're there. Then I'll go the rest of the way by myself."

Declan still hadn't told him that Pru was half black and Thomas was a Cheyenne Dog Soldier, fearing the lieutenant would balk at his orders. Guthrie would find out soon enough, but hopefully not before Declan located Thomas.

Guthrie chewed thoughtfully.

"You said it was a poor group," Declan reminded him. "I don't want to scare them. If these folks are who I think they are, a lot of them were at Sand Creek. I don't want them thinking this is another raid."

Guthrie studied him through narrowed eyes. "Indian lover, are you?"

Ignoring that, Declan pointed to a stand of aspen and spruce about twenty yards back from the far side of the creek. "You could circle around and come out of those trees. That way, if things go sour, you'll have cover behind you and the creek in front."

"While you go in alone."

"There's a better chance they'll talk to one civilian than a dozen troopers."

Guthrie chewed and thought.

Declan wanted to reach over and thump the man's head just to make sure it wasn't hollow. "No use getting your men involved unless there's good cause."

"Well . . ."

Twenty minutes later, Declan left the troopers waiting in front of the trees across from the village and rode down into the rocky creek bed. He knew the villagers had seen them, but no shots sounded and no arrows whistled through the air, and no one called out a warning as his horse clattered up the bank beside the village, so he figured he was safe. For now.

It was midafternoon, and the sun was already pressing against the mountain ridges. The women would be stoking the cook fires and pounding berries and nuts and corn into pemmican. Boys would be driving the horses to fresh grass and hobbling them for the night, and the old men would be waiting patiently for their evening meal. Any warriors that were left would step into their tipis to gather bows and rifles before coming to challenge him. Anticipating that, he held himself stiffly, looking neither right nor left, half expecting an arrow to stab into his back as he wound through the tipis toward the one with the running-horse markings.

But he saw no warriors, only tired-faced women and unsmiling children. The meat hanging over the cook fires seemed meager and stringy, and even the dogs looked half starved as they circled around him, sniffing at the deer carcass. The smell of wood smoke mingled with the reek of curing hides staked out on the tanning poles and the stench of the latrine trench behind the village. As he rode by, heads poked out of tipis and children ran up, and soon a string of curious women and children fell in behind him. When he reached the tipi he thought he recognized, he reined in the gelding and sat waiting.

After a few moments, a gray head poked out of the hide-hung door, then an old man emerged. Declan was relieved to see he was the same elder he and Thomas had spoken to four years ago. He hoped the old warrior remembered him, as well.

He dismounted and raised a palm to the old man, whose dark eyes stared back out of a wrinkled, expressionless face that boasted a lantern jaw and a nose that could filet meat. "Spotted Horse," Declan said with a nod of respect. "I am glad to find you well." He spoke in English, hoping the old man was still familiar enough with the language to understand him.

Declan's understanding of the Cheyenne tongue was spotty, at best.

The old man squinted through the smoke of his campfire. "That is a nice deer you have there."

"I would like for you to have it." Declan untied the carcass. As it slid to the ground, two women rushed forward to drag it away, trailed by a pack of sniffing dogs.

Declan turned back to find the old man studying him thoughtfully. "I remember you," the Indian said. "You are called Big Bob."

Declan nodded.

"That is a foolish name." He motioned for Declan to sit on the woven rug outside his tipi, then stiffly lowered himself into a cross-legged position across from him. "Now, Mangas Coloradas. He was a big one."

"So I heard."

"Bigger than you."

Declan nodded, wondering if there was a reason the old man was bringing up an Apache chief who'd been dead for over seven years.

"The blue coats cut off his head and sent it to your Great White Father. Do you know why they would do that to their red brother?"

"Bad people come in all colors, Spotted Horse."

The old man nodded and sighed. "This is true."

Silence. Declan heard movement behind him, but resisted the urge to look around, figuring if they had wanted to kill him, he would already be dead. He continued to sit without moving, his gaze fixed on the old man's, refusing to be the one to look away first. After a while, despite the cool breeze, his shirt felt damp against his back.

"You came before," the Indian finally said. "Seeking your lost wife."

"Yes. I came with Thomas Redstone."

"I remember. Why do you come this time?"

"I'm looking for my new wife's sister."

"You lose a lot of women, white man."

Behind him, someone who apparently understood English snickered. Heat rose in Declan's neck, but he kept his face impassive.

"Why have you brought blue coats to our peaceful village, Big Bob?"

"We mean no harm, Spotted Horse. We only seek news of my friend, Thomas Redstone, who was once a member of your tribe."

"There are not many of us left."

"I'm sorry to hear that."

They sat without speaking for several more minutes. Then the Indian pointed at Declan's waist and said, "That is a fine belt you have there."

Declan looked down at the fancy tooled belt that had been a gift from Sally the year Brin was born. "It is."

"I wish I had such a fine belt."

"Take mine." He unbuckled and handed the belt over.

The old man put it on and didn't seem to mind that it was at least eight inches too big. He showed gapped teeth in a broad smile. "It is a fine belt."

Declan nodded, hoping he could keep his pants up until he cut a length of rope to replace it.

"Thomas Redstone was here this morning," Spotted Horse said.

Declan tried to mask his excitement. "Do you know where he was going when he left?"

"After the woman you lost." Apparently pleased with his quip, he grinned again. "He thinks she is his woman."

"She is," Declan said, wondering if that was true. "I've come to help him find her."

"With blue coats."

Declan didn't respond.

"He believes Lone Tree took this woman. Do you also believe that?"

"I do."

"Such trouble over a squaw." The old man sighed and shook his head. "Will the blue coats fight him to get your lost woman back?"

It sounded cowardly, the way the old man said it, but Declan didn't rise to the bait. "If he won't give her up, then yes, the blue coats will fight. Many will die."

"Many have already died."

A gust swept through, kicking up grit and smoke and pulling long gray strands from the old man's topknot to whip across his face. Spotted Horse was a proud old warrior, but years of strife had bowed his shoulders and shrunk muscle to bone. His wrists looked frail as twigs. "We only want peace, Big Bob. We need no blue coats here."

"Then tell me where Lone Tree is, and we will leave."

It was a long time before the old man spoke. When he did, he sounded weary and sad. "Crystal River."

"What's this?" Brin held up the dress Edwina had made.

"Haven't you ever seen a dress before?" Mary Lynn Waltham snickered at the other four girls and shot a shifty glance at the three boys to gauge their reactions.

Cruelty loves company even more than misery, Edwina had found.

To their credit, none of Brin's brothers cracked a smile.

"And it will look lovely on you, Brin." Edwina forced delight into her voice, sorry that she had gone against her better judgment and allowed this birthday party. It was all Lucinda's and Maddie's idea, bless their hearts.

"I am sick to death of watching you pace and having your downcast children moping about the hotel," Lucinda had announced over breakfast yesterday morning. "So we're planning a birthday party for Brin. You're in charge of getting the boys presentable and there on time. Maddie and I will take care of the rest."

Edwina had feigned enthusiasm throughout the preparations, but anyone seeing her haggard face had probably known it for the ruse it was. Then to make a difficult situation even worse, she had stupidly invited Mary Lynn Waltham, a spiteful creature every bit as vicious as her mother, Alice.

"Where's she supposed to wear a dress?" Joe Bill asked, then looked around in confusion as more giggles erupted.

Edwina shot him a warning look that missed. Boys were so dense.

But Brin wasn't. She stared stonily at the table before her, color blooming across her cheeks.

"Church," Edwina said loudly, trying to divert attention to herself. "I think it will look lovely on her when we go to church tomorrow."

"Church?" Snorting with laughter, Mary Lynn rocked back in her chair, pudgy hands over her mouth. "They'd never let her in after last time."

"They let you in," Joe Bill said, nastily.

"I didn't bring a dead rat."

Stepping in before Joe Bill erupted, Edwina said, "Yes, church. It's a place where they teach kindness and generosity. Have you never been?"

This time, it was Joe Bill who snickered. Edwina adored him for that.

Mary Lynn stuck out her tongue at him. "Wouldn't let you in, either."

"Would, too."

"You stink."

"Don't, either."

"I think it's a pretty dress," Lucas mumbled, then blushed furiously when the Martinez twins looked his way.

With an elaborate yawn to indicate that this whole birthday thing was so tiresome she could hardly stay awake, Brin plopped down and began bouncing her heel against the leg of her chair.

R.D. yawned back and grinned.

Edwina wanted to hug him almost as much as she itched to slap that smirk off Mary Lynn Waltham's fat face.

Luckily before she did either, Maddie rushed in from the kitchen, clapping her hands. "Who's ready for cake?"

Instantly diverted, the five little girls all bounced in their chairs and squealed, "Me, me, me!" The three brothers just grinned.

Brin took advantage of the distraction to cram the dress back into the box with grim-faced efficiency.

"Why did I invite that nasty child?" Edwina muttered as she followed Lucinda into the hotel kitchen to get the cake. "She's as bad as her mother. Now I'll never get Brin in a dress."

"The rag doll was a hit," Lucinda offered in a soothing tone.

"With the other girls, perhaps. Brin was more

taken with the hat her father got her. What kind of man gives a hat like that to a child? Is she a cowpuncher? No. She's a little girl and should be treated like one."

Lucinda laughed softly. "Take heart. The hat's so big even her ears can't hold it up. Hopefully, by the time it fits she'll have no desire to wear it. Now take these and try not to hurt the children." She handed Edwina a stack of plates with forks on top. "I'll bring the cake."

The rest of the gathering passed without incident, and after the last parent came to pick up the last child, and the boys had taken Brin and the slingshot Joe Bill had given her out behind the hotel to try it out, Edwina collapsed, exhausted, into a chair. "I'm never doing that again."

"Not until the next birthday, anyway." Lucinda plopped on a chair beside Maddie.

"I think it was lovely," Maddie said, apparently unfazed by the icing smears, cake crumbs, and lemonade stains on her dress. "I love to watch children enjoy themselves."

"You would have made a wonderful mother," Lucinda observed.

Maddie's smile faltered. "Sadly, we'll never know."

"Don't be silly," Lucinda argued. "Cross your Angus off as a lost cause, announce yourself a widow, then find another man. It's not as if any-one from England or Scotland would ever find out."

Maddie looked thoughtfully out the window where Brin chased Joe Bill with a stick. "Dead is so final."

"Well, that's the point, dear. I know you cared for your husband, but really, enough is enough."

"I suppose you're right."

But she didn't look convinced. Nor did she seem to be enjoying the turn in the conversation. Hoping to steer them toward a happier subject, Edwina asked Lucinda if she had ever been married.

An odd look crossed the blond woman's face, then was quickly masked by a bored smile. "Almost. But luckily I came to my senses before the vows were said."

Maddie tsked. "Left him at the altar, did you? Not well done of you, Luce."

"Actually I left him at his lawyer's office. *After* he signed over several hundred railroad shares as my wedding gift."

"You robbed him?"

Lucinda's self-satisfied smile faded. A hard look came into her green eyes. "As he robbed the poor workers who died like flies making him rich. Waste no pity on him, Maddie. He deserved what he got, and more."

"But you *stole!*" Maddie stared at her friend as if she had never seen her before. "Why would you do such a thing?"

"Simple revenge."

Maddie looked at Edwina, her expression mirroring the same shock and bewilderment Edwina was feeling. Neither had ever seen this side of their friend. "Revenge for what?" Edwina dared to ask.

Lucinda sat forward, her clenched hand on top of the table. In a voice vibrating with a fury Edwina never would have guessed smoldered beneath that cool façade, she said, "For watching my parents die of too much toil and too little food. For being cast penniless and parentless on the streets of a dangerous city with nothing but my wits and hate to keep me alive."

As if suddenly realizing she had said too much, she abruptly sat back. Her hand relaxed. "But here I am." She made a languid offhand gesture that belied the pain still lingering in her eyes. "Very much alive. Very rich. And very happily *un*married. Revenge at its sweetest."

Blinking hard, Maddie reached over and put her hand over Lucinda's. "Oh, Luce. How you must have suffered. I'm so sorry he did that to you."

Lucinda shifted in the chair. "Not him . . . exactly. But his kind."

"His kind?"

"Fat, rich industrialists with their stinking factories. And railroaders. They're awful. All of them."

But Edwina heard something else in her voice. Regret? Was that why Lucinda was spending all her stolen money on this poor little town? To atone for what she had done? Did she care about the man she had wronged?

Maddie gave a weak laugh and sat back. "What a pitiful group of ladies we are. Edwina with a mail-order stranger for a husband. Me with my indifferent husband. And Lucinda with her almost-husband."

Edwina felt a sudden sting of tears. *And Pru?* Where did Pru fit in all this? As happened so frequently over the last days, whenever she thought of Pru and Declan, Edwina's spirits would plummet. How could they sit here chatting and enjoying cake while the two people she loved most in the world were possibly hurt or in danger? "He's not a stranger," she blurted out. "He's my husband. And I love him."

Lucinda and Maddie turned their heads to look at her.

Embarrassed to talk about such a private thing, Edwina was nevertheless driven to share with her dearest friends the intense feelings churning inside of her. "It was a surprise. He was a surprise. Like an unexpected gift that you didn't know you wanted until you opened it up and saw it and realized it was exactly what you had craved all your life."

Maddie's eyes glittered with tears. "Oh, Edwina. I'm so happy for you. Although I knew it would happen. Luce, didn't I say just the other day that those two are meant for each other?"

Lucinda didn't answer, but continued to study Edwina, her expression thoughtful. "He returns your feelings, I trust?" she asked after a moment.

"So he says." Edwina tried to cover her blush by sipping from her glass, then set it aside with a barely suppressed shudder. Despite all the lemons and sugar, the water still tasted rank. "He acts like he does."

"Ah. And by that smile I'm guessing consummation has occurred?"

"Repeatedly."

"Oh, I just love consummation." Maddie sighed. "I think that's what I miss most. That, and Angus's smile. He usually strives to be so stiff and correct, but when he smiles . . ." Her voice trailed off as that dreamy look came into her eyes.

"Stiff is good," Lucinda observed.

It took a moment for the words to sink in. Edwina and Maddie stared at Lucinda in shock, then all three women burst into laughter, which instantly swept away any lingering emotional tension. It was the first time Edwina had laughed in days, and it felt good.

"Are you truly attending church tomorrow?" Maddie asked her after the merriment had faded away. "If so, I might join you. Send up a prayer for Prudence and Mr. Brodie, as it were."

"I'll go, too," Lucinda said thoughtfully. "If we're going to have a church in this town, it should at least have a coat of paint and something other than a draped tobacco crate for an altar."

"I doubt they could afford it," Edwina said.

Tipping her head against the back of the chair, Lucinda closed her eyes and smiled. "No, but I can."

"You piss like a buffalo, white man," a voice quipped.

"Hung like one, too," Declan quipped back. Fastening the button fly on his Levi Strauss denims, Declan tightened the rope he was using in place of his belt and turned to see Thomas limping out from behind a tall spruce.

"*Haaahe*," he said, greeting the Cheyenne is his own language. He was pretty sure it meant "hello."

They had picked up the warrior's trail earlier and had made no effort to mask their movements, hoping he would hear them and circle back to see who was following him. Which apparently he had. "How's your leg?"

Thomas shrugged. His gaze flicked past Declan's shoulder. He frowned. "Your soldier friends do not look happy."

Declan glanced around to see Guthrie stomping toward him, Sergeant Quinlan on his heels. "I just now told them who it was we were following."

"And who am I, *nesene*?"

"You're a Heartbreak Creek deputy who also

happens to be a Cheyenne Dog Soldier. You don't make this any easier, you know, when you paint yourself up like that. Especially with that bruise."

"Do I frighten them?"

"Hell, you frighten me."

Thomas gave one of his rare laughs and pounded Declan on the back. *"Va'ohtama, hovahe.* I am glad to see you, Declan Brodie."

"This your deputy?" Guthrie asked, coming up. "Looks more like a goddamned savage to me."

The Cheyenne warrior graciously tipped his head. *"Nia'ish."*

"What's that supposed to mean?"

"Thank you," Thomas said and smiled.

Declan could see where this was headed. "If you two dogs are done sniffing, can we tend to business here?"

Guthrie cursed and spat. Quinlan remained silent, either accustomed to the lieutenant's bluster or struck dumb by Thomas's garish war paint.

"Lone Tree's encampment is two hours north," Thomas said. With a stick, he drew a map in the dirt, showing the ox-bow bend in the canyon that sheltered the village, where the tipis were, and how many warriors and ponies he had counted. He poked the stick into the dirt. "Cliffs rise across the river here, on the north. The river circles around the village on the east and west. South is the only way in. They will see us coming."

"Forty-five of them against fourteen of us,"

Guthrie muttered. "I don't like those odds."

Thomas tossed the stick into the brush and rubbed the dirt off his fingers. "Not all of them will fight."

"How do you know?"

"Many are from my old tribe. They will not fight me over a woman. Nor will I fight them."

"Then how do you expect to get her back?"

"I will challenge Lone Tree for her."

"No, you won't." Declan had been expecting this, knowing Thomas would feel obligated to avenge Pru since she had been in his care when the Indian took her. But this wasn't just about Pru. This was about Sally's death, and Declan's determination to keep his children and Ed safe. Besides, he'd started this mess in the first place—he should be the one to end it. "I'll deal with Lone Tree. You just keep the rest of the tribe from joining in."

"No, *nesene'*." The smile Thomas gave him carried a wealth of evil intent. "I will fight Lone Tree. I will get Prudence Lincoln back."

"Damnit, Thomas! There's no need—"

"There is every need!"

The explosive outburst startled the two soldiers into reaching for their pistols. Declan threw out a hand and told them to stand down. When they reluctantly did, he returned his attention to Thomas.

And waited.

The Cheyenne stood rigidly for a moment, then seemed to come to a decision. He let out a deep breath and said in a calmer voice, "There is every need, *nesene'*. Prudence is my woman."

It was unexpected, but not surprising. "For true?"

"Soon."

"Your woman?" Guthrie burst out. "I thought she was your wife's kin, Brodie. If I'd known she was just some damn squaw who ran off—"

Declan rounded on him with such savage suddenness the soldier stumbled back a step, almost falling into Quinlan. "Don't! Not another word."

Silence. Quinlan blinked at Declan over the lieutenant's shoulder, his mustache quivering with indignation. Or fear. Hard to tell.

Muttering under his breath, Guthrie looked away, chewing hard and fast on his wad of tobacco. "Goddamn Indians."

Declan turned back to Thomas. "You're not going in alone."

Thomas shrugged.

"Are you even sure she's there?"

"She is tied to a pole outside Lone Tree's tipi."

Declan cursed. "Bastard's using her for bait."

Thomas nodded. "He expects you to come." He smiled that smile again. "Instead he will get me."

"Then what the hell are we here for?" Guthrie demanded angrily, raring to make up for his momentary loss of backbone.

"Are you so ready to kill Indians, blue coat?"

"Hold up!" Declan stepped between the two men, palms raised. "There may be no need to put your men at risk, Lieutenant. We might be able to do this without bloodshed. Just hear me out."

Guthrie leaned over and spit tobacco, narrowly missing Declan's boot. "So, talk."

Declan talked.

That was four hours ago. Now at full dark, he and Thomas were in a stand of spruce on the south approach to the village, and Guthrie's men should soon be moving into position on the cliff across from the village.

"*Taha'o'he.*" Thomas pointed toward the dark mass of the rocky bluff silhouetted against the starlit sky.

Peering through pale bands of smoke hanging above the tipis, Declan studied the cliffs facing them from the other side of the river. High up, a shadow moved. Then, another.

Guthrie's men were in place.

Declan let out a relieved breath.

He'd had a time of it, convincing the hotheaded lieutenant this was to be a negotiation, not a bloodbath like the ones at Sand Creek and Summit Springs. Guthrie and his men were to hold their positions unless either Thomas or Declan gave the signal to fire—a dropped kerchief —or unless either of them was killed outright. The troopers were Declan's hole card, but he didn't want to play it unless the Indians forced him to.

Convincing Thomas was a lot harder. The warrior wanted to ride into the village and bury a lance in the dirt outside Lone Tree's tipi. But Declan could see the Cheyenne was favoring his leg and was still suffering headaches from the blow to his head. There was no guarantee he would survive a fight to the death. Then what would happen to Pru? And if Thomas killed Lone Tree, the Arapaho's kin might feel compelled to issue other challenges, and it could go on forever.

Besides, the responsibility for this mess was on him, not Thomas.

In the end, they compromised. The troopers would take firing positions on the bluff and watch. At dawn, Declan and Thomas would ride into the village together. But instead of going straight to where Pru was tied, they would go to Chief Lean Bear's tipi, where Thomas would try to negotiate Pru's release. If that didn't work, he would demand that a council be summoned to settle the matter. And if that failed, too, Declan would play the soldier card and hope the council would rather give up one woman than risk losing more warriors to the blue coats.

"Lone Tree has broken with the tribe before," Thomas whispered beside him. "He may not listen to the council this time, either." It was obvious the Dog Soldier needed blood on his

394

hands to avenge Pru, but Declan wanted to avoid that if he could. Too many had died as it was.

"Then I'll arrest him for abduction and my late wife's death."

Thomas's snort showed what he thought of that idea.

Declan sighed wearily. "If the council won't agree to that"—which they both knew it wouldn't —"then you can kill Lone Tree." Not that Thomas needed his permission.

After a long silence, Thomas said, "The blue coat lieutenant said Prudence Lincoln is kin to your wife. This is true?"

"They have the same father."

"Ho. Does this mean I must suffer the shame of being brother to a white man?"

"You're already grandson to a white man," Declan reminded him. "Besides, you don't know yet if Pru will have you."

Thomas laughed softly. "She will have me."

With a sigh, Declan rolled onto his back and stared up through the prickly spruce branches at the slow-moving crescent moon. He thought of Ed looking up at this same moon, and how beautiful she'd looked three nights ago, cloaked in silvery light when he'd laid her out on the mattress on the floor of the town house.

She said she loved him. A wondrous thing. Even now the idea of that amazed him and brought a smile to his face as he stared up into the night sky.

Then he remembered Pru, tied like a beast to a pole outside Lone Tree's tipi, and his smile faded.

Tomorrow, he promised himself. This would be over, Pru would be safe, Lone Tree would no longer be a threat, and he could go back to Ed— the crazy, courageous woman who had worked her way past his bitterness to wrap her gentle, joyful spirit around his distrustful heart. Then finally, the life he had always envisioned for himself could begin.

EIGHTEEN

As dawn spilled over the east canyon ridges, sending long shafts of sunlight through the haze of smoke hanging over the river from last night's cooking fires, Declan and Thomas rode toward the Indian encampment.

"You do not need to come," Thomas said yet again.

"You're not going in there alone."

"She is my woman."

Declan turned his head toward Thomas, and saw a man he greatly respected, despite their differences. A man he owed. But Thomas was a warrior first, and Declan knew the Cheyenne's first instinct was to go into Lone Tree's home ground and challenge him to a fight to the death. Reason told Declan that would only lead to more bloodshed—maybe even Thomas's or Pru's. The lawman in him was hoping for a more considered approach. The friend part of him wanted to keep Thomas safe.

"Did you let me go alone when we went looking for Sally?" he asked.

Thomas stared stoically between his horse's ears, his lips pressed flat against his teeth.

"You're not going in there alone," Declan said again.

Thomas muttered something in Cheyenne under his breath, then glared over at Declan. "Then I will speak for both of us. You will say nothing and do nothing unless I tell you."

"Sure, Ma."

Thomas frowned. "Who is Ma?"

"Just remember," Declan warned, no longer amused. "We're here to get Prudence Lincoln out. Not kill Lone Tree. You can come back later and do that if you want. But today we ride straight to the chief's tipi and try to do this in a reasonable way."

Thomas glowered at the trail ahead.

As they rode closer, Declan could see the village was awakening. Women were heading into the trees to gather firewood. Young boys were bringing the horses in from the meadow, while others headed to the latrine on the far side of the tipis. Fresh smoke rose lazily into the still morning air, and in the distance, voices called out and children laughed. A marked difference from the air of defeat Declan had sensed in Spotted Horse's camp.

The village dogs noticed them first. Rushing forward, they barked and circled, making the horses snort and sidestep, their ears swiveling. Behind them came children and gangly boys with their first bows. Several recognized Thomas and waved. The braver ones ran beside Declan's horse, reaching out to touch his knee or boot, or sometimes his horse's bridle or saddle—counting coup, adolescent style.

Then the warriors appeared, both Cheyenne and their allies and kinsmen, the Arapaho, rifles or bows in hand. None wore war bonnets or war paint, and they seemed more curious than threatening. Many, seeing Thomas, called greetings.

Thomas nodded in return, but didn't speak.

Declan kept his eyes forward.

The encampment was much like Spotted Horse's village, except the people and dogs looked fatter, and the women smiled at Thomas as they rode by. There was plenty of food, too: haunches of venison and sheep and buffalo lay on drying racks over low, smoky fires, and there was even a small patch of corn growing by the creek—a farming practice most plains tribes had abandoned years ago in favor of the horse.

It seemed a prosperous village, and Declan wanted it to remain that way.

By the time they reached Chief Lean Bear's tipi in the center of the village, the crowd following them had grown to at least two dozen, with more streaming in as word of the visitors spread.

Leaving his repeater in his saddle scabbard but keeping the Colt in the holster on his hip, Declan dismounted, then waited beside Thomas for the Cheyenne chieftain to emerge. He was aware of curious gazes turned his way, but gave no reaction. He wondered if Pru was still tied to the pole and if Lone Tree was somewhere in the crowd behind him. The thought made the skin between his shoulder blades tingle.

When Lean Bear finally stepped out of his tipi, Declan was surprised to see the chieftain was younger than he had expected. Like Thomas, he wore fringed leggings, moccasins, and a breech-cloth, over which hung a long war shirt decorated with porcupine quills, shells, and elk teeth. But instead of the topknot, Lean Bear had taken time to don a full war bonnet from which sprouted at least a dozen eagle feathers, each commemorating an act of courage or bravery.

Earlier, Thomas had told Declan he'd known Lean Bear before he became chief, but they had never been close. And listening to them greet each other now, Declan didn't hear the same warmth in Lean Bear's tone that he'd heard in other greetings as they had ridden through the village.

He hoped that didn't bode ill for the chances of getting Pru back without bloodshed.

Speaking in Cheyenne, Thomas motioned to Declan. From what Declan could decipher, he was telling the chief that Declan was the keeper of the white man's law in the mining town of Heartbreak Creek.

Lean Bear didn't respond, but studied Declan hard, his dark eyes giving away nothing of his thoughts. After Thomas finished speaking, he motioned for them to sit.

Thomas shook his head. In a voice directed at Lean Bear but loud enough to be heard by the villagers gathered around, Thomas said in Cheyenne, slowly and clearly enough that even Declan could understand, "I have come for my woman. The woman Lone Tree has stolen from me, his Cheyenne brother."

Murmurs rose from the Indians crowding close.

Indians, Declan knew, often raided and warred with other tribes, taking horses, weapons, food, and even slaves. But it was unacceptable to steal from members of your own tribe.

Lean Bear raised a hand for silence. When the murmuring stopped, he said something Declan couldn't make out. Judging by the sudden rigidity in Thomas's posture, it wasn't anything good.

"Then I demand a council," Thomas said in Cheyenne.

More murmurs from the onlookers, but Declan

couldn't tell if they were approving the call for a council or opposing it.

After several back and forth exchanges, Lean Bear nodded, and sent for the men of the council, as well as Lone Tree. This time when he motioned for Thomas and Declan to sit, they did.

Other than several young boys playing a game of ring and pin, the crowd around them settled in to wait, too, sitting quietly on the ground, the braves in front of the women, legs crossed Indian fashion, forearms resting on their knees.

From where he sat, Declan could see the bluff. But aware that Lean Bear was studying him, he didn't give it undue attention, not wanting to alert the chief to the soldiers' presence. Keeping his expression impassive, he stared straight ahead and tried not to think about Pru tied to the pole.

And waited. Again. *Christ,* he was sick of it.

The Come All You Sinners Church of Heartbreak Creek was a sad affair, boasting an out-of-tune piano played by the pastor's wife, Biddy, a pastor with wild gray hair that might have been styled by Medusa herself, two prim choir ladies, and five half-filled pews. When Edwina led in her four children, followed by Lucinda and Maddie, then Miriam and Billy, the bellboy from the hotel, the congregation instantly doubled.

Pastor Rickman was a Bible thumper from way back with such arm-waving enthusiasm for his subject—this week's being the perils of the devil's brew on the sanctity of marriage—he was sweating like a farm animal by the time Biddy pounded out the closing hymn, an off-key, but boisterously earnest rendition of "Safe in the Arms of Jesus."

It was one of Edwina's favorites. But today, when she came to the words "Only a few more trials, Only a few more tears," her throat constricted with such fear for Pru and Declan she couldn't utter a note.

"Don't worry," a voice whispered over Biddy's vigorous attack on the keyboard.

Edwina looked over to find R.D. studying her and, peering around him, the worried faces of his brothers and Brin.

"It'll be all right." He smiled, looking so like his father in that moment she wanted to throw her arms around him.

"He'll be back soon," Lucas whispered.

Edwina felt such sudden and overwhelming love for this poor, broken family—her family, now—she almost burst into tears. "Pray for them," she said in a wobbly voice.

"No need." Joe Bill's grin showed supreme confidence. "If Pa said he'll bring her back, he will."

Lucas nodded solemnly. "Pa never lies."

"Can we go now?" Brin asked, her skinny legs swinging impatiently beneath the hem of her birthday dress. "This dang thing itches me terrible."

Caught off guard, Edwina laughed out loud.

Which drew all eyes her way and apparently irritated the Lord no end, because as soon as she stepped out of the little church and into the bright sunshine, He put Alice Waltham and her demon spawn, Mary Lynn, square in her path.

"You there!"

Seeing no escape, Edwina pasted on a smile and walked toward her. "Why, Alice Waltham, fancy meeting you in a place like this. And you've brought that precious Mary Lynn." Bending down, she tweaked the girl's pudgy cheek. " 'Pon my soul, child, you look like a giant strawberry cupcake in that pretty pink dress. I could just eat you up."

"Is it true?" the flinching child's mother demanded angrily. "That Mr. Brodie has gone after that darky the Indians stole?"

Edwina straightened and, trying to maintain a smidgen of Christian charity—at least until she left the church steps—refrained from striking the woman. "If you mean Prudence Lincoln, then yes, he has gone to find her."

"And yet he wouldn't even try to find his own wife? I wonder why? Unless he had something to do with her disappearance!"

The cupcake snickered and rubbed at the red mark Edwina had left on her balloon cheek.

Facial muscles twitching, Edwina turned to nod to Lucinda and Maddie. "Would you mind taking the children back to the hotel," she asked, sweetly.

"Shall I send for Doc Boyce?" Lucinda murmured under her breath.

"Not for me." Then in a louder voice, "Children, run along with Miss Hathaway and Mrs. Wallace. I'll be there directly."

After they left, she turned back to Alice Waltham, no longer feeling so charitable. "I know you were a good friend to the late Mrs. Brodie," she began, working hard to keep her voice from shaking. "But you do her memory a disservice to spread gossip that might hurt her children—"

"I don't spread—"

"Oh, do hush," Edwina snapped. Then before the wretched woman would interrupt again, she added, "Now the facts are these, Mrs. Waltham. Sally Brodie chose to leave her family. After doing so, she and her gentleman friend were killed by Indians, as reported by the troopers who found their remains. Sad though it might be, there it is. To blame Mr. Brodie for that is wrong. It is also cruel to her children. So I am telling you to stop spreading false accusations. Immediately. Do you understand?"

Mary Lynn was so surprised, her finger slid out of her nose.

Her mother seemed more shocked than surprised, and turned the same purple color of a bruised, overripe plum. Edwina had a sudden ghoulish urge to poke a livid cheek to see if it would burst into a pulpy mass.

"You actually believe that?" Alice gave a braying laugh that made Edwina's ears ring. "You actually believe Declan Brodie had nothing to do with Sally's death?"

"I do. Fervently. As does anyone with the intellect of a gnat."

"What's fervently mean, Mama?"

Shoving her daughter aside, Alice huffed at Edwina. "Well, you're wrong! Sally loved those children. She would never leave them."

"And yet, alas, she did." Edwina shook her head, astounded by the woman's blind faith in her unfaithful friend. "She must have been a remarkable person to inspire loyalty that reaches so far beyond fact and sensibility."

"What?"

"I wish you good day, Mrs. Waltham. Do not approach me again with this nonsense." Head high, Edwina whirled and started toward the hotel.

"If Sally left, she had reason," the enraged woman called after her. "Ask yourself, *Mrs. Brodie*, what would drive a woman from the children she loved. Her husband, that's what. And now that same man has left *you* to go chasing after some nigger. Think about that before you jump to defend him."

Edwina stopped. Sighing, she sent an apology skyward. *You saw, Lord. I tried to be nice. I tried*

to show charity. But really. Enough is enough.
Taking a deep breath, Edwina turned.

The sun rose higher, beating down on Declan's back as he and Thomas sat before Lean Bear's tent and waited. Around them, others shifted restlessly and spoke in low voices. A woman crooned to a fussy baby strapped to a cradleboard, while a rangy dog licked the infant's pudgy arm. The boys grew bored playing with the ring and pin and ran through the tipis practicing their throwing skills with the hoop and dart game. Several women talked softly as they sewed porcupine quills and shells and carved beads in decorative patterns on softened buckskin.

And still they waited.

Declan felt a drop of sweat roll from under his hat, down his neck to soak into the back of his shirt. A fly buzzed around his head, but he ignored it, as well as the ache in his knees from sitting cross-legged on the hard ground. Realizing he was clenching his teeth, he made himself stop and tried not to think of water and how thirsty he was.

He didn't know how Thomas could sit there so utterly still. If it had been his woman tied to that pole, Declan didn't think he could have been so patient. But then, he doubted Thomas felt as strongly for Prudence Lincoln as he did for Ed.

He wondered what she was doing. If she was thinking about him as much as he'd been thinking about her. If she had really meant it when she'd told him she loved him. But she said it, so it must be true. If he'd learned anything in their short marriage, it was that Ed was as different from Sally as a woman could get. She didn't lie. And he thanked God for that.

Soon, he thought. They could go back to the ranch, put it to rights, and get on with their lives.

He hadn't felt so hopeful in a long time.

The council members finally arrived, grave-faced old warriors, wearing their war bonnets and roach headdresses, the decorations on their war shirts attesting to their deeds in battle. On their heels came Lone Tree, a hard set to his jaw. When his gaze fell on Declan, a shadow moved behind his eyes, something not quite human, like a demon barely glimpsed behind a gauzy curtain.

Declan stared back, forcing the other man to look away first to answer the greeting from his chief. Declan wondered why it had taken Lone Tree so long to answer the summons and hoped he hadn't done anything to Pru.

The Arapaho hadn't aged well. Muscle had withered away and there was a sallow tint beneath his ruddy skin that marked him a drinker. A band of white cut through his long, greasy hair, and the wildness in his eyes told Declan that whatever had broken inside his head during those five days in jail had never mended.

At Lean Bear's urging, the elders, along with

Lone Tree and Thomas, settled in a circle on the ground outside the chief's tipi. Declan sat at Thomas's back, the villagers fanned out behind him.

Lean Bear lit the council pipe, and the old men took turns, offering prayers or speaking of things Declan didn't understand. The scent of Indian tobacco smoke hung sweet and pungent in the still air, overriding the smell of curing hides, the latrine, and horse dung. After the pipe had made its rounds and silence had settled again, Chief Lean Bear began to speak.

Although Declan knew a smattering of Cheyenne, it was a difficult language to master with all its musical vowels and long descriptive words, so he understood only half of Thomas's words, and almost none of the chief's mumbled speech. But relying on expressions, tones, and various reactions, he caught the gist of what was said. Once Lean Bear finished explaining to the council members that they had been called to decide a matter between Thomas and Lone Tree, he invited Thomas to speak.

Tension crackled in the air as Thomas rose. He solemnly greeted the elders, then pointed at Lone Tree and began speaking so fast Declan couldn't follow. Lone Tree started to interrupt, but Lean Bear waved him to silence, and Thomas continued. When he finished, Thomas sat back down.

Then it was Lone Tree's turn.

Tension became open antagonism.

Where Thomas had spoken with calm assurance, the Arapaho gestured wildly, spit flying as he paced and shouted. Declan couldn't make out the words, but he had no trouble understanding that most of Lone Tree's ire was directed at him, rather than Thomas.

Declan wondered if he would be given a chance to answer whatever accusations Lone Tree was putting forth.

When the Arapaho finished, other braves came forward to speak. From the glares sent his way, Declan assumed they were speaking in support of Lone Tree. Two rose to speak for Thomas, but their speeches weren't long and brought little response. After all had spoken, the elders asked questions of both Thomas and Lone Tree.

As the discussion continued and tempers rose, Declan watched Thomas's back grow more and more rigid, and he knew things weren't going well. After a while, Lean Bear raised a hand for silence. When the voices grew still, he said something to Lone Tree that made the Arapaho leap to his feet, shouting.

Others rose. Finally, with a snarl directed at Thomas and Declan, Lone Tree stomped away. Declan wanted to ask Thomas what had happened but sensed this wasn't the time to distract him.

A few minutes later, Lone Tree came back. In his hand he held a length of braided leather.

Attached to the other end was Prudence Lincoln, gagged, battered, her dress torn and bloody, her tied hands clinging frantically to the leather leash to keep it from cutting into her neck. Her dark eyes were twin pools of terror in her stricken face.

A vicious yank jerked her forward and onto her knees.

Both Declan and Thomas bolted to their feet and started toward her, but at an order from Chief Lean Bear, two braves jumped forward to bar their way with rifles.

Pru looked at the faces around her, her body shuddering with fear. Then she saw Thomas. A sound escaped the rag stuffed in her mouth, and she slumped forward, her lashed hands pressed to her swollen lips.

Lone Tree said something that sent Thomas charging toward him. Declan tried to fight his way to Pru and was again shoved back. More braves rose to crowd between the two snarling warriors.

Knocked flat by churning legs, Pru curled in the dirt, hands over her head, a whimper coming through the filthy rag in her mouth.

Chief Lean Bear's shouts were barely heard over the threats singeing the air. Pointing at Pru, then at Lone Tree, he made a slashing motion. "Go," he ordered in Cheyenne.

Triumphant, Lone Tree picked up the leash and kicked at the woman curled on the ground.

With a roar, Thomas lunged.

And in that instant Declan knew he meant to kill Lone Tree, and it would mean Thomas's death, too.

"I see no blood," Lucinda observed, looking up from the register as Edwina slammed through the lobby door.

"Where are the children?"

"In the dining room." Crooking a finger at the bellboy posted beside the front door, Lucinda walked toward Edwina. "I would suggest you join them for lunch, but I'm out of raw meat. Billy, please tell the kitchen to prepare two plates and bring them to my room. The chicken, I think. And tell Yancey his nap is over."

Linking her arm through Edwina's, she ushered her up the stairs. "Don't worry about the children. Maddie is with them, no doubt regaling them with outrageous stories of British soldiers and kilted Scotsmen. One, in particular. I don't know why she left that man. She's obviously still besotted with him." Opening the door to her quarters, she waved Edwina inside, then closed the door behind her. "Let me guess," she said, steering her toward one of the chintz-upholstered chairs flanking the window, "things didn't go well at church."

Edwina sank down with a sigh. But before she could answer, Billy came in, pushing a cart loaded with two covered plates, tableware, glasses, and a frosty pitcher of lemonade.

While he set up a small table between the chintz chairs, Edwina stepped into Lucinda's private water closet to wash off the stink of Alice Waltham's accusations.

How could anyone think Declan capable of murder? For all his size and strength, he was a gentle, honorable man. A loving man.

Edwina stared at her reflection in the mirror above the washstand.

And he loves me. Edwina Ladoux Brodie. Imagine that.

Other than Pru—and in their own distracted ways, her brothers and Daddy and Shelly—no one had ever loved her. But Declan Brodie did. And that was worth more than all the others—except for Pru—put together.

Please be safe. Be safe and come back to me.

"So," Lucinda said after Edwina returned to take her place at the table. "Tell me what you did to that sweet Alice Waltham."

"Sweet like a cottonmouth, maybe." Picking up her knife and fork, Edwina stared with little interest at the food on her plate. She had no appetite but knew she should eat. She was losing weight again with all her worrying. Resolved, she cut into a roasted chicken breast atop a bed of sage dressing. "I declare that woman makes as much sense as a two-headed hen. She insists Declan had something to do with his first wife's death. Can you believe that? Naturally, I told her she was wrong."

"That's it? That's all that happened?"

Edwina took a bite, chewed thoughtfully, then swallowed. "I might have said something about her daughter's disgusting obsession with her nose, bless her heart."

"And?"

"And these green beans are delicious."

"Edwina!"

"And there might have been some name-calling. I don't remember."

"But you didn't strike her."

"Strike her? Gracious, no." Edwina popped another green bean in her mouth and smiled. "Not yet."

They ate in silence for a time while thoughts and worries and fears churned in Edwina's mind. It was intolerable—the waiting and fretting—and she knew she would make herself sick if she didn't find a more constructive way to spend her time. Then an idea occurred to her, and suddenly she was imbued with a sense of purpose she hadn't felt since Pru was taken and Declan went after her.

"I have a proposal," she announced.

Lucinda studied her over the rim of her glass. "Oh?"

"Since you seem to enjoy playing the part of Lady Bountiful with your ill-gotten gains, you might find this interesting."

Lucinda set down her glass. "Might I?"

413

"It's something Pru has talked about." Edwina's enthusiasm grew as her idea took shape. "A school for freedmen and -women. To teach them to read and write."

"I remember her mentioning it. But are there that many Negroes in Heartbreak Creek to warrant an entire school?"

"A room, then. Or one of the abandoned lean-tos down by the creek. Anything will do."

"It will take money to fix it up. My money, I'm assuming."

"Who else has any?" Edwina met Lucinda's wry look with a smile. "And it's for a good cause."

Lucinda stared thoughtfully out the window.

"The children and Amos and I can do the work," Edwina pressed, as if a rush of words would force a favorable decision. "Chick is recovered enough to help with the painting, and perhaps Emmet Gebbers will donate building supplies like he did for the town house."

"You'll need tables and chairs," Lucinda mused.

"And slates and primers and maps and books and pens and ink."

"A stove for the winter months."

"Curtains for the summer."

Lucinda sighed. Turning from the window, she gave that distant, almost-sad smile that always made Edwina wonder what had happened to smother the spark in her lovely green eyes. Had her act of revenge backfired, hurting her as well as the man she had duped?

"You want this very much, don't you?" Lucinda asked.

"I do. For Pru."

A look passed between the two women, something they didn't acknowledge by putting into words.

Pru might not come back.

"Then let's get started."

"Thomas, no!" Declan grabbed his friend from behind, using all of his size and strength to hold the shorter, stockier man back. "Let me speak!" he shouted in Cheyenne to Chief Lean Bear. "Let me speak!"

Thomas twisted in his arms, tried to snap his head back and clip Declan in the jaw, but Declan growled into his ear, "Thomas, I have to try! Think of Pru. Damnit, let me try!"

Thomas quit fighting, but Declan didn't let him go. Instead, he watched Lean Bear, hoping the chieftain would be willing to hear him out rather than have members of his tribe killing each other.

"Let me speak," he said again.

Finally, reluctantly, Lean Bear nodded.

"Translate," Declan said to Thomas and loosened his grip.

Thomas lurched forward, whirled, and gave Declan a savage look, muttering threats in Cheyenne.

Declan ignored them. "This man," he pointed to Lone Tree, "came into my village to steal this woman who is my wife's sister. Say it!" he ordered Thomas.

Thomas translated into Cheyenne.

"Lone Tree has broken the laws of the white man. He killed my first wife and now he has stolen the sister of my new wife. He must come back to answer for what he has done." Declan knew they would never let him take one of their own before a white man's judge, but they might allow him to leave with Pru, rather than press it.

As soon as Thomas gave the translation, chaos erupted. Lone Tree yelled denials. Snarling braves edged menacingly toward Declan.

"And I have not come alone," Declan shouted directly to Lean Bear over the upraised voices of his tribesmen. "Look." He waved an arm toward the bluff across the river.

The Indians turned. Threats gave way to murmurs of confusion as the soldiers rose from their positions. Guthrie had made his men remove their jackets and drape them in the rocks so that from this distance, it appeared there was double the number of soldiers than were actually there.

Lone Tree shouted something and ran from the council.

Thomas knelt beside Pru. He pulled the rag from her mouth, then carefully lifted her from the ground. She had fainted and hung in his arms like a broken doll as he glared at the faces surrounding him. "This is my woman," he thundered, then said something more Declan didn't catch.

Alarmed voices rose. Women cried out and herded children toward the tipis. Braves milled uncertainly, shouting at each other and gesturing wildly with their bows and rifles.

"What did you say?" Declan asked, using his knife to cut through the leather binding Pru's hands.

"I told them if they tried to stop me from taking her, the blue coats would shoot and many would die. Help me get her on my horse."

Thomas mounted first, then Declan handed her up. By the time Thomas had her settled in front of him, Pru was coming around. She started to fight, then saw it was Thomas, and with a cry, slumped against him.

"Go," Declan said. "I'll follow."

But before Thomas could rein his horse away from the throng of elders and braves, Lone Tree stalked forward, dragging a figure behind him.

It was a woman, small and thin, her blond hair matted around her face.

Lone Tree slung her to the ground at Declan's feet. "I did not kill your woman!" Lifting a foot, he kicked the woman onto her side. "Tell him!" he shouted in Cheyenne.

The woman scrambled into a crouch, brushed the lank hair from her face, and stared fearfully up at Declan.

Declan's heart seemed to falter in his chest.

Her fear gave way to disbelief. "Bobby?"

Jesus.

He staggered back as if struck. His lungs wouldn't work. His mind couldn't grasp what his eyes were seeing.

Oh, sweet Jesus.

The woman—a wretched, filthy creature with the look of madness in her eyes—began to laugh, a high, brittle sound that doubled her over in a coughing fit that left a red stain on her lips.

The woman.

Sally.

His wife.

Come back from the dead.

Declan looked at Lone Tree's grinning face and his fury exploded.

NINETEEN

The next few moments passed in a blur. Declan's mind in shock, his body reacted strictly on impulse, and before he knew what he was doing, he had Lone Tree in a choke hold and his knife against his chest.

"I'll kill you," he snarled into the Arapaho's ear. "I'll put you in a hole so deep you'll never see the light of day again."

The Indian twisted, his breath a hoarse gasp.

The knife shifted and a red stain spread on the Indian's buckskin shirt.

Only when he heard Thomas shouting and felt the cold press of a rifle barrel against his cheek did the red fog in Declan's brain begin to clear. Realizing that the Indian in his grip was choking and clawing at his arm, he abruptly let go and stepped back, the knife clutched in his hand, his chest heaving as he gulped in air.

Dimly through the roaring in his head, he heard Thomas shout in English. "Get on your horse. Now!"

Still dazed, Declan blinked at the hostile faces surrounding him, at the rifles pointed at his chest, at the woman still huddled on the ground.

Sally.

His wife.

He felt like vomiting.

"Get the woman," Thomas said in a hard, clipped voice. "Get on your horse and ride before they change their minds."

Slowly the words sank in. With stiff, jerky movements, he bent and helped Sally to her feet. She weighed less that his oldest son, and felt as brittle as a stick doll in his arms. His emotions were so frayed by guilt and pity and fury he couldn't even look at her. He quickly mounted, then pulled her up behind him. Gathering the reins, he looked down into Lone Tree's furious face.

"If I see you again," he said through clenched teeth. "I will bury you alive. I swear it." Then he kicked his horse into a lope and rode after Thomas and Prudence Lincoln.

He expected to feel a bullet or arrow slam into him, but none did, and no one followed.

The troopers met them as they rode out of the canyon below the bluff. When Guthrie saw Sally, he reined in beside Declan. "Two for one, huh? Who's this?"

"My first wife." The words tasted bitter on his tongue.

"The dead one?"

Declan didn't answer. Behind him, Sally clutched at the cantle, coughing so hard he could feel the heat of her breath against his back. He'd heard that wracking sound before and knew a consumptive cough when he heard one. He wanted to feel pity. He wanted to care that she had suffered and was suffering still. But all he could think of was Ed.

They rode for several miles before Declan managed to calm his racing thoughts. Turning to Guthrie, he asked him to post guards on their trail to make sure Lone Tree didn't follow.

"Already have." The lieutenant leaned over to spit tobacco, then glanced at Sally slumped against his back. "She's sick."

Declan didn't answer.

"She won't be able to ride much farther."

"I thought it best to put some ground between us and the village," Declan said. "But if you see a likely spot, we can stop for the night. Someplace easily defended."

Guthrie nodded and rode ahead to send out scouts.

Declan glanced over at Pru riding before Thomas. She seemed oblivious to what went on around her.

"Pru," he said.

She turned her head and looked at him, her eyes dull and empty.

"We'll get you home as quick as we can."

She studied him blankly for a moment, then faced forward again.

Thomas gave a slight shake of his head, and Declan saw his own concern mirrored in the Cheyenne's eyes. They were both out of their experience here, and Declan was anxious to get Pru home so Ed could help her find her way back.

Ed.

A sharp, gut-cramping pain rolled through him, leaving a gnawing emptiness in its wake. How was he to explain this to Ed? To his children?

He saw an intolerable choice looming before him. Abandon a woman who had already suffered so much and was likely facing a long, painful death—or turn away from the woman he had grown to love.

Duty or love.

He wanted to howl his despair to the heavens. Because he knew in good conscience he had only one choice, and once he made it, a lonely, bitter life stretched endlessly ahead.

They stopped in a small boulder-and-aspen canyon that offered good shelter for the women, a trickling stream, grass for the horses, and high vantage points for sentries above. While the soldiers set up camp, Declan pulled from his saddlebags a spare shirt for Pru to pull over her torn dress, a bar of soap, and a comb. Then, leading the women along the stream, he and Thomas found a private place in the aspens and left them to wash.

As they walked back to where the soldiers already had coffee boiling over small cook fires, Thomas said, "Have you told your first wife about your new wife?"

"No." He and Sally had scarcely spoken at all. She hadn't even asked about the children, which shouldn't have surprised him, but did.

"She has the coughing sickness."

"I know."

"It is a common thing in the Indian villages. A slow death."

"I know."

Thomas kicked a pebble out of their path and sighed. "It is said that desert air helps. But still you cannot stop it."

Declan didn't want to move to the desert. He

didn't want to give up Ed or the ranch or hope. He didn't want to go back to his lonely, empty life.

But he couldn't abandon the mother of his children, either.

"I am taking Prudence into the mountains."

Declan looked at the warrior in surprise, and saw the firm resolve in his friend's eyes. "Why?"

Thomas shrugged. "Two wives, four children, the two women from the hotel . . . she would be lost among so many."

Declan thought about the turmoil ahead and knew Thomas was right.

"The mountains will heal her," Thomas went on. "I will build a sweat lodge for her, and lay in the rocks to heat and a skin of water to pour over them. As the steam rises, Grandmother Earth will pull the evil memories from her mind and the pain from her body."

Declan had heard of the sweat lodge and its healing powers. He just wondered how he would explain to Ed why he hadn't brought Pru back.

Thomas stopped and faced him. He put a broad hand on Declan's shoulder and looked hard into his eyes. "She will be safe with me, *nesene'*. You know this to be true."

Declan felt a flash of resentment that Thomas had found his woman, while Declan was about to lose his. Then shamed by that thought, he put on a smile. "I know."

"We are brothers now."

In Declan's mind they always had been.

Thomas gave his shoulder a squeeze, then let his hand drop back to his side. "I will bring her back before the first snow flies."

Declan wondered if he would still be here then or if he would be headed to the desert for the winter.

They continued walking. "Lone Tree will come for you," Thomas said.

Declan looked over at him.

"You humiliated him before his tribe. He is a man full of pride but with little thought to what he does. This will not end until he is dead."

Declan had figured that.

"I wish I could be here to guard your back, but I must tend to Prudence."

"I understand, Thomas. I'll keep an eye out for him."

"You kill him this time, *nesene'*."

Declan nodded but said nothing as they stopped beside the small fire Thomas had built earlier. "Now I must hunt," the warrior said. "Prudence needs meat to make her strong again." He started away, then stopped and stared thoughtfully into the distance as if debating with himself. When he turned back, Declan saw a troubled look in his dark eyes.

"It is a hard thing you face," he said in his solemn way, "having two wives. But there is an Indian saying: 'Our first teacher is our heart.' So I tell you this, Declan Brodie. Listen well to your heart. It will show you the true path. And expect Lone Tree."

Supper was miserable, despite the four grouse Thomas added to the usual beans and hardtack biscuits. Pru ate only at Thomas's urging, and even though Sally ate well, she spoke little, and the seething resentment Declan sensed behind her watchful eyes made his own appetite wither.

The air cooled as the sun dropped. Seeking warmth, they lingered by the fire, the women using a log for a seat, Thomas hunkered beside Pru, and Declan on a stump across from them. No one spoke.

Before long, Pru was nodding off. Helping her to her feet, Thomas led her to the canvas and brush shelter he and Declan had constructed for the women earlier. When he didn't return right away, Declan figured he was staying with her until she drifted to sleep or until Sally came.

Resting his crossed arms on his raised knees, Declan glanced across the dying fire at his wife—his only legal wife, now—and found her staring back at him through a veil of smoke. She looked much better—cleaner—than she had earlier. With her blond hair combed back and her mouth pressed in a belligerent line, and that angry glint in her hazel eyes, she looked so much like Joe Bill when he was in a snit it was a bit disconcerting.

"Why didn't you come for me, Bobby?"

He'd been expecting the question. But he still didn't know how or where to start his answer. And he was more surprised than he should have been that her first words were about herself, and not the children she'd left behind.

"I did look for you, Sally. Then troopers found what was left of the stage you were on, and several burned bodies, and they said you were dead."

"You believed them?" Her voice dripped scorn. And fury.

"One of the bodies was your—was Slick Caven's. The others were too burned to tell who they were. But they showed me your bloody dress and the locket you always wore. So yes, I believed them."

She looked off, blinking against tears or the sting of smoke. Or both.

"I'm sorry about Slick," he said.

"I'm not." When she faced him again, that anger was back, brighter, harder, reflecting in her eyes like twin flames on polished glass. "He tried to save himself by trading me to them. 'Take her, take her,' he kept saying. But Lone Tree just laughed and pulled out his knife and had his fun. I wasn't sorry at all."

Declan didn't know what to say. So he remained silent, which seemed to fuel the anger until her thin body shook with it and her voice vibrated like taut wire in a high wind. "Four years, Bobby. For

426

four years I was beaten and kicked and forced and treated worse than the lowest dog. And you never came."

"I would have had I known."

"That doesn't account for much now, does it?"

He had no defense, so he said nothing.

"I'll never forgive you for that. For giving up and leaving me with them. Don't even ask me to." She started to say something more, but broke into a coughing fit that bent her over her knees, her hands pressed to her mouth. When the spasms passed, she straightened and wiped her palms, leaving red smears on her tattered buckskin skirt.

"Consumption," she said, her voice hoarse from the coughing. "Lone Tree's mother had it, and my task was to nurse her or be beaten."

"We'll go see Doc Boyce as soon as we reach town."

"Don't bother. I know what's ahead."

Silence, except for the snap of the fire and a whiffling snore from a nearby soldier. Somewhere on the picket line a horse whickered, and two men spoke in low voices as they shared a smoke. Sad, lonesome sounds.

Declan tossed a small branch onto the coals. After the flames flared in a shower of sparks that spiraled up to fade against the stars, he said the words he'd been putting off. "I took another wife."

She watched him through the smoke but said nothing.

427

"About a month ago. I needed help, and . . ." He stumbled to a stop, not knowing how to go on from there. "Her name is Ed. Edwina."

"I'm your wife. Your only legal wife."

He looked at her.

"What do you intend to do about her?"

"I don't know."

Another long silence.

"Well, take heart," she finally said, rising to her feet. "You won't have to fret over it long." Then she turned and walked into the darkness toward the shelter.

Declan continued to stare into the fire until weariness overcame him. With a sigh, he dropped his head onto his folded arms and closed his eyes. His last thought as he sank into an exhausted sleep was that Sally still hadn't asked about her children. By now, though, he was no longer surprised.

When he awoke, it was morning, Thomas and Pru were gone, and the soldiers were already breaking camp.

He roused Sally. After a quick breakfast of jerky, hardtack, and coffee, they mounted up and set out, knowing that they had a hard day ahead if they were to reach home sometime tomorrow morning.

Declan was desperate to see Ed again but dreaded that homecoming, knowing as soon as he rode up with Sally, everything would change.

•••

"Well, this is odd." Maddie frowned at the letter she'd been studying ever since bellboy Billy had brought it to the room several minutes earlier. The ladies were in the habit of taking breakfast in Lucinda's quarters, preferring the privacy and quiet there to the constant interruptions whenever the hotel owner was downstairs. "What do you make of it?"

Lucinda took the missive and read it over, pausing on the signature at the bottom. "Who is Reginald Farnsworth Chesterfield?" she asked, passing the letter on to Edwina.

"My publisher."

Lucinda poured more coffee into her cup, then set the silver pot back on the hot tray. "Do you have any idea who this person is that he says has been asking about you?"

" 'Tall, overbearing, unpleasant,' " Edwina read, then handed the letter back to Maddie. "Sounds like someone you'd do well to avoid." Picking up her fork, she cracked off the top of the soft-boiled egg perched in her eggcup. "A devotee of your work, perhaps?"

Maddie stared off into the distance, a frown drawing a ridge between her auburn brows. "Perhaps."

"Luckily your publisher didn't tell him where you were."

"However, he did say that the man was 'persistent and determined,' " Edwina reminded her. "Which he certainly proved by tracking you to your publisher even though you aren't signing your photographs with your full name. So I shouldn't be surprised if he showed up here."

"Most curious," Lucinda mused, nipping off the corner of a toast point.

"Well," Maddie said, brightly. "I shall simply have to see that my little gypsy wagon is finished as soon as possible. That way, if he does track me to Heartbreak Creek, I shall be long gone on my photographic expedition. Could you please pass the sausages?"

Lucinda rolled her eyes as she passed them over. "Pray tell me you aren't still insisting on heading into the Rocky Mountains alone."

Maddie shrugged. "How else will I find trappers, and mountain men, and miners, and buffalo hunters, and suchlike. Besides, I won't be alone. Wilfred Satterwhite is coming with me for protection."

Lucinda reared back in astonishment. "Wall-eyed Willy? You might as well take a corpse. The man must be ninety."

"He's a spry seventy-three." Maddie chewed a bite of sausage, swallowed, then grinned. "But not too spry, if you take my meaning. I would hate to have to fend off unwanted advances."

Just the idea of Wall-eyed Willy advancing on anyone with amorous intent gave Edwina the shudders. "Perhaps Declan will lend you Chick or Amos," she suggested. "They're rather at loose ends here in town, and both are deathly afraid of women."

Lucinda looked at her over the rim of her coffee cup. "Isn't Chick the one with the rather distinctive odor?"

"Sadly so. But he—"

Edwina broke off as footfalls pounded down the hall, then all three women flinched when the door burst open with such force it bounced against the wall.

"They're back!" Joe Bill shouted. "R.D. saw the soldiers coming! Pa, too, and he's got someone with him!"

"Pru!" Bolting from the table, Edwina ran out the door on the heels of Joe Bill. As they cleared the narrow rear hallway and passed the open mezzanine that overlooked the lobby, Edwina called over the railing to R.D., who stood in the open double doors into the hotel. "Do you see him? Does he have Pru?"

R.D. nodded and grinned. "I think so."

"Pa!" Brin hopped up and down on the boardwalk, the overlarge hat her father had given her falling down to her nose with each bounce. Shoving it back, she grinned to Lucas beside her. "Look! It's Pa!"

Edwina clattered down the stairs, Lucinda and Maddie close behind, charging through the door just as the troopers filed past. At the rear of the column was Declan, his wide shoulders obscuring the figure riding double behind him.

"Pa! Pa!" his children chorused.

Safe. Edwina felt such a sudden and overwhelming surge of relief her legs began to shake. Tears burned in her eyes, and she had to press her hand to her mouth to keep from bursting into sobs right there on the boardwalk in front of everyone.

Thank you, God, thank you.

Declan reined in at the hitching post in front of the hotel. He looked worn and weary and dusty and was such a joy to Edwina's eyes she almost leaped off the boardwalk and into his lap.

Then his gaze met hers, and she saw the pain and anguish in his eyes and knew instantly that something was wrong.

Please, not Pru.

Dread building, she glanced at the figure slumped behind her husband. "P-Pru? Is she—"

"She's all right," Declan cut in, his voice hoarse with weariness. "She's fine. She's with Thomas. She's all right."

"B-But . . . then who . . ."

Joe Bill stepped to the edge of the boardwalk, his body rigid, his whole being focused on the figure who clung to Declan's arm as she slid down from behind the saddle.

A woman. Blond. Dressed in a tattered, filthy buckskin dress.

"Ma . . . ?" R.D. moved up beside his brother. "Ma, is that you?"

Ma?

The woman turned.

Edwina saw a thin, sun-browned face haloed by flyaway blond hair, eyes the same hazel as Joe Bill's, a smile that matched Brin's.

Her heart began to pound. A buzzing rose in her ears.

"Yes, darlings. It's me." Bending, the woman held out her arms.

Edwina stood frozen as the children rushed past and jumped off the boardwalk, her mind unable to grasp what was happening.

Ma?

Her lungs seized. Something pressed against her chest. Openmouthed and gasping, she looked at Declan, saw the terrible truth in his eyes, and her mind spun away.

Somehow she made it to her room. Her chair.

Maddie and Lucinda hovered close by, Maddie flapping a hanky in her face, Lucinda trying to get her to drink from a glass.

The door opened. Heavy footfalls crossed the floor, and the next instant, Declan's strong, hard arms scooped her from the chair and held her curled body tight to his chest.

She smelled sweat and dust and Declan and turned her face into his neck, breathing him in.

His heart pounded against hers. Bristles

scraped her temple and warm breath fanned her cheek as he stood rocking her in his arms and whispering softly into her ear.

"I'm sorry, Ed. I'm sorry. I love you."

She clung tighter and let the tears come.

He held her that way a long time, until her tears were spent and his arms began to shake. Lifting her face from his neck, she pressed a salty kiss to the corner of his mouth. "Put me down before you drop me," she whispered and kissed him again.

After he lowered her back into the chair, he sagged into the other one, his elbows resting on his knees, his long fingers threaded through his dark hair. "Christ amighty," he muttered to the floor. "Jesus Christ amighty."

"Is there anything we can do, Mr. Brodie?"

Edwina had forgotten Maddie and Lucinda were still there. She sent up a grateful smile when Lucinda held out a half-filled glass of whiskey.

Taking it, she leaned forward and stroked a hand down Declan's arm, felt the ripple of tension there as he looked up. His beautiful eyes were as bleak and tortured as a cornered animal.

"Here," she said, and held out the glass.

He took it, tossed back the liquid in a single gulp, then set the empty glass carefully on the table beside the chintz chair. With a nod of thanks toward Lucinda, he slumped back.

"Where are the children?" Lucinda asked.

"They're with her."

"Do they need anything? Does she?"

He shrugged, rubbed a hand over his face. "Doc Boyce left her some medicine. Said he'd come by tomorrow with a tonic."

Edwina frowned in confusion, unaware that the doctor had been called. Or that the woman was here at the hotel.

The woman. Sally. His legal wife.

A hard knot of despair swelled in her throat.

"She's got consumption." His voice was weary. Defeated.

"Oh, dear," Maddie murmured.

"How bad?" Lucinda asked.

"Bad. A few months. Years, maybe. More if she goes to the desert. Apparently it's fairly common in the encampments. Lone Tree made her nurse his mother who died of it several months ago."

Years? The desert?

As if sensing her mounting despair, Lucinda rested a hand on Edwina's shoulder. "Are the children at risk?"

"I don't know. I'll talk to Doc tomorrow. Christ, what a mess."

Edwina sat numbly as the reality of the situation pressed like a weight against her chest. He would never leave a dying woman. He wouldn't abandon the woman who had borne his children. She knew Declan. She knew the kind of man he was.

I've lost him.

The realization made her throat burn and her

435

mind reel. She sat shivering, wanting to rage at God for the cruelty and unfairness of it.

I've lost him.

Lost him to a woman who didn't even love him—a woman who cast him aside for another man, and who took money to leave her children behind—a woman who would bind him to her with chains of guilt.

The pain of it stole her breath away.

She looked over to find him watching her, his haunted eyes filled with sorrow and regret.

No! Don't do this! She wanted to shake him. Make him listen. *You don't deserve a loveless life. Nor do I!*

Fearing she would burst into tears again, and knowing that would only add to Declan's burden, she took a deep breath, let it out, then forced a smile. "Tell us about Pru."

TWENTY

S he's different than I remember," Joe Bill muttered, hanging his trousers on the bedpost of his and Lucas's bed in the boys' bedroom of the suite they shared with Edwina and Brin.

"She's sick." R.D. plopped down on his narrow cot between his brothers' bed and the wall. "Besides, you were barely six when she left. You probably don't remember her much at all."

"I remember she cried a lot." Lucas tugged off a boot and dropped it to the floor. "I thought she was mad at me. She said she wasn't, but after she left, I wasn't sure."

"No one was mad at you, Lucas," Declan said, stepping into the room. He'd been standing in the hall, trying to get the energy to go in and reassure his sons. But he'd felt so drained he didn't know if he could face their questions, until he'd heard Lucas trying to take the blame for his mother's defection.

Lucas looked up, his brows scrunched in worry. Seeing that troubled frown back on his son's face made Declan realize he hadn't seen it in a while. Not since Ed came, in fact. "Then why was she crying, Pa?"

"Who knows?" Declan lifted the covers for Lucas and Joe Bill to slide in, then reached down to ruffle his youngest son's light brown hair. "Women do that sometimes. They're emotional that way."

"Not Ed," Joe Bill defended.

"No. Not Ed." Not usually, anyway. "What's this?" he asked, pointing to two unfamiliar shirts draped over the foot rail.

"Ed gave them to us," R.D. said.

"Said she meant to give them to us before Brin's birthday," Joe Bill added. "But she was so worried about you and Pru she forgot. I think maybe she figures since she's not our ma anymore she'd better give them to us now before . . ." His voice trailed off.

"Before what, son?"

Joe Bill shrugged and fussed with the covers. "I don't know."

"And look what she gave me." Lucas held up a book. "It's about watches. She said once I read it all, I could probably fix her pa's watch. It has lots of pictures."

Declan felt a jolt of unreasoning anger. Even now, in the midst of this terrible situation, Ed was thinking more about his children than their own mother was. "That was nice of her."

"Yeah." Lucas studied the book. His grin faded. "What's going to happen to her, Pa?"

"To Ed?"

"Now that our real ma is back, does she have to leave?"

"I don't want her to leave," Joe Bill burst out, not meeting Declan's gaze.

Surprised, Declan sank down onto the foot of the bed. "You want her to stay? Even though she's crazy?"

"She's not that crazy. Not crazy in a crazy way, anyway."

"Maybe Ma will go instead," R.D. offered.

Declan looked over at him. "Why do you say that?"

R.D. shrugged.

But Declan knew his son well and knew evasion

when he saw it. And with sudden sharp clarity he realized that R.D. had known about his mother all this time, and had known that Sally had run off with another man before being attacked by Indians. Declan hadn't told the children that, not wanting them to know the mother they loved had abandoned them, and it saddened him that R.D. had carried that knowledge around for the last four years.

"You could turn Mormon," Joe Bill suggested.

Declan blinked at the notion. Earlier this spring, a Mormon family had been stranded by North Creek with a busted wheel. Declan had put Amos and Chick in the barn so the family of three wives and six kids could stay in the bunkhouse while the husband rode into Heartbreak Creek to have the smithy fix the rim and make a new hub. Joe Bill had become fast friends with the oldest boy, and had thought it highly unfair that the poor kid had three moms bossing him around. "You could keep both our moms if you turned Mormon."

Declan bit back a smile, picturing how hot-tempered Ed would take to that suggestion. "I think being Mormon is more complicated than that. At any rate, it's not something you children need worry about." Rising from the foot of the bed, he said, "I have to do my sheriff rounds now, so keep an eye on Ed and your sister until I get back."

"Our other ma, too?" Lucas asked.

"Her, too."

When Declan went downstairs, he found Lucinda Hathaway and Aaron Krigbaum, the mine owner, deep in conversation in the lobby. When Lucinda saw him on the stair, she beckoned him over. "Mr. Krigbaum says he's closing the mine."

Declan sighed. Was there no end to the bad news? Now, in addition to trying to manage two wives, four fretting children, and keeping an eye out in case Lone Tree came sneaking back into town, he would have two dozen angry, out-of-work miners to contend with. Wearily he lowered himself into one of the stuffed chairs arranged around a low table on which a potted plant spread lacy fronds in all directions. "When?"

"Soon. This vein is played out." Krigbaum picked up a spittoon made out of a tin can with a wire handle, pinged a stream of tobacco juice against the bottom, then returned the cup to the floor beside his chair, unmindful of Lucinda Hathaway's look of distaste. "Heard they found placer gold along the Alamosa River. Several of my miners have already headed into the mountains, hunting the mother lode. Soon as they find it, I'll be moving my equipment up there. Just wanted you to know."

"Thank you for keeping us informed, Mr. Krigbaum," Lucinda Hathaway said.

Declan seconded that with a nod, wondering how Lucinda Hathaway became one of "us" and who the "us" was. Not that it mattered anymore. Without the mine, the town was dead. He'd be out of a sheriff job he had never wanted, and the ranch would be that much farther from supplies.

"Well." With a sighing groan from his lungs and a grateful creak from the chair, Krigbaum pushed his considerable bulk to his feet. "Best be heading home. Cynthia fixed beef tonight. Helluva cook."

"Don't forget . . . that." Lucinda motioned to the spittoon.

"Right." With another groan, Krigbaum bent and picked it up. "Ya'll take care now."

After the double doors closed behind him, Declan said, "I guess that'll be the end of Heartbreak Creek."

"Not necessarily, Mr. Brodie. If you have a moment, I'll tell you how I think we can keep this little town alive and prospering."

It was past midnight when Declan finished his rounds with his new deputy, Buck Aldrich. Buck was a capable, intelligent young man who had lost his left hand in an accident up at the mine. He had worked for a time in the mercantile, but with people moving out, business had dwindled, and Cal Bagley had let him go a month past. The young man was grateful for the deputy job and took to it well, since it required more brains than hands and would allow him to stay in the Heartbreak Creek canyon his family had called

441

home for over twenty years. It also worked well for both of them that with no wife or house of his own, he was able to take up residence in the back room of the sheriff's office, thus freeing Declan from night duty.

"I'm only guessing Lone Tree will actually come here," Declan said as they headed toward the hotel after making their stops throughout the slumbering town. "All we can do is be on the lookout for any strange horses tied up where they shouldn't be, especially at night. I doubt he'd ever come into town in daylight."

"And you think if he does come, he'll head straight for you?"

Declan nodded. "Which is why we'll be staying at the hotel until this is finished. It'll be easier to defend. Chick and Amos are taking turns keeping an eye on the house."

Stopping outside the double doors into the hotel, he added, "I found the telegram you left in the office from Judge Witherspoon. He's supposed to be through here tomorrow sometime. Let me know if you see him before I do."

"Yes, sir." The younger man pulled off his hat, tucked it under his shortened left arm, then scratched his blond head with his right hand. As he replaced the hat, he nodded to the stump where his left hand should have been. "This arm still pains me some, Mr. Brodie, so I'm a light sleeper. You need me, fire a round. I'll hear you from the sheriff's office and come running."

"I doubt I'll be sleeping all that soundly, either," Declan said wryly. "So same goes for you." Nodding good night, he stepped inside.

As he closed the door behind him, Amos rose out of the shadows, rifle in his hand.

"All quiet?" Declan asked him.

"L-L-Like my old ch-church on M-M-Monday," Amos stuttered.

Declan was relieved not to smell whiskey on the former preacher's breath. Amos was mostly a binge drinker, but he was overdue to cut the wolf loose, so Declan was keeping an eye on him.

"Where's Yancey?"

Amos hooked a thumb toward the closed door behind the front desk. "Can't you h-h-hear him sn-snoring?"

"Many guests?"

"A p-patent medicine salesman and t-two old lady tem-temperance agitators."

"Any of them using the washroom?"

Amos shook his head.

Like many small-town western hotels, the Heartbreak Creek Hotel had a washroom off the kitchen that held a copper washtub and a stove on which simmered pots of hot water. A pump inside the back door furnished cool water, and it was customary to refill the pots on the stove when you were finished, so the next bather would have hot water to warm up the tub. For an extra nickel, you could have fresh water for your bath, rather than use the water left by the previous bather. Lucinda Hathaway also furnished soap and toweling and a mirror for shaving. A real high-toned outfit.

"Any hot water left?"

Amos shrugged.

He should have known better than to ask. Amos was only marginally fonder of water than Chick was and about as talkative as an Indian totem carving. Between that and his stutter, it was a wonder he had ever managed an entire sermon. "Give me a minute to clean up, then you can head back to the house."

He moved through the dining area into the small room off the kitchen and was relieved to find fresh water in the tub and hot water on the stove. He recognized a stack of garments on a stool and realized Ed had anticipated his coming here and had left clean clothes for him, bless her heart.

He bathed quickly, dressed, and went back to where Amos dozed in the lobby. "Thanks for waiting. Go on and get some rest. I'll take it from here."

After Amos left, Declan opened Yancey's door so the old man would hopefully hear anyone who came in, then headed wearily up the stairs. He felt like it had been a week rather than fifteen hours since he'd ridden into town with Sally. It had been a long and hellacious day.

He paused in the hallway outside the suite

Lucinda Hathaway had set aside for his family. He heard nothing, and no light shone under the door. Taking out the spare key Lucinda had given him, he unlocked the door and eased it open. Moving through moonlight shining through the sitting room window, he went to the boys' bedroom, looked inside, and found all three asleep. He crossed to the bedroom Ed and Brin shared.

In the pale silvery light he could see two lumps beneath the quilt. Moving toward the biggest, he looked down into Ed's sleeping face.

So beautiful. So innocent of this mess his life had suddenly become. What was he to do about her? About their marriage? How could he live the years stretching ahead without her?

His mind as weary as his body, he slumped into the chair beside the bed, unwilling to go to his empty room.

Tipping his head back, he stared up at the shadowed ceiling and tried to figure an escape from this quagmire. He could see no way out. Only bad choices and worse choices. It would be simple if it was just him; he felt no husbandly duty to Sally. She had made her feelings clear when she'd left with Slick Caven. But what would be best for his children? Could he separate them again from the mother they clearly loved?

But hadn't they come to love Ed, too?

Christ.

Too exhausted to think about it, he closed his

eyes and let the gentle sound of Ed's breathing soothe his turbulent mind.

Tomorrow. He would make a decision tomorrow.

Hell. It seemed his life had dwindled to a series of "laters" and "tomorrows," and he wondered if he would ever get it back on track again.

Snoring awoke her from a terrifying dream about Pru and Indians and Mother. Opening her eyes, Edwina saw Declan's wide bulk slumped in the chair beside the bed, long legs outstretched and crossed at the ankles, muscled forearms resting on the upholstered armrests with his big hands relaxed and dangling off the ends. His head was thrown back and his jaw was slack, and in the faint moonlight, the cords of his strong neck showed in rounded relief beneath the dark stubble of his unshaven beard.

He had come here—to her—to find his rest.

How could she bear to live the rest of her life without this man?

She couldn't. She wouldn't.

Empty, loveless years loomed ahead. She had already lost so much—was she to lose him, too?

No. She would think of something, a way out of this wretched coil, because she wouldn't go meekly out of his life. She would fight for her husband with every fiber of her being because she wasn't going to lose Declan to a woman he didn't love, and who didn't love him.

Resolved, she pushed back the covers and rose, careful not to wake Brin. After pulling on her robe, she stepped into her slippers, then bent over her husband. Laying a hand to his bristly cheek, she whispered his name close to his ear.

He startled, his head jerking off the backrest. "What?"

"Ssh. It's me. Don't wake Brin."

"What's wrong?"

"Nothing." She kissed his cheek, then picked up his big hand. "Come with me." Gently, she urged him from the chair and out of the room. After pausing to lock the door of the suite behind her, she led him down the hall and into the room Lucinda had set aside for his use.

She closed the door and locked it, then leaving him almost asleep on his feet in the middle of the room, she crossed to the bureau and lit the lamp. When she turned back, she saw him fumbling with his belt buckle.

"Let me," she said, pushing his hands aside.

She slowly undressed him down to his drawers, which were half unions that he must have cut off to accommodate his long legs, rather than have them ride up his calves. The rough alteration was both endearing and utterly masculine in its ragged practicality and made her want to laugh and weep at the same time.

This man needed her. He needed a gentle touch in his life. Her touch.

Feeling the sting of tears, she kept her head down so he wouldn't see and tried to keep her mind on the task rather than the powerful body she was unveiling. Declan was no longer her legal husband, she reminded herself, and lying down with him would pose a risk of conception, which would only complicate an already impossible situation.

But, mercy, how she wanted to.

Leading him to the bed, she pulled back the covers.

With a deep sigh, he stretched out on his back, his arms tucked under his head. She felt him watching her from beneath drooping lids as she went to the bureau and turned off the light.

"Don't go," he said.

"I won't." Pulling off her robe, she draped it over the chair beside the bed, then slid onto the mattress beside him. Draping an arm over his waist, she rested her head on his lightly furred chest, drawing comfort from the strong steady beat of his heart beneath her cheek. "Rest," she whispered. "I'm here."

In answer, he began to snore.

Declan awoke to a pink dawn and an empty bed. For a moment, he thought he must have dreamed that Ed had undressed him and climbed into bed beside him, then he saw his neatly folded clothes on the bureau and realized it wasn't his imagination.

For several minutes he lay staring up at the ceiling, his mind sluggish and confused. But by the time the sun cleared the ridges, he knew what he had to do.

First, he would go see Doc Boyce and ask him what he could do for Sally. Then he would see if Judge Witherspoon had arrived yet, and if so, find out from him what he should do about his two marriages. Then maybe he would have a clearer idea of how to go about cleaning up this mess.

It promised to be another hellacious day.

Sally held court most of the morning.

From a table in the dining room, Edwina watched a parade of visitors head up the stairs—Alice Waltham, Cynthia Krigbaum—the mine owner's wife—Biddy and Pastor Rickman, the Gebbers, Cal Bagley's wife, and a few other faces that were familiar but ones Edwina couldn't put a name to.

"I had no idea she had so many friends in town," Maddie muttered.

Lucinda made a dismissive motion. "Morbid curiosity."

"At least this should finally put an end to the gossip about Declan," Edwina mused, staring down into her coffee cup.

"Oh, I doubt anyone believed that Waltham creature's vile accusations," ever-loyal Maddie said. "One has only to talk to him to realize what an honorable man your husband is."

Your husband. If only that were true. With a sigh, Edwina said, "I fear it's that very sense of honor that will put an end to our marriage."

"Surely not."

Edwina gave her friends a wobbly smile. "Can you truly imagine he would abandon the mother of his children, especially after she has suffered so much and is now dying?"

Lucinda stared thoughtfully out the window. "Why are you so certain she wants to stay?" Turning to face them, she added, "She happily left her family four years ago. Perhaps she will again."

"She wasn't sick then," Edwina pointed out. "Besides, she was in love with another man." Although how any woman could pick another man over Declan was incomprehensible to Edwina.

"And Declan paid her, isn't that right?"

"He didn't pay her to leave," Edwina defended. "Only to leave the children behind."

"That was rather sordid of her," Maddie said.

"Nonetheless," Lucinda went on with a smile that made Edwina uneasy. "She took the money and left. Perhaps she will again."

Maddie perked up. "You mean bribe her to leave?"

"Why not? It worked before, didn't it?"

Hope bloomed within Edwina. Then just as quickly withered. "I doubt Declan would even make such an offer in view of her illness. And we have no money, anyway."

"Perhaps not." Lucinda's smile broadened. "But I do."

After much discussion, Maddie and Lucinda decided Edwina would approach the other Mrs. Brodie that afternoon after all her guests had departed, and see what her intentions were about her marriage.

"If she wants to remain wedded to your husband," Lucinda said, not even realizing how odd that sounded, "then we will have to come up with another plan. But if she's ambivalent, perhaps we can give her an inducement to continue on to San Francisco—wasn't that where she was headed with that gambler fellow when the Indians attacked the stage?"

Edwina frowned, feeling decidedly uncomfortable with the whole idea of bribing a dying woman to abandon her family. Again. For the umpteenth time she wished her sister was here to advise her. Thomas should bring her home, rather than keep her holed up in some sweaty lodge. "I miss Pru."

Lucinda reached over and patted her hand. "We all do. But from what Declan said, she's in good hands with Thomas."

"I think they care a great deal for each other," Maddie added.

Edwina fervently hoped so. Having her sister gone left a hole inside her. Yet, oddly, it wasn't as painful as it had been at first. Perhaps knowing Thomas held her safe helped. Or perhaps she was learning to stand on her own without using her sister as a crutch.

Turning back to the discussion at hand, she said, "It just seems so . . . cold . . . paying Sally off like that."

"You'd rather she stay here with Declan?"

"Of course not."

"Then talk to her. If she seems set on staying, you needn't even make the offer."

"Oh, do it," Maddie prodded. "At least then you'll know what you're up against. And the children would be better off with you rather than her, so we must do all we can to make sure that happens."

Two hours later, Edwina presented herself at the other Mrs. Brodie's door. She was so nervous her heart sounded like calves were stampeding in her chest and her palms were damp with sweat. If only Pru were here. Her smart, levelheaded sister would know the perfect thing to say.

For long moments she stared blankly at the closed door, her courage wavering, all the carefully rehearsed words dimming in her mind. Then she remembered what was at stake here. Taking a deep breath, she wiped a damp palm down her skirt, then tapped lightly on the door.

"Enter," a voice called.

Donning a bright smile, Edwina swung open the door.

Sally Brodie was seated in an overstuffed chair that seemed to dwarf her small form. She looked much better this afternoon than she had upon her arrival the previous day. Even though she was so painfully thin her borrowed dress hung on her slight frame, her blond hair had regained its luster with a good washing, and she had a bloom of color in her cheeks that contrasted starkly with the ghostly pallor of her skin. Or perhaps that was the flush of fever. Edwina wasn't well enough acquainted with her to know.

"Good afternoon," she said, stepping into the room. "I hope you don't mind one more visitor. I'm Edwina—"

"I know who you are," the other woman cut in with a thin smile. "The children have told me a great deal about you."

Edwina shut the door behind her, then turned with her pasted-on smile. "You have wonderful children."

"Yes, I do. I've missed them terribly."

"And they've missed you. They speak of you often." Not entirely a lie. But Edwina was desperate to find a common ground with this woman so they might be able to speak freely, and she sensed the children would provide that connection. "I suppose they've changed a lot in your absence."

"Perhaps. But they're still my children."

"Of course they are," Edwina hastened to assure her. "And always will be." Hearing the combative note in Sally's voice and not wanting to further upset her before she even had a chance to say what she had come to say, Edwina strove to keep her tone light. "How do you feel . . ." She hesitated, then gave a weak laugh. "How confusing this is. I don't know what to call you."

"Mrs. Brodie will do."

So much for being nice. "Of course." Idly wandering the room while keeping her distance from the sick woman, Edwina finally stopped at the window, where bright afternoon sunlight dispelled the chill gloom that seemed to be closing around her heart. "I'm sorry for what you suffered, Mrs. Brodie," she said, facing her again. "I cannot imagine all you have endured."

"I'm sure you can't."

"And I'm very sorry you're ill," she ground out, determined to maintain civility. She understood the woman saw her as a threat. But this wasn't just about the two of them—there were children involved, and nothing could be accomplished on their behalf if she and Sally Brodie couldn't get past this distrust and hostility and at least talk to each other. "Declan said you have consumption. Are you certain?"

"Declan? How formal you are." She gave a laugh that ended in a cough. With a shaking hand she lifted a glass of water from the table beside the chair and took a sip. It clattered as she set it down. Sitting back once again, she said, "Yes, I'm certain it's consumption. I nursed an old woman who died of it."

"That must have been difficult. I'm sorry."

"Don't be. She was a cruel, hateful woman who gave birth to a monster."

"Lone Tree?"

Sally Brodie nodded.

"And you caught the disease from her?"

"Perhaps. Several in the encampment were afflicted with it."

"Do you think your children will be at risk?"

"At risk?" Bitterness flared in the hazel eyes. "I think anyone who is forced to live in a filthy tipi with little food and constant abuse is at risk!" The outburst seemed to drain her strength. She sank back in the chair, one trembling hand pressed to her chest, her eyes closed. After a moment, her breathing eased and she opened her eyes. "But you needn't fear for my children," she said in a reedy voice. "I will protect them."

How? Edwina wondered. There was no cure for consumption, and anyone in prolonged close contact with an infected, feverish person had a high chance of catching the disease. She studied the sick woman, wondering if that vindictive edge had always been there or if it was a legacy of her ordeal with the Indians.

Pity welled within her for this lost, brutalized woman. But she also felt anger. She had seen that same bitterness in her mother, and knew how it poisoned all who came within her reach. Declan and the children deserved better.

Deciding it was a waste of time to mince words with a woman determined to be her enemy, Edwina asked bluntly, "Do you intend to stay?"

Sally gave a bark of laughter that ended in another coughing spasm. She pressed a linen handkerchief to her mouth until it passed, and when she took it away, Edwina saw a red stain. "And where would I go?" she asked, once she'd regained her voice.

"San Francisco, perhaps? Wasn't that where you were headed when your stage was attacked?"

A crafty look came into the woman's fever-bright eyes. "Are you trying to run me off so you can have my husband?"

Edwina shrugged. "You don't want him."

"Perhaps not. But I'm sick. I don't have much time left or anywhere to go."

"You could go to San Francisco like you planned. They have wonderful hospitals there."

"How? I have no money."

"Money might be arranged."

Sally Brodie studied her for a long time, her

lips pressed tight, her fingers plucking at the stained linen.

Edwina tried to see past the layers of anger and bitterness to the true woman inside. Frightened. Lonely. Defeated.

"You poor thing," Sally finally said. "You're in love with him, aren't you?"

"Yes. I am."

"Then I pity you. Bobby is a man of great passion, but he has little of it to spare a wife. It's all about the ranch with him."

When Edwina started to argue, Sally Brodie made an impatient gesture with the stained handkerchief. "Fine. If you truly want him, you can have him . . . once I'm dead." Then she laughed until it dissolved in a coughing spasm, but by then, Edwina was walking out the door.

It was late when Declan headed back to the hotel. The town was dark except for a single light up at the mine and dim lamplight shining through the grimy windows of the Red Eye Saloon. No light showed in the upstairs windows of the hotel.

It had been another long day. It seemed everybody had wanted to stop and ask him what he was going to do about his two wives. Declan had tried to keep it light by saying he was thinking of turning Mormon. A stupid answer, but it was either that or break the laws he was being paid to enforce by letting his fists answer for him. But it occurred to him after a while that most folks were asking out of concern—not so much for Sally, as for Ed. She had made a lot more friends in a few short visits to Heartbreak Creek than Sally had in a two-year stay. Sort of sad, that.

A long day, but productive. He had spent most of the morning with Doc Boyce, learning what he could about consumption. Apparently, the disease was a death warrant, and from what Doc said, Sally was declining fast. Even more troubling was that Doc was convinced that whenever Sally's fever flared up or she fell into a coughing fit, she was putting everybody around her at risk of catching it, too.

"No one's quite sure how it's passed around," Doc had explained, leaning back in the oak swivel chair beside his overflowing cubby-holed desk. "Not even sure it's contagious. But from what I've read, if one member of a family gets it, then others follow. Especially the ones who do the nursing."

"Is there anything I can do?"

"Other than keep the children and yourself clear of her?" Doc sighed and shook his head. "Some say dry desert air helps. Slows it down, anyway. Strict diet. Rest. Sunshine. But nothing I know of will stop it."

Declan stared out the window, trying to imagine a life without mountains around him, a life spent nursing a woman who hated him, and worrying every day if his children would be getting sick next.

"There are also sanatoriums," Doc went on. "Believe there's one in Maine, and a few others in Europe. Germany, maybe Poland."

"Europe?" Declan gave a bitter laugh, his hopes of coming up with a workable solution fading fast. "I couldn't afford to send her to Europe."

The old man shrugged bony shoulders. "Not sure it would do any good, even if she survived the trip." Removing his spectacles, he rubbed the lenses with a scrap of cloth he pulled from his desk. After looping the wire earpieces over his protruding ears, he sat back again and studied Declan through sharply intelligent blue eyes that had lost none of their intensity despite his six decades of age. "There's another place closer by. Town called Las Vegas down in New Mexico Territory, with hot springs that reputedly have heal- ing powers. Might help. Might not. I heard there's a fellow there who runs a sort of sanatorium. More of a boardinghouse, really. Maybe you could send her there. Hire someone to watch over her." A thoughtful look came into the old man's eyes. "Unless you intend to nurse her yourself?"

Declan knew what Doc was really asking. Janet, Doc's wife, had taken a shine to Ed, and he knew the Boyces were as curious as everyone else in town about how he intended to rid himself of an extra wife.

Declan wished he knew, too. Feeling more discouraged than ever, he rose from the chair beside Doc's desk. "I'd appreciate it if you would find out all you can about the hot springs and the boardinghouse. I'll talk to Sally. Maybe going there will give her ease. Lord knows, she's suffered enough."

After leaving Doc, Declan had gone back to the sheriff's office, where he had found Judge Kelvin Witherspoon leafing through the arrests file.

When he saw Declan in the doorway, the judge showed startlingly white, perfectly aligned porcelain teeth in a smirky smile. "Heard you were sheriff again. Ranching not agree with you?" When he talked, the heavy dental plates clicked together as they moved up and down. Declan had to force himself not to stare.

"It's only temporary. I'll get back to ranching pretty soon."

"After you figure out what to do about your wives?"

Declan wondered if the judge's original teeth had been removed by a fist. He'd like to thank the fellow.

"Heard about your Indian trouble," Witherspoon went on with that smirk. "Shame."

The little dandy was a hell of a grudge carrier. Even though he had reluctantly added his endorsement to Declan's letter to Edwina through the *Matrimonial News*, he had never forgiven

460

him for releasing Lone Tree before his sentence was up. Interfering with the law, he'd called it. Witherspoon didn't like being second-guessed.

But Declan didn't want to get into that again, so he didn't rise to the bait. "That should be resolved soon. But thanks for your interest." He could be sarcastic, too.

Moving to the side of the desk, he rested an elbow on the tall, locked cabinet that housed the extra rifles and ammunition, crossed one ankle over the other and looked down at the smaller man. "However, there is something you can help me with."

"How's that?"

"You can tell me what legal tomfoolery I have to go through to get down to only one wife."

After he had his laugh, the judge had told him. Surprisingly, it wasn't that difficult to dissolve a marriage, which was sort of sad, too.

That was hours ago, and now, his rounds done and his head swimming with more information than he could organize, Declan went wearily up the hotel stairs to check on his children and Ed. If she was up, and he had the strength for it, he'd tell her what he had decided to do.

If not, he'd enjoy the quiet and watch her sleep.

TWENTY-ONE

Declan paused in the darkened second-floor hallway. He heard nothing. No light showed under the door of the room Ed shared with Brin.

He went in anyway.

The moon had risen late and now hung as bright as a gaslight globe outside the bedroom window. His wife was stretched on her back, one hand beside her face, the other resting by her hip. The covers had ridden down, and he could see the flattened mounds of her breasts beneath the worn cotton of her gown.

Unable to help himself, he reached out and drew a fingertip across one soft mound.

She shifted. Her lips parted.

Emboldened, he stroked gently with his whole hand.

He felt a shiver run through her. A soft sound escaped her that he felt all through his body.

Her lids fluttered open. "Declan."

He looked down into her eyes as he continued to stroke her, watching her body awaken to his touch. He wanted to pull up her gown and take her now, while she was half asleep and softly yielding, but his daughter slept a foot away. "Come to my room," he whispered.

Smiling a sleepy smile, she raised her arms.

Needing no more invitation, he scooped her up in his arms and carried her from the room. Yawning, she nestled against him, her wrists locked loosely behind his neck. She smelled like sleep and that rose-scented soap she favored and warm, aroused woman. At the door to the suite he stopped.

"Fish the room key out of my front pocket."

She gave him a drowsy smile. "With what? My third hand?"

"Okay." He set her down and raised his arms. "Now fish it out."

She gave him a befuddled look, then her brows shot up. "That's just plain nasty," she scolded, giving his chest a playful slap. "Which pocket?"

"Try both." Eventually, after a long and enjoyable search, she found the key, and once he'd locked the door behind them, he scooped her up again and carried her toward his room. As she reached down to open his door, he thought he heard a sound behind them, but when he scanned the shadowed hallway, he noticed nothing out of the ordinary. Until he saw the knob on Sally's door rotate slowly back into place.

A momentary sadness moved through him. He didn't want to hurt her by flaunting Ed in front of her. But he wasn't going to mask his feelings, either. Sally was part of his old life. Ed was his future.

Stepping inside his room, he gently kicked the

door closed and carried his wife to bed. After helping her out of her gown, he lifted the covers for her to slide under, then went back to lock the door.

"Light the lamp," she said.

"Why?"

"So I can see you." When he hesitated, she sighed. "Just do it."

He lit the lamp. Aware of her watching, he began to undress, feeling suddenly clumsy, and ham-fisted, and every bit the lumbering carnival bear he'd once been called.

"You're so beautiful," Ed said.

Surprised, he glanced over to find her up on one elbow, staring at him. The look in her eyes made him miss a button on his shirt. "Me?"

"No, me. I was talking to myself. Of course *you,* you silly man. Haven't you ever looked in a mirror?" She must have noted his addled expression because she laughed and waggled her fingers. "Please. Do continue. I so love your peep shows."

He fumbled two more buttons.

"I talked to Sally today," she said.

That didn't sound good. He tossed the shirt over the bedpost, then dropped into the chair to tug off his boots. "About what?"

"What her plans are."

It didn't surprise him that Ed had gone to see Sally. His sweet southern wife hid a core of steel beneath her gracious smile and wasn't one to shy away from a confrontation. But he was a little apprehensive about what his first wife might have said. There was a lot of anger and bitterness inside Sally, and he didn't want it directed at Ed, the innocent in all this.

Setting his boots aside, he stood and began unbuttoning his fly. "What'd she say?"

"That she won't let you go."

No surprise there. He stepped out of his denims, dropped his unions, and slipped under the covers. "Ed," he said, as he reached out and pulled her against his side. "I don't want you worrying about what—"

"How can I not worry?" she cut in, her voice thick with tears. "She could infect you and the children. And she won't go to San Francisco."

Sensing the ruin of his plans, Declan tried to figure out why she was crying, and how San Francisco got into the conversation, and what he could do to get her back on track. He should have moved Brin into the sitting room and made love to his wife while she was still soft and willing. Now he would have to start all over. But before he could, she started talking again, her voice rising as more tears constricted her throat.

"I don't want to lose you, Declan. Or the children. I couldn't bear it."

"You're not losing me."

She raised up on one elbow to scowl down at

him. "Aren't you listening? She won't let you go, and she won't go to San Francisco. She—"

He lifted his head and gave her a quick, hard kiss to shut her up. "You're not losing me."

"But she—"

Trapping her head in his hands, he kissed her again and kept at it until he felt her soften against him. Then, letting his head fall back, he looked into her beautiful eyes and said, "I'm divorcing her, Ed. I've already filed the papers with Judge Witherspoon."

Her mouth sagged open in shock.

As Declan watched emotion shift across Ed's expressive features, he decided the eyes truly were the mirror to the soul, although how such a thing was possible, he didn't know. Yet Ed's cornflower blue eyes truly showed it all. Disbelief. Befuddlement. Hope, joy, and befuddlement again.

"But what about the children?"

"They'll stay with us." He had hoped to explain his decision to Sally and the children first, but now that the subject was on the table, he knew Ed wouldn't let up until she'd heard it all. With a sigh, he pulled her back against his side. "I talked to Doc this morning. He said there's not much we can do for Sally except keep her comfortable and see that she gets rest, good food, and sunshine. He also says that anyone who stays close to her can catch her illness. I won't put the children at risk. I'm hoping she'll understand and accept that. Now get on top of me."

"You're sending her away?"

"Okay. I'll get on you." He did, settling happily into the warm cradle of her thighs. Rubbing against her just enough to keep things interesting, he explained about the place in New Mexico Territory with the hot springs. "There's a sort of hospital there where she can get the care she needs. I wasn't going to tell her until all the plans were set just in case that place doesn't work out and we have to find another. You cold?" He smiled down at her pointy breasts. "You look cold. Here, I'll warm you up."

"I can't believe she'll go willingly."

"Maybe not," he mumbled through a mouthful of breast. "It's her choice." He couldn't believe he was talking about one wife while he tried to make love to another. It was wrong in so many ways he didn't even want to think about it. "Is any of this working for you?" he asked, moving to the other breast.

"I feel bad for her. She's suffered so much. Lost so much. You, the children—"

Christ amighty. With a groan of exasperation, he lifted his head. "She didn't lose us, Ed," he said more harshly than he intended. "She left us. She made her decision when she rode away four years ago, and now I'm making mine. And I'm not giving you up." To punctuate that, he moved inside her, his whole body shuddering at the joy of it. "God, you feel good."

"Oh, Declan." Her long legs wrapped around him, pulled him tight. "Do you mean it?" Kisses fluttered across his cheeks, mouth, brow, nose, chin. "Truly?"

"Truly," he said through gritted teeth as he began to move. "You feel wonderful. Better than—"

"No, I mean do you really mean we can be together?"

He choked on a laugh. "We're together right now. Can't you just lie back and enjoy it instead of pestering me with questions? Christ, I'm working here."

She went still.

Realizing his mistake, he lifted his head.

It must be exhausting to be a woman, he decided, as he watched yet another emotion move across Ed's face. In the last few minutes he'd seen everything—even tears of sympathy for a woman who stood between her and the family she loved—and now hurt. It was no wonder females were so confounding.

"I'm sorry, Ed." With a sigh, he dropped his forehead against hers. "But I don't want to talk about Sally right now. I don't want to talk at all. I just want to show you how much I love you. Can we do that?" When she didn't respond, he lifted his head and found her smiling up at him.

"Well . . . if you insist . . ." And as she ran a

hand over his hip, he watched a whole new emotion take hold.

Lust. One of his favorites.

Again, he awoke to sunshine and an empty space beside him. But he smiled anyway. Today was going to be a grand day.

Hopefully, they would hear back from the man in Las Vegas, and the boardinghouse by the hot springs would have a spare room.

Then he and Doc would talk to Sally, explaining how the warm, dry climate and healing powers of the hot springs would be better for her than the cold, snowy winter in the Colorado Rockies. If she insisted the family go with her, Doc would appeal to her motherly instincts by pointing out the risks such close contact would pose to the children. Then once all the medical issues were out of the way and Doc left, Declan would tell her about the divorce.

Hopefully again, she would agree without a fuss and sign the papers so he could get them back to Witherspoon before the judge left on his next circuit. Then it would be done. Ed would be his only wife—once he married her again—legally, this time. Sally would be able to get the care she needed. And his life could get back on track.

Assuming the children could weather another parting from their ma.

And he could resolve this thing with Lone Tree.

And he could set the ranch to rights before winter.

And he would have enough cattle left to stay afloat another year.

Hell. Maybe he shouldn't get up, after all.

Edwina was in a dither of excitement most of the day. Odd, how a night with Declan always left her body worn out but her mind invigorated. She desperately wanted to tell Lucinda and Maddie about the divorce and sanatorium, but knew she had to wait until Doc heard back from the man in Las Vegas and Declan had a chance to speak to Sally and his children about his plans.

So she kept her silence and stayed as busy as she could, mending hotel bedding, making sure vacant rooms were dusted and ready for guests, and helping Brin with her letters. Again, she wished for Pru. Her sister would have had the child reciting the alphabet in record time. Probably in Latin.

She tried not to think about what Pru had suffered and why Thomas felt he needed to sequester her in the mountains in order for her to heal. Declan had said Pru seemed more shocked than injured. Edwina had noticed that same condition in the battered men wandering home after the war. Some recovered. Some didn't. But Thomas seemed a patient, gentle man, and Edwina knew he cared deeply about Pru. So for now, all she could do was wait and hope for the best. Then once this thing with Sally Brodie was over, and they were sure Lone Tree was no longer a threat, she could get back to the school she was putting together for Pru's return. That would certainly lift her sister's spirits.

Despite her chores, the day dragged. When she took a lunch plate to the sheriff's office, Declan said they hadn't heard back from Las Vegas, so Doc was looking into other sanatoriums in case this one didn't pan out. They'd also decided not to talk to Sally until they'd found a place for her.

By the evening meal, Edwina had fretted herself into such a nervous state she could scarcely muster an appetite. Which didn't escape her husband's watchful eye.

"You have to eat, Ed. You hardly cast a shadow anymore."

"Skinny as old Cooter Brown," Brin crowed, waving a carrot.

"That makes no sense, Brin," her oldest brother said as he served himself another slab of roast beef. "Cooter Brown was a crazy drunk, not skinny."

"If he was drunk all the time," Lucas pointed out in his logical way, "then he wouldn't have had time to eat, so he was probably skinny, too."

"Then she's as skinny as Mrs. Gebbers's old swayback mare," Brin argued, refusing to give up. "That nag has lips so long she almost trips on them."

Edwina ignored the unkind comment, deciding it was simply Brin's revenge for an afternoon bent over a primer, nothing more.

"Ed's lips aren't near that long," Joe Bill defended.

Near?

"And her back isn't swayed," loyal Lucas put in. "Except when she wears that butt-thing and it makes her dress poke out in back like—"

Lucinda cleared her throat. "That butt-thing is called a bustle, I believe."

"Butt-bustle then."

"Children," their father warned.

"Well, it does," Brin insisted. "Looks like she's got a pillow stuffed under there."

Maddie pressed her napkin over her mouth.

Edwina looked at the faces grinning at her, then at Maddie—still hiding behind her napkin—and Lucinda, whose green eyes were dancing.

"See what I have to contend with?" she said in mock exasperation. Then for the first time since Sally came home, she laughed out loud.

It was bath night, an arduous chore under any circumstances, but more so with Declan gone on his rounds and not available to supply intimidation. The boys went first, leaving water spills and havoc in their wake when they trooped upstairs to bed. While Edwina cleaned up the mess, Brin bathed. Once she was done, Edwina helped her into her flannel gown, then set buckets of fresh water on the stove to heat. Later she would return for her own bath. Perhaps with Declan. The idea of that made her heart dance.

"I think washing is stupid," Brin groused as she stomped up the staircase with Edwina. "Chick never bathes and Amos only does it once a month."

"Sad but true."

"And Pa never used to bathe every single day until you came. Now he sometimes even smells like flowers."

"Yes, he does." Edwina smiled at the memory.

"When I grow up, I'm never, ever going to bathe."

"I'm sure the bugs will be delighted."

"What bugs?" At the top of the landing, Brin stopped. "What's that sound?"

Edwina froze, instantly alert. From Sally Brodie's room came a faint moan, then a weak voice calling her name. Alarmed, Edwina gave Brin a gentle shove. "Go on to our room. Now."

"I can't. You locked the door, remember?"

The voice called again.

Something was definitely wrong. Not wanting to take time to go down the hall, unlock the door, relock, and come back in case the sick woman needed immediate help, Edwina made a quick decision. Putting a hand on Brin's shoulder, she said, "Stay here. I'll be right back."

The door was unlocked. When Edwina pushed it open, she saw Sally lying on the floor across the room, her head resting in a pool of blood. "Sally!" she cried, rushing forward.

The woman's eyes opened as Edwina knelt beside her. They were swollen and bruised. Blood seeped from a gash across her forehead. "What happened?" Edwina asked as she pressed her apron against the cut to staunch the flow. "Did you fall?"

Sally's lips moved. Her voice was little more than a sigh. "Run . . ."

"What?" Edwina bent closer.

The hazel eyes widened. Sally's labored breathing quickened as she looked past Edwina's shoulder. "No. Y-You . . . promised."

Edwina whipped around, then leaped to her feet when she saw a painted Indian standing inside the closed door. With one hand he pinned a struggling Brin against his body, his dirty hand over her mouth. In the other he held a knife, poised at the child's throat.

"You scream, she dies."

Edwina's knees almost buckled. When she saw the long greasy hair, the war paint, the breech-cloth and leggings, she knew she faced Declan's enemy, Lone Tree. Her heart stuttered in her chest.

How had he gotten past Amos? Why had he attacked Sally Brodie? Why was he here now, threatening a child?

Declan's child. He's trying to get at Declan through his children.

"No . . ." Sally Brodie's voice was raw and broken. "Not . . . my baby. You promised."

Promised? Edwina's mind reeled. Was Sally in league with Lone Tree? She took a step forward. "What are you—"

"Don't talk!" The knife jabbed. Brin whimpered as a drop of blood ran down her neck. Edwina retreated, terror bubbling in her throat.

"You promised . . ."

Still not comprehending, Edwina spun to see Sally Brodie trying to push up onto her elbow. Lifting a shaking hand, she pointed at Edwina. "Take her . . . not baby . . . take—" Her words dissolved in a fit of coughing.

Finally understanding, Edwina faced the Indian again.

He had his ear to the door, listening. He was filthy, his hair matted, his swarthy skin grimy with dirt. The stink of his unwashed body mingled with the smell of Sally's blood in the small room.

"Take me." Edwina's chest was so tight with fear she could scarcely get out the words. "The child will only slow you down. Take me."

"Quiet!" Straightening away from the door, he waved the knife, motioning Edwina closer. "Come now."

On shaking legs, Edwina crossed toward him, praying her knees wouldn't give way. Every instinct told her to run, to scream, to fight. But the terror in Brin's eyes reminded her she must do what he said.

When she was within arm's reach, he whipped the knife around and pressed it under her chin. "You scream, she dies. Understand?"

Edwina rose on tiptoe, trying to escape the prick of the knife. "Yes."

"You do what I say, she lives. Understand?" He pressed harder.

She felt a warm trickle as the tip pierced flesh, and bit her lip to keep from crying out. "Y-Yes."

He took the knife away. "Open the door."

She opened the door.

He peered out, then dragged Brin into the hall, his hand still over her mouth. She had quit fighting. Her eyes looked blank. Her fingers clutched at the hand clamped over her face.

"Go," he ordered Edwina, pointing the knife toward the stairs.

With him looming behind her, Edwina went down the staircase.

Where was Declan? Why hadn't anyone heard? Where was Amos or Yancey?

Then she saw Amos crumpled behind the front desk. Bleeding.

Nausea churned in her throat. She stumbled, then lurched forward when the knife pricked the small of her back.

He shoved her into the shadows of the dining room. The lingering odors of the evening meal wafted over her, momentarily overshadowing the reek of blood and musk from the filthy man behind her.

Brin started to whimper again. Oddly, that helpless, mewling cry gave Edwina the strength to keep going. Brin needed her. She couldn't weaken now. She had to keep them alive until Declan found them.

"Do what he says, Brin," she called back to the terrified child. "Papa will come. Just do what—" A vicious jab cut off her words. She staggered, gasping in pain as a warm wetness soaked into the back of her dress.

He shoved her out the kitchen door. A moment later, they were across the back alley and into the shadows of the trees behind the hotel, following a footpath that wound through the brush. Knowing every step took them farther from help and safety, Edwina choked back the scream pressing against her teeth and put one foot in front of the other.

The spicy scent of fir and pine and spruce hung in the air as the stillness of the forest closed around them. Sound dwindled to the distant rush of water ahead, the muffled thuds of their footfalls on the carpet of needles underfoot, and the harsh breathing of the man crowding behind her.

The days had lengthened as summer approached, but with high peaks rising all around them, daylight was fading fast. Edwina prayed someone would realize they were gone while there was still enough light for Declan to track them. Brin couldn't take much more of this.

She glanced back, saw the child hanging limp and glassy-eyed in Lone Tree's grip. In shock, but still alive.

Hurry, she called silently to her husband.

The roar of the creek grew louder as they moved out of the trees and into a small clearing. Ahead, a footbridge hung over the rushing water. They crossed it, then left the path and ducked into the brush. A few yards into the trees, they came to a horse tied to a sapling. It had painted markings and a feather attached beneath the braided leather of the bosal halter. Instead of a saddle, a dirty woven blanket was tied to its back, with two leather loops for stirrups.

Lone Tree tossed Brin onto the horse's back, then vaulted up behind her. He motioned for Edwina to give him her arm.

She hesitated, sensing that with the tangled brush all around them and the Indian distracted with Brin and his horse, this would be her best chance of escape. Then realizing she could never leave the child alone with this madman, she took Lone Tree's arm and swung up behind him.

She hated to even touch him, but as soon as they cleared the trees, he kicked the horse into a lope and she had no choice but to grip his waist to keep from falling. After turning onto a rough track, they climbed steadily upward in a zigzagging series of switchbacks. As they continued higher and higher, the town spread below them.

No light showed in the hotel kitchen.

No voice called out.

No one except Sally Brodie even knew they were gone.

TWENTY-TWO

Declan had just left the sheriff's office when Joe Bill ran up, his chest heaving. "She's hurt, Pa! You gotta come!"

"Who?"

"Ma—my real ma! Amos, too! I think the Indian got them. R.D. went for Doc, but she's bleeding all over the place and I can't find Ed."

He shoved his son back toward the office. "Get Buck. Bring him to the hotel. And don't leave his side!" Before the words were out, Declan was running, his bootheels thudding loudly on the boardwalk.

Lone Tree had finally come. But why would he hurt Sally? And what about his other children? And Ed?

Without breaking stride, he cleared the board-walk and raced across the street, his lungs burning for air. As he neared the hotel, he saw most of the lights were on and figures were moving in the lobby. Gun drawn, he slammed through the double doors, almost crashing into Yancey and Lucinda, who were bent over Amos, pressing a wad of cloth to his bleeding head. Judging by his groans and his efforts to fend them off, he was very much alive.

"Where is he?" Declan looked wildly around, praying he would see Lone Tree lurking in the shadows. "The Indian! Where is he?"

"Gone."

He looked at Lucinda, saw a terror in her ashen face that mirrored his own. "What happened?"

"Ask your first wife." She turned back to Amos. "He beat her. Bad. I sent your oldest for Dr. Boyce. She's asking for you."

"Christ." Holstering the pistol, he raced up the stairs, calling back as he went. "Lucas and Brin?"

"Lucas is fine."

The way she said it brought him to a stop. He whirled and looked down at her, his hand clasping the railing so tight his fingers went numb. "And Brin?"

"Gone."

His chest seemed to cave. "He took her?"

"Edwina, too."

He stood frozen, unable to comprehend it, unable to get his mind to accept what his ears were hearing. Why would he take Ed and Brin when it was him Lone Tree was after?

"Go talk to your first wife," she said again.

Her tone caught Declan's attention. What

would Sally know? Unless she was in it with Lone Tree. But why?

To hurt me. The realization knocked the breath from his lungs. *To hurt me in the worst way they could.* Rage exploded like fire in his chest. Whirling, he charged up the stairs.

She was propped in bed in a bloodstained gown, her eyes closed. Every breath was a wheezing rasp. Her skin was so pale he could see the blue vein in her neck pulse with each heartbeat. She had been beaten and by the sound of her breathing, probably wouldn't survive the night. Yet he had little sympathy—little feeling for her at all, except anger.

Movement caught his eye, and he looked over to see Miriam, the hotel maid, sitting in a chair in the corner, a handkerchief pressed over her nose and mouth.

"Go," he ordered.

She fled. After the door closed behind her, he approached the bed and glared down at his first wife.

It scared him how badly he wanted to hit her, shake her, throw her bodily out of his life. "What happened?" he demanded.

Her lids fluttered open. Her gaze wandered for a moment, then settled on his. "Bobby . . ." She reached out a skeletal hand.

He ignored it. "What happened?" he demanded again.

Her hand fell back to the bed. "He came for you. Found me . . . instead." As she spoke, a bloody foam gathered in the corners of her mouth. "Took our baby . . . took . . . Brin."

Declan leaned closer to hear her. The stink of infection almost turned his stomach. "Where did he take them?"

Tears filled her eyes, overflowed in slow, glistening trails down her sunken cheeks. "P-Promised . . . wouldn't hurt . . . children." Her eyes lost focus, stared blankly past his shoulder. "Hit me . . . made me tell . . ."

He could feel her drifting away. In panic, he reached out and shook a bony shoulder. "Tell him what?"

Her gaze swung back to his. "Fear . . . high places."

Declan pulled back, his heart thudding as the old terrors clutched at his chest. Senseless, dizzying terrors that robbed him of his will, and paralyzed his body, and sent his mind into an endless plummeting spiral.

"Waiting . . . for you."

Her voice was so weak he had to watch her lips to catch the words. "Where?" But he already knew the answer, and dread was building with every heartbeat.

"The . . . mine."

A shudder rippled through him. He fisted his hands to stop the tremors, as if somehow that might hold the panic at bay even as images flooded his mind—high platforms, spindly scaffolds, steep, sheer bluffs. Dizziness pressed behind his eyes and the terror spread, clamping like a band around his chest.

It was the perfect revenge. *Goddamn him.*

"Don't do this," Edwina cried, jerking against the ropes that bound her to a two-foot diameter upright post on the platform high above the entrance. "She's just a baby!"

Ignoring her pleas, the Indian dragged the thrashing child toward the big, barrel-sized wooden bucket perched on the edge of the platform. It was apparently used to move tools between the three levels, and he had already emptied it of shovels and picks and sledgehammers. Tied to the handle of the bucket was a stout rope that snaked up through a block and tackle on the scaffold high above them, then back down where the loose end was wrapped around a metal cleat like those used to secure a boat's mooring lines, which was bolted to the post where Edwina was tied.

Frantically, she dug at the ropes. "Lone Tree. Please. I'll do anything you ask. Just let her go."

He shoved Brin into the bucket.

Brin shrieked and tried to scramble out.

"No!" Edwina screamed when she saw the Indian draw back his arm. "Do what he says,

Brin. Get in and don't look out. Do it, Brin. You'll be safe there until Papa comes."

Sobbing in terror, the little girl huddled in the bucket.

Lone Tree untied the rope from the cleat beside Edwina and pulled.

Far above, the pulley block squealed, sending pigeons roosting in the overhead beams into fluttering flight. A grating sound as the bucket scraped across the rough boards of the platform. Another heave and it lifted off, swinging wildly out over the seventy-foot drop to the ground.

"Edwina!" Brin screamed, clutching at the wooden rim.

"Hold on!" Edwina's heart pounded so hard she felt dizzy. "Sit down, Brin! Don't move!"

Spinning and bobbing, the bucket rose higher. Brin shrieked.

"Stay still, Brin! Don't look out! Papa is coming!"

Grunting with the effort, Lone Tree heaved on the rope. Brin's wails grew fainter as the bucket rose ten feet—fifteen—swaying and rocking with every pull.

Jesus, help her, Edwina prayed, her mind reeling with terror as the bucket continued to rise. *Hurry, Declan.*

Lone Tree stopped pulling and looped the rope around the cleat, letting the loose end coil on the deck beside the post. Then, panting and slick with sweat from his exertions, he kicked the scattered picks and shovels aside, pulled the knife from the strap holding his breechcloth to his waist, and turned to Edwina.

Declan tried to calm his spiraling fears as he raced through the dwindling light. He could do this. He could overcome this senseless terror. The lives of his daughter and Ed depended on it. Yet with every thud of his horse's hooves on the rocky switchback track that rose up to the mine, his panic built. Despite the chill evening air, sweat trickled down his back. His hands shook. His head swam until his vision blurred.

What if he couldn't?

"You all right?" Buck called to him.

Declan looked blankly over at him, then forced a nod.

On his other side, R.D. grimly urged his horse faster. He had refused to stay behind, insisting he had truer aim should they get a clear shot. Declan was determined that wouldn't happen. He couldn't allow his son to take a life before he had even started his thirteenth year.

The mine loomed darkly ahead, its gangly scaffolds and open platforms perched precariously on the face of the bluff. How could men work in a place like that? How many had slipped off the edge and plummeted to their deaths?

Declan pushed the thought away before terror

overwhelmed him. In the distant part of his mind still thinking clearly, he realized the sprawling structure was too dark. There should be a lamp lit. Not that having light would make the ordeal awaiting him any easier. But there should be a watchman on duty. It shouldn't be so dark.

I can do this. I won't fall. I can't. Brin and Ed need me.

The last light of day was fading behind the peaks when they rode up to the mine entrance. No one came out of the dark overseer's shack to meet them. The place felt deserted. Then Declan sensed movement and looked up to see a figure moving on the middle platform seventy feet up.

A wave of dizziness almost toppled him from his horse.

A horse whinnied, and he looked over to see a pinto with war paint on its shoulders and rump tied in the trees. Lone Tree's.

"Check the shack," he told Buck as he dismounted. "R.D., find a place behind those rocks." He pointed to several boulders at the base of the bluff that would offer cover in case anyone started shooting from either of the upper platforms. "Don't shoot unless I give a signal. Understand?"

His son nodded, quickly tied his horse to the hitching rail outside the overseer's shack, then ducked behind the rocks with his rifle and a box of ammunition.

"Harvey Ricks is inside." Buck stood in the

doorway of the shack, an anguished look on his face. Declan remembered that he and Harvey had been friends as well as co-workers before the accident that had taken Buck's hand. "Dead. Knife, looks like."

Before Declan could respond, a man's voice called down from the platform above. "Brodie!"

Declan stepped back so he could get a clearer view of the platform and saw a woman standing at the edge, her pale skirts whipping in the evening breeze. Even in the dim light and at a distance of seventy feet, he recognized the slim form and defiant stance.

"I have your woman and your daughter," Lone Tree yelled. "Do you want them back?"

Suddenly Ed screamed and lurched forward, flailing for balance as if shoved from behind. Then just before her feet slipped off the edge, she was yanked back.

Declan could hear her muffled entreaties and clenched his fists in helpless frustration. "Let them go, Lone Tree! They have nothing to do with this."

"Come and get them, white man!" Laughter floated down. "Or are you afraid to come so high?"

Declan felt the familiar terror slide into his mind. He tried to fight it, but already his throat was so tight he was gasping for air.

Above him, Ed tottered on the edge again,

fighting for balance. "Or do you want me to send them down to you?"

"No!" Declan raised a shaking hand. "I'll come! I'll come."

"Alone. Or she falls."

"All right. Just don't hurt them."

"No guns, white man."

With trembling hands, Declan unbuckled his gun belt and let it drop. Knowing Lone Tree wouldn't let him keep his gun, he had tucked Lucinda's little pepperbox pistol into the inside band of his hat. But he would prefer to get his hands on the bastard. He wanted to feel him struggle as he choked the life out of him. He wanted to look into his eyes and watch him die.

"No coat," Lone Tree called down.

Declan took off his coat and spread his arms, shivering as the cool breeze cut through his sweat-dampened shirt. "I'm not armed."

"Then come and die, white man."

Looking around for a way up, Declan saw a rung ladder attached between two narrowly spaced uprights. It seemed to stretch endlessly above him. On shaking legs, he started toward it, speaking softly as he passed Buck, who was hidden in the shadows inside the doorway of the shack. "Is there another way up?" He knew Buck could never climb this ladder with only the one hand. "A ramp? Some way to hoist us up?" With all the ropes and pulleys hanging from the underside of the scaffolds, there had to be something better than a vertical climb up a slick wooden ladder.

"Only ladders."

Christ.

"Are you coming, white man?" Lone Tree shouted.

"I'm coming."

Declan gripped the ladder in sweating hands. With his heart pounding so hard he heard nothing but the thud of it, he began to climb.

It seemed to take forever. He had to stop several times, his arms wrapped around the ladder in a stranglehold, to wipe the dampness from his cramping hands. His jaw ached from the effort of trying to keep his teeth from chattering, and no matter how many breaths he took, he couldn't seem to fill his lungs. But slowly, surely, he went up the rungs.

Don't look down—you won't fall—don't look down.

Finally he cleared the last rung and collapsed, shaking and nauseated on the floor of the platform. When the spinning slowed, he pushed himself up on wobbly legs and looked around.

The platform was split into two wooden decks —the one closest to the bluff where Declan had climbed up—and a bigger one with no railing that hung over the long drop to the ground. Separating them was a ten-foot-wide gap running parallel to the bluff, which allowed the water cannon—now hanging limply from ropes attached to a system of oversized pulleys on beams overhead—to run back and forth along the rock wall. The decks were littered with tools and lengths of chain, and ropes so tangled they looked like a sail rigger's nightmare.

Lone Tree held Ed on the far platform.

Declan looked for a way to get to her and saw several sagging foot-wide boards bridging the gap between the platforms. The realization that he would have to cross on one of those narrow boards above a seventy-foot drop almost drove Declan to his knees.

He gulped in air. Sweat burned in his eyes. He forced himself to step forward. The platform shivered gently with his weight. He stopped, his knees shaking beneath him. "All right, I'm here," he yelled across to the Arapaho. "Let her go."

"Are you afraid to come closer?" Lone Tree taunted. "Is it too high for you?"

Eyes stinging, Declan squinted through the gloom. The Indian had one arm locked around Ed's waist, using her body as a shield. In his other hand he held a long-handled hunting knife pressed to her throat. There were dark stains on the pale fabric of her dress, but she seemed okay, although it was hard to tell in the fading light. There was no sign of Brin.

His stomach rolling, Declan took another step.

Lone Tree laughed. He started to say something,

but Ed cut him off, her words coming out in a rush. "Brin's up there. In the bucket."

"Quiet!" Lone Tree cracked the butt of his knife against her temple.

She sagged, then caught herself.

Declan looked up and saw the barrel-shaped bucket suspended halfway between this platform and the one above. "Brin!"

"Pa!" a muffled voice cried. A small head rose over the rim of the bucket. "Pa, help me!"

Declan almost choked when he saw the bucket tip as she moved about. "Be still, Brin! Don't move! Sit down and be still!" After her head disappeared from the rim, he turned furiously to Lone Tree. "Is this how an Arapaho fights his enemies? Hiding behind women and children?"

"This is how an Arapaho avenges his dead family!" the Indian said savagely. "You killed my woman and child! Now you watch as I kill yours."

"No!" Declan lurched forward, then stopped when the boards beneath his feet groaned and trembled. "I didn't kill them! A flash flood killed them."

"While I was in your cage!" Suddenly the Indian gave a high, jittery laugh that had the sound of madness in it. "But I will give you the chance you never gave me, Brodie. I will let you try to save them. Come." He motioned impatiently with the knife. "Or is your fear so strong you will let them die?"

Declan glanced down at the gap at his feet. Dizziness assailed him. Acid burned in his throat. He slid one foot forward onto the spanning board, then the other, and tried not to think about the emptiness below.

"How does it feel, white man? Are you afraid? Are you sorry you locked me in your cage?"

"I let you go. Early. Before your sentence was up." Declan sucked in air and chanted silently in his mind. *Don't look down, don't look down.*

"Faster, white man. I tire of waiting."

Staring down at his boots, Declan took another step. The board bounced under his weight. *Jesus.* He felt himself tip and flailed for balance. As if from a great distance, he heard Ed's voice.

"Don't look down, Declan. Look at me. Don't look—"

Her words ended abruptly. Declan looked up to see her crumple onto the floor amid a tangle of picks and shovels. "Ed!" he shouted, then froze when the board shifted beneath his feet.

"Now you have lost one," Lone Tree called as he began to unloop a thick rope wrapped around a cleat bolted to the post. "Will you come in time to save the other?"

Declan took another step, arms outstretched, his heartbeat roaring in his head. Then another.

Lone Tree slipped the last loop from the cleat and wrapped the rope around one forearm, while gripping the loose end with the other hand.

"Hurry, white man." He began to play out the rope.

Brin screamed.

Declan watched in horror as the bucket started a jerky descent. "No!" he shouted and took another step.

The board bounced. He tried not to over-compensate as he fought for balance. Blinking against the sting of sweat seeping from under his hat, he crept forward, Ed's voice echoing in his mind.

Don't look down. Don't look down.

Terror churned in his gut. Air hissed through his clenched teeth.

He focused all of his mind on the end of the board stretching forever ahead of him. He was distantly aware that Brin had quit screaming, but he didn't dare look at Lone Tree to see if he was still playing out the rope, afraid any movement of his head would throw off his precarious balance.

The end of the board edged closer. He tried not to rush the last few steps, but suddenly he was lunging for the safety of the deck. He found it, went down hard on one knee, but welcomed the pain because it helped bring his mind back in focus. Chest heaving, his mouth so dry his lips stuck to his teeth, he straightened.

Lone Tree stood by the edge, still holding the rope. The bucket swayed gently five feet above him. Ed hadn't moved. The light was so faint now Declan could barely make out the scattered tools, ropes, and leavings of workers who wouldn't be back.

"All right, Lone Tree," he said, still struggling to catch his breath. "I'm here. Do you have the courage to face me like a man?"

The Arapaho laughed. The bucket dropped a foot, then halted with a jerk. Brin's whimper cut like a blade into Declan's heart.

"Closer, white man. So you can watch her fall."

On wobbly legs, Declan came closer. His foot twisted on a discarded pick hammer, but he caught himself before he fell and continued on. If he could get inside five feet, he had a shot.

As long as the gun didn't jam.

As long as he was within reach of the rope when the bullet struck.

As long as the momentum of the dropping bucket didn't pull him over, too. Realizing how slim the chances were of any of that happening sent Declan's mind into a helpless spiral. *Jesus, help me. Help Brin.*

As he crept forward he kept his gaze pinned on Lone Tree's hands, terrified the Indian would let go and send Brin plummeting.

Just a little closer. Ten more feet. Eight.

Movement behind the post caught his eye, but he steeled himself not to look that way, fearing the moment he did, Lone Tree would let go of the rope. He prayed it was Ed. Prayed she was still alive. Prayed he could reach Brin in time.

"Closer. To the edge. So you can see when she hits."

The bucket slipped lower.

Seven feet. Six. When five feet separated them, Declan stopped. "Please." Keeping his movement slow, he lifted a shaking hand to wipe sweat from his face. "Don't do this, Lone Tree. Don't bring this shame on yourself." As he spoke, he eased off his hat and continued to wipe sweat from his brow. "You're not a coward who kills women and children." He slid his hand inside the crown.

"I am an Arapaho warrior," the Indian snarled.

In a single motion, Declan dropped the hat and lifted the pistol to point at the Indian's head. "Not anymore."

For a heartbeat the two men stared into each other's eyes. Gone was Declan's fear, overshadowed by an unshakable resolve that steadied his hand and calmed his thundering heart. "Tie off the rope, Lone Tree, and you can walk away from this alive."

The Arapaho looked at him, his dark eyes reflecting the last pink glow of the evening sky, his mouth twisted with hate.

"Do it now, Lone Tree. Or I pull the trigger."

Something shifted behind the Indian's eyes. He showed broken teeth in a mocking smile. "Then pull the trigger," he said and let go of the rope.

The bucket dropped.

Brin screamed.

With a roar, Declan flung the gun aside and lunged, grabbing for the rope as it snaked past the edge of the platform. He hit the deck belly first, almost knocking the air from his lungs. Feet spread, he hung over the edge, grabbing frantically at the rope.

It slipped through his fingers. *No!* The pulley whined, caught, then screeched as the rope whipped through.

Above him, Lone Tree laughed.

A cry tore through Declan's throat. Then his fingers felt rough hemp, and suddenly the rope was in his hands. But the bucket continued to fall, the rope searing away skin on his palms, his fingers. Blood slicked the twisted hemp. He gripped harder, air rasping through his teeth.

Jesus Jesus Jesus.

The bucket bounced at the end of the rope, sending a jolt of pain up his arms, almost pulling his shoulders out of their sockets. Then it stopped, twirling slowly ten feet from the ground.

"Brin," he cried, just as a moccasined foot slammed into his side. He grunted as another kick drove the air from his lungs. He felt himself roll toward the edge. More kicks. Something popped in his shoulder as he struggled to hold on to the rope.

Then a high-pitched scream like nothing he had ever heard—a clanging thud—and suddenly a heavy body stumbled over him and crashed to the deck on his other side.

Lone Tree.

The Indian grappled for a hold as his body started over the edge. Grimy fingers tore at Declan's shirt. Fabric ripped away. Nails clawed into the flesh of his arm. Declan tried to pull back, afraid for one horrifying moment that he would go over, too. Then with a guttural cry, the Arapaho slipped over the edge.

Declan watched him fall, narrowly missing Brin's bucket and almost crashing into Buck, who stood watching from seventy feet below. A sickening thud as his body struck the earth and then lay still.

Gasping, his arms in agony, his mind in shambles, Declan tilted his head up to see Ed standing beside him, a shovel clutched in her hands like a club, her hair flying all around her ashen face.

"Got him." She started to sway.

"Don't faint!" Declan ordered. "Don't you dare faint now, Ed!"

"Okay," she said and dropped like a stone.

"Ease her down," a voice called.

Declan looked over the edge to where R.D. and Buck waited with arms raised toward the bucket. Apparently sent by Lucinda and Doc, other men from town had arrived and were running to help.

"Go slow. We got her."

His arms and hands burning with the effort, Declan slowly played out the rope, then groaned at the sudden release of pressure when they took on the weight of the bucket. Once he saw Brin was safe and they were clear of the falling rope, Declan forced his sticky fingers to let go. Shuddering with pain and terror, he cradled his wrenched arms and bloody hands to his chest and rolled away from the edge. He looked over at Ed.

She was sitting up, her hands clutched to her head.

Something twisted in Declan's chest. Tears of relief and gratitude clouded his eyes. "You okay?" he asked hoarsely.

Ed let her hands fall. "I c-couldn't watch. Is B-Brin?"

"She's safe. Lone Tree's dead."

She blinked at him, then her face seemed to crumple. She crawled toward him, sobbing. "Oh, Declan, you did it."

"*We* did it." He gave a shaky laugh as she cradled his head and pressed wet, salty kisses to his sweating face. "But I think my arms are broken."

It took five stout men and a makeshift sling to get Declan back to the ground. His arms weren't broken, but he did have a dislocated shoulder and little skin left on his palms. Luckily Doc was at the hotel when they arrived, and with Buck and R.D. helping, and Ed's tears egging them on, they were able to doctor his lacerated hands and pop his shoulder back into the socket before Declan vomited from the pain. He would have to wear a sling for a while and bandages on his hands, but other than bruising from the kicking, he was fine.

As was Ed. Her knife cuts didn't require stitching, and the two lumps on her head weren't threatening, although she would have headaches for a while.

Brin was shaken, but aside from a few scrapes and bruises, she was unharmed. Physically. Doc said that only time would tell how her mind dealt with the experience. For now she was content to be cuddled in Ed's arms and suffer the attentions of her brothers and Lucinda and Maddie.

Sally was still alive, but fading fast. Apparently the beating had further damaged her weakened lungs, and she had been coughing up blood steadily.

"She's asking for you." Doc glanced from Declan to Ed. "Both of you." Dropping his voice, he added, "She's said her good-byes to the boys. Since Brin doesn't even remember her, I think it best if we don't put her through that. But it's up to you."

He and Ed decided to spare Brin another difficult confrontation with her mother. Declan didn't want one, either. But knowing it was necessary if they were ever to put this horror behind them, he and Ed reluctantly went up to her room.

Sally looked even worse than the last time Edwina had seen her. The damage from Lone Tree's beating showed in livid bruises and swollen, seeping cuts. Seeing the two bright spots of color on her sunken cheeks and the glittery brightness in her eyes, Edwina guessed her fever had worsened. Her breathing was so labored it sounded like a farrier's rasp scraping across a horse's hoof. The corners of her mouth were crusted with blood.

Doc was right. It wouldn't be long. Even now the room stank of death.

"Sally," Declan said, standing at the side of the bed.

Even though the sick woman's eyes were open, Edwina wondered if they saw anything. It took them a moment to find Declan. "Brin . . . ?"

"She's safe. Lone Tree is dead."

Her smile left red smears on her teeth. But when her gaze shifted to Edwina, the smile faded and an intense yearning came over her face. Her mouth opened and her breathing quickened, but no words came out.

Edwina stared back, not sure what to say to this broken, defeated woman. What did Sally want of her? Why had she even asked to see her? She sensed unspoken messages hanging between them but didn't know what they meant.

"Please . . ." Sally whispered.

And finally Edwina understood. "I'll take care

of them, Sally. I promise." She glanced at the man beside her and added, "All of them."

A look of relief came over the dying woman's face. Her features softened and grew slack, giving Edwina a glimpse of the pretty woman she might have been before disappointment and bitterness and disease had taken their toll. That fevered gaze shifted to Declan. "For . . . give me," she whispered as the light faded from her eyes.

"I do, Sally."

They buried her the next day. Doc was concerned that even in death Sally's body might be able to transmit the disease. At his further suggestion, there was no wake or formal gathering at the church but a processional from the hotel out to the little fenced cemetery beside the church on the flats at the edge of town.

Out of deference to the dead woman, Edwina hadn't moved with the rest of the family into the sheriff's house the night before. Declan and the children needed time to come to grips with this second good-bye. For that same reason, she held back now, and flanked by Maddie and Lucinda, walked to the graveyard behind Sally's family. This was their loss. Their grief. It wasn't her place to intrude.

Besides, she wasn't a wife anymore. Sally's return had negated that. The judge had been adamant that she and Declan would have to marry again if they wanted their union to be legal.

The strains of the ragtag band—minus the piano —wafted back as the marchers left the narrow canyon and followed the road onto the grassy flats. As they cleared the trees and the sky opened above them, Edwina studied the thunderheads building behind the peaks. It would rain later, she guessed. Perhaps that was the Lord's way of washing away all the heartache and sorrow. She hoped the ceremony would be over before it came.

On a distant ridge, a lone horseman rose silhouetted against the sky. He had stopped to watch the train of mourners walking behind the buckboard carrying Sally's casket. He sat stiffly, his back ramrod straight. A huge dog stood beside his horse. She wondered idly who he was, and where he was headed, or if he sought his future in Heartbreak Creek. She wondered if Heartbreak Creek even had a future. Or if her sister would be home by the time she and Declan married again.

She had to be. Edwina wouldn't marry without Pru by her side. Perhaps it would be a double wedding . . . assuming Cheyenne Dog Soldiers even believed in marriage. Meanwhile, Edwina would get to work on the little shack that would house Pru's school for Negroes and anyone else who wanted to learn.

And life would go on.

She let her gaze travel over the broad back of the man walking ahead of her. That sturdy back was hers now—hers to touch, to lean on, to run her hands down when he moved over her in the night. She smiled, her fingers tingling at the idea. Despite the solemnity of the day, the future stretched gloriously ahead.

By the time Pastor Rickman said his final prayers, the lone horseman was gone, the air had cooled, and the wind was blowing hard out of the west.

A storm was coming, for sure.

TWENTY-THREE

Three weeks later, leading a string of four horses, Declan rode his big bay down into the rocky creek bed, wincing at the pull of the lead rope on his shoulder and across his gloved and barely healed palm.

Several braves waited on the bank, rifles or bows in hand, their expressions ranging from curious to wary to menacing. Ignoring them, he rode up the low bank, forcing them to step aside. Looking neither right nor left, he rode on into the heart of the Cheyenne-Arapaho village.

Despite the yapping dogs, and curious children and women gathering around, he kept the restive bay at an unhurried walk until he reached the tipi he sought. There he reined in and dismounted.

After a moment, Lean Bear stepped from behind the deer-hide door flap. He looked at Declan without speaking, his face twisted in a scowl. Or maybe that was the scar.

Declan held out the rein on one of the unsaddled horses, Lone Tree's stocky pinto with fading war paint on its shoulders and rump, and wearing a bosal halter with an eagle feather. "For his family," he said in broken Cheyenne, knowing not to speak the name of the dead. Turning, he motioned to the three other unsaddled horses beside his bay. "For his tribe. To ease the loss of a warrior."

The chief's gaze flicked from Lone Tree's pinto to the three young horses restlessly kicking up dust. Declan had pulled them from his own small herd, wanting to show good faith and hoping if the chief accepted this offering, it would put an end to this sorry business once and for all.

Lean Bear finally motioned to a young brave. As the grinning boy led the horses away, the chief nodded to Declan. "It is well," he said in his slurred voice.

Declan nodded in return. Feeling as if a great burden had been lifted from his shoulders, he remounted and rode out of the village toward the shadowed silhouette of the Raggeds.

It was over. Finally. "Later" had come and now he could start his life anew. Grinning, he nudged the bay into a ground-eating lope.

• • •

He was still a day from home, crossing a low aspen-topped ridge, when he saw movement in the draw below him. He reined in. Two riders were working their way up a switchback trail toward the bench where he sat watching. The rider in front was quite a bit larger than the one following and wore the traditional Cheyenne topknot. There was something about the way he sat his horse . . .

As they drew closer, Declan grinned and spurred his gelding to intercept them as they reached the top of the ridge. "Ho, Thomas," he called, riding toward them.

Thomas reined in. The second rider stopped beside him. Pru.

As he pulled the bay to a walk, Declan studied Pru's face, hoping she was recovered and had returned to the pretty, smiling woman she had been before Lone Tree had abducted her.

The bruises had faded. The swelling was gone. She was smiling, and as pretty as he remembered. But as he stopped before them, Declan saw her smile lacked animation, as if it had been carved into her face with a chisel, and there was a wariness in her dark eyes that hadn't been there before.

Thomas showed as little expression as he usually did, but Declan recognized the weary droop at the corners of his mouth, the exhaustion and worry in his eyes. It was apparent things hadn't gone well, and the sweat lodge hadn't accomplished what they'd hoped.

"You're early," he said to Thomas. "I didn't expect you for another month."

"Prudence wanted to return to her sister."

"Ed will be glad." Declan smiled at Pru and added, "She's missed you. We all have."

Pru acknowledged that with a nod, but her fixed smile remained unchanged. "I have missed all of you, as well."

"You are far from your ranch," Thomas said.

"I'm headed there now. I was visiting Lean Bear." As their horses fell into step down the trail, Declan told them about Lone Tree coming to the hotel, Sally's beating, and that gut-churning scene on the platform at the mine. "He would have killed all of us if Ed hadn't hit him with a shovel."

For the first time, true emotion flashed in Pru's eyes—fear. "She killed him?"

Declan gave a wry smile. "She just hit him. It was the seventy-foot fall that killed him."

A shudder rippled through her. "And Brin is all right?"

"She's still skittish, and I doubt we'll ever get her on anything higher than a chair, but the nightmares have stopped."

"Poor child."

Thomas said nothing, but the way his mouth tightened indicated his disappointment that he

506

hadn't been the one to take care of the man who had hurt Pru and endangered the little girl he loved like his own blood.

They rode in silence for a while. Then Declan said, "We buried Sally last month. She never recovered from the beating Lone Tree gave her."

"Perhaps her spirit can rest now."

"How are the children taking it?" Pru asked.

"It's complicated things," Declan admitted. "More so since her being alive made my marriage to Ed illegal."

Prudence gave him a sharp look. "You're not married?"

"Not anymore."

"What does Edwina say about that?"

Declan reached down and brushed a horsefly off the chestnut's neck. "Haven't talked to her much lately. She's been staying at the hotel ever since Sally's passing."

"She's not with you and the children?"

Hearing the anger in Pru's voice, Declan took heart. If the poor woman could worry about Ed, then she hadn't completely shut herself off. "It was her idea. She thought the children might adjust better to their mother's death if she wasn't there to confuse the issue."

"And you agreed to that nonsense?"

Definitely angry. "I've been pretty busy lately," Declan defended, "getting the new sheriff up to snuff, and moving out of the house in Heartbreak

Creek, and doing repairs at the ranch. But I suspect we'll talk soon."

"Men." Prudence said it like a cuss word. "You all think you know best. But you don't. You just make everything worse."

Surprised at the vehement tone, Declan glanced past Pru to meet Thomas's troubled eyes.

At the unspoken question, Thomas gave a small shake of his head and looked away. But Declan had seen that shadow of sadness behind those dark eyes and knew it was as he had suspected; things hadn't gone well at the sweat lodge, and apparently Prudence Lincoln was nursing anger about more than just Lone Tree.

Late the next day, Edwina was sweeping the boardwalk in front of the hotel when she noticed two riders coming down the street. Raising a hand against the afternoon glare, she studied them, then gave a whoop when she recognized Thomas and Pru.

Flinging the broom aside, she yelled through the double doors to Yancey at the front desk. "Get Miss Hathaway and Mrs. Wallace! They're back! Pru and Thomas are back!" Then she rushed to the edge of the boardwalk, one hand gripping her apron, the other waving frantically.

Tears blinded her. *Thank you, God. Thank you, Thomas.*

By the time the Cheyenne reined in at the

508

hitching post by the step, she was sobbing and babbling uncontrollably. "Pru! Thank the Lord. I've been so worried!"

Lucinda and Maddie rushed onto the boardwalk behind her, and soon all three women were laughing and crying and talking at once.

Pru smiled back, her own eyes shimmering.

Thomas slid down and went to help her, but Pru had already dismounted and was rushing toward Edwina.

Edwina grabbed her the moment she came up the steps, wrapping her so tightly in her arms she could feel the thud of her sister's heart against her own. "Oh, Pru. I feared I'd never see you again." She laughed, tears running down her face. "Have you truly come home? Are you all right?"

"I will be when you stop choking me." A final pat on Edwina's shoulder, then Pru pulled out of her grip and stepped back. "And yes, I'm home."

Swiping tears from her eyes, Edwina studied her sister from head to toe, desperate to assure herself that Pru was truly all right.

She looked weary and dusty and odd in those buckskins. She had also lost weight and her smile seemed a bit strained, but that was no doubt because she was tired. Pru wasn't much of a rider. Yet when Edwina looked past her sister's shoulder to greet Thomas, she saw such a troubled look on the warrior's face, she knew something was wrong. But before she could question him, Thomas turned back to his horse.

"Wait!" Edwina rushed down the steps toward the Cheyenne. "Where are you going?"

"I have fulfilled my promise, Edwina Brodie. I have brought Prudence Lincoln back to you."

"And that's it? Now you just ride away?" Edwina looked back at Pru, willing her to speak up. But her sister wouldn't meet her eyes and quickly turned to speak to Maddie and Lucinda. Puzzled, Edwina faced the warrior. "I don't understand. What happened? Why are you leaving?"

Thomas studied Pru's back, a look of yearning softening his stern features. "If Prudence Lincoln needs me to stay, I will." He said it loudly enough for Pru to hear, but her sister never turned to face him.

His face grim, Thomas gathered the reins on his bosal bridle and vaulted up onto the horse's back.

Panicked and confused, Edwina put her hand on the horse's rein. Lowering her voice so the others wouldn't hear, she said, "You can't leave. She needs you, Thomas. She may not want to admit that right now, but she does. We all do. You're part of our family."

"I will not be far. Good-bye, Edwina." Reining away from the hitching rail, he kicked his horse into a lope. Only then did Pru turn. And as she watched Thomas ride back the way they had come, Edwina saw in her sister's face that same look of yearning she had seen in the Cheyenne's.

• • •

"Well, where are they?"

At Edwina's words, Lucinda looked up from the curtain she was threading on the wooden rod. "Are you referring to Pru, Thomas, or Declan and the children?"

"Either. Any. All of them. We shouldn't have to do all this by ourselves." Edwina frowned at the half-painted walls, the rough floor that needed sanding, the windows awaiting curtains. "This is her school. She should be helping."

And usually she was. Pru was as excited as any of them about the school and seemed at her happiest within these rough walls. But this morning she had already been gone when Edwina awoke, and was still absent when the ladies walked to the little school on the outskirts of town.

Maddie brushed back an errant auburn curl, leaving a smear of white paint on her cheek. "Perhaps she and Thomas are busy."

"Busy doing what?" Edwina groused. "They don't even speak."

She was peeved, irritated, hurt, and so worried she was chewing her nails. She hadn't seen Declan and the children in weeks, and whenever she tried to talk to Pru, her sister avoided her. She felt like a pariah.

"I've seen the way they look at each other." Smiling wistfully, Maddie dipped her brush into the bucket of whitewash that Edwina had coerced Cal Bagley into donating. "And sometimes looks say more than words."

"Not to me," Edwina muttered, fitting a new sheet of sandpaper into her sanding block.

Lucinda looked over at her. "She still won't talk to you about what happened when she was abducted?"

Moving to one of the tall windows, Edwina knelt down. "No," she said, rubbing the sanding block over the sill. "Every time I bring it up, she changes the subject."

Which was only partly true.

After Pru had first come back, Edwina had tried to talk to her about her ordeal, hoping if she could get her sister to share those terrors with her, then maybe that lost look would leave her eyes. But Pru had cut her off each time Edwina had broached the subject, saying curtly that "some things were best forgotten."

When Edwina had tried a different tack, asking why she was so upset with Thomas, Pru had been ever more snappish.

"He hovers. You know I don't like that. I don't need his help. I just want everything to go on as it was before and for everyone to quit pestering me about it."

She must have seen the shock on Edwina's face, because she had tried to cover her sharp words with a half apology. "I know everyone means well. Thomas, too. But I'm not ready for that right now. Perhaps I never will be."

"Ready for what? Is he pressuring you?"

"No, of course not. Thomas would never force me to do anything." She gave a laugh that sounded false. "Except crawl into that stifling sweat lodge. What a disaster that was. It's just that . . . well . . . he wants something from me that I can't give right now. Or perhaps ever."

Edwina studied her sister, seeing such a mix of emotions move across her usually serene face she could scarcely sort them out. But one seemed especially prominent . . . one Edwina had rarely seen there. Fear.

"He wants something you can't give, Pru? Or offering something you won't take?"

"Both. Neither. I don't know what you mean." Perhaps realizing how confusing that sounded, Pru had reached out and patted Edwina's arm. "Please, Sister. Don't press me about this. Perhaps soon we'll talk. But right now I can't bear to think about it."

That was almost two weeks ago. And Pru still hadn't spoken about it. She still avoided Thomas, and still cried herself to sleep every night. And Edwina still waited for her beloved sister to return.

Poor Thomas. Edwina rubbed harder on the rough wood, and the smell of raw pine rose from beneath her sanding block.

Thomas had seemed as confused as she by Pru's silence. Yet he hadn't given up. Many times Edwina had seen him seated on the bench across the street, arms folded, his expression set, his gaze fixed on the front door of the hotel, as if expecting Pru to come to him or perhaps letting her know he was still there, watching over her. And like Edwina, waiting.

Last week, Edwina had gone to speak to him, determined to get some answers. Plopping down beside him on the bench, she had said, "She won't talk to me, Thomas. It's like she's pretending nothing happened. Yet at night I hear her crying, but when I ask her about it, she just brushes me off. So what am I supposed to do? I want to help her, but I don't know how."

"Prudence will speak when she is ready."

"And we're just to wait?"

Thomas had turned his head and looked at her then, and Edwina had seen a wealth of wisdom and patience and certainty in his dark eyes. "When it is time, she will come to me. So yes, I will wait."

And waited still.

Edwina sighed and waved a fly away, showering her nose with fine sawdust. *If only Declan would show such devotion to me,* she thought for the umpteenth time. But he seemed to have forgotten her existence, which made her own nights as restless and tearful as Pru's.

Feeling a familiar churn in her stomach, she pulled her bowl closer, closed her eyes, and breathed through her nose. When the queasiness passed, she resumed sanding, her irritation shifting away from her sister to her . . . what? Lover? Once-and-nearly-husband? The man who had ignored her for over a month? *That lump.*

Granted, she had wanted Declan and the children to have time together to come to terms with Sally's death. But really. It had been almost five weeks since the funeral. She hadn't meant for them to completely ignore her. *Forever.*

She had seen him only once during that time—the day he had turned over the sheriff's job to Buck Aldrich and had gone to pack up the contents of the little house beside Elderberry Creek. Through Lucinda and Maddie, she had learned that soon after, Amos and Chick and the children had left in a wagon creaking under the weight of window glass, milled boards, assorted building materials and furniture, while Declan had ridden off into the mountains with a string of horses.

Then nothing. Not a word, other than Thomas's assurances that Declan would come back when he could. *Men.*

It wasn't fair. She deserved an explanation of why they had deserted her, didn't she? As if to punctuate her aggravation, her stomach rolled. Dropping the sanding block to the floor, she shot to her feet, barely getting her bowl in position before her stomach cramped. Luckily the cramping didn't last long and produced no result. Leaning dizzily against the wall, she waited for the churning to stop.

"You poor dear." Maddie paused in her painting to give Edwina a look of sympathy. "I wish there was something we could do for you."

Edwina weakly waved her away. "It'll pass."

"I think it's revolting. The whole thing." Wobbling on the stool, Lucinda rose on tiptoe to fit the rod into the bracket above the window. "God must surely hate women to put them through that."

"Just wait until the birthing starts," Maddie called gaily, then caught Edwina's glare and hastily added, "A miracle, I've been told. A woman's grandest achievement."

"Really, Maddie." Lucinda tugged on one side to even the hem, then nodded in satisfaction. "You make her sound like a brood mare."

"This isn't God's fault." Anger replacing nausea, Edwina set the bowl on the windowsill. "It's *his*. He just had to consummate, and now look at me." She scowled down at her midriff, which at six weeks was still flat, especially with all the weight she had lost. Yet she felt as bloated as a spring tick.

"You look wonderful," Maddie gushed, slapping on another brush full of whitewash. "Glorious. Glowing."

"Oh, please, Maddie. She just vomited."

Edwina felt tears start and kicked at her sanding block in disgust. If she wasn't heaving, she was crying. Maybe Lucinda had a point. "I can't believe this is happening! Why is he ignoring me? Has he changed his mind? Does he not love me anymore? Is that it? Why else would he—"

A thought struck her, one so unexpected and terrifying it almost buckled her knees. What if something had happened? What if he was hurt or the children were sick or the Indians had come again? What if he was out there now waiting for her to come to him?

Oh, Declan.

Panic sent her mind in flight. "I have to go! Now!" She raced toward the door just as it swung open and Pru stepped inside.

"Pru!" Edwina cried, rushing her sister before she could close the door. "Did Thomas bring you? Is he still here?"

"He might be. He said he—"

Edwina bolted past her, saw Thomas walking away. "Thomas!" she yelled, charging toward him. "You have to take me to the ranch! Now!"

Pru insisted on going, too, and if there had been enough room in Lucinda's smart four-wheeled buggy, Lucinda and Maddie would have joined them, as well. As it was, the three of them were quite crowded. Oddly enough, despite the jostling and bouncing, Edwina's stomach remained calm, and only once did she have use of the bowl she held in her lap throughout the daylong journey.

Thomas set a fast pace. Now that they were full into summer, the days were longer, and even with the late start, they crossed Satan's Backbone well before dark. Leaning forward, Edwina peered down through the trees, trying to catch a glimpse of the house. Thomas had repeatedly tried to reassure her, but she needed to see for herself that it was still standing. When she saw that it was, she breathed a sigh of relief.

Forty-five minutes later, Rusty barked in welcome as they pulled up in front of the house. Before the dust settled, children were tearing out of the parlor door.

"Thomas!" Brin cried, bounding down the steps. Then she caught sight of Edwina and abruptly stopped. "Oh, no! Look who he brought!"

"What are you doing here?" Joe Bill demanded, stopping beside her.

"You've ruined everything," R.D. added.

Even Lucas, hanging back on the porch, greeted her with a frown.

They didn't want her. They didn't love her anymore.

Burying her face in her hands, Edwina burst into tears.

The buggy rocked as Thomas, then Pru climbed down. Voices rose and fell, but Edwina couldn't hear them over her own sobs.

After a while, silence. Even Rusty quit barking, and all she heard was the occasional stomp and jangle of harness as the horse shifted in the traces. She took a deep, hitching breath and, using the hem of her skirt, wiped the last tears from her face.

"Are you getting down or not?" a familiar voice said, startling her.

She looked up and saw Declan leaning against the front panel, his elbow resting on the dashboard. He was smiling. *The dog.*

"No." She continued to wipe her face even as new tears threatened. How could he smile when her heart was breaking?

The buggy rocked on creaking springs as he climbed in and settled on the seat beside her. He was so close she could feel his heat, smell his sweat, hear his breath move in and out. She wanted to hit him.

"Why are you crying?"

She stared stoically out the other side of the buggy, wondering how she had ever loved such a dense man. "I'm not crying."

"You were."

She didn't respond, refusing to admit her heart was breaking in a thousand pieces. She had some pride left.

"Nice buggy," he said after a long silence.

"It's Lucinda's."

"I figured."

Another long silence. It finally wore her down. "Apparently my coming was a mistake. I apologize for upsetting the children."

He shrugged, his shoulder bumping against hers. "They'll get over it. What's the bowl for?"

Ha! As if she would tell him now. She might be in a pickle, but she wasn't desperate enough to trap a man with that old trick. She'd suffered enough humiliation. "Since I haven't heard from you in a while"—seventeen days, in fact, and even then he'd been in such a rush to get his wagon of supplies back to the ranch before dark he had hardly spared her five minutes—"I was starting to worry that perhaps something had happened."

"Everything's fine. I've just been busy."

She contemplated striking him but was saved from making a decision when the parlor door opened and Brin shouted, "We're ready!"

Ready for what?

Declan climbed down, then turned to assist her. He was grinning again. "Come on. They've been planning this a long time."

Edwina hesitated. "Planning what?"

"You'll see." Taking her waist in his big hands, he swung her down, but instead of letting her go, he tucked her hand in his elbow and escorted her toward the front porch. "You know I love you, don't you?" he said as they walked toward the porch.

Edwina almost stumbled. "Well . . . I . . ."

"I wasn't sure I could love again," he went on. "Especially after the mess I made of my first marriage. I didn't expect a second chance. And I sure didn't expect it to come with a woman like you."

Wondering what that was supposed to mean, Edwina just stared up at him, her heart daring to hope.

Once on the porch, he stopped. Letting go of her arm, he took her face in his big, rough hands and kissed her. Then he kissed her again, and finally a third time. When he lifted his head, he might have been smiling but Edwina couldn't tell because she was tearing up again.

"I don't deserve you, Ed," he said in a solemn voice. "But I'm not going to make it without you, and the children aren't, either. So, I hope you'll love us back." He let go of her face and grinned. "Prepare yourself," he whispered and opened the door.

A fistful of mountain daisies was thrust into her face. Several fistfuls. Four, in fact. "Surprise!" the children shrieked.

Edwina glanced from one face to another. Beautiful, hopeful, beloved faces. Even Pru, standing beside Thomas by a new settee, was smiling as she hadn't in weeks. Above their heads, hanging from the rafters by bright colored yarn, was a crudely lettered sign: WELCOME HOME, ED. Other signs, pinned about the room, all carried the same words: SAY YES.

Edwina's heart seemed to swell in her chest.

She looked up through tearing eyes to find Declan grinning down at her, his beautiful eyes dancing. "Will you marry us, Ed?"

She tried to smile, but her mouth was wobbling. "A-All of you?"

"All of us!" Brin shouted, waving the daisies and sending up a cloud of pollen that made Lucas sneeze. R.D. nodded. Joe Bill did, too, showing the gap of another lost tooth in a big grin.

"Well . . . let me think . . ."

The children sent up a chorus of pleas. Pru sent her a chiding look and Declan laughed softly, his eyes promising retribution.

Edwina shivered at that delicious prospect.

"You almost ruined the surprise!" Brin shouted. "But I'll still bake you a cake! All by myself!"

"And we fixed the house," R.D. added proudly. "It took forever."

Joe Bill hooted and danced a jig with Lucas. "No more stink!"

Only then did Edwina see other changes in the parlor, the new furniture, the special touches here and there. For her?

"In that case," she blubbered, laughing and crying at the same time, "of course I'll marry you. All of—"

Suddenly the ground shifted. Her stomach rolled. Clapping a hand over her mouth, she looked frantically around.

"She's gonna spew!" Joe Bill cried.

Daisies flew. Children fled.

"Holy hell," Declan muttered, as his wife started to heave. He looked anxiously at Pru, saw her standing there laughing like a loon, and was so shocked he couldn't move.

Then realization came.

"Does this mean what I think it means?" He looked down just as his beautiful southern wife vomited on his boots, and all he could do was laugh.

Thus, the true courtship of Edwina Ladoux Brodie began.

And in the nick of time.

About the Author

Kaki Warner is an award-winning author and longtime resident of the Northwest. Although she now lives on the eastern slopes of the Cascade Mountains in Washington, Kaki actually grew up in the Southwest and is a proud graduate of the University of Texas. Kaki spends her time garden-ing, hiking, reading, writing, and soaking in the view from the deck of her hilltop cabin with her husband and floppy-eared hound dog.